PRAISE FOR
THE VAULT OF DREAMERS

"A mixture of science fiction and contemporary fiction, this novel is an interesting addition to both genres."

—*School Library Journal*

"Like viewers of *The Forge Show*, readers will want to keep watching Rosie."

—*Publishers Weekly*

"A sharp novel about the ways in which everyone can be manipulated, either through editing or one's own desire to go the easiest path."

—*The Bulletin*

"An amazing escapade into a 'be careful what you wish for' world . . . sending Rosie and the reader into unchartered territories."

—*Children's Literature*

"Like O'Brien's Birthmarked trilogy, this dystopian, sci-fi, psychological-thriller hybrid raises ethical and moral questions about science. . . . With a likable narrator who is thoroughly unimpressed with herself, it works."

—*Booklist*

BY CARAGH M. O'BRIEN

The Birthmarked Trilogy
Birthmarked
Prized
Promised

The Vault of Dreamers Trilogy
The Vault of Dreamers
The Rule of Mirrors

THE VAULT OF DREAMERS

CARAGH M. O'BRIEN

SQUARE
FISH

ROARING BROOK PRESS
NEW YORK

SQUARE FISH

An Imprint of Macmillan
175 Fifth Avenue
New York, NY 10010
fiercereads.com

Library of Congress Cataloging-in-Publication Data

O'Brien, Caragh M.
    The vault of dreamers / Caragh M. O'Brien.
        pages cm
    Summary: Rosie Sinclair, who attends an elite arts school where students are
contestants on a high stakes reality show, skips her sleeping pill one night and
discovers that the school is really a cover-up for the lucrative and sinister practice
of dream harvesting.
    ISBN 978-1-250-06825-5 (paperback)   ISBN 978-1-59643-939-9 (ebook)
    [1. Reality television programs—Fiction.   2. High schools—Fiction.
3. Schools—Fiction.   4. Dreams—Fiction.   5. Science fiction.]   I. Title.
    PZ7.O12673Vau 2014
    [Fic]—dc23
                                                                        2014013322

Originally published in the United States by Roaring Brook Press
First Square Fish Edition: 2016
Book designed by Elizabeth H. Clark
Square Fish logo designed by Filomena Tuosto

1   3   5   7   9   10   8   6   4   2

LEXILE: HL680L

For my husband,
Joseph J. LoTurco

CONTENTS

THE VAULT OF DREAMERS

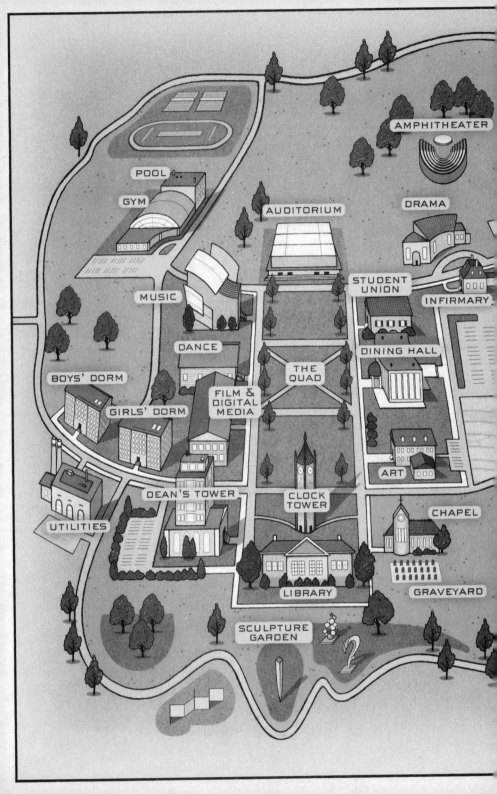

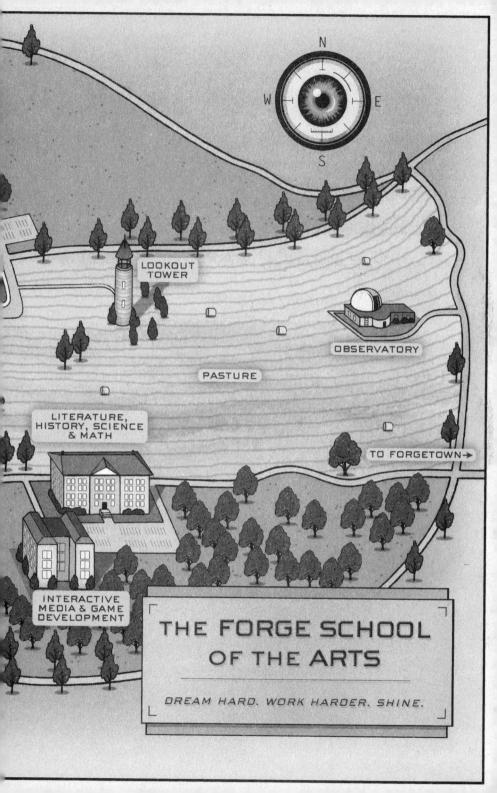

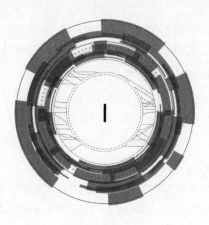

NIGHT

I MISSED NIGHT. I had other reasons to disobey, too, like wanting to escape the cameras, but most of all, I missed the deep, vacant darkness of night.

We lined up as usual, shivering in our bare feet and night-gowns. Rain streamed down the windows, obscuring the gray view of the prairie, and the patter sounded gently on the vaulted roof overhead. Orly passed out the pills, starting at the far end, and I watched as each girl obediently swallowed, climbed into her sleep shell, and slid her lid closed with a soft swoosh.

When Orly reached me, I took my pill like the others but faked tossing it back. Instead, I lodged the disk up alongside my gums before I took a sip of water and opened my mouth for her inspection.

She turned and went on to the next girl.

I'd won. I climbed in my sleep shell, spit the pill into my hand, and wedged it under my pillow.

"Close your lid," Orly told me.

"Do I have to?" I asked. "I like the sound of the rain."

"You can open it again after your brink lesson if you want," she said. "Sleep well."

When Orly switched off the lights, the room went the soft, gray color of childhood naps. I pulled my lid closed to watch the brink lesson cast across the glass: a scene of a woman laying bricks, tucking them evenly in a row. What I was supposed to learn from it, even subconsciously, I couldn't tell. Afterward, I slid open my lid again and rolled over on my pillow. Across from me, the next girl fell asleep easily and completely, and from the uninterrupted sound of the rain, I knew forty-eight other girls fell asleep on schedule, too.

Myself, I was secretly, deliciously awake. As the hour brought the darkness closer, I lay fidgety with hope and relished how it felt to be alone, stealing back the real me. The windows darkened like a gift until I could see the faint, blue reflections of our domed lids in the glass. A nearly invisible glow fell over the dormant faces, making the girls' skin gleam with faint phosphorescence, as if they had been chalked and scanned under a black light. I slowly waved my fingers before my face, testing. The glow gave my fingers a staggered trail of black shadows, like cartoon lines of motion, tracks in the air.

Deep night came at last, bringing me more awake than ever. After nine nights of drugged sleep, my nerves seemed to have lost the trick of falling asleep naturally on their own, and now they worked in reverse, lighting me up within. To watch the night out my window was not enough. I wanted more.

It was a risk, breaking the rules, but following them hadn't done me much good, either. I had to face facts. With the fifty cuts happening the next day, this could well be my last night at Forge. I didn't want to waste it sleeping. From outside, the bells of the clock tower tolled midnight, until the twelfth bong resonated away to nothing.

Slowly, I sat up to look around the room.

No alarm went off. No warning lights. Orly did not come running. Our fifty sleep shells, with their paneling below and full-length glass lids on top, were lined up in two rows as straight and motionless as so many coffins. Cameras had to be picking up my movements, but either no one cared that I was breaking the rules, or the night techies didn't watch carefully. A third possibility didn't then occur to me: someone cared very much, was watching very closely, and still let me continue.

Clutching my nightie close, I tiptoed the length of the room, past the other girls, and peeked through the doorway to where the hall was dark, empty, and cool. Barefoot, I crept across the smooth floor to the stairwell and touched a hand to the banister. Downward, a wide, dark staircase led to the floors for the older students, but upward, an old, narrow staircase led around a corner I'd never noticed. I took the old steps up to an attic, where the roof was close and alive with the rain's pattering.

I breathed deep. The aged, still air was faintly sweet, as if the missionaries who had raised the roof long before had also left behind a trace of incense in the wooden beams. I had just barely enough light to see, which also made me trust that the attic was too dark for the cameras to find me. I was effectively offstage for the first time since I'd arrived on the show, and the privacy was so palpable, it made me smile.

Two large, old skylights glowed in the slanted roof, setting edges to my blindness, and I wound my way gingerly past a number of storage bins. Rivulets of rain were slanting down the glass. With a hand on a rafter, I leaned close to the first skylight and peered out. To the left, the dean's tower was dark except for lights on the top floor, where I'd heard the dean lived in his penthouse. The techies who worked in the building must be gone for the night. It made sense, I realized. They couldn't have much to do in the twelve hours of night while *The Forge Show* was on the repeat cycle, rebroadcasting the feeds of the previous day.

With a shove, I pushed the heavy skylight upward on its hinge and propped its bar in the opening. The rain dropped in a perfect curtain just beyond my touch, releasing a rush of noise and tropical mist. The drenched roof tiles smelled unexpectedly like the metal of the boxcars back home, or maybe I was smelling the wet grid of a catwalk I spied running below the skylight.

I ached to go out and feel the soft blindness of the night touching my skin with the rain. It would make me strong.

When I rolled up my sleeve and reached a hand out, clean, colorless droplets fell upon my skin. They were warm and irresistibly inviting.

Using a bin for a step, I hitched my nightie around me and crawled gingerly through the skylight to the catwalk. I gasped. The rain drenched me instantly, and I hunched against the downpour. It was so wonderful, so surprisingly not cold, that I had to laugh aloud. After nine days of guarding myself, trying fruitlessly to please the teachers and cameras, I was free.

I grasped the railing of the catwalk with one hand and pushed my wet curls out of my eyes. This was good. Light from the dean's tower cast outlines on the sloped roof of the film building next door and beyond that, I could see the sharp roof of the clock tower. A row of lamps illuminated the edge of the campus and separated us from the darkness of the plains beyond. Except for the faintest flickers, the lights of Forgetown were lost in the rain to the east, and my home, to the southwest, was impossibly distant.

I looked, anyway, employing my filmmaker trick. I imagined my gaze forward, high speed between the drops, to the boxcar where my kid sister was sleeping in the top bunk. I zoomed in large to picture her rosy cheeks and her eyelashes. Then I scanned past the curtain to the living room and put my stepfather in a stupor on the orange plaid couch. My mother I bent over a calculator, with some paperwork from the cafeteria, while the lamplight limned her profile. Home. In the next instant, I released them all to dissolve in the rain, and I was back at Forge.

My homesickness wasn't truly for home, I realized. It was for something more elusive. A silent, low-grade, unnamed yearning persisted inside me. It was always there, a reaching feeling that grew stronger when I was alone and listened for it. The rain understood what it was.

I spread my arms wide and tilted my head back to let the night splash into my mouth. Too little of it fell in to actually quench my thirst, but the few drops that passed my lips tasted sweeter than anything from a glass. This moment was real, at least. This was worth remembering. If they cut me the next day and I left Forge as a failure, ashamed, I could always recall my invisibility on the roof in the rain this night, and I would know this moment was my own.

"You like that?" I said, facing the sky. "Is that good enough?"

It was for me.

And the next second, it wasn't. The truth was, I would do anything to stay on the show.

A gust of wind blew me into the railing of the catwalk. This was a mistake. My stupidity astounded me. Why did I think, at any level, that doing something at night when the viewers weren't even watching could possibly help my blip rank?

I turned back to the skylight. Getting in was harder than getting out. I had to grab my drenched nightie up around my waist, and then I crawled backward into the skylight, reaching with my toes for the bin below. As I carefully reclosed the skylight, the chilly air clung to my nightie and set my skin prickling. I wrung out the fabric as best as I could and flicked drops off my legs with my fingertips. Then, quietly, I descended the stairs again.

Wet and chilled, I raced silently along the length of the dorm. I hung my drenched nightie on a hook in my wardrobe and swiftly pulled on a dry one. Soon I was back in my sleep shell, burrowing into my quilt, and I waited, in dread, for someone to come for me.

It took a long time. The rain made it hard to listen for footsteps, but finally, a quiet voice came from farther down the room. I tried to calm my heart and breathe normally. Another voice answered, just distant and soft enough that I couldn't grasp the words. I waited as long as I could, listening, and then I turned toward the voices and slit my eyes open to see.

Down the row, a man and a woman stood by one of the sleep shells. The lid was open, and their figures were dark in contrast to a soft light that shone on the student. I hadn't made friends with any of the girls, and this one, Janice, I knew only slightly. She was twitching in spasmodic, unnatural tremors, though from her silence, I guessed she was still unconscious. The man, an older, bearded guy with a potbelly, held a tablet and a pole with an IV bag. The translucent line glowed as it led down to the girl's arm.

"Too much, do you think?" he said.

"No, she'll be all right," said the woman. "She'll settle. Just wait."

She leaned over Janice's face, propping up her eyelids to shine a pen light in one eye, and then the next. A cushiony

7

bar had been wedged between Janice's teeth. The man touched his finger to the tablet, indicating something.

"Just wait," the woman said again.

When she set the back of her fingers tenderly against Janice's cheek, and then her forehead, the sleeve of the woman's red cardigan took on a garish, flickering hue. Together, she and the man peered at the tablet again. The woman's smooth dark hair slid forward, covering her earphone as she waited, and her expression stayed watchful.

After a few more moments, she said, "See?"

"Yes," said the man.

Janice's trembling diminished, then stopped. She never once opened her eyes. The man straightened, relaxing. The woman reached to skim a finger over the tablet, tapped it, and nodded quietly.

"That was close. I'll admit it," she said.

"I'll say. These new ones. You never know." The man reached for the absorbent bar in Janice's teeth and gently worked it free.

The woman in the red sweater took out Janice's IV, handed it to the man, and pressed a cotton ball to Janice's arm. With her free hand, she touched her earphone. "There's no need. She's fine for now," she said. And then, "Right. Of course." She made a sign to the man, and then a circle with her finger that encompassed the room.

The man turned, and I closed my eyes.

"Yes. Of course. We will," said the woman.

I held very still, feeling my heart pounding, as the sound of footsteps spread out around the room. Soon I inhaled a faint trace of perfume. I could feel the presence of the woman hovering at the end, near my feet, and I breathed as evenly as I could.

"This one?" It was the man's voice, very soft. "What's her blip rank?"

"Ninety-three."

"A shame."

There was a faint rubbing noise of fabric.

I waited for more, a touch or a sound. A reply. I listened inside myself, too, distrusting my own body. Would a seizure hit me soon? My ears stayed primed, but I heard no reply, only the continued pattering of the rain high above. It took forever before there was another faint sound, a clicking from far down the room near the door. I exhaled in relief. I didn't dare open my eyes again, didn't turn my head or shift even when I felt the gentle tickle of a hair against my cheek.

I'd forgotten my wet hair. They must have seen it. They knew what I'd done.

But they'd said nothing.

>>>>>>>>

When the morning alarm awoke us at six, I sat up slowly. My hair was dry in thick, post-rain clumps, and my mouth felt fuzzy. Orly checked in for a minute to be sure we were all up, but she paid no special attention to me. As I headed toward the bathroom with my shower kit and fresh clothes, I looked over at Janice, who was talking to one of the other girls. She seemed fine. She pulled her blond hair high over her head in a ponytail, and when her sleeve shifted, I saw a scab mark on her forearm.

Do you tell someone she's had a seizure in the night? You don't, not if it would mean admitting your own crime of being awake. I passed her by without speaking, but I wondered how Janice could not instinctively know about her episode. She should at least notice the pinprick where the IV had gone into her skin. I pushed up my sleeve and glanced down at my own arm, and that's when I saw it: a faint, healing track mark in the crook of my left elbow.

They'd done it to me, too.

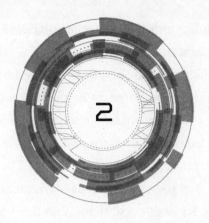

2

THE DISHWASHER

SHOCKED AS I was, I knew not to show it. Cameras were following my every move from a dozen different angles. I headed straight into a bathroom stall for privacy, locked the bolt, and closely inspected both my arms. One mark was all I had, and I couldn't tell how old it was, but they must have given me an IV, too, sometime fairly recently.

I didn't understand. Was I sick without knowing it? I felt okay. I also didn't get why I wasn't in trouble for breaking the rules during the night. Possibly they were waiting to call me in for discipline at a time that would be optimal for the show. I had no idea when that might be. In the meantime, the only thing to do was pretend everything was normal.

I flushed my sleeping pill down the toilet, unlocked the

door, and headed into the one other place we also had privacy: the showers.

This was the day of the fifty cuts, a Monday when my life would be decided. *The Forge Show* posted minute-to-minute blip ranks for every student at the school, with the most popular in each grade ranked #1, for first place. We had one hundred first-year, tenth-grade students who had been on campus for ten days, but today, half of us were getting cut, which meant anyone scoring worse than 50 at 5:00 p.m. would be gone. The eleventh- and twelfth-grade classes, each with fifty students already, were safe. If I stayed at the Forge School, on *The Forge Show*, I'd have a shot at a dream life of fame and art. If I was cut, I'd be lost to the dead-end boxcars of Doli. Not to put too bleak a spin on it.

Considering that my blip rank was 93, my chances didn't look good.

I toweled off, threw on my favorite skirt, boots, and a tee shirt, and headed to the dining hall for breakfast.

>>>>>>>>

A crash behind the serving line of the cafeteria made me look up just as the cook pummeled his fist into a guy's face. The guy staggered back, out of my line of vision.

"I wouldn't do that," the cook said, lifting his big hands in warning.

"It was an accident," came the guy's voice.

"That knife's no accident," said the cook. "No way am I getting attacked in my own kitchen. Put it down."

Others in the kitchen moved warily nearer, but I still couldn't see the guy who had been hit. A clatter came as something dropped on metal. The cook stepped out of my sight. I heard another smacking punch.

"Clean it up, you royal bastard," the cook said. "You hear me?"

A shuffling clank and a stream of indecipherable words came next.

"What's that?" the cook demanded.

"I wasn't going to use it," came the guy's voice, clearly.

Smack again.

The girl beside me gave my tray a nudge. "You're holding up the line," she said. "Let's go."

"The cook just hit somebody," I said, edging farther along.

"You're kidding. Really? Where?" she said.

I craned to look back in the kitchen, and when I caught a brief glimpse of a brown-haired guy crouching near to the floor, cleaning something, I stopped again.

"Back there. He just hit him, hard," I said. I had the tense, flayed feeling that I was supposed to do something about it, even though it was none of my business.

Other students went around us and kept picking out food.

"I don't see anything," the girl said, bumping my tray with hers again. "They have banana pancakes. Sweet."

I slid my tray down the poles and peered through the next

counter slot, trying to see the guy once more, but instead, the cook's sweaty face blocked my view. He looked casually across at me through wafty sizzles of sausage smoke, and I felt the same vicarious burn of anger that came whenever my stepfather clocked me.

I ducked my head and moved down the cafeteria line, but I hardly noticed the food anymore. First Janice, then my own track mark, and now this flash of violence in the kitchen. They were like cracks at the edges of *The Forge Show*, cracks that made me question the appearance of everything on the stage around me. I paused by one of the wooden pillars with my tray.

Morning light dropped in the big windows, glinting on saltshakers, and the dining hall buzzed of coffee and sugar. In a corner beneath an abstract wall sculpture, Janice was eating with a couple of guys. She smoothed her long blond hair from one side of her neck to the other, like an angel spreading its glittery wings, and with my mental lens, I saw how naturally she projected a photogenic presence. She wasn't the only one, either.

We were the show. I got that. I knew that coming in, just like everybody else, but accepting the constant cameras wasn't the same as liking them, let alone performing for them. The Forge School was an elite arts academy, while *The Forge Show* was the reality show that tracked and broadcasted the activity of each individual student at the school. It was a smart, interactive system. Viewers at home controlled who they watched by selecting their favorite students' feeds. The feedback of their viewing choices, in turn, determined student blip ranks.

To sweeten the value of popularity, banner ads linked to each blip rank were incrementally more expensive as the ranks rose toward #1, and students banked a fraction of what the advertisers paid, receiving the funds at graduation. For the most popular students with the highest blip ranks, their banner ad funds after three years of high school could top a million dollars.

I'd certainly watched the show before, from home, back when my dream to come here had seemed impossible, but until I'd arrived on campus, I hadn't fully understood how the stage aspect of the school pervaded everything. The other new students like Janice were perpetually projecting extra-watt versions of themselves for the cameras. For them, it seemed effortless. They even thrived on it. But to me, who preferred the other end of a camera, the super-visibility was exhausting.

A big, old-fashioned tally board on the wall made a flipping noise while it updated the blip ranks of every student in the school, and I watched as my name settled in at 95th place. Great. My oatmeal was skimming over as it cooled. It was no use. My appetite was shot, and food wouldn't settle my restlessness, anyway. I left my tray at the counter and stepped outside to the terrace.

Breathing was immediately easier. The rain had stopped, leaving a layer of moisture in the air and an overcast sky. Far off, between the buildings, the Kansas plains turned blue as they approached the horizon. Nearer, the sheep pasture was a deep, soggy green, as if the mud beneath carried its lifeblood up each blade of grass.

On impulse, I walked between the dining hall and the art building, toward the pasture. A clattering came through the sieve of the kitchen window screens, and I smelled coffee cake more distinctly than I had when I was inside. A Forge Farms Ice Cream delivery truck was parked by the loading dock, tucked up close so the driver could load the big cardboard tubs onto his dolly.

Ahead, half a dozen sheep made a constellation of white against the green of the pasture, and I mentally framed them up in a bucolic shot. Artsy me. Farther east, beyond the short stone wall that edged campus, a sky-blue water tower labeled "Forgetown" overlooked a rambling assortment of small homes. Just inside the campus wall, on a knoll of its own, stood an old observatory with a gray dome. To my left, a wood and stone lookout tower rose dark against the gray sky. At the top, big camera lenses gleamed like black, mismatched eyes. The semisphere of a microphone dish with its lacework grid of metal could be aimed to pick up sound from any direction, including mine.

Just then, one of the cameras swiveled to aim directly at me, and I swear, it tempted me to do something asinine. It really did. You'd never believe how annoying it was to be watched *all the time*, even when you were doing *absolutely nothing*. It put me at war with myself all the time: behave. Don't behave. Behave. Don't.

The toe of my boot bumped against a rock. I picked it up

and hurled it. The rock soared, shrank to a speck, and plum-meted into the grass far from the sheep. *Face it*, I thought. *You're getting cut.* No matter how ideal it seemed, I shouldn't want to stay at a place where students had secret seizures at night, but stupid me, I did anyway. I wanted to stay at Forge so badly I could gnaw it in my teeth. I just couldn't see that anything I could do would make a difference. I backed around, searching for one last rock to throw before I went to class, and then I paused.

Behind the art building, leaning against a giant, paint-spattered wooden spool, a guy was pressing an ice pack to his face. He was all Adam's apple with his head tipped back, and a white bib apron protected his shirt and jeans. I picked up another rock and ambled slowly across the gravel lot.

"Hey," I said. "I saw, in the kitchen before. Are you okay?"

He lowered the ice. His bruise was a defined crescent, and the skin near his eye was ruddy and shiny from the cold. He might have been my age, fifteen, or a little older. His dark hair partially hid a row of three rings in his ear, and after one mea-suring glance, he hefted the ice pack and put it back on his bruise, closing his eyes.

"I'm not interested," he said. An accent gave his words an extra clip. "Go find someone else."

"For what?" I asked. When he didn't explain, I went on. "If you want to report the cook, I'll back you up. I saw what he did. He shouldn't have hit you like that."

"That's cute," he said.

"I mean it. Is he always like that?"

17

"I don't need you to make a report," he said. "Fortunately, no one gives a crap about what happens in the kitchen."

"What did you do, anyway?" I said.

He shifted the ice pack and opened his good eye. "Spilled his precious eggs. Pulled a knife on him. It was instinct. Stupid." He gave me a little wave. "Okay, enough. You can go now. You've got your spike."

"My spike?"

"You know. For this compassionate little outreach of yours." He did a double jerk of his thumb, like a hitchhiker, to indicate the cameras.

It took me a sec to follow his logic from the cameras to the viewers to a likely spike in my blip rank. "You think that's why I'm talking to you?" I asked. "For my blip rank?"

"The fifty cuts are tonight," he said. "Students will be pulling stunts all day today to get their blip ranks higher. It happens every year. It's pathetically predictable, actually, especially among the doomed."

I dropped my rock and brushed my hands. "Actually, asswipe, I just wanted to be sure you were okay," I said. "My mistake." I turned and started toward the quad.

His voice came after me. "Your name would be?"

"Seriously?" I paused to stare back at him and braced a fist on my hip. "That's an apology?"

He lowered his ice pack again. He didn't bother to smile and I didn't either. Then he gave the slightest shrug.

"I beg your pardon," he said. "It hasn't been my best morning. I'm Linus Pitts."

18

I frowned, considering him, and then I took a couple steps nearer again. "Rosie Sinclair," I said.

"We meet at last."

His voice was so deadpan I couldn't quite tell if he was being ironic. That was when I noticed something really was wrong with his eye. I came nearer to inspect him. The pupil was a murky color instead of clear black.

"Can you see all right?" I asked.

"As it happens, I can't. I think there's blood in my eye."

"Let me see." I looked closer while Linus aimed his eye-balls at me. It looked like red liquid had spilled inside his left pupil. I didn't know that was possible. "Shouldn't you get that checked?"

"Probably."

"Like now?" I said.

He closed one eye slowly, and then the other. "This happened to me once before. It'll clear in a few days."

I laughed. "So you're half-blind and it's no big deal?"

"I'm not keen on doctors."

"Neither am I, but I like to be able to *see*."

"Like I said. It'll clear."

With a beeping noise, the ice cream truck backed up from the dining hall next door and drove away.

"How long have you worked here?" I asked.

"Me? Three years."

"That's a lot of dishes," I said.

"What makes you think I only wash dishes? I do a lot of prep, too."

He resettled the ice pack against his bad eye and shifted so he could see me with the other.

"Where's your accent from?" I asked.

"I'm Welsh, by way of St. Louis."

"Why aren't you in school yourself?"

"Because I quit," he said.

"To work kitchen prep?"

His eyebrows lifted. "You're a regular charmer. You know that?"

"Sorry," I said. "There's nothing wrong with kitchen prep. I'm just wondering."

"How do you feel about getting cut tonight?" he asked. He pushed off from the giant spool and ran a hand down his apron, catching his thumb where the string wrapped around to the front.

"I said I was sorry. You don't have to be vindictive."

He let out a laugh. "Not bad, Sinclair. You almost make me want to watch the show."

"You don't?" I asked. "Seriously? But you work here."

"Exactly. It's too much of a good thing. Franny likes to run it in the kitchen, and I always work facing the other direction if I can help it."

I couldn't believe it. He worked on the staff of one of the most popular reality shows of all time, and he didn't watch it. Actually, that was pretty interesting. "Cool," I said.

"Tell me something," he said. He lowered the ice pack and turned it in his fingers. "All that compulsory sleep every night. What's that feel like?"

20

"It's a little weird," I said. I glanced around to see a mic button on the top of the giant spool. Every inch of this place was wired for sound. I leaned back against the spool in the place where he had been, and tugged idly at my necklace.

"Do you dream a lot?" Linus asked. "Can you actually feel yourself getting more creative?"

"Not really."

"That's the theory, though, right?" he asked.

It was. One of the principles of the school was that our creativity was increased by our sleep because it cemented the learning from the day. It puzzled me, though, why we needed a full twelve hours. I wondered if Linus knew anything about what happened at the school at night.

"I didn't know it was such a tough question," he said. He had a way of smiling with his eyes narrowed in concentration, like he was serious even more than he was happy. I found it oddly inviting.

"It's weird," I said. "I miss the night. I miss who I am in the night."

"That's not so weird," he said. "Go on."

"I don't dream at all anymore, either." I glanced out at the sheep again. "I miss that, a lot. I also miss feeling like I'm asleep. I *know* I'm asleep. I know the time goes by because when I wake up, it's daylight again. But I don't *feel* like I'm sleeping here, you know?"

"That sort of makes sense," Linus said.

It was hard to explain what I didn't fully understand myself. I put the toes of my boots together and examined them.

"I think it's connected to the cameras. I feel like I'm always on," I said. "Like they've pushed a button and I'm always on. Night is completely skipped. When I wake up, I'm continuing directly from the evening before when I climbed in my sleep shell. Like I haven't had a break. Like I've been cheated." That was it. I felt cheated. I wasn't simply asleep. Someone was stealing my sleep *and* my privacy from me, until I existed only for the show. "It's like being robbed."

"That can't be good," he said.

I did the double thumb jerk to indicate the cameras. "I'm not sure I'm supposed to talk about this."

He smiled. "You can talk about anything. People say negative things about Forge all the time. You're only being honest."

I felt a tingle of apprehension. "It feels like a mistake."

"It adds authenticity. Viewers love that," he said. "Besides, if you dislike it so much, you should be glad to be going home."

"Don't say that!" I said, alarmed.

"Why not?"

"I want to stay here so badly, it hurts," I said. "It'll kill me if I have to go, but every time I look at my blip rank, it's worse."

"So you're a pessimist," Linus said. "How refreshing."

I laughed and half squirmed at the same time. "Are you doing this on purpose? Tormenting me?"

"Not at all," he said. "Why do you want to stay? You want to be a big star? Is that it?"

I couldn't possibly explain this hungry thing inside me. I needed to make films, real films about real people. It was the

22

one way I knew, the one, complete way to get to the truth and show what really mattered. If I had to go back to Doli now, without an education, realistically I'd end up working at McLellens' Pot Bar and Sundries, or at the prison school like Ma. I'd be dead my whole life.

"Have you ever heard of Doli, Arizona?" I asked.

"No. Should I have?"

"We're the poorest zip code in the country. Half the people don't have jobs. My school is a farce and I'm on the pre-prison track there. It's teaching me nothing, let alone anything about film," I said. "And don't ask me why we don't leave Doli. It's still my home."

"I didn't ask you," he said quietly. He leaned a hand on the wooden spool. "You can't seriously be here for the education."

"Crazy, huh?"

He drummed his fingers for a second. "What's your blip rank?"

I lifted my gaze toward the horizon. "Last I checked, it was ninety-five."

"That's quite lousy."

"Exactly." I took a deep breath and tried to smile. "The worst is going to be facing my little sister. She believed in me so hard."

He sloshed the ice pack in his hand and then chucked it with a clank into a garbage can. "You're good. I'll give you that," he said.

I wasn't sure what he meant. Linus took a step backward and waved up at the tower where the big cameras were.

An old guy with a mustache looked around from the back of one.

"Hey, Otis! How's it going?" Linus said, and waved again.

"Where are my smokes?" the old guy called down.

"I'll bring them at lunch!" Linus yelled back.

Otis vanished again.

"What are you doing?" I asked.

"Otis is a sharp old bastard," Linus said. "You want to get him on your side."

"You can't just flag down the camera guy," I said.

Linus slid a hand in his back pocket. "Why not? Get this, Sinclair," he said. "I may not watch *The Forge Show* anymore, but I get how it works. It's a *show*. You're a performer on a TV show. That's what matters. Not your fancy education part of it. Your entire value is measured by how popular you are to the viewers."

"You mean for the banner ads," I said.

"You won't even be *eligible* for a banner ad unless you pass the fifty cuts," Linus said. "You have to think about the audience every minute between now and five o'clock. You have to plan for them and calculate their reactions. You need a strategy."

I straightened away from the spool. "Just because you work here doesn't mean you know what it's like from my side. I've *been* thinking about the cameras. I've followed all the rules, but it doesn't work for me. I can't explain it. I never feel like myself here."

"You don't understand," Linus said. "Forget the *cameras*.

24

Think about the *people watching*. That's the difference. The *people* out there care about you, or they would if they felt like they knew the real you." Linus ran a hand back through his hair. "Look. I can help you. I do know what works here."

"And what's that?"

"Honesty. Integrity."

I laughed, thinking of all the Janice types on the campus. They didn't strike me as honest, but they had high blip ranks. "What else?"

"You could take the talent show approach," he said. "That works if you're phenomenal. What's your art? What did you do to get in?"

"I made a documentary about my sister Dubbs," I said. "She's seven. I want to make films."

"Oh, *films*," he said, in a snobby drawl. "You can't exactly make a film in a day."

"I could, actually, but it wouldn't be any good," I said. "Next idea."

He opened a hand. "Hang out with one of your friends who has a high blip rank," he said. "You'll get a shadow effect."

I didn't have any friends. I had acquaintances, but it took me longer than ten days to make what I considered real friends. "Next idea," I said.

"What's wrong?"

"Nothing. What else?" I asked.

"Betray your boyfriend. Or girlfriend. Whoever. Go for personal drama."

"I don't have a boyfriend," I said.

"Then find one." His eyes stayed serious, as if he were testing me. "Think tryst," he said. "Cut out later and meet up with a humble dishwasher with a festering black eye. It'll add a good ten points to your blip rank."

He was neither humble nor festering, obviously.

"You are a very misguided person," I said.

"I'm just right. You know I am."

"Why would meeting you be worth a spike?" I asked. "Because I'm a student and you're on the staff? Is that supposed to make us special?"

"Don't be dense."

I searched back and forth between his mismatched eyes, waiting for something in his words to make sense.

He smiled slightly and spun a hand back and forth between us. "We have this," he said.

"This what?"

"You know," he said softly.

I did not know. The fine, expectant buzzing in my chest had nothing to do with him.

And then it did.

His eyes warmed. "See?"

I took a step back. The buzzing had exploded into wild wings of surprise.

"You're smiling," he said.

"I'm not."

"I'll be here at quarter to five," he said. "Just in case. I'm telling you, personal drama's good. It gets viewers to care about you."

26

I backed up some more. "Get your eye checked."

"You do bossy very well, Sinclair," he said, covering his heart. "Irresistible."

He was impossible. But he was also right about one thing. As I turned and ran for the film building, I was grinning and primed with hope.

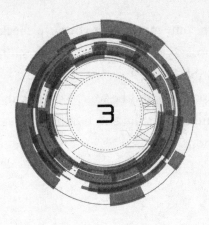

3

FISTER

"TARDINESS IS A sign of disrespect or overinflated ego," Mr. DeCoster said as I stepped into my Media Convergence classroom.

"I'm sorry," I said. Out of breath from running, I started toward the back where I usually sat.

"No, sit here," Mr. DeCoster said, clearing a box off a desk in the front row. It was closest to the windows, directly in front of the teacher's station where hiding was impossible. Great.

I plopped in my wheelie chair and turned on my computer. The large screen above was controlled by a smaller touch screen below. The guy on my right glanced over. I peeked at his screen, which briefly showed the green and gray terrain of a game world before he switched windows to an editing program.

Forge students took three classes and a practicum daily, six days a week. I had Media Convergence, a required class for all incoming sophomores, followed by The Masters, where we studied artistic geniuses of the past, and then Space, my Math/Science elective. My practicum followed after lunch. Since everything had to be crammed into twelve waking hours per day, every minute counted. On Sundays, we were encouraged to call home, attend a religious service on campus, and relax, which didn't come naturally to many. We also had myriad performances scheduled on Sundays, not to mention impromptu ones, like when students started singing in the laundry room.

None of the schedule was going to matter if I was sent home, but for now, it did. Linus hadn't done me any favors making me late.

Mr. DeCoster was explaining how to sync audio and video tracks if they uploaded with a timing glitch. Such glitches could happen with low-grade field uploads, and he gave us each a fifteen-second clip with the sound off by a couple seconds. It was a persnickety, retro type of skill, and I didn't see the point of it.

"You'll notice I've customized each of your clips," DeCoster said. "Check in your E files in the K:Cloud under 'SynchClog,' as in s-y-n-c-h."

The pun evoked a chorus of moans and a brief laugh from the guy on my right.

I glanced his way again. He was a husky black guy with glasses and thick, uneven hair that was long enough to tuck behind his ears. At his feet, his backpack had a pair of swim goggles looped around a strap.

"This is a waste of time," I said.

"Questions, Rosie?" DeCoster said.

"There's got to be an automated program for this," I said.

"I want you to do it by hand," he said. "It'll open up different possibilities for you. Give it a shot."

When the teacher's back was turned, I clicked open a new window on my computer and pulled up *The Forge Show* to check my blip rank: 85. It was up ten points since breakfast, and my heart did a little jig. Linus had been right about a spike.

"That's doom in a noose, you know," said the guy beside me. He had a southern cadence to his voice. He nodded at my large screen as he kept skimming his hand over his touch screen. "Watching yourself. The viewers hate that. It's cliché."

My Forge profile showed a live image of me facing my computer, and when I leaned forward, the image of me did, too, of course. I tried a wave and aimed it toward the active camera somewhere to my right. I leaned sideways and felt slowly through the air toward the camera lens so I could watch my hand get bigger on my computer screen.

"Hey now," said the guy.

I'd entered his no fly zone.

"One sec," I said.

I kept going, leaning farther over him, watching in my screen as my hand grew monster-attack large until I finally touched the camera lens, a button on Mr. DeCoster's desk lamp. On my screen, my Forge profile switched to a new camera angle that showed me practically in the lap of the guy beside me. He was still working, peeking around me to see his own screen.

"Any day now," he said.

"Sorry," I said, laughing, and settled back. "I just had to do that." On my computer, I closed out of *The Forge Show*.

"I know," he said. "I did it myself, back on day two."

He didn't stop working to talk. He was splicing tracks, unlinking them, and shifting them around like bricks in a fluid wall. I watched him collapse the field, skim it sideways, and expand another section to drop in a segment of film from his closet.

I felt a flicker and remembered last night's brink lesson about laying bricks. It seemed suddenly like it could be related to editing. "How did you learn to do that so fast?" I asked.

"Projects back home."

I'd been working with videos at home for a couple of years, using the editing options within my camera, but I couldn't do half what he was doing.

"What's your name?" I asked.

He shoved his glasses up his nose. "Burnham Fister."

"I'm Rosie Sinclair," I said.

"Hi," Burnham said.

I pulled my SynchClog file out and sat back as the first shot of the film clip appeared in my editing program. To my surprise, it was from my documentary on my sister, the one I'd used to apply to the Forge School. The first close-up shot of Dubbs's face brought me instant delight.

"Who's that?" said Burnham.

"My sister."

"Nice. How old is she?"

"Seven."

I leaned closer to get lost in the monitor. I knew this section. I'd filmed it myself and watched it a million times. Every frame was precious and familiar to me.

It began with Dubbs's face up close, bobbing up and down as she rode her bicycle straight toward the camera. I'd filmed her five times so I could splice together the shots at different angles, and she'd been totally into it, every time. Next, the film showed her complete body in profile on the bike, bumping along the road in front of our train, with the orange light of the sunset coming through the gaps between and under the boxcars. Every color and shadow was deep and strong. I'd added a shot of my sister's tan legs and her bare feet on the pedals. Her short red skirt swirled out behind her. The next shot showed her profile, and then came another three seconds of her face again, head on, until her hair flew across her lips as she turned to look to her right. There the clip froze, ended.

Beauty shines out of my sister. You'd have to be blind to miss it. If you put her in a playground with a hundred other dusty second graders, all loud and teasing and running around, in all the commotion, your eye would light on her.

Something inside me cracked open and homesickness poured

in. At the same time, I ached to prove to her that I was good enough to stay at Forge.

"She looks like you," Burnham said.

"No."

Dubbs is the delicate, light-footed, blond sister, while I'm the dark, sturdy one. Her crooked smile is openly charming and unselfconscious. My eyebrows are black, my eyes hazel, my teeth straight except for a gap in the front. In short, Burnham couldn't be more wrong.

"She does," he said. "Around the eyes."

Maybe he meant how Dubbs looked determined. I turned to find Burnham watching me.

"She's my half sister," I said. "We have the same mom."

He nodded. "Let's hear the audio," he said. "May I?" And he plugged his earphones into my spare jack.

It was only fair, considering I'd practically sat in his lap. I put on my headphones and turned up the volume. It was natural sound, with the voice of my stepfather coming from off-screen. My sister called, *"Coming, Dad!"* and then rang her bike bell. The audio was delayed by a full second, and it was going to be a job to line it up again.

Burnham unplugged. "Nice stuff," he said.

"Thanks." I lowered my headphones and nodded politely at his screen. "What do you have?"

He skimmed his touch screen and a dimly lit, underwater world appeared, with softly waving kelp below and the dark underbelly of a small boat above. There was just enough grainy blue light to see. A figure dove from the boat and a shimmer of pale, tiny stars trailed around his strokes as he swam down to the bottom, touched down, and sprang back up toward the surface.

"How did you do that effect?" I asked.

"It's bioluminescence. It's for real," he said. "My brother and I went swimming last summer and I caught this."

"You shot that yourself?" I asked, amazed. "From the bottom of a lake?"

"The sea. Yeah," he said.

And he thought my film was good. This was the sort of person I was competing against. I thunked my head down on my desk. "I'm dead."

He smiled. "Maybe you could switch to the drama queen department."

"Are you worried about getting cut tonight?" I asked. "Like, *at all*?"

"No."

I laughed at his confidence and straightened up.

"I don't believe in worry," Burnham added. "It doesn't change the outcome, but it makes the now miserable, so I don't do it."

"The now. That's very Zen of you."

"I'm a third child," he said, smiling again.

He awed me. "What's your blip rank?" I asked.

"Last I checked, sixteen."

"Sixteen!" I said. Who was this guy? "That's why you're not worried."

"Ranks can change," he said. "They'll fly all over the place today. No one's safe, and you shouldn't give up hope."

"You're too nice," I said. "But thanks."

He flipped to the window with the computer game again. Squat cartoon knights brandished axes and maces. A little dragon came on and spouted purple fire. It was distracting, at first, to have Burnham whizzing around with his computer beside me, but after a while, I got into my synching assignment. I sank my chin into my hand, rested my left elbow on the desk, and sprawled while I worked the touch screen with my right hand.

"Where are you from?" he asked.

"Doli, Arizona," I said. "How about you?"

"Atlanta."

His clicking distracted me again, and I looked over to see a strange sketchpad box where the dragon fire changed from purple to green.

"Wait," I said, frowning. "Are you *making* that game with the dragon?"

"Yeah," he said absently. "I'm still working out the kinks. I didn't create the engine or anything. I just developed the game."

Okay, this was a boy with serious skills.

"What do your parents do?" I asked.

"They're Fister Pharmaceuticals."

"Come again?"

"My mom's a biochemist. She started the company," Burnham said. "My dad invested and expanded it."

"You should get them to supply the sleeping pills for the Forge School," I said. "They'd make a mint."

"They already do."

Of course they do, I thought. I was such a genius. How did I not put this together? Fister was a major advertiser on the show.

Burnham took off his glasses and polished the lenses with the bottom of his shirt. It was an old shirt, a button-down that had once been red, but had faded to a soft, cottony color. He also wore an analog watch with a rectangular face. Nobody wore watches except old men. And Burnham, apparently. Burnham had to be richer than he looked. A lot richer. Burnham could wear whatever he pleased.

"Awkward," I said.

He squinted as he put his glasses back on. "Might as well say it. You think I'm here because of my connections."

"Actually, I was just wondering how rich you are. How classy is that?"

"Real classy," he said, laughing.

"Do you take the same pills the rest of us do?" I asked.

"Yes, of course. Why?"

"I don't know." I was thinking about Janice's seizure again, and the track mark in my own arm. "Is it purely the sleep that's supposed to make us more creative, or is there something in the pill that does?"

"It's just the sleep," Burnham said. "If the pill could make people more creative, we'd be selling it by the millions."

"You don't sell a lot just as sleeping pills?" I asked.

"Well," he said, "we do."

I laughed. I had a ton of questions, now that I thought about it. "Why does the school make us sleep for twelve hours?" I asked. "It can't be just for the convenience of the repeat cycle." One of the distinctive features of *The Forge Show* was that it showed the exact same footage twice, once as it happened live during the day, straight through for twelve hours, and again at night, while the students were asleep. Viewers could watch the same or different student feeds the second time through, focusing on their favorite moments of interaction.

"The twelve hours came out of a study the Forge School commissioned back when they were trying to find the optimal amount of sleep for creativity," Burnham said.

"When was that?" I asked.

"Back before we were born. I'm thinking eighteen or twenty years ago?" he said. "The rationale is that we're on a kind of hyper-life during the day while we're here. We'd burn out without enough sleep. You get tired by six, don't you?"

"Yes," I said. "Definitely."

"There you go."

I wondered if Burnham had any idea why a student would have seizures, but it seemed unwise to ask him in front of the cameras. I glanced out the window. Across a narrow courtyard, inside the glass walls of a ballet studio, a class was practicing at the barre. The dancers arched their arms over their heads, all in synch, like models for a Degas painting, but without the tutus. I wished I had my video camera with me to capture the movement.

"Can I try something with your footage?" Burnham asked.

"Sure."

He reached for my touch screen and swiveled it closer to himself. He pulled up a still frame of Dubbs. Then he pulled up a color wheel and started sweeping in bits of purple and blue around the shadows of the boxcar and its wheels. He worked so quickly and fluidly, it was almost like he was painting directly on the photo. A few minutes later, after a final click, he stopped and slid his hand away. He hadn't touched Dubbs herself, but by deepening the colors and darkness that framed her face, he'd made her even more luminous than before.

I stared, absorbing the effect, wondering how he'd done it. I touched a finger to Dubbs's cheek, wishing I could have her with me in person. We walked on the train tracks together sometimes. She liked to hold my hand and randomly tug downward for an inside joke.

"You like it?" he asked.

"It's very cool. Can you teach me how to do that?" I asked.

Mr. DeCoster approached behind us. "Rosie, I've had a call from Dr. Ash," he said, indicating his earphone. "She wants you to stop by the infirmary after lunch."

I clenched the edge of my chair. They had caught up with me. I swiveled to look at Mr. DeCoster. "What for?"

"She didn't say."

A student called him from the other side of the room, and I glanced over to see Janice with her hand raised. Mr. DeCoster reminded us to save our work before he headed off.

"Are you sick?" Burnham asked.

"No. I have no idea what that's about," I lied. I glanced at Janice again and wondered if she would be called to the infirmary, too.

"You look, how shall we say, a bit constipated," Burnham said.

I let out a laugh. "It isn't that. But thanks for the compliment."

"No problem."

The bell rang, and around us, students shuffled up with their backpacks and turned off their computers. I hadn't finished my synching exercise. I wasn't sure if I'd ever be back to complete it.

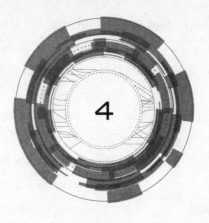

4

THE BLIP RANK BOARD

BY LUNCH, I was starved, and my anxiety about the cuts was gnawing at my gut. Every time I'd stolen a chance to check my blip rank, it was hovering around 85. All the other first-year students were checking their ranks perpetually, too, and some of them looked even more frazzled than I felt. From a distance, the older students gloated good-naturedly, as if they'd never gone through this torture.

As I passed along the cafeteria counter once again, I peered into the kitchen for Linus. He was working at a back sink between mounds of dirty trays, scrubbing in water so hot it steamed up against his face. His red arms disappeared into yellow gloves, and his white shirt clung.

A couple of students shifted out of line before me, and I realized the girl ahead of me was Janice. I couldn't think how to ask her if she'd also been called to the infirmary, but I could at least try to get her talking.

"Hey," I said. "You're in my Media Convergence class. Janice, right?"

"That's right," she said. "DeCoster chewed you out for being late. How did you do with the synching?"

"It was okay. I didn't quite finish."

"Really?" she said. "You always look so badass in that class, like you can't see anything but your screen."

I laughed. "You're kidding. Me?"

She smiled, and for the first time, I wondered if, in my own way, I was as intimidating to the other students as they were to me. Janice kept talking about class, and we went through the line together. Brightly lit stations made French fries glow and green nubs of broccoli shimmer in their cheesy sauce. I still couldn't get over how much food was offered to us every day, and in such a variety.

When we came out of the line, the tables were nearly full, and I scanned for empty seats. Janice hovered beside me. Above, designer LED lamps dropped down between crisscrossing beams of wood. I didn't have to look closely to know the room was riddled with cameras, little button ones affixed to window frames, booths, and napkin dispensers. The blip rank board flipped its mini panels in another update, and I could feel how the fluttering noise fanned the anxiety in the room as students turned to check their ranks. I was at 87.

Someone called my name. I turned to see Burnham sitting at a round table with a couple other first-year students. They'd found a sunny place near the windows, and Janice and I wound our way over to join them.

I set down my tray across from Burnham, and Janice took the place between him and me. "This is Janice," I said.

"Burnham Fister," he said, half rising to offer a hand. He was the first guy I ever saw who made shaking hands look natural and not weirdly grown up.

"I think we've met before. At Camp Pewter," Janice said. She smoothed her long hair over her shoulder.

"That's right," Burnham said, smiling. "I didn't think you remembered. Do you know Paige and Henrik?"

Paige, slouching in a black leotard, said a quick hello. Her eyes were ringed with black, her dark complexion was flawless, and her lips were a deep, pouty red. Henrik had close-cropped brown hair and a chin-strap beard, and his thin summer scarf made me think *Europe*, especially when I picked up a slight accent. He was methodically adding sugar to the four cups of coffee on his tray.

"You know, Paige, it doesn't mean you're any less of a person if you get cut," Henrik said. "Viewers watching from home have no way to judge our inner worth."

"That's not true," Paige said. "Our inner worth is directly connected to the behavior we show on the outside. That's why it's going to hurt. It's the ultimate rejection."

I glanced doubtfully at the two of them while I spread cream cheese on my everything bagel. Burnham, I noticed, was chewing the end of a straw.

"But they've only been watching us for ten days in this

totally bizarre, surreal place," Henrik went on. "This isn't who we really are."

"No? I don't know about you, but I've been spilling my guts out on the dance floor," Paige said. "This *is* who I am. This is *everything* I am."

"Are you saying a bunch of strangers knows you better than your own family?" Henrik asked.

"I'm just saying they're picking their feeds based on what they see, and this is who I really am," Paige said. "Whether I make the cuts depends on if they want me or not. It's that simple. Why can't you accept a true meritocracy?"

Henrik leaned over his coffee cups with a red swizzle stick. "If it's that simple, everyone who's rejected tonight will go home and slit their wrists."

"Holy crap," Janice said.

Paige smacked her hand on the table. "You have to put everything of yourself out there," she said. "That's the point. That's art. You can't hold back."

"Oh, please," Henrik said. "Art is not all guts on the dance floor. Can you imagine the mess?"

I let out a laugh.

Paige glared at me. "What?" she demanded.

"It's just, guts *would* be sort of slippery," I said.

Paige leaned back, crossing her arms, and stared at Burnham as if to ask him, *who is this moron?*

Burnham smiled around his straw.

"Fine," Paige said. "Laugh."

"Come on," Henrik said, starting on another cup of coffee.

"No, you have to admit Paige has a point," Burnham said, taking out the straw. "It's hard not to feel like our entire worth is wrapped up in our blip ranks. But Henrik's right, too. If we exist only for our ranks, we'll cease to exist once we leave. That can't be right, Paige. There has to be something more."

"Why? Art is already more. That's what we're being judged on," Paige said.

"Your art and your blip rank are connected, but they're not the same thing," I said. "If you say your rank is all that matters, Paige, then you're saying people with low ranks or no ranks, like people working in the kitchen, have no worth at all."

"That's not what she's saying," Henrik said.

"No, that *is* what I'm saying," Paige said. She stirred her yogurt. "Why be afraid to admit it? We're on the show because we're better than them. We're more creative and interesting. And if we make the cuts, that says we're worth more than the students who get cut. We're intrinsically more valuable people."

I sat back with my lemonade and stared at her. Paige was crazy mean, but I sort of admired her elitist guts, the ones she put on the dance floor. I also hoped she'd get cut.

"You probably think the hyper-rich are intrinsically more valuable, too, just because they're rich," Henrik said.

Paige opened her hand. "Survival of the fittest. They've figured out how to rule the world. Ask Burnham."

I choked on my drink.

"Can I strangle Paige?" Henrik said.

Burnham's dark cheeks had taken on a deeper hue, and he looked stiff. "Be my guest," he said lightly.

Henrik threw an arm around Paige's neck and wrestled her into a headlock. She did something to him under the table that made him let go. "Hey!" he said.

"All's fair," Paige said.

"Which is this? Love or war?" Henrik said.

"Take your pick," Paige said, and took up her sandwich.

From across the dining hall, the big blip rank board fluttered with another update, and I was surprised that none of my companions glanced over at it. I couldn't resist. I was at 83. Janice, Burnham, Henrik, and Paige were all in the top twenty-five. I caught Burnham watching me, and focused again on my bagel.

"Can I have your swizzle sticks, Henrik?" Janice asked.

Henrik passed them over. "Why?"

"I like them," Janice said.

"They've got a whole can of them over by the coffee," Henrik said.

"I like them used. That way they're not wasted," Janice said, drying them daintily on a napkin.

"What do you do here?" Henrik asked her.

"I'm an actor, *obviously*," Janice said, drawling out the word. "Speaking of the cuts," she added, reverting to normal, "I heard people can hack into the *Forge Show* database and falsify the blip ranks."

"Like who?" I asked.

"Backers and advertisers," Janice said. "Gamblers."

"Everything's encrypted," Burnham said. "The computer security has a ton of layers, and they change the encryptions regularly so people can't hack in."

"How do you know about it?" I asked.

He shrugged.

"Have you tried to hack in?" I asked.

His gaze met mine. "I have cameras on me all the time," he said. "When would I have the chance to try?"

"You could have tried before you came here," Paige pointed out.

"That would be highly unethical, wouldn't it?" he said.

He wasn't saying it was beyond his abilities, though.

I sucked a dab of cream cheese off my thumb. "If a person wanted to influence the blip ranks legally, would there be a way to do it?" I asked.

"Sure," Burnham said. "One way would be a group effort. We have a lot of influence ourselves, actually. If the five of us made a direct appeal to our viewers and asked them, point blank, to start following one person, that person would gain a major chunk of our viewers all at the same time. They'd see a serious spike in their blip rank."

"Could we try it?" I asked.

They all turned to me, and I felt a knot of apprehension. I was way too uncool.

"Never mind," I said quickly. "Forget it."

"No. It's not a bad idea," Burnham said slowly. He studied me a moment. "The effect would be even more conspicuous

46

with a low-ranking student, and, no offense, Rosie's rank is low."

Paige laughed, sitting back. "You want us to endorse little Miss Rosie here?"

"Why not?" Burnham asked.

"I don't even know her," Paige said. "Why should I use my influence for her?"

Burnham smiled easily, but there was an edge to his voice. "You may be an elitist snob, but you're also interested in a social experiment."

Paige considered me with her black-rimmed gaze as if I were some seven-legged bug.

"You guys don't have to," I said. "Really."

"Why? Is it mortifying to be a guinea pig?" Paige asked. "Let's all do it at once."

"It's not mortifying, Rosie. It's just an experiment. Let's try it!" Janice said. "What do we do? Hold hands?"

Henrik was shaking his head at Burnham. "Man, you are something."

"Keep it simple. Just look right at one of the cameras," Burnham said. "Ask your viewers, straight up, to check out Rosie's feed. Ready? On your mark, get set, go."

The four of them each turned to a different camera button and recited some version of "Follow Rosie."

Burnham slid his phone into the center of the tabletop and pulled up my Forge profile. Everyone hunched over it to see, and correspondingly, my profile showed us all hunching to-gether. My blip rank put me in 82nd place. Then it jumped to

80, and then 78. It hovered there a moment. On the wall across the dining room, the big blip rank board began to flicker again with another update. I turned to watch it, holding my breath, as the numbers and letters spun, and when they settled, my blip rank was up to 69.

I let out a laugh of disbelief.

"My rank's up, too," Henrik said. "So is Paige's. We all went up."

Paige was gaping at the big board. "Burnham's at number nine." She turned to him. "Unbelievable."

He shrugged.

"Does this mean we all just got spikes for helping Rosie?" Janice asked.

"Looks like it," Henrik said, laughing. "I guess that blows your theory, Paige. Niceness trumps art."

"Don't worry. It won't last," Paige said, rising from her seat.

The others laughed and started getting up, too.

"Thanks, you guys," I said, pushing back my chair. "I mean it." Despite what Paige had said, I was beyond thrilled. "You especially, Burnham. Thanks."

"You never know," Burnham said. He reached into his back pocket. "Hold on. I've got something for you, if you want it." He passed over a piece of paper, folded in quarters to make a kind of booklet, and I opened it to find a picture of Dubbs. He'd printed off a screenshot from when he'd played with the colors around her face. I held it up to peer at it closely, loving how cool it was.

"You like it?" he asked.

I hardly knew what to do with such thoughtfulness.

"Are you always this nice to people?" I asked.

"It's no big deal. Really," he said, and with a jog of his glasses, he turned and made his way between the tables.

Janice grabbed my arm to hold me back. "That dude totally likes you," she said.

"He just met me," I said.

"Yeah, but still. Do you have any idea how rich he is? I can't believe he's even at this school," Janice said.

Burnham was kind of cute. I almost said it out loud before I remembered the cameras. It wasn't just the viewers stopping me this time. Anything I said could make its way back to Burnham, and also to anyone else in the school. I glanced back toward the kitchen.

"I'm supposed to go to the infirmary," I said.

"How come?"

"I don't know. The doctor wants to see me," I said.

Janice obviously hadn't had the same request to report to Dr. Ash. For a second, I considered showing her the track mark on my arm to see if she might notice hers, but then what? I still didn't want to admit, on camera, that I'd been awake at night.

"It's probably nothing," Janice said.

"I hope so."

We left our trays at the return counter, and I lingered a second, looking back into the kitchen for Linus. His pile of trays was gone, and he was on to washing a stack of pots.

"Can I help you?" The chef stepped into my line of vision. "Chef Ted" was embroidered in blue cursive on his white jacket, and his jowly face was mismatched with a lean, wiry body. When I scanned his hand for bruising, I saw nothing but hard knuckles.

"I was wondering if Linus is okay," I said.

"How's that?" the chef said, turning an ear toward me.

"Linus," I said, louder. "I wondered if Linus's eye is okay. From when you punched him this morning."

Linus didn't stop working, but another one of the kitchen helpers, a frizzy-haired woman with a potato peeler, looked my way. A young man behind her set down a big tub of applesauce to watch, too.

"Pitts!" Chef Ted called.

Linus turned, and I saw the discoloration around his eye was worse.

"I told you to get that checked out," Chef Ted called.

"I'm going to. Right after—"

"Go now," Chef Ted said. "And go to the infirmary, not the clinic in town."

Linus glanced toward me, his expression unreadable. He turned the hot water off. He started peeling off his gloves.

"We appreciate your concern," Chef Ted said to me. "You have a nice day now, hear? Good luck with the cuts."

Linus turned his back to me. From the angle of his elbows, it looked like he was untying his apron. I hesitated, waiting for another look from him, but it didn't come. Why did I feel like I'd made a mistake? I'd only used my leverage, such as it was, on his behalf. He stepped out of view. I waited a bit longer, expecting him to come out of the kitchen and join me. Then finally I realized he must have gone out the back door.

We were both going to the infirmary, but we were each going alone.

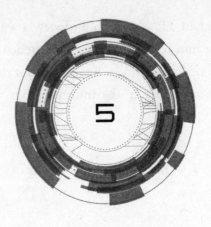

THE INFIRMARY

THE INFIRMARY WAS an older, ivy-covered building with shiny wooden floors and a clock on the mantel. No one was manning the receptionist's desk, but I could hear voices down the hall. I stood patiently, noting the retro phone next to the computer, and a few of the usual camera buttons inconspicuously mounted on the window frames of the waiting area.

"Hello?" I called.

No one answered.

I wondered how long it would take someone to react if I started down the hallway, so I did. I wasn't exactly sneaking around if thousands of viewers knew where I was.

The first door showed an empty bedroom with a high ceiling and a heavy, old-fashioned radiator. In the next two rooms,

I heard voices and I glimpsed patients lying half-concealed behind curtains. The next door was ajar, and a familiar voice came from inside. I tapped to announce myself.

"Hello?" I asked, and pushed the door open.

Books crammed shelves from ceiling to floor, and a red cardigan was draped over the back of a desk chair. I paused on the threshold, inhaling a trace of perfume. An old desk piled with papers was tucked between two tall windows. When the voice came again, I recognized the woman who had been in my dorm the night before, but she wasn't in the room. The sound came from the computer, from a speaker. Linus's voice came next.

"Once before," he said. "Same eye."

"And how did that happen?" asked the woman. The doctor.

"Same way."

I was eavesdropping, wicked little me. The computer had to be wired to a microphone system in the building, apart from *The Forge Show*, because Linus wasn't a student on the show. I looked over my shoulder, but the hallway was still empty. A camera on the hallway ceiling was aimed toward me, but inside the office, I couldn't see any.

"A fight? When was this?" asked the doctor.

"Three years ago, in St. Louis," Linus said.

"You could have mentioned it."

"I didn't see that it would make any difference," Linus said.

"When I think I know everything about a patient and then

it turns out I don't, it's disconcerting," she said. "You don't want to go around collecting hyphemas. Your eye hasn't given you any trouble since that time?"

"No."

I gave the door another nudge and took a step in. A large screen covered most of the third wall. It was divided into a grid much like the viewing setup of *The Forge Show*, but the squares did not show live feeds. Instead, they were filled with pictures: a brown castle teetering as it melted into the sea, a green caterpillar eating a sky scraper, a blindfolded child with red curls standing on top of a Ferris wheel. A dozen fantastic, impossible images created a kaleidoscope of color.

"How long has it been since Otis tapped you?" the doctor asked.

"What's that have to do with my eye?" Linus said.

"Just answer me."

"Only two weeks," he said. "I'm not due again for a month."

"And you're not selling your blood to anyone else?"

"No."

"Linus," she said gently. "You don't have to let them tap you. You know that, right? I'm sorry for Parker, but I can't see that it's making any difference for him. I've told Otis that many times."

"Are we done here?"

"We're not," she said. "Hold on. I'll be back in five minutes. Here, tip your head back again. Right."

The conversation puzzled me. It sounded like Linus was selling his blood to someone who was getting no benefit from it, and Otis, the cameraman from the tower, was involved. Waiting to hear more, I peered again at the grid of pictures. One was a black-and-white Hamlet in a red scarf. The next showed a black boy who looked like a younger Burnham. He was sitting by a campfire, staring into the flames.

A voice startled me from behind.

"For goodness's sake. What are you doing here?" she said.

I spun to see the dark-haired woman who had tended Janice the night before. I backed up nervously as she stepped around me. She swiped her hand briskly across the touch screen to turn the monitors dark.

"What is all this?" I asked.

"You're off-limits," she said. "Come back on camera. Did Mr. Ferenze let you back here? Where is he?"

"No one was at the desk," I said. "What were those images?"

"Oh, those," she said, with a self-effacing wave. She was slender, of Asian heritage, and up close, she seemed younger than she had in the dorm. "It's just my hobby. I'm experimenting with photography. It's hard to work here without getting inspired." She laughed, but she also kept crowding me back toward the hallway until she could close the door. "I'm Dr. Glyde Ash. Thanks for coming in. Right this way."

She led me down the hall and gestured me into an examining room.

"What am I here for?" I asked.

"It's nothing serious. Have a seat." She patted a paper-covered bench. "One sec. I'm with another patient, but I'll be with you shortly." She stepped out, and I listened as her high heels clicked down the hallway. "Ferenze?" she called.

I hitched up onto the bench to sit and let my feet hang. A button camera on the windowsill aimed at my face. Another was on the ceiling. Out the window, I could see Otis's look-out tower. I hung my head and knocked my boots together a few times. Then I flopped back and covered my eyes with one arm, trying to look bored.

Inside, I was dying of curiosity. What was Linus's connection to Otis? And Dr. Ash's pictures were definitely weird. I didn't buy that they were just a photography project. These glimpses off the edges of the show were baffling. Worst of all, I dreaded having the doctor ask me point-blank about last night, when I'd been out of bed. If only I knew how to play this.

Dr. Ash returned a few minutes later and washed her hands at a little sink. "Sorry to keep you waiting. Busy day here. Lots of stress-related issues."

"What's wrong with me?" I asked.

"Nothing serious, I'm sure," she said, ripping a paper towel from the dispenser. "I just want to follow up on some readings we had the last couple nights."

Here it comes, I thought.

She took out a penlight. "Look up," she said, and shone it in my right eye, and then my left. The glare half blinded me. "Good. Now down."

"What kind of readings?" I asked. I would play dumb as long as I could.

She looked in my ears next. "Elevated heart rate and

breathing. Just because you go to sleep at six o'clock doesn't mean we stop caring. Some of our new students have a mild reaction to the sleeping pills. We monitor you all very carefully, and at the first sign of an irregularity, we're right there."

"So I had a problem?" I asked. "Does that mean you have to send me home?"

"No, no. I wouldn't say it's a real problem," she said, with a smile. She rolled a temperature gauge along my forehead. "You were very restless. Having a bad dream, no doubt. It happens, but it doesn't mean you aren't fit to stay, provided you make the cuts. Finger, please."

I held out my finger, and she put a white clamp around it. It sounded like she was giving me a warning. Maybe that was all this was.

"I don't have any dreams here," I said.

"You do. You just don't remember them." She lifted the back of my shirt. "Take a deep breath."

I did. The cold disk of her stethoscope on my back made me flinch.

"Again," she said.

I took a few more breaths, as directed. She pulled my shirt down and took the stethoscope out of her ears to loop it around her neck. Then she took a small, triangular hammer and beat it against my knee. My leg jerked. She did the other knee, too, and then took the clamp off my finger to inspect it. She backed up to tap into her tablet.

"Have you had any dizziness? Nausea? Headaches?" she asked.

"No."

"Appetite normal?"

"Yes."

"Déjà vus?"

I laughed.

"I'm serious," she said. "Have you had any déjà vus recently?"

"No. I haven't had any déjà vus," I said.

She took my blood pressure, and the cuff made a little hiss in the silence. The scab on my arm was visible, like a secret test between us, but the doctor didn't touch it or mention it. She released the rest of the blood pressure cuff with a whoosh of air.

"You're fine. Totally fine," she said. "A little stressed, but nothing to be concerned about. That's perfectly natural."

I looked directly at her. We both knew Janice had had a seizure in the night. That shouldn't be hushed up. Then again, the doctor wasn't saying on camera that I'd broken the rules, and mutual silence made for an odd form of trust. I decided to take a chance.

"I have a question, actually," I said. "What's this?"

She brought her face close to inspect the crook of my elbow, and ran a finger over my track mark. "That's from an IV," she said. "Most students never even notice. It's a standard precaution to put one in. Ninety-nine percent of the time, we don't even have to use it, but I like it ready."

"What happens the other one percent of the time?" I asked.

"You know, sleeping medication is just not something we take chances with," she said. "If someone's in trouble and we need to bring them around, we can."

"So you have an antidote to wake someone up from the sleeping meds?"

"Yes," she said. "But like I said, we almost never need to use it."

"You could have warned us about this," I said.

"We did. It's in the fine print. You and your parents signed the contract before you came," she said. She wrapped up the cord of the blood pressure cuff. "Honestly, Rosie. This is about the safest place you could ever be, and you're perfectly fine."

I got it. This was definitely a warning disguised as a reassurance. I had read my contract, of course. It stated clearly that I was supposed to take my pill each night, and it contained all sorts of cover-their-butts legalese about risks and potential death. I had never thought any of that was a real possibility, though. Now I wasn't so sure.

A tap came on the door, and a man in a white coat looked in.

"Doctor? We're ready for you," he said.

Dr. Ash looked toward me. "Any last questions?"

"Why did you need to check me out? I could be gone in a few hours," I said.

"That's true," she said. "But I'm a stickler for following up, and while you're here, you're under my care, no matter how short or long that is. Good luck with the cuts."

I had Practicum for two hours next, followed by an original one-act play some older students put on, and afterward, around 3:30, I went back to the girls' dorm to pack.

All first-year students were supposed to pack and have their belongings piled at the ends of their sleep shells before the fifty cuts. In theory, this was to make the removal of half the students quick and easy after the cuts. In practice, it made the fourth floor of the girls' dorm a miserable place to be. The big room was hushed when I arrived. Some girls had come and gone already, leaving their mute, tidy piles behind. I passed several other girls who were quietly folding their things and tucking them in suitcases. A few were passing around their phones to exchange numbers, with big tears and promises to keep in touch. Looked fake to me, but whatever.

It took me five minutes, total, to drop everything in my duffel bag and zip it closed. No way was I going to wait around and swap daisy chains with the other contestants.

"This is decidedly unfun up here," I said to Janice, pausing by her sleep shell. "I'm going for a run. Want to come?"

She shook her head. "I told my parents I'd call them."

"Where's Paige?" I asked, scanning the room.

"She went to dance," Janice said. "You know. Art and guts."

"And niceness," I added. "Thanks again for the spike at lunchtime."

"No problem. Actually, I've been remembering Camp

Pewter, from when I knew Burnham before," she said. "He was kind of a chubby do-gooder back then."

"He's not chubby now," I said, leaning a hip into the end of her sleep shell.

Janice laughed. "No. He's not."

"Were you friends?"

"Not exactly. But I definitely remember him." Janice folded a yellow sweater, adding it to her suitcase. "On the last night of camp, everyone went down for the last campfire out on the point. It was this special tradition, right? With all these nice songs and prayers and readings? It was great until I got some ash or something in my eye. It wouldn't come out, so I started back to my cabin to get a mirror, and one of counselors saw me going." Janice slowed down. "I thought, you know, he was coming along to look after me."

"What happened?" I asked.

"This counselor, he kept putting his arm around my shoulder," she said. "I shrugged him off, and then he put his hand around my waist. It was really creepy. 'What's your hurry? Watch your step,' he kept saying. 'Listen to the crickets.' Like it was a nature walk, but it wasn't."

Janice slowly raked a hand back into her hair.

"Creepy," I said.

"I know, right?" she said. "Then one of the boys came running along the trail behind us. He caught up with us, and I was so glad. He said he had to use the biffy. That's what we called the bathroom. He walked with us all the way back to the cabins and the slime ball counselor didn't touch me again."

"Let me guess. It was Burnham."

Janice picked up her brush and absently pulled a matting of hairs out of the bristles. She gave a crooked smile. "We passed the biffy and he stayed with us the whole time until I went into the nurse's office. I think he knew. I think he was protecting me."

"How old were you?" I asked.

"Like, twelve?"

"Didn't you become friends after that?" I asked.

"No," she said. "I was kind of embarrassed, and camp ended the next day anyway. I hadn't thought about it in ages. Then I saw him here."

"All grown up and not chubby," I said.

"Yes. But still nice."

I absently fingered my necklace. "Do you think he remembers?" I asked.

"I have no idea."

I wondered where Burnham was now. Probably working on his computer game. I recalled the image from Dr. Ash's office of a young, Burnham-like kid, gazing into a campfire. It was odd to think Janice could have seen him that way once. The elusive connection was enough to be inspiring.

"Maybe I'll take some footage instead of going for a run," I said.

"Footage for what?" she asked. "You only have a couple hours. Not even."

"I don't know yet," I said, but I was already getting ideas. I had the mini video camera my old science teacher had given me. Sometimes I liked to just collect footage, though I hadn't done it since I'd come to Forge. It wouldn't actually be a documentary, but it could capture my last hours here. Like a journal. I'd be making meaning for myself.

I checked my blip rank on the panel by the clock. My rank had dropped to 72 from my high of 69 at lunch. Scores were moving around a lot, just as Burnham had said they would. I looked at the last name on the list: 100 Anna Mezzaluna. I didn't know her, but I was getting an idea.

"I'm going to take some footage of the losers," I said.

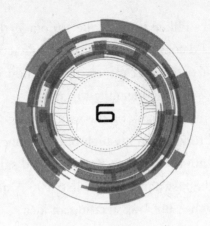

THE LOSERS

"LIKE THAT'S NOT sick and cruel," Janice said. She did the double jerk of her thumb to indicate the cameras. "I wouldn't."

"I would," I said. "It's reality. There's nothing wrong with that. Do you know Anna Mezzaluna?"

"She sleeps there," Janice said, nodding at the sleep shell beside hers where three black, matching suitcases were neatly lined up by size. "She's a classical cellist."

"Can you find her for me? Look up her profile on *The Forge Show*."

"I don't have to," Janice said. "She's always in the practice rooms at the music building."

Perfect, I thought. "Come with me. Please? You know you don't want to sit around here."

I completely expected her to say no.

Janice zipped the closure on a bag of earrings. "I still have to call my parents," she said. "I'll meet you at the music building. Just give me ten minutes."

"Fine," I said.

"What exactly are you going to do?" she asked.

"I don't know yet," I said. "Trust the process, right?"

I ran past the other sleep shells and down the stairs, passing the floors for the older girls. I took the back door out of the girls' dorm, cut behind the dance building, and hurried to the music building, where I followed arrows to a warren of practice rooms under the auditorium. The hallway was stuffy and smelled like cork. Each door had a small, narrow window and a sign-up schedule. I could faintly hear the muffled sound of jazz piano from one room, but most of the others were dark and silent as I passed.

At the last room, I caught the clear, crooning notes of a cello, and I peeked in the little window. A girl's slender back was toward me, with the curving wooden knob of her cello over her shoulder. It gleamed beside her smooth black hair. I considered just filming her from the window, but then I'd be no better than an anonymous *Forge Show* camera. I knocked.

The music stopped. The girl looked over her shoulder, and I saw her small, pointed face for the first time. She reached to open the door without rising.

"Yes?" she asked.

Panels of white cork lined the walls, soaking up her voice until it was wispy thin. She was alone in the little room, with

65

nothing else but her cello, her cello case, a chair, and an empty music stand. Four camera buttons were discretely positioned in the corners.

"I'm Rosie. I'm getting some footage from the last hour before the fifty cuts," I said.

"And?" she asked.

I wasn't sure what to say. It suddenly seemed like a horrible idea, what I was doing. I couldn't tell her she ranked dead last.

"Can I film you playing?" I asked.

She looked at me a long moment, and her expression broke into a pained little smile. "It won't make a difference," she said.

"I know," I said. "But can I?"

She gave a wave with her cello bow. "Be my guest," she said.

I sidestepped into the corner, scooted down on my heels, and lifted the camera to my eye. The girl, Anna, set her bow on a string, positioned her finger on the same string higher up, and closed her eyes. For a moment, she was still, and I hardly dared to breathe. Then the bow began to move, and music resonated into the tiny room.

She didn't know me. I'd never met her before. She had no reason to give me anything, but she played with such soul-searching tenderness that the song spilled into me, filling places I never knew were empty. I didn't dare move. I hardly breathed. Long minutes later, when she finished and the last note faded into silence, she rested her bow hand on her knee.

I lowered my camera.

"I'm speechless," I said.

66

"Thanks." She opened her eyes but didn't look at me.

"I wish I'd met you earlier," I said.

She examined the calluses on her fingers. "You met me now," she said.

"That's true," I said.

The quiet was as empty as the music had just been full, but it wasn't sad. It was powerful. Defiant. Anna nodded at my camera. "Good luck with that."

Her approval meant a lot to me. A knock came softly at the door and I looked over to see Janice outside the little window. As she opened the door, a welcome influx of cooler air stirred against my neck.

"Did I miss anything?" Janice asked.

"Yes," I said. I switched off my camera. "Do you want to come with us?" I asked Anna. "We're going to find someone else to film."

"No. I'm good."

"You sure? Come with us," I insisted.

She shook her head. "I want to be here."

Janice beckoned me. I slipped around Anna to the door.

"That was wonderful," I said.

Anna balanced her bow again in her hand. "Thank you," she said. "Close the door."

I did, stepping out into the hallway. Faintly, from inside, I heard Anna starting another piece.

"What happened in there?" Janice asked, whispering.

"It was incredible," I said. "She played for me." I'd never been next to a cello like that. I had no way to describe how

Anna had sucked me into her music, or the power in the silence afterward. She'd given me a perfect gift just when I was ready to receive it, and somehow it felt even more generous because we were strangers.

"Can I see?" Janice asked, reaching for my camera.

"No," I said. "We have to find the next person."

"I bet that boosted Anna's blip rank," Janice said, pulling out her phone. "She's up to eighty-two!" Janice said. "That's a huge jump!"

"Who's at one hundred now?" I asked, looking over her shoulder at her phone. Someone else must have slid down to take the bottom rank.

Janice skimmed her phone. "Terry Fieldstone. He's in the library. It looks like he's reading or sleeping."

"Let's go find him," I said.

We did. In worn boots and a plaid shirt, Terry was sprawled in one of the low armchairs near the windows. It turned out he was reading Shakespeare and memorizing the "But soft, what light from yonder window breaks?" speech from *Romeo and Juliet*. When I asked if he would recite it for me to record, he tilted his head back in his chair and his gaze went far away. He spoke the words tenderly, effortlessly, as if he were remembering a dream he'd once had, and it lifted a brush of goose bumps along my arms.

When I lowered my camera, he still didn't move. Janice was spellbound.

"That was awesome," she said.

Terry eased out of his concentration and rubbed both

hands in his hair. "I've seen you in acting class," he said to her. "You're good."

"I can't do better than what you just did," she said. "That blew me away."

He laughed. "Yeah, whatever. I'll be back to driving my aunt's tractor tomorrow. This was fun."

"You're a farmer?" I asked.

"Yep," he said. "In Montana. My aunt wanted me to try out for this, though. Never thought I'd get this far."

"But you'll keep acting once you get home, won't you?" Janice asked. "You can't give up."

"Well, now, I'll think about it," he said. He gave her a smile. "I'll be following your career, no doubt about it."

The charm was too smarmy for my taste, but Janice blushed. She pushed up the sleeves of her blue dress and adjusted the strap of her purse over her shoulder while she chatted. I tried to duck out and leave them to it, but Janice gave him a wave and came along with me.

Once we were around the corner, she pulled me up short and took out her phone.

"He's up to eighty-six! That's a lot better than one hundred," she said.

"It's probably you brushing off on him," I said. "Who's one hundred now?"

"Let's check your blip rank," she said.

"Not yet. I don't want to know," I said. "Tell me who's at one hundred."

We used Janice's phone to guide us on a sort of scavenger

hunt around the campus. The next student to drop to the lowest blip rank was an artist who was working on a graphic novel with pages and pages of drawings. Hunched over an easel in the top floor of the art building, he had a radio blaring and smudges of ink along the sides of both hands. After him, the next student with the lowest rank was a costume designer we found ironing fabric in the drama department. Then I filmed a dancer who was working solo before a bank of dusky mirrors.

Despite their lowest blip ranks, they weren't losers at all. The whole system was an arbitrary, capricious farce, and with each artist I met, I felt my biggest mistake had been in not trying to get to know more of the people here, and I felt a growing disgust for the fifty cuts.

Finally, we located Ellen Thorpe, a singer, in the girl's bathroom of the chapel. When I heard retching in one of the stalls, I fingered my camera but didn't turn it on. Janice softly backed out the door, beckoning me, but I shook my head.

"Do you need anything in there?" I called through the stall door.

There was no immediate reply. I glanced around the bathroom. Cameras in the sink area weren't aimed to view in the stalls once the doors were closed. The mics picked up voices, but as long as Ellen was silent, she was essentially invisible to the show, and I had to think that was by choice.

Janice signaled to me again. *Leave her alone*, she mouthed silently.

"No," Ellen said.

"You sure? Some water?" I asked.

The rush of a toilet flush came from inside. "No, thank you," she said. Her voice was low and husky. Not what I expected for a singer. "It's just the nerves. I'll be okay."

"It's getting late," Janice said quietly to me. "We're supposed to meet in front of the auditorium by quarter to five."

It was a decent enough excuse to leave, but I hesitated when Ellen's voice came again.

"They're putting everyone's profile up on the outside of the building," Ellen said. "I saw them there."

"On the big screens?" I asked. "Is that something new?"

"Yes," she said. "It'll be extra humiliating."

I glanced again at Janice, who was still bracing the door open to the hall. I could see the last pews of the chapel around the corner.

"Come with us, Ellen," I said. "We'll go together."

"I'm dead last, aren't I?" Ellen asked.

Janice glanced at her phone and then nodded to me.

I didn't know what to say, but I couldn't just leave her there. "Come on out," I said, tapping the stall door again. The beige was an industrial, impersonal hue. "We can't talk to you through the door."

"I'll be okay. Just go," she said. A choking, stifled sob came next.

Crap, I thought. I tiptoed nearer to Janice. "This isn't good."

"I know," Janice said.

"Go get somebody."

"Who?"

"I don't know. A teacher? Someone from the infirmary? Anybody."

"What are you going to do?" she asked.

"Talk to her, I guess. But hurry."

Janice slipped out.

"Ellen?" I asked. I propped my dormant camera on a shelf by the sink and tapped the door again, trying to listen inside. "You still in there?"

"You don't understand," she said. "I've got nothing after I'm cut."

I had a flash memory of our refrigerator back home, with two eggs and a jar of horseradish inside.

"Tell me," I said.

"My mom," she began, and then her voice strangled off again.

Double crap. I gave my skirt a hitch. Then I dropped to my elbows and knees so I could peek under the door. Ellen was sitting on the tile floor before the black-seated toilet with her knees drawn up and her head buried in her arms. By her feet, a pink purse with a kitty on it rested beside a paring knife.

"Ellen," I said softly.

She wouldn't look at me. She shifted to press the heels of her hands against her eyes, and her mouth stretched in a grimace.

"This is so stupid!" she said.

I didn't know this girl. She terrified me. But nobody deserved to be this unhappy. I ducked my head and crept bare-kneed under the door to squeeze into the lonely space beside

72

her. I wished I knew what to say, or if I should touch her. I'd been unhappy before, but not this miserable.

"That's a nice purse," I said.

"I *hate* this purse," she said.

Okay, I thought. *Wrong tack.* "Sorry. That was stupid," I said.

She wiped her eyes with her arm, and turned to me with a bleary gaze. "Who do you even think you are?" she demanded.

I went very small inside. Very still. If Ellen knew what I'd been doing for the last hour, she might think I was in for the kill, catching people at their lowest. She was still glaring at me, expecting an answer.

"I'm Rosie?" I offered.

She stared at me another long, hard minute. Then she closed her eyes and seemed to deflate. Her eyebrows crumpled together in a pleading way. "I'm just so tired," she said.

"I know," I said. "Me, too." And I was, suddenly.

She put her face down on her knees, curled her arms around her head again, and held herself there. The knife was still an inch from her shoe. I was afraid to move. I didn't know what else to do. We dropped into an isolated morass of time that had never begun and would never end, where my sole job was to listen to her breathing and stare at the beige tiles on the floor.

It took forever, but I heard the outer door open and then footsteps.

"Rosie?" Janice asked.

I exhaled a silent sigh of relief. "In here," I said. "I think we're okay." I had no evidence of that whatsoever. I looked at Ellen. She slowly pushed the hair back behind her ears.

"Can you open the door?" asked another voice. Dr. Ash.

"Give us a sec," I said.

I pulled off some toilet paper and handed it to Ellen. She wiped her nose.

"Ready?" I asked.

She nodded. I got up, brushed off the back of my skirt, and helped her up, too. I handed her the kitty purse and left the knife on the floor. Then I straightened her shirt along the shoulders, like that would help. I tried to meet her eyes, but she wasn't looking at me.

Finally, I pushed over the lock and pulled open the stall door. We had to edge around it one at a time. Beside Janice, Dr. Ash and a couple of medics were crammed in the space near the sinks. The team quickly, gently surrounded Ellen, and in a surprisingly short time, they guided her out. One of the medics collected the knife in a little bag and looked back at me as he held the door.

"Are you all right?" he asked.

I nodded.

"You certain?" he repeated.

"Yes. I'm fine," I said.

Janice reached for my camera on the shelf. "Do you want this?" she asked.

I didn't want to use it anymore, and I didn't have a decent pocket. "Can you stick it in your bag for me?" I asked.

"Sure."

I needed some air. We headed out of the chapel, and I saw an ambulance pulling away. A light drizzle had begun to fall, and the shrouded light turned the buildings and the lawns all the same slate gray. At the base of the clock tower, the rose garden was a bleak tangle of thorns. I stood under the chapel awning with Janice beside me.

"I think you saved her life," she said.

I didn't want to talk about it. Ellen had rattled me in some dark place below words.

"Look at the time! It's almost five," Janice said. "We're supposed to be over by the auditorium."

I glanced up at the clock tower, where the school motto was etched around the face of the clock: *Dream Hard. Work Harder. Shine.* We had seven minutes until the fifty cuts. Down the length of the quad, at the far end, I could see lights shining near the auditorium, and I felt a conflicted rush of emotion. I still wanted to stay at Forge, but I was also completely disillusioned about the cuts.

"Come on already!" Janice said. She went running down the quad sidewalk, holding her bag over her head for shelter from the rain.

I hunched my shoulders and followed after.

Students were dodging the rain as they ran, and a crowd had gathered beneath an overhang of the student union. I ducked under, too, just as the rain began to fall in earnest. I lost track of Janice. Through the downpour, the giant screen panels that covered the façade of the auditorium were aglow with the live broadcast of *The Forge Show.* All one hundred

75

of the first year students' profiles were up, magnified to five times life-size. They were bright enough that the rain only added a shimmer of streaks before them, and they were organized by rank, with the top fifty students bordered in bright green. Every twenty seconds, like a fancier, faster version of the big blip rank board in the dining hall, all the profiles shifted to show their updated rank.

Cheers and gasps came from the students around me. More students were sheltered near the doorways of the dance and music buildings, anywhere it was dry enough to see the big screen, and their voices cut across the quad, too, like an echo.

Dreading what I would find, I scanned the profiles until I found mine in the sixth row: a thin, wet, bow-legged girl standing under a rainy awning. I was in 54th place, the highest I'd ever been, but it wasn't high enough. Janice's blip rank was up to 26. Burnham's was 7. Ellen, the girl from the chapel bathroom, was now ranked at 70. Her profile showed a still photo of her smiling, and I was puzzled until I realized they must have cut her live feed when she entered the ambulance and drove off campus.

The screens flickered and refreshed again. Another burst of cheers and groans surrounded me. I was down a notch to 55.

My fate was right there on the wall, impossible to ignore, and still, stupidly, I couldn't accept it. This idiotic hope of mine wouldn't die. Despite everything I'd learned about Forge today, I still wanted to stay.

In four minutes, the time would hit five o'clock, and the scores would be finalized.

A gust of wind blew a spattering of rain on my face, and I winced.

I couldn't stand still watching helplessly.

I bolted out into the downpour and turned sharply, sprinting alongside the student union. Completely soaked, I cut behind the dining hall. Behind the art building, the two giant wooden spools were dark with water and more drops bounced off their edges. I ran toward them, splashing loudly in the wet gravel. A garbage can pinged under the cascade of drops. I peered around the parking lot, then through the rain toward the pasture and the tower, seeing no one.

He wasn't here.

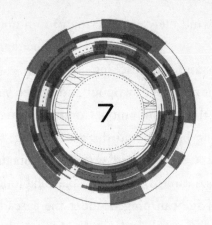

7

THE FIFTY CUTS

I HUGGED MY arms around my wetness, closed my eyes, and tilted my face to the pouring sky.

"Rosie?"

I spun around and squinted toward the back of the art building where Linus was striding forward. Under a baseball cap, he wore a dark patch on one eye.

"Where've you been?" he asked.

My throat choked up and I could barely talk. "It looks like I'm going home," I said. I wiped my nose with the back of my wet hand and let out a laugh. "All the real artists are fine about it. Except this one girl Ellen. She's a mess. And me. What did I do wrong?"

He came a step nearer, and as he did, I discovered a hug was what I wanted more than anything. I leaned near him uncertainly. His white tee shirt was wet. Lightning flashed, and I shivered, expecting thunder. When it finally came, the sky opened up harder and the rain fell with a punishing noise into the gravel.

"Hey," Linus said, bending near to my ear. "They can't hear us."

When I peered up to him, he took off his hat and put it on me so the brim sheltered my face.

"I don't want to go home," I said.

"Then stay," he said.

"I can't. It's too late. Listen." I could hear the clock starting to bong. It was so unfair to want it most just as I was losing it.

"You know what to do," he said, and his gaze dropped to my lips.

Fear shot through me. I'd never kissed anyone before. I didn't know how. It felt like despair to even try, and I didn't know why he wanted to help me. But he was giving me a chance. I had to take it. I clenched my fists and leaned into him a little bit more.

I didn't know his mouth would be warm in the coolness of the rain. I didn't know I would shift myself a little nearer to feel the right pressure, or that when I did, a tiny jolt inside me would erase the rest of the world. I didn't think to unclench my fists. He didn't do more than touch his lips to mine for a slow moment, but when he finally backed up a little and I could breathe again, I hardly remembered how.

With his one good eye, Linus was watching me closely. I felt hopelessly wet and self-conscious in my clinging shirt.

"I think this had better be our secret," he said just over the noise of the rain.

"What?" I asked.

He curled a hand to his mouth and leaned close to my ear. "I mean, that this matters," he said.

I searched his expression, and though he couldn't have come up with a more perfect thing to say, it riddled me with guilt. Our kiss had been completely contrived. A zillion *Forge Show* viewers had just seen it, and even now the last toll from the clock tower bonged through the rush of the rain. No matter how much I'd liked kissing him in the moment, it was all fake, right?

Linus was frowning. "Was that your first kiss?" he asked.

"You could tell."

His smile was genuinely warm. "Yes."

"It wasn't yours, I take it," I said.

He laughed. "No. But it was my first in a very long time. It was my first with you."

I withdrew half a step, letting the rain fall between us. "And probably last," I said. "It's past five o'clock."

"Let's go see if you're cut," he said. "They'll have the news in the kitchen."

We turned together to dodge across the puddles, and another flash of lightning burst around us as we hurried up the steps to the loading dock. Linus held open the kitchen door for me and I stepped inside, hunched and dripping.

Half a dozen kitchen workers turned to face us and let out

a rousing cheer. The frizzy-haired cook pointed to a TV screen on the wall.

"You made it!" she said to me. "Blip rank fifty. You're in! Congratulations!"

I let out a squeak of joy and instinctively grabbed Linus's arm.

Linus grinned and took back his hat. "Nice," he said.

At the front of the dining hall, laughing, jubilant students were streaming in from the quad. Cake and punch had been set out for the celebration. A young man handed me and Linus a couple of towels to sling around our shoulders, and Chef Ted gave me a nod.

"Go on out and join the other winners," he said. "You've earned it."

I glanced back at Linus, who was still smiling. In his wet shirt and eye patch, he looked like a pirate just in from a storm.

"Great job, Sinclair," he said. "I'm happy for you."

"Come with me," I said.

"No," he said. "I'm good."

"I owe you," I said.

"Yes," he said. "You do. Go on."

I gave a wave to the rest of the kitchen staff and headed through the doorway to meet up with the other students. Other winners from the auditorium were streaming in, laughing as if they couldn't contain their delight. Teachers and older students filed in, too, until the place was packed and the windows steamed over.

Janice nearly attacked me. "You made it!" she said, and gripped me in a hug. "It was so exciting! I nearly died! Who is that hot, hot guy from the kitchen? Is he here? When did you meet him?" She rose on tiptoe, looking past my shoulder toward the kitchen.

I peeked back to where Linus was ruffling his hair madly in the towel.

"His name's Linus," I said, blushing. "I met him this morning. Quit staring."

"Way go to, Rosie. I mean, really." Janice dropped her voice. "Way to pull it out of the bag."

"It wasn't exactly a premeditated plan," I said.

"Whatever. It worked, right?" Janice said. "Burnham made it, too. And Paige. And Henrik. Holy crap. They have chocolate cake. Check out that frosting." She passed me a piece and started in on her own. "I'm starving," she said. "Who knew anxiety could make me so hungry?"

"You weren't seriously worried for yourself," I said.

"Are you kidding? I've been a mess," she said. "Plus of course I just started my period. Whoops! Too much info. Man, this is good."

Following her cue, I tried a forkful of cake, and the sweetness dissolved in my mouth. It was insanely good, a taste of pure happiness, with a thin, gooey line of bittersweet frosting between the spongy layers of cake.

"You should have seen the losers," Janice said. "Number fifty-one was destroyed. It was awful. Dean Berg's saying goodbye to them."

"Where's Burnham?" I asked.

"I don't know." Janice pulled out her phone. "It's my mom," she said, looping her blond hair to one side. "Excuse me." She snagged another piece of cake as she shifted away to talk.

I scanned the crowd and absently rubbed my arms with the towel I'd kept. Henrik and Paige stood talking in the far corner, but I couldn't find Burnham. I wanted to celebrate with him, especially since he'd helped me at lunchtime, but instead I felt a letdown. I didn't see any of the students I'd shot for my footage, either. In terms of passing the cuts, it hadn't made a difference for any of them, but I had to think it had helped me. That hadn't been my intention when I'd started out, not consciously, so it shouldn't have made me uneasy. But now it did. Ellen wasn't going to be easy to forget.

"My parents say congratulations," Janice said, coming back over. "Have you talked to yours yet?"

"No," I said. I didn't have a phone, but there were a couple of landline phones in the student union next door.

"Here. Use this," Janice said, handing me her phone.

"Really?"

"Go ahead," she said. She was still smiling happily, and another girl came up to give her a hug.

I took her phone and dialed my home number. Turning away to face the rainy windows, I waited while it rang.

"Ma?" I said.

"Rosie! We're so excited!" my mom said. Her voice came over the sound of partying in the background. "You made it!

We've got the McLellens and all the neighbors here. We're so proud of you!"

I felt a mix of pride and loneliness. "I'm happy, too. Is Dubbs there?"

"Who was that boy? Are you seeing him?" Ma asked.

I glanced down at my wet boots and stuck a finger in my other ear.

"Maybe. I don't know," I said. "I can't really talk now. The cameras, you know."

"Oh, yes!" she said. "Oh! There you are on the TV right now, in that towel, talking on the phone. Isn't that amazing? Can you wave?"

I waved.

She squealed.

"Ma, I've got to go," I said. "Give my love to Dubbs, okay?"

From the background, my stepfather yelled something that was greeted by shouts of laughter.

"We're so excited for you, Rosie," Ma said. "Be a good girl, okay? Wait, your father wants to talk to you."

A clicking and mumbling ensued. "Rosie!" my stepfather called into the phone.

"Hi, Larry," I said.

"You're a big star now, huh kid? What happens next?"

"What do you mean?" I asked.

"How do you win? When's the next elimination? Next week?"

How he could possibly not know this was unbelievable to me. It was as if he'd paid zero attention to what I'd been doing, all that time I'd talked about the show and prepared and applied.

"There are no more eliminations," I said. "These were the fifty cuts, just now, tonight. That's it. Now we stay on for the rest of the school year."

"But then, how do you win? How do you get the big bucks?" he asked.

"It's not about winning," I said. "It's about getting an education."

"Don't pull that," he said. "You said there was money."

He'd paid attention to that much, at least.

I wasn't in the mood to explain this. "Ask Dubbs about it. She understands."

"I'm asking *you*," he said. "What, are you too much of a big shot now to talk to your dad?"

Stepdad, I thought. A bumping noise came from the other end of the line, and my mother came back on.

"Don't worry about him," she said. "I'll explain it all to him. You'll do fine. Just fine, Rosie. We love you so much. This is an incredible opportunity for you. Give me a smile, would you? Let me see that little gap of yours."

My family had bought a cheap tablet so they could watch me on the show, and I could picture Ma holding it up for the others to see. I didn't know which camera was focused on me, but I lifted my head and tried a smile over my shoulder, toward the center of the room. I was extra conscious of the gap in my teeth.

"How's that?" I asked.

"Beautiful," my mom said. "My baby." More voices were cheering behind her.

"I've got to go, Ma," I said.

"Of course," she said. "Thanks so much for calling. Don't forget to thank Dean Berg for letting you stay on the show. What a very attractive and distinguished man he is. So brilliant."

Across the room, Dean Berg had entered with Mr. DeCoster. The dean struck me as a sandy-haired, clean-cut, Scoutmaster type, more boring than attractive, but there was no accounting for Ma's taste.

"They're so lucky to have you, sweetheart," Ma said, with a wistful sigh.

"Got it," I said. "Thanks, Ma. I love you, too. Bye."

The phone buzzed with party noise for another second while I found the end call button. I hoped I wasn't too abrupt with her. I loved my mom, but I never handled sappy from her very well.

"Thanks," I said, handing the phone back to Janice.

Most of the other students were heading out of the dining hall, and it hit me again that I got to stay. Instead of going home to that staticky world on the other end of the phone, I was fully admitted to the Forge School, a place to dream and work and shine. I was deeply grateful and excited, but I couldn't quite ignore what it had taken for me to earn my place.

I glanced across the room to find Dean Berg regarding me thoughtfully. Our eyes met for too long to pretend otherwise, and I wasn't sure how to respond. He broke into a genial smile and lifted his glass to me briefly before his gaze moved on.

Weird, I thought. I hugged my damp towel around me and turned away.

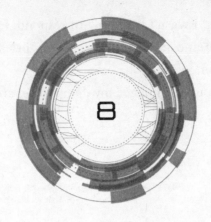

8

THE LAST BOXCAR

IT WAS RAINING the day I was sent home from Doli High for fighting. The road was so flooded, I had to walk my bike the last mile, which made me muddy on top of irritable. I stashed my bike under the boxcar and stomped up the steps to slide open the door with a careless bang.

"Shut that thing!" my stepfather yelled from the couch.

I stayed outside, peering in, while the rain drummed down around me and splashed in the ruts of the door. Tempting as it was to leave again and avoid Larry, I was hungry and I had nowhere else to go. I stepped in and rolled the door partway back on its wheels, leaving a gap.

Larry twisted his head around so that creases showed in the back of his neck. "What are you doing home?" he asked.

I shucked off my muddy shoes and reached for the dishtowel

looped on the cutlery drawer. Before I patted at my soaked shirt and hair, I took my video camera out of my backpack and checked to see that it was dry. My skirt was wet through, dripping down my legs.

"I asked you a question," Larry said.

"I got sent home."

"What for?"

"Fighting," I said.

"You don't fight people," he said.

I did when they started it.

I tossed the towel in the sink and looked down at my hand, flexing my fingers. They didn't hurt too much anymore, but I checked the freezer for some ice. The ice tray contained little square puddles of water, proof that the freezer had stopped working. I checked the fridge, which was still cold, but it contained only a jar of horseradish and a couple of eggs. Nothing else. I started water to boil for tea.

"Did you tell your ma?" Larry asked. His gun parts were spread over the coffee table on a layer of newsprint. Since the chemical factory was on strike, he cleaned his weapon a lot, ostensibly for relaxation, though I never saw that it worked.

"I tried to," I said.

"What's that mean? Didn't the principal call her in from the kitchen?"

"He did. She couldn't stay long. Once she saw I was okay, she had to head back to work."

"Let's have the story," Larry said.

I leaned back on the counter and crossed my arms.

To my left, a red curtain hid the bunk beds I shared with Dubbs, and to my right, a wall of bookshelves separated off my parents' bedroom. The center section of the boxcar, where we cooked and lived, hummed with the rain on the metal above. In the corner behind my stepfather, a busted TV sat on a dresser under a rack of antlers. A drip fell from one of the skylights into a rusty coffee can.

I resisted an urge to sag.

"I'd say I don't have all day, but I do," Larry said.

"It wasn't a big deal. A couple of seniors were picking on one of the fat kids," I said. "She was taking a shower after gym and they hid her clothes. One of the older girls took out her phone and videotaped the fat girl when she came out naked, like that was real funny. They were going to post it online."

"So what did you do?"

I plucked slowly at my wet shirt, remembering, feeling my rage again. "The naked girl was begging them not to post it, but the seniors were laughing hysterically. So, I laughed too, and I asked to see, and when the senior girl passed over her phone, I dropped it in a toilet."

Larry briefly shook his head. "Mistake."

It had felt great, actually.

"Yeah, well," I said. "That's how I got in a fight."

"Did you explain all this to the principal?"

I shrugged.

"Did you hit someone first?" he asked.

"I don't know. I guess."

90

"You guess?"

"All right, I did."

The whole thing still pissed me off. The older girls tried to make me reach in the toilet for the phone, but I wouldn't. They shoved me, so I fought back. The whole time, the fat girl had had nothing to wear, no towel or anything, and she went scrambling through the stinky stuff in the lost and found box. Jill. That was her name. It wasn't like I'd expected her to thank me or anything, but she yelled at me as if I was just as bad as the others.

I would never videotape someone like that. I would never defile my video camera with footage that mean.

The water was boiling now, adding steam to the damp air.

"I think I'm in trouble," I said. "School has a zero tolerance policy for violence."

"Meaning what?"

"The principal's considering his options," I said.

"How about the other girls? Are they in trouble?"

I clicked off the burner.

"Rosie?" Larry said.

"I don't know," I said. "That doesn't really matter, does it?"

>>>>>>>>

By the time Ma and Dubbs came in, I'd cooked half a box of spag with some stewed tomatoes, and I was setting the table. Dubbs ran and gave me a hug as if she hadn't seen me in days, so I knew Ma had told her I was in trouble. I lifted her up for a kiss, inhaling the scent of glitter glue.

"Ma says she's quitting her job," Dubbs said.

"What for?" I said.

Larry looked over from the couch. "Nonsense," he said.

My mom dumped down her purse and sat heavily to take off her shoes. She was a big woman who moved slowly even when she wasn't tired. She was allowed to eat whatever she wanted at work in the school cafeteria, but she couldn't take anything home, not even if it was past its expiration date. The policy drove her crazy, but she never broke the rules.

"You didn't really quit, did you?" I asked.

"No, but I will," she said. "I'm not going to work at a place that won't educate my daughter."

"What did the principal decide about me?" I asked.

A brown hairnet pinched along Ma's forehead, and when she took it off, it left a faint pink line in her skin. "You're supposed to pay for the phone you ruined, and you're getting switched to the N.I.P. track."

"What's that?" Larry asked.

"Needs Improvement slash Parole," I said.

A few years back, Doli High had merged with the low-security prison in our town to form the Doli High School and Incarceration Institute. On the N.I.P. track, I would be required to wear an ankle bracelet and take classes with the student-inmates. Forget that.

"You're not quitting over this," Larry said to Ma.

Ma laughed. "No?"

"You're not," he insisted.

"For how long? How long am I supposed to be in N.I.P.?" I asked.

Ma winced. "It's permanent," she said.

"What?" I shrieked. I'd be derailed from the College Prep track, with no chance of getting back on. "That's completely unreasonable! I might as well drop out right now."

"Will she be eligible for any scholarships on the N.I.P. track?" Larry asked.

"Nobody goes to college from N.I.P.," my mother said. "It's a dead end. That's why I'm quitting. Can you see Rosie here, living like this for the rest of her life?"

Dubbs was watching with worried eyes. "Can we eat?" she asked in a small voice. "I'm hungry."

I looked across at my mother, who didn't move. I wasn't sure she'd even heard Dubbs. I wanted to explode, but instead, I brought over the pot and took my place at the table. Ma and Larry sat at either end, and Larry dished out the food. Opposite me, Dubbs led grace and we dug in. There wasn't enough. Fuming as I was, I still managed to eat slowly, conserving my noodles, and when Dubbs finished hers, I silently reached over and pushed the rest of my food onto her plate.

"Thanks," she said.

Ma put her fork down. She started to cry. My stepfather kept eating.

"When's your next pay day?" he asked.

"Thursday," Ma said.

I looked at him, at the way he was forking up his food while Ma wiped at her eyes.

"Maybe you should get a job," I said to him.

He backhanded my face so hard I flew crashing to the floor.

Dubbs screamed.

"Larry!" my mother said.

My mind reeled. I could barely breathe, let alone think. My stepfather leaped around the table. He grabbed my hair and jerked me up. Bile rose in my throat.

"Don't you throw up," he said.

I gritted my teeth, forcing the bitterness back down.

"My hair," I whispered.

He released me. I fell again, and he backed up a few inches, pointing at me the way a master tests a dog to see if it will stay. For a moment, we fixed like that. Then he flexed his hand and turned away.

"Pawn the gun," he said quietly to Ma.

Then he reached for his hat and walked out the back door, closing it after himself.

>>>>>>>>

I didn't exactly hate my stepfather. I more despised him. Either way, he was just another part of my life of rolling, low-grade injustice that I couldn't change. Yet.

An hour after Larry hit me, Ma passed me a napkin filled with warm chocolate chip cookies. She'd walked up to

McLellens' with the gun and come back with the baking ingredients, and she'd made a cheese omelet, too. Dubbs, at the other end of our orange plaid couch, was ripping an old red shirt into thin, stretchy strips so she could tie them in loops for a weaving craft she liked to do, but she paused to reach wordlessly for one of my cookies.

My nose was scratched across the bridge and swollen, too, but it wasn't broken. I could hold a cold cloth to my face and eat cookies at the same time without too much trouble, though the cookies took on a damp taste.

"Any better?" my mom asked.

"Yeah." I sounded muffled. "Why doesn't Larry get a job?"

"The workers are still technically on strike," Ma said. "If he gets a different job, they'll take his name off the roll, and he won't get any of his back pay if they rehire again."

"But it's been a year."

"It's our problem to worry about, Rosie. Not yours," Ma said. "Just try not to exasperate him, okay? You want the rest of this?"

She passed me the mixing bowl before she turned back to the kitchen area. I ran my finger inside for a gob of cookie dough, and Dubbs crowded over to poke her finger in, too. I licked down smooth heaven: buttery, sweet, and chocolaty. Sometimes, it felt good to let my mom indulge me like a kid, but it didn't erase what had happened. She might want me to leave the problems to her, but my parents' problems had become mine, too. Whatever trapped them trapped me.

I'd been running errands for the McLellens as long as I could remember. If I couldn't get a decent education, I'd end up working at their pot bar and sundries shop for the rest of my life, or turning into my mother, which terrified me. I loved her, but still. I didn't want her life. She'd loved my birth father, her first husband, and they'd been saving up to move before he went MIA in the Greenland War. Then, after my dad had been declared PD—Presumed Dead—she'd ended up marrying his best friend, Larry, and having Dubbs.

Sometimes, like tonight when my nose hurt, I looked up through the skylight and dreamed about how my life would have been different if my own dad had never died. The only thing was, I'd never give up my little sister.

"Where'd you get that, Dubbs?" my mother asked.

"From the school library," Dubbs said. She had pulled out a tablet and, with layers of red strips still woven through her little fingers, was skimming the touch screen. "Remember you signed the permission slip? I get it for one night for free."

"Don't let your father see that."

"It's not a phone," Dubbs said. "He won't care."

Larry was paranoid about cell phones. He thought the government used them to track every citizen, so he refused to have one. We had to be the last family in town with a land-line phone, and half the time it was disconnected because we didn't pay our bill.

I sat up slowly, and Dubbs settled close enough that our arms bumped. She tapped up *The Forge Show*, which I hadn't watched since our TV broke. A menu along the bottom of the screen ran a tally of the top ten students in each grade, in blip rank order, so it was easy to track the popular students. Another menu listed links to spin-off commentary, interviews, and merchandise. Since the hour was after six, the show was on its repeat cycle, looping through the feeds from earlier in the day. It was showing that morning, around 8:00 a.m., when the students were dancing, singing, and studying in their classes.

"Who should we watch?" Dubbs asked. Each time she clicked on a student profile, it enlarged to fill three quarters of the screen, shrinking the other profiles to smaller boxes along the margin and muting their audios.

"Him," I said, pointing to a senior student with a goatee.

He was standing in a recording booth with a female student, coaching her on how to sing. He wanted her to be more internal and private with her characterization of a voice she was doing for a cartoon he was animating. As they talked, he urged her to feel it more, and he warned her that the mic was picking up her extra breaths. He left the booth for the other side of the glass while she gave the song another try.

The whole process fascinated me.

Dubbs flipped through different feeds, following her scattershot whims into ballet studios, art ateliers, and music practice rooms. Ma looked over the back of the couch.

"Do they ever take regular classes?" Ma asked.

"They have to take some electives in lit, history, science, and math," Dubbs said.

I laughed. "You know a lot about it."

"My friends watch it all the time," Dubbs said. "You'd be great there, Rosie, except it's too far away."

"Thousands of people apply every year," I said.

"So? You should at least try," Dubbs said.

"We could never afford it," Ma said.

"They have scholarships," Dubbs said. "They won't care if you're in N.I.P. It's based on talent."

"What would you study there? Film?" Ma asked.

"Of course film!" Dubbs said. "Really, Ma."

My inner longing expanded at the idea, and my gaze shot automatically to the top of the refrigerator where I'd stashed my video camera. I mentally framed up the shot of my sister and my mother together, with Ma leaning over the back of the couch, watching me, and Dubbs all pink-cheeked. A second later, I jumped over the back of the couch and grabbed my video camera to start shooting.

Dubbs took another bite of cookie and stuck out her tongue at the camera.

"That's the charm," I said. "Give me more."

"Where'd you get that old thing, anyway?" Ma asked.

"My science teacher gave it to me. He said I could keep it if I could fix it," I said.

I'd found a way to rig a penny in the battery pack. It wasn't perfect, but I loved that video camera. It gave me an excuse to stare close up at whatever I wanted, but it allowed me some distance, too, because I was never quite in the scene when I was filming.

I turned the video camera upside down as I aimed it at

Dubbs and focused in on one of her eyes. Her lashes were huge. "Say something brilliant, Dubbs," I said.

"I need to fart," she said.

"That's good," I said, laughing. I zoomed out again to frame up both of her eyes. Her lashes were still huge.

"No! I've got it!" she said. She made her little voice serious. "This is my brilliant message: you have to dream."

My sister said that. My little sister.

I lowered my video camera so I could see her in real life. She killed me sometimes when she was right.

Then she farted.

We both laughed. I set my video camera aside so I could wrestle her into a squashed, squirming shape beneath me. "You're disgusting!" I said, and exhaled cookie breath in her face.

"Stop!" she said, laughing harder.

I did. Eventually.

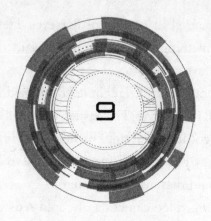

9

THE FURNITURE MOVERS

MY FIRST ELATION at passing the fifty cuts soon faded.
I paused as I stepped into our dorm room that Monday evening. It had always been a large, uncomfortable space, more
like a drafty barn than a bedroom, but now it veered toward
the ominous. With their lids dim and closed, the sleep shells
of the cut girls were interspersed among the remaining ones
like great, hulking coffins.

"This is creepy," I said.

"Forgive us if we can't move twenty-five sleep shells out of
your room in under an hour," Orly said dryly. "They'll be gone
by morning. Hurry, now, and get ready for bed. Pills in ten
minutes."

I hadn't seen her standing by the door. Orly was a big-
boned woman who favored gray, high-necked blouses, and

she retained a dour air despite the general cheer of the rest of the staff. I glanced toward the other girls who were getting ready for bed, and then back to Orly.

"I didn't mean to criticize," I said.

"You, of all people, should be grateful you're still here," she said. "That was quite ruthless, making a project of all those losers. Not to mention using that kitchen boy like you did."

Her words stung.

"I didn't use Linus," I said.

"No? What was that, then? Spontaneous chemistry?"

Orly was laying out small white paper cups on a tray for the evening pill-taking routine. I didn't understand why she had a grudge against me, but wittingly or not, she was giving me a chance to defend myself before the cameras.

"I had no idea what I'd find when I went to take footage of Anna and the others. I was just trying to capture an important time," I said. "And I happen to like Linus."

"I'm sure you do," Orly said. "I've seen it all before, believe me. You're certainly not the first to stage an opportunistic romance."

I squared my feet. "What's bothering you? That I filmed those other students, or that I kissed Linus?"

Her mouth went prim as if she weren't going to answer. Then her eyes went snappish. "That kiss was trashy," Orly said. "It cheapened both the school and the show. Maybe nobody else will tell you so, but it's the truth. And Linus is little better than catnip for that old goat in the tower."

"Excuse me?" I said.

"It's their business, I'm sure," Orly said. "Not mine."

My thoughts leapt and just as instantly reversed. I couldn't believe she'd said such a thing on camera. Orly turned her back before I could respond, and I looked awkwardly around at the other girls. The nearest ones were acting like they hadn't overheard, but they weren't chatting like normal, either.

I headed down the length of the room, toward my wardrobe. I was acutely uncomfortable. Orly obviously didn't think I deserved to stay, but my blip rank proved her wrong. My viewers had multiplied enough for me to stay. That was all the vindication I needed.

It wasn't until I had changed into my nightie and brushed my teeth that I realized I was judging myself by my blip rank, using that to bolster my confidence. I wasn't any better than Paige.

I was supposed to take my pill and go to sleep like everyone else, but I didn't want to. I had too much to contemplate. I needed time alone, to think, to settle, and I couldn't do that properly with the pressure of the cameras. So, after Orly distributed the pills, I climbed into my sleep shell and closed my lid. Then I curled into my pillow, shifted my quilt around my face, and took the pill out of my cheek where I had hidden it. I slid it into my pillowcase.

"Good night, girls," Orly said from the far end of the room. "Sleep well."

The vaulted room dropped into murky twilight as she turned off the lights, and half of the sleep shell lids glowed with brink lessons. The one to my right side stayed dark. My brink lesson showed a pair of hands folding a square of silver paper into an origami shape, and at the end, the person blew into the paper to expand it into a cube. It was a clever play on dimensions, and it made me smile.

Dubbs would like a cube like that, I thought. I missed my sister. I wanted to make her proud. When my brink lesson ended, I slid my lid open and listened to the hush in the room. I vowed to do everything I could to make the most of my time at Forge, and I wouldn't do anything reckless again like go out on the roof at night, no matter how tempted I was. I was incredibly lucky that Dr. Ash had given me another chance. I wouldn't ignore her warning.

The rain stopped, leaving drops clinging to the glass of the nearest window like colorless ladybugs.

I didn't realize I had dropped into a doze until a low, rolling noise awakened me. The overhead lights were on again, but it wasn't morning. I listened, hearing more rumbling from the other end of the room, near the door. Without rising, I shifted just enough to take a peek.

Workers were quietly moving the extra furniture out of the dorm. Pairs of people rolled the sleep shells and eased them, one at a time, out the doorway and around the corner. Others tilted the dressers on dollies to guide them out. I counted six movers, plus Orly, who was giving directions.

The process was marked by extended gaps, and I guessed that the elevator couldn't handle more than one sleep shell at a time. The movers were also bringing in simple wooden chairs and rugs, like midnight magicians or the set crew for a play.

I closed my eyes to feign sleep as the noises gradually worked their way down the room toward me. When I heard Linus's voice nearby, I nearly jumped.

"Touch her and you're dead," Linus said.

"Come on," said another guy. Some nasal quality of his speech reminded me of a weasel. "She'd never know. They're completely asleep."

A brief squeak came from a rolling wheel.

"All right," said the same weasel voice. "I was only curious. Take it easy."

"I don't even know what you're doing here," Linus said. "I thought you stuck to the fifth floor."

"It's good extra money. Besides, I wanted to see my girl in person. Check her out," said the weasel guy. "Why do you suppose she leaves her lid open?"

"I don't know. Don't touch it."

"It has been one crazy run. Victor couldn't believe it when I came in at fifty. You heard about my bonus, right?"

"I don't care about your pissant competition," Linus asked. "Watch your foot there."

"Victor sure cares," said the weasel guy. "This was the first time in three years he wasn't in the top fifty. Bummer."

"You got lucky being assigned to Rosie," Linus said.

I was surprised to hear him use my first name.

"No, *she* was lucky to get *me*," said the other voice. "Picking the angles is an art form. It's so ironic, filming a girl who calls herself a filmmaker. The students get all the credit, but they wouldn't be stars without us."

Okay, he was a jerk, but still, it was totally cool to realize this guy was one of the techies who managed my profile for *The Forge Show*.

"Is that so," Linus said.

"The better I know her, it's like I can read which way she's going to turn, and then she does," the weasel guy said. "She moves right into my picks, like we're dancing together. Except she doesn't know it. She beamed that smile at her mother last night? And bam, I was right there to get the gap and all."

"She doesn't even like the cameras, Bones," Linus said.

The weasel guy, Bones, laughed softly. "They all like the cameras, idiot, or they wouldn't come. What did she say when you kissed her?"

"Let me check my notes and get back to you," Linus said.

"So funny. Truth be told, the visuals were tough with the rain," Bones went on. "I only had four decent camera angles to choose from, and I didn't want to spin between them too often. Pacing's everything, especially when you're respecting an intimate moment. I had to choose between Otis's wide shot from the lookout tower and a button close-up from behind her head. The close-up had no lips, so I went with Otis's. The man's an ace for framing it up, but I could have killed him for not going in closer."

"Incidentally, I don't give a crap about your angles," Linus said.

"You know, I should have mic-ed you," said Bones. "Why didn't I think of that?"

"Possibly because I'd beat your brains in before I'd ever let you mic me," Linus said.

Their voices were moving farther away. I itched to take a look and see what the weasel guy looked like. I didn't dare move, though.

"What if Berg insisted on it?" Bones said. "I'm surprised he didn't. Maybe next time. I'll talk to him."

Next time? Dean Berg? A chill spread over my skin. If Dean Berg could make Linus wear a microphone, what else could he make Linus do? He couldn't have sent Linus to kiss me, or to meet me in the first place. No. Of course not. Linus was on staff, but that didn't make him a puppet. I was way too suspicious.

I kept listening to the quiet movement of furniture, hoping to hear Linus's voice again. Once I heard my techie Bones again, speaking to Orly, and once, later, I heard steps coming near that I thought might be Linus's. I expected he might say something. My ears strained for a clue to where he was, and how near. I opened my mouth slightly to take in extra air, and a faint tingling in my lips reminded me of how it had felt when we'd kissed.

It was a strange kind of suspense, not being able to open my eyes, and not knowing if I was imagining that he was there.

"That's enough, now, Pitts," Orly said clearly from the other end of the room. "We've got the boys' dorm to do still."

I felt a faint tremor, as if a hand was set on the end of my sleep shell, and then I heard footsteps retreating. A minute later, the lights went out again. I took a deep breath and rolled over to my other side, waiting forever for my pulse to calm.

It was almost as if Linus had known I could open my eyes. As if he'd dared me.

I needed to get some solid sleep or I'd be dead the next day. I let myself go, willing my muscles to unclench. I tried to recapture the feeling I usually got from my sleeping pill, the way a warm, easy calm soothed through my veins, wicking through my neck and shoulders, relaxing my hips and knees. My mind slowed, my fingers went limp, and the brown mist slipped gently in.

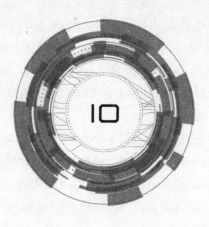

10

FANS

A TRACE OF dream clung to me as I surfaced into Tuesday morning, a shadow twin who stretched out from my feet, farther and farther ahead of me along the railroad tracks, until she detached and slipped away.

Languorously, I smiled and rolled over. It was the first hint of a dream I'd had since I'd come to the Forge School, and I loved remembering dreams. I'd missed them while I was on the pills.

The bells from the clock tower were still tolling six as I opened my eyes on a transformed room. Half the sleep shells were gone, and each of us had been given a straight-backed chair, a small bedside table, and a braided oval rug. For the first time, the dorm room felt, if not quite homey, at least less oppressive. Best of all, the clouds outside had finally cleared.

My sleep shell had stayed at the end of the room, but Janice's had been shifted next to mine in the line. She was leaning on the edge of her sleep shell, running her bare toes over her rug. Sunlight dropped in the windows around her, bouncing off her blue quilt and bright hair.

"This is a vast improvement," she said.

I eased over to the nearest window and with a finger on the glass, I located the pale gray façade of the dean's tower. It was the most modern building on campus, morphing out of an older, shorter building. I counted up five stories to the row of windows where Linus had said my techie worked, and I wished I could see inside.

"Did you ever watch one of those Forge specials about the people who work behind the scenes?" I asked.

"Sure," she said. "With the tunnels and stuff?"

"I'd like to get in the dean's tower sometime," I said.

"I'd rather go to Forgetown. I heard last year, after the seniors graduated, they all went into town and partied with the techies." She cupped her hand in a princess wave. "Hello to you, techie," she said, and laughed.

"He's probably choking on his coffee right now," I said.

"I think of mine as a her," she said. "I don't know why. She's very kindly and soulful."

I thought of mine as an arrogant weasel named Bones.

The upbeat voices of the other girls made a nice change from the stress of the day before. Paige was doing ballerina stretches between her rug and a chair, extra wide splits that hurt me to look at her. Janice began getting dressed.

I examined my arms for new marks, and found none. It was a relief.

Maybe I was going to be okay here now. I could hope.

>>>>>>>>

I saw Linus in the kitchen when I went through the cafeteria line, but he was busy with the meat slicer, and it wasn't the right time to flag him down just to say hello. He was wearing his eye patch again, and I wondered how much sleep he'd gotten the night before. The blip rank board in the dining room had been reconfigured for the new total number of students in the school, fifty in each class of tenth-, eleventh-, and twelfth-graders, and it was satisfying to see myself listed there even though I was still number 50, the new last rank for our grade.

After breakfast, when I walked into Media Convergence class, a number of the usual students were gone, cut from the show, and others had been switched in. Burnham sat at a desk near the back, next to Henrik, and after a moment's hesitation, I took a seat beside Janice, near the front.

She put a hair binder in her mouth and reached up with both hands to twist her blond hair into a sloppy bun. "Kill me now," she said, wrapping the binder in place. "I ran into this guy from acting? He hears we're doing the coolest gender flip thing. I want to be Hamlet."

While she chatted, a few other students came in, and then Mr. DeCoster appeared carrying a metal coffee mug. He paused at the door to speak to his earphone, and Paige edged in around him.

"Okay, everybody," Mr. DeCoster said. He pointed to a couple of big tables that were pushed together. "Circle up the chairs around here. Time to talk."

We all scooted our swivel chairs toward the tables, like swarming racer bugs. I ended up with Janice on my right, and Burnham next to her. Mr. DeCoster pulled his chair up across from me and slid a shallow cardboard box onto the table. Inside was a jumble of seashells, twigs, and stones. Today Mr. DeCoster wore a silver and turquoise bolo tie over a black shirt, and he looked a lot cooler than usual.

"First of all, let me congratulate you all on making the fifty cuts," he said. "I couldn't be happier you're still here. We've combined a couple sections to adjust for the cuts, and you'll notice a few other changes, too." He gave the box a little shake. "Take one and please introduce yourself, with your art."

Paige, on his right, selected a dainty, pearly shell shaped like a spiral, and told us she was from Houston and danced. Henrik, it turned out, was a percussionist from Berlin, Germany. The group also included a playwright, a painter, a singer, and half a dozen others. The singer, Mae, asked if Mr. DeCoster knew anything about Ellen, and he reported that Ellen was home with her family. I glanced at Janice, who gave me a sad little smile. On my turn, I chose a small, black stone and kept it short: Doli, Arizona. Filmmaker.

When Burnham introduced himself—Atlanta, Interactive Media and Game Development—he smiled at everyone else except me, and I got an uneasy feeling that something was wrong.

After introductions, Mr. DeCoster spoke up in a louder voice. "Up until now, we've focused on learning specific, hands-on editing skills," he said. "They had value for everyone, whether they were staying on the show or getting cut. Now it's time for a different focus. Your next assignment is to create something that's bigger than you are. Something at which you'll fail."

I waited for him to elaborate, but he reached for his coffee and said nothing more. Students started looking around the table.

"Like save the world?" Henrik said, laughing.

"That would work," Mr. DeCoster said.

Paige fiddled with her shell. "Dance can save the world."

"You could fail at that," Henrik said.

"Or not, you sad little drummer," Paige said.

Burnham pointed his finger at Henrik and smiled. "Burn."

"The answer is yes, your project can be dance," Mr. De-Coster said.

"How about a computer game?" Burnham said.

"Fine," Mr. DeCoster said.

"Are you serious? He gets to play a game?" Henrik asked.

"Burnham designs games," Mr. DeCoster said. "It's not the same as playing them."

"I fail at it a lot, too," Burnham said. "In fact, most of the time."

Mr. DeCoster swept his attention around the table. "This

is a good time for experiments that don't work. For fun. For the things you used to dream up when you were a kid on a playground or in a fort under a chair. Imagine anything and try to make it happen."

I'd never had an assignment like this before. Not even close.

"What materials can we use?" Janice asked.

"Anything you can find or borrow," Mr. DeCoster said. "The shop is full of gear: swords, black lights, costumes, explosives, paints, paper, cameras, you name it."

"Explosives? Seriously?" Paige said.

"You hear your voice there?" Mr. DeCoster said. "That's a good starting point."

The others laughed again. I was starting to like Mr. DeCoster.

"Can we work in teams?" Henrik asked.

"You can do whatever you want, as long as you fail," Mr. DeCoster said. "The more spectacularly, the better."

"Do we have any deadlines?" the painter Harry asked.

"Your failure is due at the end of the marking period, on October thirty-first," Mr. DeCoster said. "I want to see a portfolio of progress every Friday, and by portfolio, I mean whatever pieces of work or disasters you have to show at that point."

I looked down at the smooth, black stone I'd chosen, and rubbed its cool surface with my thumb. I didn't even know how to start thinking about this assignment.

"How about you, Rosie? Any questions?" Mr. DeCoster asked.

I glanced up. "Do we keep these?" I asked.

"You can. Why did you choose yours?" Mr. DeCoster replied.

"It's pretty," I said. "It makes me think of the sea."

He smiled. "Have you been there?"

"No," I said. "Not yet. I want to someday."

"How about the rest of you?" Mr. DeCoster asked. "Why'd you pick your objects?"

"My parents have a summer place on Nantucket," Janice said. "We go there every year." She'd chosen a speckled shell, I noticed.

The others talked on. Burnham had another black stone, much like my own, though the hue of it seemed different against his dark fingers. I glanced up to find him regarding me steadily through his glasses, and an odd, slow trickle ran through me, like I was taking a long swallow of cool water. He couldn't be mad at me, I reasoned. Something else was going on. He tapped his stone once lightly on the table and sat back, unsmiling, still watching me. *What?* I thought, but his gaze shifted to his stone, and he turned it over on the table.

"This box may not seem related to your project, but it is," Mr. DeCoster said. "We're always choosing things, every minute—how we spend our time, what we think about, what object we pick out of a box. Forge students are incredibly focused, driven people. Each time we choose, however, we're also choosing to reject or neglect something else."

"Like viewers choosing who to watch," Henrik said, and the others laughed.

114

"Take the next leap with me, please," Mr. DeCoster said. "Making choices is natural. It's human. Over a lifetime of choosing, we train our minds to select and focus, and we think of that as a strength. But what happens when you try to think differently? To dream?" He gave the box a little shake and I saw half a dozen items had been left inside. "Your customary thinking patterns can become a trap. Creativity isn't rigid."

"You want us to think outside the box, obviously," Paige said.

"That phrase itself is a box," Mr. DeCoster said. "Think how tidy it is, how cliché. I want you to see where the edges of your box are, or redefine the box itself. What if instead I said think outside the room? Think outside the school?"

Think outside the solar system, I thought. Closing my eyes, I began to see stars, to feel the cool pull of the purple sky that floated between them. The air began to thin, the molecules to separate, and I expanded my lungs to fill them while I still could. This could work for me.

"This assignment is a test, isn't it?" Burnham said.

I opened my eyes, surprised.

"How do you mean?" Mr. DeCoster said.

"You're testing us to see who's most creative," Burnham said.

Mr. DeCoster smiled. "So? This is an art school, after all. Creativity's part of the curriculum."

"It's a reality show, too," Burnham said. "We're competing with each other for our blip ranks and banner ads. What's your payoff? If our blip ranks go higher than the ranks for some other class, do you get some kind of kickback?"

"Easy, man," Henrik said.

I'd only known Burnham a day, but cynicism from him just seemed wrong.

Mr. DeCoster's face was impassive. "It's my job to push you however I see fit. And yes, a percentage of your banner ad monies come to me. I doubt it's ever been put that baldly, but it's no secret. Does that make my teaching methods any less valid?"

Burnham spread his hand on the table. "No. It's just nice to know where we stand." And he looked at me.

I stared back at him while my mind flew. He was competing with me. Or he was saying I competed. Either way, he didn't mean it nicely. I felt a flare of resentment.

"Where we stand," Mr. DeCoster echoed slowly. "Let me explain something for you. Twenty-three years ago, the Forge School was nothing but an obscure prep school with an outdated campus at the edge of civilization. But it had a film teacher, an inspired film teacher, and she kept turning out one famous director after another."

"Yes, sir," Burnham said, as if he'd just recalled his manners. "We know this story."

"You don't know the story," Mr. DeCoster said. "You haven't really listened to it, or you wouldn't have asked about my payoff."

"Go on," I said, crossing my arms. "I want to hear."

"Thank you, Rosie," Mr. DeCoster said. "One of the

famous director alums decided to do a documentary on the teacher who had inspired her, and that teacher, Miss Lavinia, refused. She said to spotlight her students instead. So the director made a film about the students at Forge." Mr. DeCoster took another sip of his coffee. "Then what, Burnham?"

"I guess it expanded from there," Burnham said.

"You would be right," Mr. DeCoster said. "First, Miss Lavinia noticed something unexpected. The students who were being filmed began to work much harder. They took bigger risks. They began to excel. The camera eye, itself, was influencing their performance."

"Oh, right," Janice said. "I remember this. Wasn't she the one who asked to have cameras installed in her classroom?"

"She did, and she sold the feed to the local cable network, with even more striking results," Mr. DeCoster said. "Half of the other teachers wanted to kill Miss Lavinia, but the other half wanted in, and then the school ran a pilot program following a batch of the students everywhere, twenty-four seven."

"That's how *The Forge Show* was born?" Henrik said. "I never knew that."

"What too many people fail to remember is that this place exists for you. For the students," Mr. DeCoster said. "At its purest level, the show serves the school, not the other way around. We've been under pressure countless times to spice up the show with hot tubs and guest stars and cheap what have you, but we've held to Miss Lavinia's principles, always putting you first. You and your art. Why do you think people watch this show?"

It was wildly popular, but I'd never tried to put my finger on why people watched. Burnham stubbornly refused to reply.

"They're bored," Paige said.

"They're bored," Mr. DeCoster repeated. He closed his eyes as if in pain. When he opened them, he tweaked his earphone. "Sandy? Are you there? Can you come on the speaker, please?"

I scanned the ceiling, and then a speaker near the doorway came to life.

"What can I do for you, Robert?" said Dean Berg.

"Could we have a sampling of some fan clips, please? On the overhead?"

"Sure. One minute. Let me patch in Xing Lao. Xing Lao?"

A second voice came from the speaker. "I heard," he said. "I'll pick a few that came in last night after the cuts. Will that do?"

"That should be fine," Mr. DeCoster said.

He reached for a remote. Blinds in the windows swiveled to dim the room, and the screen at the front of the classroom flickered on. Up came a menu of icons, presumably controlled by Xing Lao, who flew through layers of options to pull up a video of a young black woman, maybe twenty years old, with wet eyes and a gleaming smile. She was hugging a gray kitten and looking straight into the camera.

"Hi," she said in a scratchy voice. "I just watched the fifty cuts, and I just have to say, I'm so happy Paige made it. She's exactly like my sister. Exactly. Only my sister died last year from leukemia, and I miss her so much. When I watch Paige dance, it's like I get Megan back for a minute. I mean, of course, I know she's not really Megan, but she's just like Megan would be if she was here to keep dancing." She kissed her fingers and touched them to her heart.

Paige's mouth went agape in surprise. Before I had time to react, another face came up on the screen. Two faces, really. A couple of old guys in plaid flannel shirts. They hadn't shaved lately, and a mangy caribou head was mounted on the wall behind them.

"Howdy. This here's Jim and Joey Johansen from Nome," said the man on the left. "We wish to offer our congratulations to all the kids who passed the fifty cuts. We've been following your progress most days—"

"Every day but Sunday," said the second man.

The first one nodded. "Every day but Sunday, that is. Our friend Rhonda—"

"She works over at the diner here in town," said the second man.

"Our friend Rhonda told us to try your show. She said we'd like it for the art, and she was right. We'd like to say we appreciate the energy of you young people. I don't think it's too much to say you give us hope. For the future."

"For humankind," said the second man.

"That's right. For humankind. So best of luck to you now."

The two men nodded solemnly.

I glanced over at Janice, who was watching the screen, spellbound. Nobody snickered, and I was glad.

The next clip showed a boy of twelve or thirteen, sitting in a hospital bed with an oxygen tube running under his nose and back around his ears.

"I got it, Mom," he said, and then smiled straight at the camera, which jiggled once. "Hi! This is Billy!" He breathed in thickly. "I'm so excited! I've been watching your show three years now, and this year is the best year ever, with the best people ever. My favorite students are Burnham Fister and Henrik Plashcka and Rosie Sinclair." He took another deep, thick breath. "If you ever see this and just give me one quick wave or thumbs up or whatever, that'd be great."

The frame froze on him giving a thumbs up, and I stared at him, unblinking. On instinct, I gave him a wave, and looking around the table, I saw others doing it, too.

The voice of Xing Lao came over the speaker again. "Want a few more?"

"Thanks. I think that will do," Mr. DeCoster said.

"My pleasure. Anytime," Xing Lao said.

"All good, Robert?" Dean Berg asked.

"Yes, thank you," Mr. DeCoster said, touching his earphone again.

A soft crackle came from the speaker, and then it went quiet. The window shades hummed as they tilted to let the light back in.

I stared around at the other students, who sat humbled and silent in their seats. Not one of us spoke.

Mr. DeCoster set down his remote and opened a hand upon the table. "Questions?"

Henrik cleared his throat. "How many of those clips do you get?"

"Hundreds," Mr. DeCoster said.

"Why don't you pass them on to us?" Janice asked.

"Because of the pressure it would put on you, and the distractions it would create when you felt you had to reply," Mr. DeCoster said.

"That last little guy was cute," Henrik said.

"It's terrifying," Paige said. "Who can live up to that?"

Some of the others were muttering to one another. Burnham was quietly turning over his stone in his fingers.

Mr. DeCoster took his box of shells and put a lid on it. His gaze shifted toward Burnham, and then to me, and then he pushed back his chair. "I have one other thing. I'm moving our class to the basement of the library. There's a den down there with a couple of old couches and a Ping-Pong table. I find it more conducive to thinking, plus it's closer to the shop. Meet me there tomorrow. A little help with the chairs, please."

We rolled our chairs back toward the computer desks, and Mr. DeCoster took his coffee cup. A couple of students lingered to ask him a few questions. Janice said she was heading over to the drama building. As if he planned to stay a while, Burnham turned on a computer at the back of the room. I slid my stone into my skirt pocket, and then I walked over and took the swivel chair next to his.

"Hey," I said. "What was that about?"

"Nothing."

"You sure?"

"Yes. I get it."

"Get what?" I asked.

Burnham skimmed a finger over his touch screen, and a black world with purple, winged guys shifted onto his larger computer screen.

"Right. Ignore me. That's real subtle," I said.

"I'm trying to work on my game here, if you don't mind."

"Okay, wait a second," I said slowly. "I could be wrong, but yesterday I thought we were friends."

"I thought so, too."

"So why aren't you talking to me?"

"I am."

He was too smart for stupid games.

"Is this because I kissed Linus?" I asked.

He let out a brief laugh. "That is a totally girl thing to say."

"I *am* a girl, in case you haven't noticed," I said. "You're acting incredibly weird. Yesterday you weren't like this."

"Why would I care if you kissed anybody?" he asked.

"That's what I want to know." I pulled his touch screen out from under his hand.

"Seriously? I am not going to fight you for my touch screen," he said.

"Just tell me, Burnham," I said, leaning over him and holding the touch screen tight. "Yesterday, you were nice to me. Was that some kind of stunt? Is this the real you now?"

"*I* was not doing a stunt. *You* were the strategy queen," Burnham said. He turned to face me and folded his arms. Behind his glasses, his eyes were hard. "Make friends with someone who has a high blip rank. Use your special talent, like make a film of losers to get everyone's sympathy. Have a personal drama. Sound familiar?"

Guilty alarm rose in me. "You know what Linus told me to do to stay on the show?" I said.

"That's right," Burnham said, nodding. "My brother watched your scene with him from yesterday morning and told me about it. He thought I'd be interested."

I quietly set down the touch screen. "I did everything Linus said," I said, half-amazed. "But I wasn't following his advice. It wasn't like that."

"Ellen's tragedy must have been pure luck," Burnham said. "Then again, you had to be laughing your head off when I got everybody at lunch to do our spike experiment."

"You actually think I masterminded yesterday," I said. "You think I was using you and everybody else." I felt a horrible twinge of conscience. The spike at lunch *had* been mainly my idea, but I hadn't set out to use the others at our table, and they had benefited, too.

"You're good, Rosie," Burnham said. "A far better actor than Janice, in my opinion. And now you've made the cuts. I fully expect you to claw your way right to number one."

"That's awful," I said furiously. "I wasn't thinking about what Linus said. I was just being myself."

"And yet you managed to kiss him at five o'clock, *in the rain*," Burnham said.

"Now the weather is my fault, too?" I demanded.

"Cut the righteousness," Burnham said. "Just admit you

123

played me and be done with it. Just admit it, and say you're sorry, and I'll admit I was stupid to believe you were just a nice, awkward kind of girl, and we'll be even."

"Awkward!" I said, and my voice strangled into incoherence. I narrowed my eyes to slits. "You know what?" I said. "I know what I did yesterday, and why I did it. I don't need to justify myself to you or anyone else."

"That is not an apology," he said.

"You're right. It's not. Because I didn't do anything wrong."

"You cheated and manipulated to pass the fifty cuts," he said. "You set me up and used me."

I glared at him, seething. "I did not. You're just saying that because I'm not the meek little awkward thing you thought I was."

"So it's my fault, then?" he said. "Fine. Believe that. And now I'm sick of being nice." He pushed his watch farther up his wrist and started swiping on his touch screen.

"I hate to tell you this. You're not nice," I said, and left.

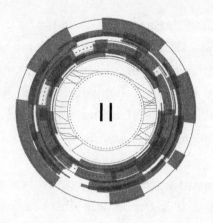

THE CLOCK TOWER

BURNHAM'S DISAPPROVAL STUNG. I couldn't believe he'd thought I was just a nice, awkward sort of girl, but it was even worse that he thought I was a manipulator. I kept reviewing what had happened at lunch the day before, and I knew I'd asked, in so many words, for him and the other students at our table to try to get me a spike in ratings. But he was the one who had proposed the theory of influencing spikes, and the others had seen their blip ranks improve, too.

I hadn't filmed the losers to be cunning and vicious. I'd had no idea that Ellen would be in meltdown. I certainly hadn't planned on kissing Linus for a premeditated finale.

"What's wrong with you?" Janice asked me later, when I went up to the dorm to change for a run. "You're all moody and quiet."

"No, I'm not." I turned my back to the room and changed into shorts and a shirt as quickly as possible. The techies were notoriously discreet about not broadcasting nudity, but me in my bra and undies was fair game. I could have gone to a bathroom stall to change, but I wasn't shy and awkward like some people might think I was.

What had given him that idea?

"Do I seem awkward to you?" I asked Janice.

She set her shell on her bedside table beside a collection of swizzle sticks. "You seemed a little aloof before I got to know you," she said. "Maybe a little introverted, but driven, too. Why?"

"I'm just wondering."

She pulled up a ratty old paperback of *Hamlet* and flipped through the pages. "Remember the simple old days, when all boys were obnoxious and clammy?" Janice said.

"I don't want to talk about boys," I said.

"Fair enough. It was just a shot," she said. And then, "Burnham was pretty weird around you earlier."

I reached for my sneakers and frowned over at her. "Okay. Do you think he's jealous because I kissed Linus?" I asked. "I've known him for *a day*. Could he be that cliché?"

"It's remotely possible," she said. "He did have a chivalrous gleam in his eye where you were concerned."

I laced up one foot. Then the other. "That was yesterday. Now he thinks I'm a manipulative cheater."

Janice set a finger to hold a place in her book. "He actually said that?"

"He did."

"That's not very like him," she said. "I'd say he's more of a hero type. He likes to save people. Besides, he seemed happy about your spike at lunch."

It was true. He'd given me the picture of Dubbs then, too.

"He won't be saving this girl," I said. I didn't want to think about him anymore. I certainly didn't want to talk about him and have his pesky watching brother get back to him about it. My eye caught on Janice's shell again, and I remembered what she'd said in DeCoster's class. "What's it like on Nantucket?"

"Pretty. The light feels like afternoon all day long," she said. "I miss it."

Here I'd been blabbing on about myself without ever giving her a chance to talk. I pulled my thick hair back in a ponytail. "Do you have any brothers and sisters?" I asked.

"Just my little sister, Amy," she said. "I miss her, too. Want to see?" She reached for her phone and pulled up a photo to show me. The two sisters had their faces cheek to cheek, and they were basically adorable.

"You have the same smile," I said. "What do your parents do?"

"Mom's a minister, and Mami's a pediatrician," Janice said.

Two moms. And a minister's daughter, too. "What's that like?" I asked.

"Which part?" she asked, still gazing at her photo.

"The two moms."

"I don't know. What's it like having different sex parents?" she asked, glancing up.

I smiled. "You have a point."

"What's your family like, though, really?" she asked. "The typical mom and dad? Golden retriever?"

I shook my head. I didn't like talking about my family, especially on camera. I wasn't exactly ashamed of my parents, but I could never be sure what I was revealing about Larry, and I couldn't explain what it was really like living in the boxcars. "I live with my mom and my stepfather and my half sister, Dubbs. She's seven. She's pretty cool."

"Do you have a picture?"

I reached into my backpack and took out a little notebook. Tucked inside was a small paper photo of Dubbs and me at the Grand Canyon from three years ago. Behind it was the picture Burnham had given me of her. I handed Janice the one with the Grand Canyon, and looked again at the other, wondering if he still wanted me to keep it.

"Nice," Janice said. "She has a sweet face."

I looked down at both images before I tucked them away again. "Yeah," I said.

The bonging from the clock tower came through the window, and I leaned against my wardrobe to stretch out my calf muscles.

"I'm going for a run before dinner. Want to come?" I asked.

"Gads no," she said. "Maybe it will help if you go talk to that guy."

"He's too mad at me."

"Not Burnham, genius," Janice said. "The hot kitchen guy."

I hadn't talked to Linus all day. I frowned down at the floor. "It's too weird with all the cameras," I said.

She laughed. "Get used to them, girl."

"I mean, Linus could have seen my conversation with Burnham this morning."

"He probably did. Burnham can watch you with Linus, too. He could be watching this right now, come to think of it. Either of them could."

"Burnham's not watching me. He's far too cool for that."

"Should we check?" she asked and reached for her phone.

"No!"

"I'm just teasing you," she said, laughing.

Just what I needed. "Thanks. You're the best."

"Anytime."

>>>>>>>>

I was *obviously* heading to find Linus, but for my pride's sake, I took my run first. Running usually settled my nerves, but this time, my nerves fueled my run instead, and I started out way too fast.

I was not an athlete. Far from it. I didn't even have decent shoes, but that never stopped me. I cut north between the gym and the amphitheater, and hit a steadier, more realistic stride as I started counterclockwise around the campus loop. Echoey voices and a lifeguard's whistle came through the windows of the pool. Big, loose clouds were locked in place, dropping patches of muted silver on the solar farm beyond the campus to the west. With my sneakers drumming a regular beat, I zigzagged through the sculpture garden and past the graveyard with its tilting markers.

By the time I reached the sheep pasture, I was panting hard, but I pushed on to the old, defunct observatory. A twenty-foot ladder led up the limestone building to a narrow metal catwalk that ran around the gray dome. On impulse, I sidestepped the DO NOT ENTER sign and climbed the ladder hand-over-hand to the top. When I finally stopped, I braced my hands on my knees and sucked air.

"Okay," I said.

My mind was clearing and my body felt deliciously loose-limbed. I straightened, leaning back against the base of the dome, and soaked in the vastness of sky. The prairie stretched out for miles, wide as an ocean, with flowing ripples of wind blowing through the grass. A pair of swallows flew overhead, and I joined them, soaring and dipping above the green.

I had to smile. I'd found my favorite new place.

A satellite dish was propped beside the dome, aimed toward the universe. I seriously doubted if the quirky, anachronistic building even had a functional telescope inside anymore, but I was glad it hadn't been torn down to make room for something useful, like a parking garage. I'd heard someone had died inside the observatory, but on such a pretty afternoon, that was hard to believe.

I walked around the dome, liking how the slanting light

130

fell on the curved surface. The opening for the telescope was sealed. No doubt the entrance down below was locked, too, but I could imagine the darkness inside, with its cache of privacy. How I'd love to get in there. I glanced up the pasture to the lookout tower, and sure enough, Otis's big camera was angled at me. I waved, and was surprised to see the old man wave back.

I climbed down the ladder, careful of the chain near the bottom, and headed up the pasture path. At the service entrance of the dining hall, I jogged up and peered inside the screen door, looking for Linus. Two other kitchen guys and the frizzy-haired woman were working, but I saw no sign of Chef Ted. Hoping I wasn't too much of a sweat ball, I straightened my shirt and rapped on the door frame.

The woman came over and undid a hook inside.

"Hi. Is Linus here?" I asked, entering.

She called over her shoulder. "Linus! You have a visitor!"

Linus came out of a back room carrying a white plastic barrel. His eyebrows lifted as he saw me, and when he hefted the barrel onto a counter, he smiled. His patch was gone. A shadow of bruise circled his eye, but he looked better.

"Hey," he said to me. And then, "Look, Franny love. It's Rosie. Fancy her stopping by the kitchen all uninvited."

Franny put a fist on her hip. "If that's your way of saying 'I told you so,' it's not very subtle."

Linus untied his bib apron and ducked out of it. "Rosie, this is Franny. Franny, Rosie."

"Hello," I said, and she gave me a nod.

"Do you think you can hold the place together for ten minutes without me?" Linus said to Franny, and tucked his white tee shirt loosely into the waist of his jeans.

"Oh, please," she said with a dismissive flick of her fingers.

He smiled and pushed open the door, holding it for me. We headed down the back steps and cut right, toward the back of the art building where we'd met before. The big, paint-spattered spools were dry, their wood warm in the sun. I hitched myself up on one and let my sneakers dangle. Linus stayed on the ground and picked pebbles out of the gravel to pitch toward the pasture.

"Franny's been warning me all day you wouldn't come by," he said. "She started running your feed in the kitchen just to prove she was right."

"You knew I'd come, though, right?" I asked.

He shrugged. "I hoped."

I smoothed my shorts more comfortably under my legs. "Can I ask you something? Do you think I'm a big manipulator?"

"I don't care if you are," he said. "It was fun to see you work your way on."

"Burnham thinks I use people," I said.

"Fister uses people, too. He just doesn't know it. Come on." He held up a hand to me.

"Where are we going?" I asked. "I like it here."

"You'll like it inside the clock tower, too."

"I didn't know you could get in." I took his fingers as I hopped down.

"It's kind of cool. I'll show you," he said, and we headed uphill, toward the quad.

The late afternoon sunlight was striking the clock tower sideways, adding long shadows to the hands on the face of the clock. The rose garden, with a scattering of late blossoms, was far more inviting now that it was free of rain, and I fingered the soft petals of a flower as we passed. At the side of the clock tower was a small wooden door.

"Watch it!" Linus said.

A Frisbee soared past my head, and Linus caught it out of the air. I jumped, looking back over my shoulder. A guy yelled an apology, and Linus threw it back in a smooth arc. For an instant, Linus was just like one of the other students, and I felt a wavering in the line that separated us, a line I hadn't even realized existed.

Then he reached to open and hold the door for me, and the impression was gone.

"After you," he said.

"Are there cameras in here?" I asked

"Yes. Watch your head," he said. He propped the door open with a wooden kick wedge so the sunlight and air could come in.

I went up a couple steps and ducked a low-hanging beam. Sparse windows cast beams of spindly, dust-shot light into the tower and illuminated a dozen chains that hung from the mechanism of the clock high above. The chains fell level to where we stood and below, even lower, into a pit. I stepped to the railing and peered down into a deep, dim shaft, spotting four of the clock's weights before the chains vanished into darkness.

"Cool, isn't it?" Linus said. "The guy who designed the clock made it so it only has to be wound once every five years."

"Really?"

Linus pointed to a cylindrical weight that was suspended some distance above our heads. "It runs on gravity, by weights and gears. Even the LED light at the top of the tower is powered by gravity. Otis explained it to me once."

I could see a delicate, horizontal wheel spinning far above in the main mechanism, but everything else looked motionless.

"And what's this?" I asked, looking over the railing again. Metal rungs were bolted to the inner wall and descended down like they were disappearing into a bottomless well. The clock chains had the smoothness of old, oiled metal, and I wondered if bugs or dust ever got caught in them.

"The pit is just for the weights," he said. "It's thirty feet deep."

"Wow."

"I knew you'd like it." Linus leaned sideways into the railing and passed me a pebble. "Go ahead."

I weighed the little stone in my fingers, and then dropped it, listening while it vanished down through the silent blackness until it finally hit with a faint, distant clink.

"Deep," I said.

He laughed. "Yes."

I glanced up to find him smiling at me.

"Is your eye better?" I asked.

"Yes. Dr. Ash did some minor surgery to it, after all," he said. He closed one eye, and then the other. "I can see a little better, actually, though things are too bright. That's supposed to go away."

"You seemed like you didn't want to go to the infirmary, yesterday in the kitchen," I said.

"I didn't. But it turned out okay."

I remembered what I'd overheard about him selling blood, but I didn't see how to ask him about it. Instead, I shifted nearer to examine his eyes, and he held still, waiting. The pupil in his left eye was bigger than the other, but the difference was slight. His irises were a rich light brown, very like the honey-eyed color inside the tower.

"I wish we could talk," I said softly.

"I know," he said. "But there's no way to be private."

I thought of what Bones had said in the night.

"You aren't wearing a microphone, are you?" I asked.

I glanced down at the neckline of his shirt, and then up to find him regarding me oddly.

"No," he said. "There are mic buttons on the wall."

"I suppose we could meet in some bathroom stall. That's private."

Linus laughed again. "Or a shower."

"They'd hear us anyway," I said, reconsidering.

"What do you want to ask me, anyway?" he said.

"Just regular stuff."

"Then ask away," he said. "I don't care about the cameras."

I hesitated. "I don't exactly have a list ready to go."

"Okay. Then I'll start. Tell me about your necklace," he said, and touched his finger to the token I wore.

I looped my thumb through the leather cord and lifted the little disk for him to see better. "It's an old subway token from New York City. Isn't it cool? I found it near the tracks where I live," I said.

"And where's that?"

"Doli, Arizona." I remembered the day with my sister. It had been so bizarre to find the vintage coin with the pentagonal hole in our own backyard, as if it were a ticket to a distant place or time. "We live in the boxcars at the edge of town. The train was abandoned there after an earthquake made it too expensive to repair the bridges for the rails, so people started moving in. My sister Dubbs and I find all kinds of things along the tracks."

"When was the earthquake?" he said.

"Back in twenty-forty-five," I said.

He smoothed my token lightly back in place. "You know, the token's no good anymore."

I laughed. "I like it anyway. I've worn it so long now, I'd feel weird without it."

"You could give it to your sister."

I was startled by the idea, and pleased. "Do you have any sisters or brothers?" I asked.

"No."

"Do your parents work in Forgetown?"

Linus shifted to lean his elbows on the railing of the pit.

136

He clasped his hands over the void. "They're dead," he said. "My ma died back in Wales, and my dad brought me to St. Louis to live when I was eleven. He died a couple years later, and after that, I was on my own."

"I'm sorry," I said.

"It's okay," he said. "I have an aunt back in Wales. She's my next of kin, but there was some hassle with the transit papers, and then we stopped hearing from her, so the state put me in a couple foster homes."

He spoke with such little concern, he could have been reading the weather report.

"Did that work out?" I asked. I smoothed my hands along the railing of the pit.

He glanced at me sideways. "Not really, and nobody looked too hard for me when I cut out on my own."

"So, how did you end up here?" I asked.

"Otis brought me. I have a good setup with him," Linus said. He gave a half smile and did the double jerk of his thumb to indicate the cameras. "You're right. This is a little awkward."

"Would you go back to Wales if you could?" I asked.

"And find my aunt?" He turned and leaned back against the railing. "I think about it. It would take a ton of money, more than I'm ever likely to see. But I would. I sometimes wonder if she's ever watched *The Forge Show* and seen me here, in the background."

"Wouldn't she contact you?"

"I'd like to think so."

It occurred to me that he might be more visible now that he was on my feed with me. That could be a good thing. "You're earning something here, right?" I said. "You could save up to go see her."

He laughed with genuine mirth. "Yes."

"So, maybe it will take a while, but you'll get there," I said.

He looked at me curiously. "You're really a dreamer, aren't you?"

"What's that mean?"

The clock made a shifting noise above us, and then the bells tolled out the four-note sequence of the quarter hour.

I hunched, pressing my hands to my ears and grinning. The reverberations filled the space of the clock tower. In the din, Linus took a step closer to me and leaned near to my ear. I lowered my hands.

"You were awake last night, weren't you?" he whispered. "When I was in your dorm."

I shot my gaze to his. I nodded. I leaned close, cupping my mouth to his ear. "Something's going on here at night. Something wrong. I have to figure out what."

He stared at me hard a moment. Then he leaned close once more. "Like what?"

"I don't know," I said. The last of the bell resonance was fading to nothing, and I knew the microphones would pick up our voices again.

Somehow his hands were on my waist and the tips of my sneakers dovetailed with his shoes. With a start, I realized how close we were standing. I knew that we had no privacy, but the air around us *felt* private.

"I could be wrong, but I think you're the same girl who kissed me yesterday," he said.

"That's right," I said. "Or you kissed me. Technically it was more of a mutual thing. With rain."

He smiled. "You're nervous."

"No."

He nodded and silently mouthed *yes*.

I lifted my fingers to his tee shirt where he was warm and strong under the fabric. He shifted a little, bringing me an inch closer, and I couldn't decide whether to look at his eyes or his mouth, so I glanced at his nose, and then I just closed my eyes.

I could feel better with my eyes closed, it turned out. This time, I was happier, and a little more certain, and his lips met mine with just the right pressure. The tingly, tiptoe nonsense I'd heard about kisses pretty much came true, only now it was mine, with Linus. I started to smile, until I discovered that kissing and smiling at the same time didn't work so well. When Linus mumbled a laugh, it lit me up inside.

His lips moved against my ear and his voice came as the softest whisper. "You're safe as long as you stay in bed."

I couldn't breathe. Then he kissed my cheek and reached for my hand, moving easily as if nothing was wrong.

"Come on," he said at regular volume.

I broke out of my shock and stumbled after him, holding hands. I blinked rapidly as we left the clock tower and stepped into the sunshine.

"You look properly dazzled, Sinclair," he teased.

"Sunlight will do that."

He smiled and tucked my hand more firmly in his.

We shared a secret now. We couldn't talk about it, but he knew for certain I'd been awake. His warning to stay in bed was a promise that he'd understood me. This might have been small to him, but to me, it felt huge.

I had an ally.

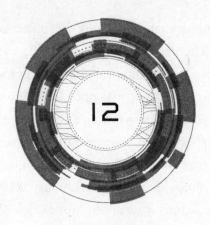

12

FISH TANK

THE MORE I thought of it, the more Linus's caveat
piqued my curiosity. If he'd thought a warning would make
me take my pill like a normal student, it actually did the opposite. He might have been simply reminding me that I risked
getting sent home if I disobeyed the rule to sleep, but it was
also possible that he knew something dangerous was happening at Forge. I couldn't find out what that was if I slept.

So that Tuesday night, for the third time, I skipped my
sleeping pill. Again Orly checked my mouth and didn't catch
me. When my brink lesson finished, I opened my lid and listened to the quiet as the other girls grew still.

Out the nearest window, the topmost leaves of a tree were
silhouetted against the darkening sky. When they were no
longer visible, I slipped out of my sleep shell, fluffed my quilt

around my pillow so it didn't look so empty, and stepped to the window. The dean's tower was visible to my left, and without any rain to obscure it, I could see in the lit windows of the fifth floor. The angle was poor but not impossible, and half a dozen techies were working at computers. How nice it was to spy on them for once instead of the other way around.

Or maybe they were still watching me. Just because night scenes at the Forge School were not broadcast to viewers didn't mean the cameras went dead for twelve hours. I looked at a few button cameras and up toward the camera at the apex of the ceiling, but I could barely make them out in the darkness. Dr. Ash herself had explained to me that we were closely monitored at night, but apparently, for some reason, whoever was watching wasn't reporting me for being out of bed.

I couldn't make sense of it.

Maybe they didn't notice immediately. Maybe the techies were less vigilant after the fifty cuts. Like me, a few of the other girls now slept with their sleep shells open, and since they were less visible without their faintly lucent lids over them, I figured it was the same for me. Then again, it could be that the techies had spotted me, but they were waiting to see how far I'd go. I wished I knew.

My feet grew cold as I kept watching. Around midnight, the techies reached for purses and sweaters, and soon after, the lights on the fifth floor began going out. I was about to get back in my sleep shell when a light came on in the penthouse, and Dean Berg passed before one of the windows. Instinctively,

I drew back a little. He loosened his tie and walked out of sight again. I waited, watching for him to reappear. I felt like quite the devious spy, and I hoped he would do something worth staying up for.

Long minutes later, Dean Berg walked past a different set of penthouse windows and stopped beside a fish tank. He had taken off his blazer and tie, and undone a few shirt buttons. He appeared to be talking to someone I couldn't see, pausing occasionally to take a drink from a gray mug. Dean Berg shifted out of view again, and a slender, dark-haired man in a white shirt and jeans stepped into view beside the fish tank.

Linus. He was Linus. I about died. He stood with one hand in his back pocket and appeared to be concentrating on the fish. Then he shook his head, turned, and spoke. The dean walked slowly back into view with his mug.

My heart thudded as I watched. I desperately wished I knew what they were discussing. Neither one was smiling, but I couldn't discern any visible friction or tension between them, either. The dean occasionally nodded. He paced back a step, talking, and Linus absently linked a hand around the back of his neck while he listened. A minute later, Linus passed out of view. He showed up once more, at a different window, holding a tray of dishes, and then he was gone.

My curiosity was going to kill me. I pressed closer to the window, trying to see the front of the tower where Linus would come out, but the corner of the building obscured my view. I was ready to sneak out and find him when I heard a noise. Footsteps in the hallway.

I flew back to my sleep shell, and burrowed under my quilt. Someone was entering the dorm room. I labored to even out my breathing, and I listened hard as the footsteps advanced and then stopped. A slight, shifting noise sounded from the middle of the room and then a whispered voice. A squeak followed, and a rolling noise moved away. I almost exploded with relief. They were taking someone else. I turned my face and opened one eye a slit.

Down the room, a couple of people were rolling Paige's sleep shell quietly toward the door.

I shut my eyes again, trying to think what to do. Should I stop them? I could demand to know where they were taking Paige. But if I spoke up, I'd be discovered breaking the rules. I would jeopardize my education and get kicked out of Forge before I'd discovered any real information about what was going on at night. That would be more stupid than brave.

When the noise stopped, I guessed they had taken Paige down the elevator. I was just starting to relax when I heard soft footsteps again. They were coming back, whoever they were.

And this time, the steps progressed down the full length of the room to me.

My sleep shell vibrated with a slight touch, and my pulse skyrocketed. I lay as still as possible, breathing deeply, willing my muscles to relax. A moment passed. Then another. In excruciating suspense, I waited for another sound or hint of movement.

Finally there was a soft rustling.

"Rosie? Are you awake?" a man asked. "It's okay to tell me. It's not your fault."

I recognized his voice. He was the bearded man who had assisted Dr. Ash two nights before, when I'd seen them tending to Janice. Apparently, someone *had* noticed I was out of my sleep shell.

I kept my face slack. Every inch of my body was alert, expecting him to touch me, and I didn't know if I could keep from jumping. I sensed brightness through my eyelids as a nearby light was clicked on. I heard soft rustling again, and a clink. Then a ripping of paper.

"Okay," he said. His voice was very quiet and calm. "If you can hear me, I'm just adjusting your meds. It's nothing to worry about."

I felt a hand on my wrist. I kept my arm limp. It took all my concentration not to resist. Next I felt a rubbery, binding tightness around my upper arm, and a couple of taps on my forearm. A swipe of wetness along my skin came next, and a moment later, the pinch of a needle.

Liquid entered my vein, surprisingly cool, and a sense of easy security washed along my arm and into the rest of my body, erasing my tension. My face tingled, my jaw went loose, and in a simple, complete flood, everything in my body and mind let go. My last, clinging worry disappeared. I was out.

Moments later, it was morning.

I shot up in my sleep shell.

The dorm was totally normal. Down the row, Paige was

up and doing her ballerina stretches. Janice lay in her sleep shell beside mine, rubbing her arm over her face.

"What day is this? Wednesday?" she asked.

My heart was still pounding. Normal morning light was dropping in the windows, and outside promised to be another clear day. The other girls were getting up. Janice gave a great, loud yawn, and then smacked her lips. She reached for her shower caddy.

"How'd you sleep?" I asked.

"Good," she said. "I think I'm getting an idea about how to play Hamlet in the scenes with her mom." She wiped her nose with the back of her hand. "I left your camera in your wardrobe, by the way."

"Thanks."

She shuffled off toward the bathroom in her fuzzy, polka dot slippers.

I checked my arm, knowing before I looked that I would have a scab, and I did, right where the needle had pinched me. It was faint, barely noticeable, and utterly real. I felt dirty. Violated.

Angry.

I climbed out of my sleep shell and checked its orientation beside my bedside table and my rug. The difference was so small I never would have noticed it if I wasn't looking, but I was certain my sleep shell had been moved in the night, like Paige's. We'd been taken somewhere. Something was being done to us while we slept.

I had a choice to make. If I spoke up about what I knew,

I'd reveal that I was awake at night, which was enough to get me kicked off the show. If I remained silent, I was basically accepting the night treatment not only for me, but for Janice and Paige and any other student they chose to wheel out. I didn't know what to do.

The other girls, who were heading off to the bathroom and getting dressed, all seemed fine. Totally and completely fine. Maybe whatever they were doing to us wasn't that bad, but if it was harmless, *The Forge Show* would have no reason to keep it secret. It occurred to me that the bearded man had entered the dorm only after the techies had left, so maybe the other staff didn't know about it.

Linus had met with Dean Berg in the night. Linus might know something. If I could find a way to talk to him, maybe that would help. Or I could confide in Janice. I would have to talk to her in the shower, which would be weird, but possible. Then again, I wasn't sure exactly what to tell her. Until I knew more, I had to pretend that I knew nothing.

I stood to reach in my wardrobe for clean clothes and found my video camera hanging on the hook where Janice had left it.

Too bad it wasn't on during the night, I thought. *With the door ajar.* I gazed slowly around the room again, locating all the button cameras on the windows and furniture.

Why couldn't I do the surveillance backward? I was a film-maker. I could film *The Forge Show* from the inside. In a place where everything was exposed, no one would think another lens mattered. Or two. I leaned back, letting my mind run. I could have a dozen of my own cameras if I could get them from the shop, and DeCoster had said we had endless supplies there.

I let out a laugh.

I could aim cameras wherever I wanted and leave them on all night. It would take work, and I would need a cover project to justify what I was doing, but I could figure that all out. I could pretend I knew nothing and be normal, just like everyone else, but all the while, I could find out what was really happening here at night.

Yes. I had a plan.

>>>>>>>>>

After a quick breakfast with no Linus sighting, I headed into the library and down the steps for Media Convergence. I followed voices and the pattering of a Ping-Pong ball to the first room on the right, where Paige and Henrik had a game going. A domed lamp hung above the green table, just begging to get hit by a lob ball.

"Eight, six," Paige said, and let loose a serve.

To my right, in the longer leg of the L-shaped room, students lounged on a couple of old, faux-leather couches before a fireplace. Their feet were up on an oval coffee table, along with a deck of cards, a Rubik's Cube, and battered boxes of Dominion and Settlers of Catan. A dozen windows near the ceiling let in a view of passing feet, which underscored how the room was half-submerged below ground.

In the corner, Mr. DeCoster sat behind an old desk, idly peeling pistachios as he watched his computer. He had pulled out the lower drawer of the desk and propped his feet on the edge so I could see the soles of his oxfords. Today, his bolo tie was made of some dark stone, maybe onyx.

A dozen other computers lined the inner walls, and Burnham was working at one of them already. I figured he would ignore me, but he glanced over at me once before he began the ignoring for real. Like that wasn't awkward.

Janice came in behind me and flopped over one end of a couch. "Sweet."

"I know. It's nice down here," I said, and stretched out in my jeans.

"Hey, Mr. DeCoster. When are you going to start class?" Janice called.

"I already did. Yesterday," Mr. DeCoster said.

Paige caught the Ping-Pong ball, and the silence hung.

"Well, crap," Henrik said conversationally.

Janice moved toward a computer, and some of the other students paired up in teams.

"Mr. DeCoster," I said. "I need some gear from the shop."

"Fine," Mr. DeCoster said. "Tell Muzh I said you could browse the shelves."

That sounded promising. I left my backpack by the couch and headed off.

The shop, like our new room for Media Convergence, was in the basement of the library, but at the other end of a cement hallway. It had a half door with a ledge at waist height, and it reminded me of the athletic cage at Doli High where a student could sign out a basketball. A woman in a helmet stood at a workbench, soldering something in a vice. When she pushed up her helmet visor with her glove, I saw she was young with delicate, Indian features.

"Are you Muzh?" I asked, wondering if that was a first or last name.

"That's right."

"Mr. DeCoster said to tell you I could browse," I said.

"Fine," Muzh said. "Are you looking for anything in particular?"

"Explosives," I said. "Just kidding. I'm looking for cameras."

Without releasing her soldering gun, she reached to open the door for me. "Aisle five, left side. Help yourself," she said.

She lowered her helmet again, and with the noise of her working behind me, I went in search of my gear. The shop was a cross between a hardware store and a flea market, with light fixtures and ceiling fans side by side with garage openers and toasters. The camera selection filled a wide, compartmentalized shelf, and the gear ranged from big, shoulder-harness film cameras to old, flip-open phones. I picked up one of the phones. It didn't turn on, but it might if it were charged. A smudged cardboard box had a couple of old-fashioned gadgets and baby monitors in it, some so ancient they didn't even have USB ports.

I took the box, adding an assortment of the small cameras. Then I took a slow walk through the other aisles and picked

150

up some duct tape, on principle. I lingered over the explosives and fireworks, curious about a small box of glow worm pellets that promised to turn into black worms of ash with the light of a match. *Stay focused.* I gave the box a little shake and set it back.

When I returned to the front, Muzh took off her gloves. "Any luck?"

"I could stay down here all day," I said.

She inspected each item, ran a scanner over the QR codes, and called up a list for me to sign on an electronic pad.

"Does everything work?" I asked.

"Most likely. It all did when it was stored." She opened the back of one video camera and blew some dust out.

"What are these?" I asked, lifting a couple of gadgets that looked like old-fashioned toy phones.

"Walkie-hams," she said. "They're an inelegant cross between walkie-talkies and ham radios. They're susceptible to rogue interference, but they're slightly better than two cans on a string."

I pivoted one of the little walkie-hams, which was about as heavy as a pack of cards. "Do you have a normal phone I could take?" I asked. Having one would be great. Other students could text one another when they had something private to say. I couldn't.

"Don't you own one already?" Muzh asked.

"No," I said. "My stepfather won't let me. He thinks the government tracks us and spies on us through our cell phones."

Muzh nodded slowly. "He's not alone in that theory. In

any case, we don't loan out phones." She gave my box a poke. "What are you trying to do, bug the place?"

"More or less."

"What for?" Muzh asked. "The last student who took out this many cameras was looking for paranormal activity. Tell me you're not that misguided."

Muzh was brilliant.

"I'm exactly that misguided," I said. "Do you have any ghost sensors?"

"None that work," she said dryly.

I bundled the box into my arms. "Thanks."

"Here, wait," she said, and handed me a box of old-style batteries and a charger. "You'll need these. The old devices guzzle electricity. You'll have to rotate in fresh batteries frequently."

"Thanks."

"Good luck," she said, and reached for her gloves again.

As I made my way back to class, a heavy door swung open, and a thickset man backed into the hallway, maneuvering a dolly of boxes. "Excuse me," he said, pulling it aside to let me pass. Through the door behind him was a long, beige hallway.

"Is that one of the service tunnels?" I asked.

"That's right," he said, letting the door go.

I caught the knob just before the door closed.

"You can't go in there," he said. "That's off-limits to students."

Reluctantly, I let the door close. There was a scanner

beside the knob. The man had a swipe key hanging from a loop on his hip. I wondered if Linus had such a swipe key. The man spun his dolly before him and headed away down the hall, and I continued to the Ping-Pong room with my box.

>>>>>>>>

At lunchtime, I looked for Linus in the kitchen. He gave me a brief wave, but he was busy with dishes again and couldn't talk. When I took my tray out to the dining area, Janice was sitting with Paige. Burnham and Henrik were nowhere to be seen, and I secretly hoped they wouldn't show up and join us. I glanced reflexively at the blip rank board and saw I was listed at 48. It was better than 50.

"Hey," I said, sliding my tray onto the table opposite Janice's.

The girls looked up from a phone that lay on the table between them.

"You have to see this," Paige said. "It's so cool."

Janice pushed the phone over toward me. "Paige's doing a thing on aging dancers, and she found this face recognition app, Ace Age."

"It searches the Internet for the face of a famous person, back through time, and puts the photos in chronological order, with the same eye spacing, so you can see the person growing up and aging over the years," Paige said.

"Really?" I asked, angling to see.

Janice pushed a button, and a teen girl's face began

evolving gradually through a series of shots. Her cheeks and hair had a rippling, flickering quality, but the constancy of the face stayed strong, right up to the most recent picture of a woman in her midthirties.

"That is so so cool," I said. I had to see it again. I sat back, amazed. "Who else have you done?"

"Movie stars. Politicians," Janice said. "Anyone public."

"What about private people?" I asked.

"They don't have enough pictures," Paige said. "It doesn't have the same effect."

"What happens when you try?" I asked.

"Let's see," Janice said. "Who do you want to do?"

"You," I said.

"No," Janice said, covering her face.

Paige laughed, taking the phone. "That's good. Put your hands down, Janice," Paige said sternly, aiming her phone at Janice.

Instead, Janice ducked her head under the table.

"Okay, then, you," Paige said, and before I knew it, she swiveled my direction and took my picture.

"No!" I squeaked.

But Paige leaned back, working the phone with her thumbs. Janice popped back up. She bumped her shoulder to Paige's, and the two of them peered at the phone together.

I had no idea what the app would find.

"Cute!" Janice and Paige squealed at the same time.

"Let me see," I said, holding out my hand.

They didn't seem to hear me.

"Oh," Janice crooned. "Little pumpkin face."

I moaned.

They were silent another moment, watching the phone, and then their smiles faded. They glanced up at me at the same time, as if they'd never seen me before.

"What?" I asked.

The two girls exchanged a glance.

Then Janice smiled doubtfully. "You were a cute kid."

"Let me see," I said.

Paige slowly passed over the phone. The app had frozen on the picture of me that Paige had just taken, but by tapping the little circular arrow, I could set it back through the progression from the start. To my surprise, the first picture it found was one of me in third grade, with two pigtails, frowning in the front row of my class picture. The close-up in the app only showed my head and shoulders, but I remembered when it was taken, and how the guy on the riser behind me kept bumping my butt with his knee. From there, I aged through school photos, and it snagged for a second on one at a pumpkin farm we'd visited for a school trip. All the other kids had a parent meet them there, and I kept watching for my mom to show up, but she never did.

After that, the pictures went downhill. A blur of homely middle school pictures merged into a dozen miserable images from Doli High. They were little better than mug shots. A slew of happier, more recent ones from *The Forge Show* couldn't offset the bleak sequence from before. No wonder Janice and Paige had looked dubious.

"I guess the Internet has a long memory," I said. It was weird to think how many pictures of me were in the public domain, and I wasn't famous at all, or I hadn't been until I'd come to Forge.

Paige reached for the phone. "I've got an idea," she said. She turned toward the kitchen, where Linus was standing at the salad bar with a big bowl of lettuce.

"Paige, no," I said.

But she had already snapped his picture and was hunching over the phone, giggling.

"Paige!"

"You want to see or not?" she asked.

My cheeks were burning. I glanced back at Linus, hoping he hadn't seen, but he was watching us now. When I shrank down in my seat, he lifted his eyebrows. He switched out the lettuce bowls and headed back into the kitchen.

I wanted to die. "This is wrong," I said.

"Get over yourself," Paige said.

"Tell me there's nothing on him," I said.

Janice's expression lifted in surprise. "Holy crap," she said lightly. She blinked at Paige, and then they both nudged close to the phone.

Paige cleared her throat and sat back slightly. "Well," she said. "They're tasteful, at least."

"Let me see that," I said.

Paige did not let go of her phone until I tugged hard.

The photos of Linus did not go back far. In the earliest, he was no older than eleven or twelve, about the age when he'd come to the States, and there were only a few photos from those early years. Around the time he was thirteen, his face began a seamless transformation through dozens of pictures. All of them were shot in a distinct black-and-white clarity that indicated they had come from the same camera. Sometimes he smiled. More often, his expression was neutral or serious. The app showed only his head and shoulders, but since his shoulders were always bare, it gave the impression he never wore clothes.

The photos kept advancing toward the present, through countless sessions of the black-and-white pictures, until they finally jumped back into color and flickered more like mine had, with his dark hair changing lengths, and he was usually wearing the white shirt of his kitchen garb. Then the picture stopped on the image Janice had just captured.

Paige cleared her throat. "I'd say our hot kitchen guy has a sordid little past," she said.

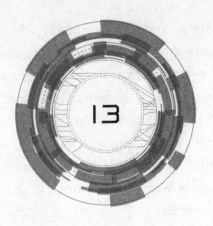

GORGE ON FORGE

"BE QUIET," JANICE said.

I was stunned. I hurt for Linus. I wanted to watch the app again and go back to those black-and-white pictures. I wanted to track down where the series had come from and skewer the person who had shot them all. Still worse, I wanted to know how far down Linus was naked. My cheeks were burning, and I felt the shame of trespassing into some horribly private mess.

Paige gingerly pulled the phone out of my hand. "I didn't know it would find that sequence," she said. "You know that, right?"

I didn't know what it meant. I didn't want to jump to conclusions, but I wasn't completely naïve, either. Orly had said something nasty about Linus being catnip for Otis. I remembered him up in Dean Berg's penthouse, after hours, and then I felt sick at myself for what I was imagining. There could be a perfectly good reason why someone had taken dozens of artsy photos of Linus with no shirt on and posted them online.

I closed my eyes and thunked my forehead in my hands.

"Boys," Janice said.

"I know, right?" Paige said. "I hope he got paid well."

"This is not helping," I said.

The bell tolled out in the quad, and students at the tables around us began getting up.

"Look, it's no big deal, Rosie," Janice said quietly. "So what if some perv took a bunch of pictures of the kitchen guy? It's who he is today that matters."

"His name's *Linus*," I said. Who he was today was most likely watching this very exchange on the screen in the kitchen. I put my head up and straightened my spine. "I have to get to class. Remind me to run that app on you sometime."

"It's just a thing," Janice said, looking at me strangely. "Don't be mad."

"He's not even on the show," I said. "He deserves some privacy."

"Listen, I'm not the one making out with him," Janice said.

"*You're* the one who's drawing attention to him," Paige said to me. "If he wants his privacy, all he has to do is stay away from you. Have you thought about that?" She stood and dropped her napkin on her tray. "Maybe he has something to gain from you. He can get famous without even being on the show."

Behind me, the blip rank board started to update with its flipping noise again. I looked back and forth from Paige to Janice.

"Seriously? You think that's why he's hanging out with me?" I asked.

"I don't know," Janice said.

"Not everyone wants to be famous," I said.

Paige pushed back her hair and picked up her tray. "No, but it can't hurt. Check out your blip rank."

I looked over my shoulder. I'd spiked up three ranks to 45. I was appalled.

Paige grinned at me. "Welcome to *The Forge Show*."

>>>>>>>>

I could think of only one reason why my blip rank had spiked. Viewers liked to see me upset. The next thing they would do was look up the Ace Age app. And Linus.

I couldn't bear to think about the pictures of him I'd seen on Paige's app, but I couldn't stop, either. They bugged me all through my practicum that afternoon, making me sad and worried for the kid Linus had been. At the same time, Paige had started me questioning his motives. I'd thought Linus had done me a favor by helping me get my blip rank high enough to stay on the show, and in the clock tower, I hadn't thought twice about why he was kissing me. I'd thought he liked me, but now I had this needling doubt. He might get something else, something bigger out of being with me.

The whole thing stank.

In the end, the only way to quit obsessing was to focus on my work.

After my practicum, I went back to the Ping-Pong room to check on my cameras, which I'd left there to charge. Their batteries were full. Now I just had to figure out where to place the cameras to best spy on the campus at night. My dorm room was a given. I stuck everything in my backpack and started out the door, only to encounter Burnham on his way in.

He shifted politely to let me pass, but I backed up, doing the same thing.

"Hey," I said.

"Hello," he replied, and after some awkward seesawing, he edged in past me. He flipped on the overhead lights and headed toward his favorite computer.

"Are you working on your project for DeCoster's class?" I asked.

"That would be why I'm here." He eased into his chair and turned on his machine. A small yellow leaf was stuck to the back of his red sweater, but it wasn't my business to tell him so.

"You could work from the K:Cloud anywhere," I said.

"And yet, I'm here."

I gripped my thumb under my shoulder strap. "How long are you going to be mad?" I asked. "I'm just curious."

"You realize, of course, how irritating it is to be falsely accused of being mad," he said.

Oh, boy, I thought. "That's real mature."

"If you'll excuse me, I have work to do."

"Well, that's even more mature. What are you? A grandpa?"

His fingers froze over his touch screen, but he didn't turn.

"Sorry," I mumbled, and I backed out of the doorway.

I couldn't let him goad me into being sarcastic. It made me feel horrible and small. It wouldn't happen again.

>>>>>>>>>

I put one of the cameras up in the attic of my dorm, aiming out the skylight toward the dean's tower. I planted more aiming at the quad, the infirmary, the security office in the student union, and the roads entering the school. Others I planted in whimsical places that fit my ghost theme: the graveyard, the chapel, the clock tower, and the pasture with the lookout tower in the background. At one point, I stopped in the girls' room, hid in a stall, and experimented with the two walkie-hams, whispering in one and listening with the other against my ear to be sure they worked. Then I wrote a note: *8:00, channel 4*, folded that around one of them, and slid it in the pocket of my jeans.

I had set up all but my last two cameras when I veered to the dining hall and found Linus vacuuming the dining room. He wore no apron, and his white tee shirt had come untucked from his jeans. He was dodging the chairs that were upturned on the tables like he'd vacuumed beneath them a million times. A long orange extension cord snaked out behind him, a dense roar filled the room, and I was seriously tempted to take footage as I walked toward him.

"Busy?" I called.

He turned off the vacuum, and silence rippled out around him. He turned to face me, panting a little, and didn't smile.

Now that I had seen his features from when he was younger, he looked different to me. His cheeks had outgrown a certain fullness, and his eyes had become cautious at the corners. He was Linus, today, but underneath he was also the boy from the black-and-white photos.

"Not cool, Rosie," he said.

Blushing, I glanced down at the orange cord. "You mean the app," I said.

"I mean the whole thing. Looking me up. If you want to know something about me, ask me." Linus gave the cord a yank, and way on the opposite wall, the plug came out of the socket.

"Okay," I said.

He started wrapping the long cord in circles around his arm, fist to elbow. "It's not just okay," he said. "You know that spin-off site for Forge fans? Gorge on Forge?"

Everybody knew it. "Yes?"

"They've uploaded the pictures of me that you and Paige found," he said. "The entire sequence is right there for any-one to watch. You should see some of the comments. I guess I'm gay now. And looking for a sugar daddy. Those are the nice ones."

I felt terrible. "I'm sorry," I said. "Those people leaving comments, they don't know you."

"Neither do you, really."

"No," I agreed. But I wanted to. I should have come to apologize earlier. I fiddled with the straps of my backpack. "I'm really sorry, Linus. It wasn't my idea to do you. I had no idea what Paige would find. I wish I could have stopped her."

Linus plugged the ends of the extension cord together. "I know it wasn't your fault exactly," he said. Then he added, "I'm not hanging out with you for any stupid fame."

So he'd heard that, too. I couldn't believe I'd let Paige make me suspect he wanted to use me for his own visibility. Someone back in the kitchen banged a pot, and voices rose for a second. Linus glanced over his shoulder.

"You told me once to ignore the cameras," I said.

"I was an idiot. They're impossible."

I laughed. "Do you want to come walk with me?" I asked. "It's nice out."

"I can't. But thanks."

I could tell that any second Linus was going to drag the vacuum toward the kitchen, and I'd lose my chance to give him the walkie-ham. I stepped nearer.

"Whoever took those pictures of you had no right to put them online," I said.

"I signed away my rights."

"Kids can't sign away their own rights," I said. "With the right lawyer, you could sue the pants off the original photographer, plus Gorge on Forge. Who owns that site, anyway?"

"I think it's a *Forge Show* affiliate, actually," Linus said.

"Seriously?" I said. "Does Dean Berg know about this?"

Linus considered me thoughtfully. "I'm guessing he does now."

A phone rang back in the kitchen.

"Don't you have any privacy rights as someone on staff here?" I asked loudly.

"I do normally, unless I step onstage. Like this, with you," he said. "Then they're forfeit."

"I would say whatever you did before you came here was offstage, wouldn't you?" I asked. "How old were you in those pictures?"

"Thirteen," he said.

"Thirteen!" I said.

Chef Ted leaned out from the kitchen. "Pitts. There's a call for you. It's the dean," he said.

Linus moved toward the kitchen, and then turned back toward me.

"Thanks," he said.

I stepped near to hug him, and when he slowly hugged me back, I slid the walkie-ham between us and jabbed it hard at his belly. I felt his surprise, but he said nothing, and when we moved apart, he caught the transfer easily and covered it by maneuvering the vacuum before him.

"I'll see you later," I said.

"Okay, good," he said.

"You coming, love bird?" Chef Ted called.

Linus took off toward the kitchen while I headed out the door. I could not wait to talk to him for real, by walkie-ham.

I still had two more cameras to place, and so I went down

the pasture toward the observatory. I stepped past the DO NOT ENTER sign and climbed up the narrow ladder. The dome was a brighter gray in the sunlight today, and the view was as pretty as ever. From the catwalk that went around the base of the dome, a second ladder rose higher, to the five-foot-wide satellite dish that pointed toward the sky. Perfect.

With the thighs of my jeans against the metal edge of the satellite dish, I leaned toward the center and duct-taped my camera to the pod in the center of the dish. A strange whisper of noise skimmed over the white surface, deeper than crickets, surprising me. I flipped the camera on. I expected that it would record nothing but sky for the visual track, but I had no idea what it might collect for audio.

Alien voices were probably too much to hope for.

>>>>>>>>>

That Wednesday night, under the cover of getting ready for bed, I set up my last video camera, my old one from home. I placed it inside my wardrobe and aimed it out toward the room. Then I turned it on and nonchalantly left the door ajar. I also managed to slide my walkie-ham under my pillow while I was folding a few clothes. After Orly distributed pills, I climbed into my sleep shell, took out my pill, watched my brink lesson, and pretended to sleep. This time, I kept my lid closed.

Stealth was getting to feel like a routine.

I was dying to see if Linus would come on my walkie-ham. I lay still, waiting while the clock tower bonged the interminable quarter hours into the night. When at last it approached eight, I rolled over and hugged my quilt softly to my ear. Then I pulled out my walkie-ham. I clicked on the little black device and turned the volume as low as possible, just to listen.

Faint static buzzed from the speaker, so quiet it was barely discernible. By eight, it was still without a voice. *Come on, Linus*, I thought. *Be there.*

I pushed the talk button and spoke so softly I didn't believe any mic in the room could pick me up. "Hello?"

Then I released the button to listen again. Still nothing. I kept waiting, trying not to be disappointed. He might be still working, or walking home, or busy with Otis.

By eight-thirty, I was bummed, but I dialed slowly through the ten channels, listening carefully to the static on each one and checking back often with channel four. At nine, my hope plummeted. Maybe the walkie-hams didn't have enough range to reach between the dorm and Forgetown. It couldn't be that Linus didn't want to talk to me.

Disheartened, I flipped through the dial once more, and at a blip of noise, I stopped. On channel seven, a voice came in dimly, but it wasn't Linus's. A woman had an accent that I couldn't identify, sort of Norwegian and British. I rolled over, keeping the walkie-ham hidden under my quilt, and I turned it up enough to hear.

"Very amusing," the woman said. "Now, let's be reasonable. That last bit was exactly what I've been looking for. Invigorating. Intoxicating. I feel ten years younger. Don't tease me with this nonsense of her being too fragile to mine for more."

A second voice came in, laced with annoyance, and it took me a moment to recognize Dean Berg. I'd never heard him as anything but congenial. "You weren't supposed to use it on yourself. Did you even *try* to duplicate it?"

"There was too little. I told you. Send more next time."

"You're impossible. I swear. Do you remember what we said before, about trust?" Dean Berg said.

The woman laughed. "I do love it when you get righteous. How does the minister's daughter like her seed?"

"I don't seed my patients," Dean Berg said.

"Don't you mean your *students*?" she said. "Come on, Sandy. This is me you're talking to. When are you going to realize you have a gold mine right there already? Forget clinical medicine. Go for the entertainment potential. You could rake it in if you let a couple of us dabble in seeding your students. To watch them live it out! I know a guy or two who would get a real kick out of playing god. You can't keep all the fun for yourself."

"You know the problem with you, Huma?" Dean Berg said. "You think everyone else is as ruthless as you are. Stick to the dead and leave the living to me."

"My clients aren't dead," she said. "And you're no one to talk." Her humor was gone.

The voices were fading, and I didn't hear Dean Berg's reply. I tried shifting the walkie-ham to bring them in clearer.

"I need more of the Lo Eight," said the woman. "We've had some very nice results with that and I could use a fresh batch."

"How nice?" Dean Berg asked.

"Nice enough. I'm getting more inquiries than I can possibly keep up with. I'm having to turn people away. It's tragic. Please tell me you're at least reading your students for potential mining. Give me that much."

"We do read the students," Dean Berg said. "I'll concede that. But only to learn from their healthy minds. Nothing else. Their dreams, as you can imagine, are exquisite."

"See? Was that so hard? I could help you so much if you'd just confide in me."

Then the voices were gone. I tried the channels again, anxious to hear more, but however the walkie-ham picked up the rogue signal, it wasn't under my control. It killed me not to know more about the mining and seeding they'd discussed. Who was Huma? I couldn't even be sure I'd heard her name right.

Frustrated, I dialed back to channel four.

I did know that the minister's daughter had to be Janice. And he was reading us, whatever that meant. The dean was studying our minds. I found that ridiculously exciting. And terrifying.

"Are you there?" a voice asked.

I clenched the walkie-ham to my ear. "Linus?" I asked.

"I thought you'd be asleep by now," he said.

I smiled into the darkness. "I'm not."

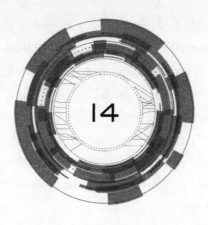

WALKIE-HAMS

I CLICKED THE button to keep our channel open.

"I tried to reach you from home, but I got no signal," he said. "I'm in the lookout tower. You should see these stars."

I rolled to look out my window, seeing just enough sky over the dark tree branches to tease me.

"Are you still upset about Paige and the face app?" I asked. I curved my hand around my mouth and pitched my voice barely above a whisper.

"Guys don't get *upset*," he said. "Besides, you were right. It wasn't really your fault. Gorge on Forge took down the footage of me, for what that's worth. Are you awake every night?"

"Yes. Since the fifty cuts. I skip my pill."

"You know that defeats the whole purpose, right?" he

said. "I mean, it's great to be able to talk to you, but you have to sleep for your creativity to get the full effect."

"I know that's what they say, but I'm not so sure that's the reason. Why did you say that thing about how I'm safe as long as I stay in bed?"

"Because students who leave their beds get sent home," he said. "I don't want that happening to you."

But I've been out of bed, I thought.

Around me, the faint blue glow of my sleep shell had its familiar, surreal shimmer. I moved my fingers before my face, watching the black tracks that followed in the air.

"You haven't been sneaking out, have you?" he asked.

"No," I lied quickly, shielding my mouth again. "But strange things have been happening here. I saw them giving Janice an IV in her sleep a few nights ago. Sunday night, I guess. She was having some kind of seizure. Dr. Ash told me later that they put in IVs just as a safety precaution, but I don't believe her. Last night, they took Paige out of the room in her sleep shell, and I'm pretty sure they took me out, too."

"You don't remember?"

"I was asleep again. A man came in and gave me more sleep meds, intravenously. And my sleep shell wasn't in the same place this morning."

"You're sure?" he asked.

"Positive," I said. "I'm not imagining these things. And just tonight I overheard a very, very weird conversation between Dean Berg and some woman through my walkie-ham."

"Weird how?"

"They were talking about mining and seeding people."

"Mining people?" Linus's voice lifted. "Are you sure they said that?"

"Why? Do you know what that means?"

Linus didn't answer.

I curled my face into my pillow again, keeping the walkie-ham under my quilt. "Seeding somebody sounds so evil," I said. "Like they're planting something inside. Mining sounds even worse."

A distant beeping sound came over the walkie-ham, like a truck backing. Linus still didn't reply.

"Linus? Are you there?"

"I'm just trying to think," he said. "It doesn't make sense. There's no way Dean Berg could be mining or seeding people. That isn't even real."

"What is it?"

"It's a scam," Linus said. "I heard about it back in St. Louis, when I sold my blood. This quack at the Annex said he could mine people's dreams and seed them into someone else, like a drug, for a high. He was always looking for donors."

"But it wasn't real?"

"Of course not," he said. "It was just a way to get guys unconscious. He always picked young boys. They'd be gone all night and come back the next morning with a wad of cash."

I listened uneasily. "You never went, did you?"

"No. I didn't have anything to do with it."

"What is this Annex place?" I asked.

172

"It's a sort of emporium where you can buy anything you want."

"Anything like drugs?"

"Drugs. Sex. Guns. Planes. Body parts for surgeries. Private islands. It's a kind of exchange. You've heard of those places."

I had, but I'd thought they were all at the Canadian and Mexican borders, not in St. Louis.

"Did you work there?" I asked.

"No," he said. "I was a kid. I just sold blood there."

"Your own?"

He laughed. "Yes. Who else's?"

I didn't know, anymore. He knew all about a world I'd only vaguely been aware of. "Is that where you were photographed?"

"You really want to know?" he said.

"Not if you don't want to tell me."

A little clicking noise came from his end, like he was tapping something, and then he spoke. "It started a couple months after I ran away from my last foster home. A man came to the park and said he was looking for swimsuit models. He hired me and a couple of the other guys a few different times."

"That's all?"

"It was a little creepy, but he never touched me. He would just tell me politely to turn my head or lean back or whatever."

"Weren't you scared?" I asked.

173

He laughed. "I was hungry. I didn't know any better."

It sounded awful to me. "I can't believe you went back more than once."

"No?" Linus was quiet a moment. "I did a lot of dumb things before Otis found me. I'm probably lucky to be alive."

That I believed.

"How did you meet Otis?" I asked.

"He came to the Annex to pick up some blood for Parker, his partner, and he tracked me down. Parker has Alzheimer's, and Otis likes to give him transfusions of young blood. He says it stimulates him, and he seems to think Parker responds better to my blood than the generic pints."

"I didn't know there was any difference in blood, beyond the basic types."

"I didn't either," Linus said, and laughed. "My guess is Parker just happened to have a good day after one of my pints. It makes him happy, though."

"Otis?"

"Both, I guess."

"So, wait," I said. "Did Otis bring you here so you could keep donating blood for Parker?"

"It's my rent," Linus said.

I wasn't certain I'd heard right. "Your what?"

"I pay my rent with my blood. I know. It sounds strange, but it works."

I tried to imagine Linus living in a household with old Otis and his partner with Alzheimer's. "Are they your family now?" I asked.

Linus was quiet for a moment. "I don't know what family is anymore."

A stillness spread through me, a quiet more lonely and sad than I'd let myself feel in a long, long time. I wished I could reach through the walkie-ham and touch him. *You have me,* I thought, but I couldn't say it out loud.

"I think family starts small," I said.

He laughed. "You're probably right."

I closed my eyes, trying to picture him in the top of Otis's tower. "It will be strange seeing you in the day and not being able to talk openly," I said.

"We have to remember to act like we haven't had this conversation," Linus said. "Technically, you haven't heard about Parker, or dream mining, or my fun times in St. Louis."

"Good point. I'll try to keep it shallow," I said. I curled my knees up and shifted more comfortably. "Can you tell me one more thing?"

"Sure."

"Why were you in Dean Berg's rooms last night?"

"How did you know about that?" he asked.

"I saw you through the window," I said. "I can see Dean Berg's penthouse from my dorm."

The tapping came again before he spoke. "I wanted to know if I could become a techie."

That was the last thing I'd expected. "Really?"

"They're paid well," Linus said. "I don't have the background for it, but he told me he'll think about it. I might have to go to university for a few years first."

175

"That's good, right?"

"It's just complicated. I've been saving up, but still I don't have much. I'd need my GED."

"You could get that," I said.

"Right." He paused. "This is your fault, you know."

"Why?"

"You and your dreams," Linus said. "You asked me about going home to Wales. It started me thinking about what it would take to actually get there."

I wanted to jump in and cheer him on. He could totally make it. But something in his voice warned me not to overdo it. Instead, I said, "Hope is a weird thing."

"Yes, it is," he said.

I pictured him in the tower, still gazing out at a sky full of stars. I found the brightest star in my window and fixed my eyes on it.

"You want to know something?" he asked.

"Sure."

He spoke quietly, as if divulging a secret. "When I first saw you? I thought you were too good for this place."

I couldn't figure out why he'd think so. "You mean that morning, behind the art building?" I asked. "You didn't even like me."

"No. Before that, when you first came to campus with the other new students," he said. "You were different from the others. You kind of kept to yourself, watching everyone, and you hardly ever smiled. But you were polite, too. You thanked me for carrying your duffel."

"I did?"

I hadn't even noticed Linus then. That first day, I'd been so awed just to be at the school. I had been so conscious of the cameras, and so nervous about doing the wrong thing. I wished I had paid attention to him. We might have become friends sooner.

"You're still too good for this place," he said.

"Go on," I said, smiling.

"I mean it. Don't forget that, Rosie," he said. "Sweet dreams."

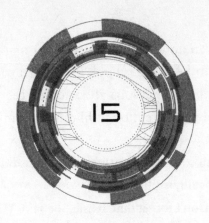

THE NOOSE

A SEA OF distinct, blueberry-like droplets of water is steadily rising, overlapping the dock where I stand. Above, the sky is a noxious violet. I'm barefoot on the planks, trying to retreat, but the strange water droplets lap up to clutch at my ankles, pinning me, and I can't escape. The droplets swarm up at a vicious pace and as I inhale, they crowd into my mouth to drown me. Something pokes my ribs and I surface.

Squarely into the dorm.

"Are you okay?" Janice said. "You didn't wake up."

I breathed hard and filled my lungs with precious air.

Janice tipped her head, frowning at me. "Could something be wrong with your sleep meds?" she said.

"No, I'm good." The last of the blue droplets trickled away, taking the fear with them. "I'm good," I said more certainly.

"If you say so," she said.

I didn't believe in trying to interpret dreams. Nightmares, either. Nevertheless, I got the impression my subconscious was not entirely at ease.

A bit later, when I went over for breakfast, I looked for Linus, but Franny told me he was out running errands for the chef. Afterward, I collected a few of the cameras I'd posted around campus so I could check out the footage in Media Convergence. The morning was clear and cool enough that I half wished I'd worn jeans instead of a skirt.

I was retrieving a camera from the graveyard when Burnham walked out of the IMGD building. The early sunlight streamed in behind him and highlighted the artful mess of his hair, making me wonder if he just naturally looked cool all the time, or if he had to work at it. Our non-friendship was like an itchy scab I couldn't resist picking at.

"Hi, Burnham," I said.

He slowed on the other side of the spiky iron fence. "Good morning, Rosie."

"You heading to the library?" I asked, coming through the gate.

"Yes."

We fell into synch walking together, but with enough space for an elephant between us.

"I love these intimate exchanges we have," I said. "Don't hold back."

"I was never mad at you," Burnham said. "I don't like being misunderstood."

"You called me a manipulator."

"But I wasn't mad."

"What was that, then? A calm opinion?"

"It was a mistake," he said. "I apologize."

I turned fully in his direction, astounded. He looked perfectly serious.

"Where is this sorriness coming from all of a sudden?" I asked.

"My brother told me I was a tool," he said.

I let out a laugh. Other students ahead of us were taking the steps into the library, and Henrik gave us a curious glance.

"Let's hear it for brothers," I said. "This is the same one who told you about my conversation with Linus? When I hatched my masterly, diabolical scheme?"

"Same brother," Burnham said. "Are we good?"

I wouldn't have minded a little more explanation and groveling, to be honest. It would have been just fine with me if he took back that "awkward" insult.

"Sure," I said.

"Great." He strode into the library ahead of me.

Guys. It was so tempting to generalize about them. But Burnham was one of a kind, and he mystified me.

Down in the basement classroom, I picked a computer as far from him as possible and unloaded my cameras. It was not a good idea to watch the one from my wardrobe. If it had caught any suspicious activity, I would rather discover that in secret, which meant I would have to view it at night, in my sleep shell.

I lined up four of my other cameras on the counter and

advanced each one to six o'clock the night before, when all of us students went to bed. The quad camera showed the campus growing dimmer as the sun went down, but very few people were about. A few techies and a cleaning crew went by, and then a security guy in a slow-moving golf cart. The attic camera showed the lights going off on different floors of the dean's tower until only the fifth floor was lit. Shortly after midnight, that went dark, too. Later, lights went on in the dean's penthouse, and still later, in the background behind Otis's lookout tower, an ice cream truck arrived at the loading dock of the dining hall.

It was all painfully dull.

I slumped my chin into my hand, my elbow on the table, bummed that I didn't have a faster, more efficient way to watch the footage. Henrik and Paige were playing Ping-Pong. Janice had taken a computer beside Burnham, and other students were working, too. Mr. DeCoster was back in his corner with his pistachios.

"I need to go out and put my cameras back up," I said to him.

Mr. DeCoster glanced up. "What are you working on?"

"I'm looking for ghosts," I said.

He tossed a shell at his coffee cup and missed. "You believe in ghosts?" he asked.

"I don't, but I want to look for them," I said. "It's a fruitless quest, fraught with failure."

He nodded slowly. "I suppose you've got the graveyard."

"Yes."

"You might try the observatory," he added.

"I already put a camera on the roof."

"Inside is where you want to go," Mr. DeCoster said. "One of the old-timers hanged himself in there. If I were a ghost, that's where I'd be."

Funny way of putting it.

"How can I get in there?" I asked. "It's locked."

"One sec." Mr. DeCoster sat up and touched a finger to his earphone. "Sandy? Who would have a key to the observatory?" He glanced toward the windows, frowning absently. "Okay." He leaned back. "Dean Berg can meet you there."

"Himself? What, now?" I asked.

"You want to go in, right? He'll be there in five minutes."

It was weird to think of going to the observatory with Dean Berg. I couldn't guess why he would drop everything to help me personally, but I couldn't exactly argue.

"Okay," I said.

"Go on, then," Mr. DeCoster said. "The dean should have a good perspective for your project. He knows everything about the school, onstage and off, forward and back."

I collected my cameras in my backpack and headed out.

〉〉〉〉〉〉〉〉〉

I passed the lookout tower as I strolled down the sheep pasture. It spiked up against the sky, and as usual, Otis was working the big black eye of a camera lens toward me. I was more curious about him now that I knew he was Linus's landlord and vampire. Or Parker was. When I waved, he lifted a hand back.

Grasses at either side of the path skimmed my shins, and I covered my eyes to squint down the pasture. The sheep were absent today, but a gray cat lay in the road to Forgetown. As I rounded the corner of the observatory, the area near the door was vacant, so I turned back toward the pasture to look for Dean Berg. He had said five minutes, but I knew important adults had trouble keeping time, so I sank down to wait on the sunny gravel path that circled the observatory.

Farther downhill, Forgetown huddled beneath its water tower, with prairie stretching out in either direction. I pulled out my video camera and panned the little town from left to right. A man was hanging laundry on a line, and a pair of people were working on the solar panels of the dairy barn. I had no way of telling where Linus lived, but I picked a yellow house with gray shutters and imagined it was his.

I swiveled to aim my camera back toward campus and focused in on the clock tower. The Roman numerals were sharply vivid, and so were the carved letters of the school motto. *Dream Hard. Work Harder. Shine.* I always liked the way a dream was either a hope to be longed for, or an elusive flight of sleep.

"Hello. Sorry to keep you waiting," Dean Berg said. "Something always seems to hold me up."

I scrambled to my feet and dusted off the back of my skirt. "That's okay."

I stashed my camera in my backpack while he pulled a ring of old-fashioned metal keys out of his pocket.

Appearance wise, Dean Berg always struck me as blandly forgettable, and now I tried to figure out why. He was a fit, plain man somewhere in his early forties, I guessed. Carefully trimmed, sandy-blond hair, pale eyebrows, and soft-looking, ruddy cheeks gave him a healthy, tidy look. He wore a green tie with ducks on it, a tweed jacket, and the obligatory earphone. Altogether, he was the last person I would suspect of masterminding anything, but when I recalled his phone call I'd overheard, I knew his looks were deceiving.

The trick was going to be acting like I didn't know anything.

"How are you liking Forge?" he asked in a friendly voice. "Does it live up to your expectations?"

"Yes. It's great."

"I understand you're looking for ghosts," he said.

"It probably sounds a little silly," I said.

"I've learned to go with our students' ideas. You never know where they might lead. This, let me tell you, is one of my favorite old buildings on campus." He pointed the key toward the door. "Just give me a minute to be sure the cameras are up and running inside so our viewers can come along with us. Wait here," he said, and pushed open the door.

I stood on the threshold while he disappeared into the dark space. A moment later, lights flickered on, accompanied by a flapping noise, and Dean Berg was talking into his earphone. "Bones? We good here? How about to my right?" He called back out to me. "Rosie? Come on in."

184

I stepped in slowly, scanning around the cramped, stuffy interior. The space was smaller than I'd expected, with large, boxy computers crowding in from the walls, and a narrow staircase that led up to the telescope platform. The black, cylindrical machine was aimed directly upward, like a stubby rocket set to launch. I felt a faint, interior shimmer of familiarity, as if I'd been here before, and then I went up the steps. The interior of the dome, above, was a dark, steel color, and another fluttering noise startled me.

"Wouldn't you know. Doves," Dean Berg said. He touched his earphone. "Bones? Ask Leroy to send over a work crew, will you? They'll need to find and patch the hole. See if they can relocate the nest outside."

Guided by a mess of droppings that streaked one wall, I peered up to a ledge where the dome met its lower circle. The nest explained why the stuffiness had a tinge of feathery rot to it. A bird flapped its wings loudly and then darted out of sight. My déjà vu of familiarity grew more intense.

I stayed near the telescope while Dean Berg paced around the lower circle.

"I remember when the astronomer hanged himself," he said. "A terrible pity. It happened during my first year here as dean. Clarence Smith, his name was. He was nearing a hundred."

A cool shiver slipped along my skin, and I looked up again, instinctively searching for a likely hook or beam for a noose. Without effort, my imagination summoned an image of an old man in black, hanging straight and still, his shoes tugging at his limp feet. I could even picture his knobby ankles.

"What was he like?" I asked, and I half knew how the dean would answer.

"He was a quiet man. Kept to himself," Dean Berg said. "No family to speak of. He loved the stars, though. He told me many times that making you all sleep so long was an egregious mistake. He said you would miss the night."

"He was right," I said.

"Unfortunately, there's no way around that," he said, still pacing.

"I suppose not," I said.

He tapped his key on the lower railing, and the pinging grated on my ears.

"You're an interesting student, Rosie," the dean said. "You're an observer by nature. We have that in common, actually."

"I just want to make films," I said.

"I notice you aren't filming now," he said. "Do you want to set up one of your cameras?"

I didn't want to. The space was feeling claustrophobic. Lights flickered at the edge of my vision as if I'd stood up too fast, and my sense of déjà vu grew stronger. "Can we open the dome, do you think?" I asked. I needed light and air.

Dean Berg pointed to the telescope before me. "There should be a button."

To my right was a panel of buttons and switches, so old they had punch-labels on them. Half of the labels had buckled or fallen off, but one green button said OPEN on it. I tried it, looking up expectantly. Nothing happened. My déjà vu told me the failure was entirely normal.

"It doesn't work," I said. My voice was both muffled and echoey.

"There's probably a master switch somewhere," Dean Berg said.

I didn't see one. I didn't know where to look. The air seemed thicker than ever.

The dean's voice dropped to a low, dragged-out bass. "Don't you want to know where the astronomer killed himself?" he asked.

I couldn't have heard him correctly. His question was too bizarre. Suddenly, I wasn't sure he'd spoken at all.

My déjà vu might have supplied his words.

"Excuse me?" I said.

"Rosie? Are you all right?" The dean's voice came from far away.

I didn't want to know where the body was. I wanted to get out of there. I shook my head, but at the same time, I was busy anticipating the next thing he would say.

"Can't you guess where we found the body?" whispered through my mind.

As if compelled by a deep command within me, I lifted my gaze upward, expecting to see a gray knuckle of a hook for a noose, but before I could locate it around the rim of the dome, a sudden dizziness hit me. I reached for the stair railing to catch my balance, but missed. I lurched forward, grabbing blindly, and gripped a knob on the telescope, just barely. Sweating and unsteady, I held on tight and closed my eyes.

"Rosie!" Dean Berg said sharply.

I focused all my energy into my grip, fighting to stay conscious. I could feel the dead man's invisible feet overlapping with my face, stifling my nose and mouth so I couldn't breathe. Gravity shifted sideways.

A quick noise came behind me on the stairs.

"Come here," Dean Berg said.

Stars exploded behind my eyelids in spikes of pain. The dean's arm came around my waist. I tried to pull away from him, but he held me tighter just as I lost balance completely. I pitched forward, and he caught me hard. My knees gave out from under me, but the dean, with surprising strength, lifted me in his arms and carried me swiftly outside.

"Bones, send Dr. Ash," the dean said. Then to me, as he set me on the doorstep, "Steady on. Have a seat. Keep your head down. Let's get this off."

He helped me out of my backpack and I leaned forward over my knees.

My head was still swimming, and I focused on breathing. Dimly, I registered that Dean Berg was talking into his earphone, calling again for Dr. Ash. I had never come close to fainting before now. My fingers were trembling, and my throat felt tight. The dean was asking me questions, but I couldn't reply. I was too busy watching the gravel between my shoes, trying to stay conscious, and at the same time, my heavy head felt like I was stuffing a roomful of feathers into a small, airless breadbox.

"Let's get you to the infirmary," the dean said.

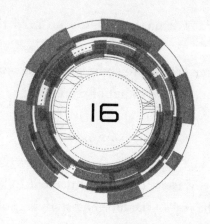

NEW FAVORITE

DR. ASH'S EXAM of me was thorough, but she found nothing to explain my sudden faintness. She noted my reflexes were a little slow, but she wouldn't say whether that was a cause or an effect. She suggested I might have been dehydrated and advised me to eat well. Stress, she said, could cause unexpected symptoms.

"I don't faint," I said.

"Maybe not," Dr. Ash said. "But you came close to it today. I suggest you take it easy for a day or two. I wouldn't take up any new activities that require a lot of balance, like tightrope walking or bouldering. Not until you're feeling better."

"I'm feeling better now," I said. "It was just stuffy in the observatory. Some doves had a nest in there."

I didn't tell her about the déjà vu.

She smiled. "Fortunately, there's no need to go back in there."

She made me promise to come see her the minute I felt any dizziness again, and I was out of there.

>>>>>>>>

I'd missed my Masters class, but I made it to Space on time, and I spent the rest of the morning studying solar flares with my classmates. I tried not to think about how weird my time with Dean Berg had been. My group was doing a report on the Flare of 2032, which had started wildfires on three continents, fried two-thirds of the telecommunications satellites, and disrupted half the cell phone service in the Northern Hemisphere for over three months. On the plus side, it saved the landline phone industry and instigated an international medical alliance on solar radiation poisoning and related cancers. One of the students in my group, a girl named Rebecca with sturdy knees and blue-tipped hair, wanted to turn our report into an interpretive dance. I finally gave up trying to tell her we were in a math/science class.

At lunch, Linus was out on the terrace of the dining hall, serving ice cream for students with Franny and another staffer. They all wore cheery red bib aprons for the occasion, and Linus put his arm into the work of scooping. He passed me a big bowl of chocolate-chunk-coffee-cinnamon-swirl and abandoned his post when I came through the line.

"Where are you going?" Franny asked him.

"Shirking, obviously," Linus said.

"I can see that," Franny said. "For how long?"

"Long enough to drive you mad, love," Linus said, and took a second bowlful for himself.

I caught Franny shaking her head and fighting a smile.

Linus and I strolled over to one of the benches under a tree, where Linus straddled one end and I sat normally, so I could keep my short skirt decent. Students relaxed in clusters on the lawn while a campus tour group passed by. The day had warmed up considerably, and the cool sweetness of the ice cream was pure heaven in my mouth.

"How's the dizziness?" he asked.

"Gone completely," I said, and licked my spoon. "I'm fine."

"What happened?"

"I don't really want to talk about it." On camera.

"Right," he said.

A couple of guys with bongo drums started playing across the quad, which was all the invitation Paige and a couple other dancers needed to head over and start improvising. I was happy talking with Linus and watching the lithe figures as they bent and twirled over the grass. This was what I'd hoped Forge would be like, and in the brightness of a sunny day, I could almost forget about Dean Berg and my nighttime anxieties.

"Where's your camera?" Linus asked "Don't you want to film them?"

I shook my head. "Sometimes its better to live in the moment."

As we finished eating, he took my bowl and set it with his in the grass.

"That's my new favorite ice cream," I said.

"Mine, too." He leaned near and gave me a coffee-flavored kiss. He touched my waist, lightly, and then kissed me again. "You taste nice," he said. "How'd you manage that?"

"Beats me."

I ran my fingers along his forearm and skimmed a dried drip of ice cream from when he'd been scooping. When I saw the fine hairs lift in goose bumps along his skin, I smiled at his sensitivity. I thought we might kiss again, but he held very still, even when I drew my thumb along the pocket of his tee shirt where a thread was frayed. The red of his apron did something vivid to his eyes, and his bruise was now almost completely healed. I leaned shyly away and scanned my gaze around the quad. We had cameras *and* real people to watch us this time.

"So many witnesses," I said.

He laughed. "Tell me about it." He got up from the bench, hitched at his apron, and reached for our bowls.

I couldn't wait to talk to him for real, at night.

>>>>>>>>>

I lived the rest of that Thursday impatient for bedtime, when my second life could begin again. It was such a routine by now, faking my pill swallow, that I grew careless when Orly was checking in my mouth and almost showed her the pill.

Though Orly had overseen the removal of the extra furniture from our dorm the night of the fifty cuts, she never indicated that she knew about any other activity in our room at night. I was trying to put together who knew what, without much luck.

Dr. Ash, for certain, knew what was going on at night. The bearded guy who'd given me intravenous sleep meds had to know, too, and so did Dean Berg. But Mr. DeCoster and the other teachers, did they know? Did the maintenance staff and the techies? If they did, then Dean Berg had an entire network of people keeping secrets. It just didn't seem possible.

As soon as it was dark enough, I turned on my video camera under my covers and reviewed my footage from the previous night. It showed me tossing and turning during the time I'd been listening to my walkie-ham, but the walkie-ham itself never showed. I simply looked restless, and then I went still. I fast-forwarded through the rest of the night, but nothing disturbed the dorm room.

No one entered the dorm while we slept. No sleep shells were rolled out. I wasn't exactly disappointed, but I wasn't completely reassured, either. I would have to try again.

I turned my video camera off, stashed it farther under my quilt, and checked my walkie-ham to see if it was dialed to channel four. A tiny buzz of static broke for a voice.

"Rosie?" Linus said.

I clicked the button to keep the channel open. "It's me," I said, so relieved and happy to hear him. "Where are you?" I arranged the walkie-ham so I could speak into it with hardly any voice. I had left my sleep shell lid closed, too.

"Back in the lookout tower," he said. "This is the only place

193

we seem to get decent reception. Listen, I'm worried about you. What really happened to you in the observatory today?"

"It was so, so weird," I said, and I tried to explain how creepy it had been inside with the stench and the doves and the dean. "He was talking about the dead astronomer, and how he'd hanged himself in there. I could practically see the body."

"That's strange, all right."

"I was having this weird déjà vu, too," I said. "Like I'd been there before."

"In the observatory?"

"With Dean Berg there," I said. "He was part of it. At one point, it seemed like he was offering to show me exactly where they'd found the body, but I'm not really sure if he said something, or if I just *thought* he did."

"You couldn't tell?" Linus said.

"I *thought* he really spoke, but the whole thing was too morbid to make sense," I said. "Could I have been hallucinating? Just thinking about it again is kind of freaking me out."

I heard a faint tapping from his end of the line.

"Okay, I'm just going to throw this out there," he said, "but maybe you shouldn't be skipping your sleeping pills. Maybe it's messing you up."

I was shocked. "Linus, I can't just sleep. This place is dangerous. Somebody has to find out what's going on."

"But it doesn't have to be you," Linus said.

I couldn't believe he was telling me to back off, to follow the rules. "Did Dean Berg ask you to say this? Did he tell you to tell me to take my pills? Or Dr. Ash?"

"Rosie, no," Linus said.

But I was doubting him. "Did the dean tell you to meet me, that first day behind the art building? Did somebody send you out to the spools on purpose to tell me how to pass the fifty cuts?"

"What are you talking about?" Linus sounded irritated now. "What is this?"

"I don't understand this place," I said. "I don't know what's happening to me."

"Nothing's happening to you. Listen," he said, and I could hear him making an effort to speak calmly. "I get that you're scared. You almost fainted today. But you're kind of working yourself up, too. I'm not part of some big, complicated conspiracy here. Maybe you need to quit eavesdropping on conversations that don't concern you, and take your pills, and get your sleep like the other students. You're hardly giving this place a chance."

I felt a screw of worry tightening inside me. "You're the only one I can talk to, Linus. If I sleep at night, we can't talk."

"We can still talk during the day."

I let out a laugh. "Like that's any good."

He was silent a moment.

"I mean, having ice cream with you was great, of course," I said.

"Glad to hear it."

"Linus, I'm sorry. That didn't come out right. It's just, I want to be able to really talk to you."

"We might have a problem with that," he said. "Otis has

been asking me what I've been up to. He doesn't want me up on campus at night."

"Did you tell him I'm staying awake?"

"No, but he's not dumb. He doesn't want me to get in trouble, and he doesn't want me blamed if *you* get in trouble."

"We aren't sneaking out," I reminded him. "We're just talking."

"But is it really doing you any good?" he asked. "I think I'm making it worse for you. That's what I'm saying. Maybe you'd be better off if you took your pill."

I got what he was saying. Sort of.

"Does Otis know anything about what's happening here at night?" I asked.

"I don't think so. Do you want me to ask him point-blank?"

I had to think about that. I trusted Linus, more or less, but I was pretty certain Otis's loyalties would have to lie with Dean Berg.

"No. Not yet," I said.

"It's up to you," he said.

"Thanks." I shifted my quilt around my head and the walkie-ham again. "Could we talk about something else for a while? Something nicer?"

"Like what?"

"Anything."

"Okay," he said slowly. "Guess what's on the repeat cycle of *The Forge Show* right now? I'm watching it on my phone."

"What time is it?"

"Twelve-thirty," he said.

The repeat cycle ran twelve hours straight through, so midnight in real life matched up with noon on the show. On the show he was watching, it had to be just after lunch. "Ice cream?" I asked.

"Yes. And guess what your blip rank was when you had ice cream with me."

"I have no idea."

"Thirty-five. You'll get decent banner ad money in that range," he said. "That's going to add up."

It was nice to know I could get a spike during happy times, too, and not just when I was upset. "My stepfather will be glad to know," I said.

"What's he like?" Linus said.

"My stepfather? He's fine," I said. "He's had some bad luck with his job, but he's tight with the other strikers. What else. He likes to hunt. And read mysteries."

"You don't like him," Linus said.

"I don't want to complain. You don't have any parents at all."

"He must be a total jerk."

I laughed. "Okay, truthfully? I can't stand him," I said. "My mom works two jobs and still she does all the cleaning and stuff while Larry sits on the couch, scratching his hairy belly. It drives me crazy. And he's mean. He's just ugly mean, for no reason."

"How mean? Does he hurt you?" Linus asked.

I hesitated. "No." It felt bad to lie, but I couldn't tell him.

"I take it you don't miss home."

"I miss my mom," I said. "She's great. And my little sister Dubbs. She's great, too."

"Dubbs is the one you walk along the tracks with?" he asked.

He remembered.

"Yes."

"What happened to your birth dad? Is he in the picture?"

Long before I walked the tracks with my sister, back when I was little, I used to walk them with my dad. I could feel his big, calloused hand holding mine as I stretched my strides to land on each railroad tie. The wood gleamed with old tar under the dust, and the rails were rusty bright in the sunlight. My sneakers were small and red beside his boots, step after step. He liked to whistle. That was what I had left of my dad.

"He's dead," I said. "I was four when he went MIA in the Greenland War, and he was declared presumed dead four years after that."

At that moment, I heard a noise from the hallway. I froze.

"Linus, I have to go," I said.

"What's going on?" he asked.

"Someone's here."

Before he could reply, I shut off my walkie-ham and stuffed it in my pillowcase. I scrambled under my quilt for my video camera and turned it on. I didn't dare pull it out to capture any video, but the microphone would pick up the audio in the room if it was loud enough to be heard through my lid. I held super still, trying to breathe softly.

Brisk but quiet footsteps came in the far end of the room and came on steadily in my direction. I kept my fingers limp, my shoulders loose, and then I heard a muffled click nearby. Not a word was said, and then a faint, weighty rolling noise headed back toward the door. I waited through a long minute of silence. Then I opened my eyes and shifted just enough to see down the room.

Janice. The space for her sleep shell was empty. This time they'd come for Janice.

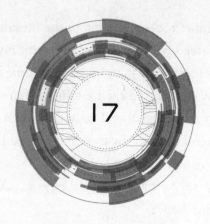

17

THE GAME

FOR ONE MOMENT, I hesitated, full of fear, and then I thought, *Forget this. She's my friend.* I had to find out where they were taking her.

I slid open my lid, climbed out of bed, and grabbed my video camera. I aimed it briefly at the empty space where Janice's sleep shell had been, and then I flew past the others to the doorway. I peeked out. The upper hallway was dark and empty, the elevator doors closed. I ran for the steps and raced down in the dark, flight after flight. I heard no hint to indicate where they'd left the elevator until I reached the basement, where the heavy click of a closing door sounded clearly.

A service tunnel was most likely where Janice had been taken. I paused to listen for any more sound, and I lifted my video camera. Through my viewfinder, I saw that the EXIT signs glowed just enough to illuminate patches of the basement, which meant that the instant I left the deepest shadows, I would probably be visible to the school cameras, too. I had to get offstage as quickly as possible.

I hurried past the washers and dryers in the laundry area, and past an elevator, scanning every wall and corner until I found, around the farthest bend, a solid steel door with a swipe lock.

A swipe lock. I was stuck. I gave the door an experimental tug. It didn't budge. I yanked again harder. It was no good. I couldn't get any farther. Without a swipe pass, I couldn't get through the door.

I would need to get one. That was all.

I hurried back through the basement and up the stairs, filming as I went and dodging the glows of the EXIT lights as best as I could. At the fourth floor, my dorm level, I looked up the last flight toward the attic, teetering between caution and the urge to know more.

On impulse, I climbed up the old, narrow stairs to the attic again. The space under the eaves was silent tonight, and through my viewfinder, the scene was utterly black except for the slanting windows. I felt my way cautiously forward, toward the nearest skylight. A chill came through the rafters, and when I looked out, the stars had an extra crispness. Across the way, the dean's tower was dark. Not even the fifth floor was lit, nor the penthouse. I could find no hint that they'd taken Janice over there.

Then I noticed a dim glow on the sixth floor, in the corner.

I adjusted my video camera and used the zoom to close in. A solitary man was leaning back in his chair, watching an array of screens. He had his chin in his hand, and he appeared to be lost in contemplation. He didn't move, or reach for his touch screen. He barely seemed to breathe, and with only a faint reflection of light from the screen animating his face, it looked more like a mask than a true visage. Only when he finally turned did I recognize that he was Dean Berg.

He pivoted his chair, slowly, until he was facing out the window, toward the girls' dorm. Toward me.

While I held my camera perfectly still, my heart began to pound. He knew where I was. He knew I was watching him. Button cameras covered this attic, just like they spied on every other place at this school. I'd thought it was too dark for me to be visible, but I had to guess I was discernible to someone who knew where to look.

The dean obviously did.

He must have been watching me all along.

What are you playing at? I thought.

If he expected me to say something, or freak out, he was going to be disappointed. A few of the pieces suddenly clicked together: the way I was allowed to sneak around at night, the way he'd personally helped me to get into the observatory, the way he was watching me right now.

I didn't have to understand every nuance to grasp that I was in a game, a weird, one-on-one game with Dean Berg. The school, the show, and the other students were all part of it, too, but they were mainly the board and the other unwitting pieces. I was the only student who suspected something wrong was happening at night. My opponent was the dean. I just didn't know yet what the stakes were, or what it would take to win.

>>>>>>>>

I was exhausted and thick-headed when I woke the next morning. Janice's sleep shell was back in place, and Janice herself looked as healthy and bright as a sunbeam. The other girls were thriving, too.

But I came to a resolution. The situation was too twisted and weird for me to handle on my own. I planned to show my footage to Mr. DeCoster in front of all the other Media Convergence students, so the viewers and Janice's parents could ask for an explanation as to why Janice's sleep shell had been removed in the night. After that, it would be out of my hands.

Responding to a couple of friendly greetings by rote, I rolled my video camera into a towel to conceal it and headed for the bathroom. I just needed to check that my footage clearly showed how Janice's sleep shell was gone in the night. I would face consequences for being out of bed myself, but hopefully, the school would be lenient on me.

In the privacy of a stall, I checked the index of my video camera. The most recent clip started with the darkness from under my quilt. I skimmed forward, searching for the first flicker of when I'd brought the camera out of my sleep shell to film the dorm. But the video clip stayed dark. It didn't show the dorm room without Janice's sleep shell, or the stairs I had run down, or the basement, or the attic. The entire clip was a deep, unfocused brown-black.

I didn't understand. I checked the time stamp on the clip: 9.19.2066:00.43. Last night. After midnight. I knew what I'd seen, and I knew what I'd filmed, but my camera showed nothing.

I gasped and fumbled with my camera, dropping my shower kit to the floor.

"Are you okay in there?" one of the girls called from the other side of the stall door.

The only explanation terrified me. Someone else had erased my footage. Someone had come to my bed while I was asleep and taken my video camera out from under my covers and changed the footage.

"Rosie?" the girl said, knocking. I recognized Rebecca's voice. "Is that you?"

"I'm okay," I said. "I just dropped my stuff. I'm fine."

I grabbed my things and wrapped my camera in my towel again. I clutched everything to my chest and tried not to hyperventilate. My mind scrambled for a better explanation, but there wasn't one. When I was in the attic, Dean Berg had turned to watch me from the dean's tower. He'd known all about where I was and what I'd been doing. Was it crazy to consider that he'd come to the girls' dorm and taken my camera and messed with my footage?

I let out a strangled laugh.

I was coming unglued.

I reined in my panic, thinking fast. I needed to be careful. Very careful. I didn't know what to do yet, but until I did, I had to hold on to one thing: I couldn't tell anybody what was happening.

They'd never believe me.

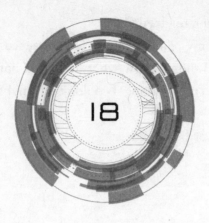

18

THE LADY KNIGHT

I WAS TOO terrified not to behave like a good student. That day, Friday, I worked hard in my classes, kept my nose down, and went for a run. In the cafeteria, I made a point of taking lots of vegetables and protein, as if I could fortify myself against my fear of getting back in my sleep shell by eating a healthy dinner.

As I pressed the metal bar of the milk dispenser with my glass, Linus came out from the kitchen. He leaned his hip into the counter beside my tray.

"Hey," he said. "I saw you're studying Del Toro in Masters."

"Yes," I said, and moved my cup to the chocolate milk to make a mix. "I'm supposed to compare him to Poe and Mustafa as an innovator."

"That sounds cool."

I moved around him toward the canisters of silverware. "I'm trying to make the most of all my opportunities here."

"I can tell." He put a napkin on my tray for me and smiled. "Very admirable. Want some of that ice cream? I saved some for you."

I wanted to tell him I wouldn't be calling him anymore. I needed to sleep. I needed to be good. "Thank you, but no."

"I thought it was your favorite."

"It is, but I don't want it every day. That might spoil it," I said. I was so bad at lying. I smiled tightly. "I think the pace here is catching up with me. I'm actually looking forward to going to sleep tonight."

He tilted his head back slightly. "You don't want to burn out."

"No," I said. I gripped my tray. I didn't know why it was harder to pretend to be a normal student when I was with Linus, but it actually hurt that I couldn't tell him what was really going on. I gazed past his shoulder, spotting Janice, Paige, and a couple of the other girls, Mae and Rebecca, together at a round table.

Linus followed my gaze, and then looked back to me. He thoughtfully rubbed a knuckle to his eyebrow. "I've got plenty of work to do myself. A little studying, too."

"Really?"

"Turns out I need to learn geometry for the GED. Who knew?"

I laughed. "Good luck with that."

He gave my shoulder a squeeze and then leaned in to kiss my cheek. "See you around."

"Hold on. Not so fast," I said, and shifted to make sure I got a real kiss, with actual lips meeting mine. Linus obliged. I thought it would be fast, but it kind of slowed down, and edges blurred, and then, through lingering, I forgot where I was.

He smiled. "Don't lose your dinner, Sinclair."

I glanced down to see he was steadying my tray for me. I felt right for the first time all day.

"Thanks," I said.

"Anytime."

>>>>>>>>>

For the next few weeks, I took my sleeping pill every night like everybody else. There was no way I could face getting in my sleep shell unless I knew I'd be unconscious there, and it was a relief to escape my fears and wake physically rested and refreshed. Part of me longed to forget what I had seen at night and accept the bright existence of my daylight hours. Days at Forge were certainly full enough without me also trying to unravel the puzzle of what was happening at night.

But as time passed, I felt increasingly restless and unlike myself. Without the night to clear my head, I felt an insidious poison crawling just beneath the surface of my conscious mind. It made me tense, and irritable, and the more I tried to smile and pretend it wasn't there, the more false I felt to myself.

I couldn't fully bury the possibility that Dean Berg had put his hands under my covers to take my video camera, but I couldn't come up with another explanation for my deleted footage, either. Maybe he'd sent Dr. Ash to take the camera, but that was only marginally less creepy. I tried setting my video camera to spy on the dorm out of my wardrobe, but it never caught anyone coming in. It seemed to prove that we were undisturbed at night, but I still wasn't reassured. I kept checking the other cameras I had set up for my bogus ghost project and they, too, yielded nothing.

Dean Berg scared me. All I had to do was see his smiling, youthful face—and he could show up anywhere on campus—and I had to fight not to cringe and flee. He made me feel dirty, ashamed. It was bad enough that I suspected he'd come to my sleep shell in the night, but I also felt like I'd capitulated to him. I couldn't tell anybody about what I knew because they'd think I was just a crazy kid who skipped her pill. Without ever making a threat, he had trapped me into secrecy.

As an added frustration, sleeping at night also meant I couldn't have a candid conversation with Linus. I saw him almost daily, whenever our schedules allowed, but aside from assorted kisses, which were brilliant, our exchanges were superficial and inhibited. It was often easier not to see him than to pretend I wasn't hiding anything. I felt like a puppet performing for the cameras with my puppet boyfriend.

On Sundays, when I called home, my parents sounded busy with their own lives. Larry pestered me about my blip rank, which gradually drifted back down to the forties. Ma worried that I looked tired, which wasn't remotely possible since I was sleeping my full twelve hours a night. Only Dubbs was good to talk to, and her bubble of conversation always left me smiling. "I miss you," she'd say. "When are you coming home? You're famous enough now." She mailed me a drawing of a purple shark which I taped to my wardrobe.

One Monday afternoon, for Practicum, I had an assignment to film scenes in a gradation of color, from black and white, through pastel, to super vivid. I started with the dome of the observatory, and recalled that I still hadn't retrieved the video camera I'd put in the satellite dish. The place evoked an unpleasant memory for me now, and I had no urge to climb up it today.

Next, I filmed some of the tilting gravestones in the cemetery, and then a chapel window, interested by how dull the stained glass looked without any illumination behind it. The chapel reminded me of Ellen, with her knife and her kitty purse. It still disturbed me to think of how upset she had been when I joined her in the bathroom stall. I felt like I had sat beside an abyss of despair instead of a living girl. A gust of wind moved through the graveyard, ruffling the grass between the stone markers. I hoped Ellen was okay.

When I met up with Janice in the dining hall, even though the room was as bright and noisy as usual, I was still preoccupied by my mood of gray scales.

"Do you ever think about Ellen?" I asked.

"Who?" Janice asked.

"The singer in the bathroom the night of the fifty cuts," I said.

"To be honest, not really. No," Janice said.

She had another swizzle stick to add to her collection, and her dinner consisted of cole slaw and fries. Without even trying, I had loaded up my tray with comfort foods: a Sloppy Joe, mashed potatoes, macaroni and cheese, green beans, and applesauce.

"Do you think she's okay?" I asked.

"Why are you thinking about her?" Janice asked, smearing a fry in ketchup.

"I was by the chapel taking footage. It reminded me of her," I said. "I was wondering if she went to the chapel for the acoustics, to sing."

"I think she probably went there to be alone," Janice said. "She knew she was getting cut."

I idly spooned up some applesauce and sucked it through the gap in my teeth like I used to do when I was little. "Let me borrow your phone," I said.

Janice had it on the table, and I drew it across to me. It didn't take me long to do a search for Ellen Thorpe. To my surprise, the top listing was an obituary for a girl of the same name, and then I realized it wasn't a different girl. It was the same Ellen. I had to check again twice before I could believe it. I passed the phone back toward Janice.

"Did you hear about this?" I asked.

Janice frowned, scanning the article, and her eyes went wide when she looked back up at me. "That's awful. You'd think they would have told us." She typed on her phone, and then studied it for a long moment. "She died in a car crash. She was driving alone at night and hit a tree."

"Is there anything more?" I asked, trying to see upside down across the table.

She shook her head, typing again. "There's no condolence site. She's not on Facebook. I wonder if her family took all her stuff down. What do you think?"

"It's sad," I said.

Janice passed the phone back to me, and I scanned the related news articles. It only said Ellen's car had hit a tree at seventy miles per hour. I felt kind of freaked out. I had sat next to this girl only a few weeks earlier. I had thought she was home, getting help.

"It's really sad," Janice agreed. "She was pretty bummed in the bathroom. Didn't she have a knife?"

I glanced up and wondered if she was thinking what I was thinking.

"Do you think it was suicide?" I asked. "I heard a lot of teen driving accidents are actually suicides but nobody can prove it."

"That is seriously sick."

Sick or not, I couldn't help wondering how much Ellen's death had been an accident, or if there were others like her. I felt kind of ill. "How many Forge alums kill themselves?" I asked.

Janice tucked her chin back and made a face. "Somebody really got up on the dark side of the bed this morning."

"You had to sign that paperwork when you came, right?" I asked, remembering the waivers my parents and I had signed.

Dr. Ash had mentioned them, too, the day of the fifty cuts. "Was your mom the doctor concerned at all about side effects from being here?"

"No." Janice looked both revolted and concerned.

I wound my finger around a twist of my hair and pulled it taut. "You feel totally fine, don't you? You never feel the least bit weird or stressed or anything here, do you?"

"Okay, maybe I should take you over to the infirmary," she said.

"Just because I'm asking questions doesn't mean I'm sick or crazy."

"No, but if you *were* sick or crazy, you'd be acting a lot like you are right now," Janice said.

I took a good, hard look at my friend. Janice oozed confidence and energy. I'd thought, when I first got to know her, that she was a little East Coast prim. These days, she laughed easily and had tons of outgoing theater friends. She'd cut her long blond tresses into a wispy, wild hairdo, and she wore what she called her Hamletta scarf wherever she went.

I glanced past her shoulder at the rest of the room. Henrik and Burnham were flicking a triangular paper puck across one of the tables, aiming at goals made with their pinkies. At that moment, Paige trapped the puck under her hand. Then she dropped into Henrik's lap, draped her willowy body around his, and kissed him before she gave back the puck. Other students around us were laughing and lively, too, glowing in the hotbed of creativity that was Forge.

The contrast to my own stifled condition hit me in the

gut. What I felt most, unexpectedly, was envy. What on earth was wrong with me? I was taking my pills like everyone else. Why wasn't I turning into an artistic genius? Why was I the only one who was unraveling?

As the blip rank board on the wall began its flipping noise again, I covered my ears with my hands and closed my eyes. I didn't let go of my ears until it stopped.

"It's no good trying to hide," Janice said. "The blip board knows all."

I looked up then to see I was ranked fiftieth.

"You're fifty," Janice said.

"Thanks."

"To clarify, you're absolute last," she said.

"I got that. Really."

"Look, whatever's going on with you, you need to figure it out," she said. "I mean it. This isn't a place that lets students fall apart. Honestly? I'm surprised no one's onto you."

"Unless they want me to fall apart," I said.

"Come again?"

I sighed. At some level, I'd never stopped worrying about what was happening at night. Inside, I was half-unglued, and apparently it showed because the board, like a magic mirror, never lied.

"Maybe it's good for the show, altogether," I said. "Maybe they like having one student in crisis so the rest of you look good."

She scratched her head. "They haven't done that in past shows."

"Maybe it's new for this season," I said.

"Are you admitting you're in crisis?" she asked.

"No."

I slouched my arm out along the table and laid my cheek along my arm. This way, my eyes were close to my fork when I twirled it in a morsel of Sloppy Joe. I was serious about wanting to know how many Forge alums committed suicide or otherwise died young. How to figure that out was the question. I got an idea.

I sat up straight and made a slow-motion princess wave with my hand.

"If anyone out there in viewer land can tell me how many Forge alums kill themselves or otherwise die young, I'd be grateful for the info," I said. "Same about kids who get cut in the fifty cuts. Feel free to send me an email. R-Sinclair-at-TheForgeSchool-dot-com."

"What are you doing?" Janice said. "I do not approve."

"I'm just putting it out there," I said. "There's freedom in being dead last. And incidentally, for the record, even though I've actually said the word *suicide* out loud, I'm perfectly fine." I slumped back on my arm and fed myself a cold, waxy morsel of Sloppy Joe.

>>>>>>>>

On Tuesday, after classes, I headed down to the basement of the library. Most of my cameras for my ghost hunting project had reached capacity on their memory, and I needed a way to

215

store the footage or lose it. So far, I'd watched only a fraction of what I had. Even though I seriously doubted that Dean Berg would allow me to record anything to incriminate him, I still had to try. I also needed to use the footage for DeCoster's class.

I chose a computer near the windows, and I was uploading my footage when Burnham came in.

"Hey," I said.

He scooped up a Ping-Pong ball by the net and strolled slowly nearer. "It's Rosie, at it again."

His hair was wet and his blue shirt looked fresh, like he'd just come from a shower. "Is this seat taken?" he asked, pointing to the place beside mine.

"Go ahead," I said.

He swiveled into the chair, turned his computer on, and set the Ping-Pong ball in a paperclip on his desk, where it couldn't roll. It was a little weird having him near me since we were still barely speaking. I glanced to see if anyone else was coming in, but we were alone.

"How's your project going?" I asked.

"Not bad."

A gaming program came up on his screen, with panels for settings, rules, and characters. I watched him skim through various screens until I saw a bird's eye view of a clock tower and a quad.

"Are you making a game of the school?" I asked.

"Sort of."

"*Are* you?"

"Sort of."

He was. How totally cool. I leaned closer, intrigued. He even had the benches in the quad and the fence around the rose garden configured in 3-D so they shifted appropriately whenever he swiveled angles.

"That is so cool," I said. "Who are the characters?"

"I'm still working on them."

"Let me see. Are they us? That looks like a knight." I hitched my chair closer to his so I could point. "Does that guy have a name?" I asked.

"She's a lady knight," Burnham said.

"Really?" I said, peering closer.

He pointed. "She has boobs."

I laughed.

"It's a little hard to tell under her armor, but they're there," he said.

"For the discerning gamer," I said. "The boob-seeker."

"Exactly."

I gave the character a closer inspection. "Did you mean for her to look like me?"

"No."

"She does," I said. "Curly brown hair. Nasty, nasty scowl. That's totally me."

Burnham nudged his glasses and leaned toward the screen, examining his own artwork as if he'd never seen it before. "You're full of it," he said.

I looked down at my own cleavage and straightened my violet tee shirt. "If you say so."

He frowned over at me. "I hear you're looking for ghosts?" he asked politely.

"Yeah. I know. I don't believe in them, either, but there's merit in an impossible search," I said. "The problem is trying to sort through all my footage. If I watched it in real time, I'd have to watch 'til I'm forty." I swiped a couple of files on my touch screen.

"Why are you spying on Forge?" he asked.

"Like I said—"

"No. Why? I'm curious." He planted an elbow on his desk, swiveled in my direction, and waited like he expected a real answer.

I opened my mouth and no words came out. A flash of panic hit me. Since he could guess I was spying, he ought to know I couldn't explain my motives on camera.

"I'm just attempting to fail, like Mr. DeCoster said," I said.

The lie was so obvious between us, it was almost a form of truth. Was this why he had sat next to me? To ask about this?

"And you're doing it with all your heart?" Burnham asked.

"That's the goal. To fail with all my heart. Remember the assignment?"

He lifted one of my video cameras, the one from the grave-yard. I'd taped a cross to it so I could keep track. "Are these all the cameras you have? Nine?" he asked.

I glanced at my row of video cameras. I had hours of foot-age that showed moonlight shifting over the quad, and a se-curity guard passing in a golf cart, and cleaning crews going by with barrels of garbage. The one useful thing I'd discovered was that the techies consistently headed home around mid-night, after which I could expect hours of nothing. "I have one more camera on top of the observatory," I said.

"Why there?"

"It's haunted."

He picked up the Ping-Pong ball and rolled it between his palms. "To start with, if you want full coverage of the school at night, you need to plot out the angles of what the cameras are covering," he said. "Then you need a system to review the footage efficiently."

I noticed he'd gotten past needing to know why I wanted the coverage.

"How would a person review the footage efficiently?" I asked.

"It's easy," he said. "You could use ten computers simultaneously to load the footage and dump it in the K:Cloud, and then combine them in your editing platform."

I had been stuck on the technical limitations of the up-loading, but his idea made perfect sense. I glanced again at his game, and remembered my pretend motivation for filming the school at night. "I could add a little ghost to some of the scenes, and move it from screen to screen," I said.

"That would be *faking* a ghost sighting, which isn't what you set out to do," he reminded me.

"True, but it would be fun," I said. "Fun's worth something and projects evolve. I don't suppose you'd help me."

He leaned back in his chair, still rolling the small white ball. "Possibly, I could," he said slowly. And then, "Catch."

He tossed me the ball and I caught it. For the first time since before the fifty cuts, he smiled at me for real, and I smiled back, relieved. Burnham's gaze shifted toward the door behind me.

I turned to see Linus framed in the doorway.

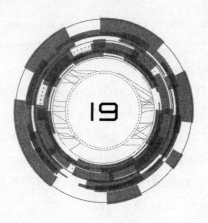

THE LOOKOUT TOWER

LINUS'S HAIR WAS shorter, and he was wearing a dark jacket I hadn't seen before.

"Hey, Sinclair," he said. "You busy?"

I smiled and set the Ping-Pong ball back on Burnham's paper clip. "Come on in. Do you know Burnham?"

Linus stayed where he was in the doorway. Burnham swiveled his chair around and said hi. Linus said hi back.

It wasn't awkward at all.

Linus hooked a hand around the back of his neck and looked toward me. "I was wondering if you wanted to come do something," he said. "I've got a half hour."

"It'll take me a minute to pack up," I said.

"I can watch your stuff," Burnham said.

"Are you sure?" I asked.

Burnham reached over to swipe my touch screen, and nine bars showed the uploading progress of my footage. "No problem," he said.

"Thanks. I'll be back soon," I said, and zipped up my backpack to leave it tidy by my chair.

Linus and I climbed the stairs to the main door of the library and pushed out into the fresh air. Though it was still sunny, the temperature had dropped, and I could hear a breeze rippling the trees along the quad.

"You cut your hair," I said. He'd taken out a couple of his earrings, too, I noticed.

"It's too short," he said.

"No, it's good." I examined the back of his neck where the trim little hairs looked soft and sharp. He looked older, somehow, with the shape of his head more defined. "It's definitely good."

"Thanks. Want to watch the storm come in?" he asked.

I glanced over my shoulder at a dark bank of clouds. "Sure."

"I know just the place," he said, and reached for my hand. "You're cold."

"A little," I admitted.

He shrugged out of his jacket and put it around my shoulders.

"But then you'll be cold," I protested.

"No, I'm fine," he said. He had only his white tee shirt on, and I could see goose bumps all up his arms.

I protested again, but he insisted, and when I reluctantly

slid my arms into the sleeves of his jacket, I could feel his residual body heat in the fabric.

"Okay, I'm never giving this back," I said.

He laughed. "I've missed you," he said.

"You saw me yesterday."

"Even so."

I lifted my gaze quickly to his. He meant he missed me at night.

"I have to be in class sometimes," I said.

"I know."

We moseyed between the chapel and the art building. He leaned over sideways and put a kiss on my earlobe.

"You're cute in my clothes," he said. "Want my pants?"

"Like that'll happen," I said, laughing.

"You wouldn't have to actually *wear* my pants," he clarified. He nodded at the chapel. "We could always take a couple blankets behind the organ."

I'd heard about that. "But there are still cameras back there," I said.

"I know. It's not ideal."

"And everyone would know what we're doing."

"They would, yes," he said, smiling. "They would absolutely know."

"Are you teasing me?" I asked.

"Maybe."

"Just how old are you?" I asked.

"Seventeen," he said. "How about you?"

"Fifteen."

"When's your birthday?" he asked.

"December."

"December whath?"

"December fifth," I said. "Why?"

"I don't know," he said. "Sixteen just seems like a good age."

"For what?"

"For teasing somebody."

I laughed again. We were walking behind the art building, past my favorite wooden spools, and I glanced up at the lookout tower where a big camera lens was, predictably, aimed at me. Linus drew me over to the base of the tower.

"Hey, Otis!" Linus called up. "Drop us the key!"

The old man with the mustache peeked out from behind the camera. "A storm's coming."

"Yeah, I know," Linus called. "That's why we're coming up."

"Stand back," Otis said.

A moment later, Otis tossed out a small, spiky object that fell in a long arc to the gravel at our feet. A trio of metal, old-fashioned keys was attached to a mini rubber duck. I peered toward the top again.

"Watch that ninth step," Otis called.

Linus worked the key in the lock, pushed open the thick door, and held it for me.

Inside was a dim, dusty stairwell that smelled of cool stone and old wood. I moved farther in to peer up the center column of the stairs, liking the ascending, octagonal spiral.

"I should have brought my video camera. You know all the coolest places," I said. "Are we still on the show in here?"

"Of course," he said, and pointed out a camera. "Only people who have Otis's permission can come in the tower, though."

"So you had to use your special connections."

"That's right."

Our shoes made hollow noises on the steps, and the railing was dusty under my fingertips. With each window I passed, the scene outside dropped lower. One window showed foreshortened little people between the dining hall and the student union. The next overlooked the infirmary roof. At the top, the staircase ended in an open lookout area and as I turned to meet Otis, I found he had turned one of the long-range cameras inward to aim at me. The black lens was as big as a pie plate.

"Hello," I said.

The old man shifted from behind the camera. "Forgive the overkill. I don't usually have guests," he said.

"Otis, this is my friend Rosie Sinclair," Linus said. "Otis Fairwell."

"How are you?" I asked.

"Fine, thank you," Otis said. "It's a pleasure."

He made no move to shake hands, and I wondered if he was deliberately staying off camera or if he was naturally shy. Short and thin, he was dressed in a thick camo jacket and baggy trousers. His eyes were sharp, with deep squint lines, and he wore a typical Forge earphone. A hunting cap, the same gray hue as his mustache, fit his scalp with worn familiarity.

At his feet, a sleek golden retriever panted at me and gave a thump of its tail. Its nose was gray with age.

"This here's Molly," Linus said, and crouched down to rub the dog's furry neck. "Hey, girl. Good dog."

"How old is she?" I asked.

"Fourteen," Linus said.

"She has trouble with the stairs," Otis added. "Linus carries her up and down for me. Go on, now. Admire my view."

I braced a hand on the railing and peered out. "Oh, wow."

"Nice, right?" Linus said.

The air was incredibly fresh. The land stretched away for sweeping miles all around us. Far out on the horizon, a streak of sunlight dropped down and lit up a shimmering, narrow patch of prairie green. In the other direction, to the west, black clouds piled high over a giant, slanting curtain of gray rain.

"I don't allow any other view in all of Kansas to be prettier than that there," Otis said. He flicked a match and cupped it to light a cigarette between his lips.

"Can we see your house?" I asked Linus.

He pointed toward Forgetown. "It's that gray one, the second one behind the water tower."

"With the dog house?"

"Yes, and the black shutters," he said.

"Nice," I said.

Linus smiled at me, and then turned to Otis. "Want a hand with the windows?"

"Just those six," Otis said, pointing. "Leave the other two up."

Linus reached to unhook the big windows, which swung down on their hinges, and I helped to fasten them closed. As we finished the sixth, a wash of drops darkened the sidewalks and roofs below, and the sound pelted against the glass.

"Fun," I said, laughing. "Has the tower ever been hit by lightning?"

"Thirty-three times that I've recorded," Otis said. "We've got a rod. It's safe enough, but you can feel the shake of the power, that's for sure."

I believed him. A framed photo of Otis with his arm around another man's shoulders was nailed to a post. Down a couple of steps, behind a tidy curtain, I glimpsed a little washroom with a sink. Another corner had a minifridge, a Hot Pot, and a spindly begonia. A hammock was looped on a hook.

It struck me that this was the place Linus called me from when we were talking on our walkie-hams.

"It must be nice up here at night," I said.

Linus smiled. "It is."

He came to stand beside me as we looked out one of the open windows. I bunched up the sleeves of the jacket Linus had loaned me and slid my hands into the pockets. My fingers came up against a hard ridge.

His swipe key was in the right pocket.

Excitement flared inside me before I realized I would be stealing. I had no idea how mad he would be if I took his key.

Probably very. Guilt hovered in my fingertip but I already knew what I was going to do.

A rumble of thunder shook the windows.

"Your lips are a little blue," he said. His eyes frowned while his mouth smiled. "Let's see."

I tipped my face up for his inspection and hoped he couldn't see my agitation about his swipe key. Then I felt his finger touch lightly to my lower lip.

"They don't feel cold," he said, and brought his mouth to mine.

I could never get used to kissing Linus. He was sweet and unnerving every time, especially now, when I felt a twinge of shame for what I was going to do. He shifted both his arms around me, snuggling me against him. My feet went pigeon-toed to fit between his. Where his jacket on me came open between us, the feel of him made me suck in my stomach and want to be even closer.

A discreet "ahem" alerted me to Otis standing there with his monstrous camera, not ten feet away.

"Ignore him," Linus said.

"I can't," I said, blushing.

I leaned my forehead against Linus for a moment, and then I glanced over my shoulder at the old man. "Does Linus bring all his girlfriends up here?" I asked.

"Yes," Otis said.

Surprised, I spun back to Linus.

"Are you going to explain for her, Otis?" Linus asked.

"You're doing a good enough job explaining, I guess," Otis said.

Linus kept me near. "You're the only one."

I studied him. "Really? Wait, I'm the only girlfriend you've brought here, or the only one you've had?"

"Both," he said simply.

I was still uncertain. "But you kissed somebody before. I distinctly remember you telling me that," I said. "These things matter, Linus."

Linus laughed. "She wasn't exactly a girlfriend. She was more of a neighbor, looking to practice."

I just bet she was.

"It's better practicing with you, needless to say," he added. His hand slid to my waist under the jacket, and he kissed me once more. At the next rumble of thunder, he leaned close to my ear. "Would you please stay awake tonight and call me?"

I jumped inside.

"Are you afraid of thunder?" he asked at normal volume.

"Only when it's really loud," I said, and when another crash of thunder came just then, I laughed and covered my ears.

"We should go," Linus said. "Chef Ted expects me back. Your friend's waiting for you in the library, too."

I'd forgotten about Burnham, but Linus was right.

"Thanks for having me up here," I said to Otis.

"It's funny. I've only met a handful of students over the years," he said. "I think I know you from the cameras, but it's

229

different once you know me back, even a little. Come up again anytime, with or without Linus."

His invitation surprised me. "Thanks."

Linus gave Molly another friendly petting, and we started down the stairs.

In the dimness, it was simple to move his swipe key to the pocket of my jeans. When we reached the bottom, I opened the door and paused at the prospect of all the rain, now that I was going to have to run through it.

"Otis liked you," Linus said.

"I liked him, too," I said. I slid off Linus's jacket and passed it back to him.

"No, keep it. You'll get all wet," he said.

"I'm fine. Really," I said. "You have to go to work. You don't want to be wet all night, and I can run back to my dorm and change and get my own jacket."

"That's ridiculous. I'm two paces from the dining hall."

I backed up, smiling, and stepped into the rain so I was already drenched. "Too late," I called, and I took off sprinting, with his swipe key in my pocket.

>>>>>>>>

Back in my dorm, I was able to hide Linus's swipe key under my clean sweatshirts while I was changing, and once I was in dry things, I took an umbrella and headed back to the library. Burnham had loaded all of my footage onto the computer and organized it in my editing program so I would be able to watch it efficiently. I hardly knew how to thank him.

We went over to dinner together. When we were joined by Janice, Paige, and Henrik, I liked the relaxed friendliness of our circle, especially when one of them teased me about my blip rank. It had risen into the thirties again without any special effort from them. Once, I looked up to see Linus working in the kitchen, and I felt a complicated hitch of guilt, half for him being an outsider, and half for stealing his swipe key. I didn't know when he would notice either.

Later that evening, when Orly came by with the pills, I faked swallowing mine for the first time in nearly a month. As soon as she was gone and the lights were out, I took the pill out of my cheek and put it in my pillowcase. Then I closed my hand around my walkie-ham, weighing my options.

On one hand, Linus had asked me point-blank to stay up and call him. I could picture him in the lookout tower, surrounded by Otis's gear and the stars, waiting for me to connect. The problem was, I'd stolen Linus's swipe key. He might even be in trouble for losing it. I didn't think he'd tell on me. Not at first. But I might only have one chance to use it before it was deactivated, assuming it wasn't already.

If I called Linus, I would have to admit I'd done something wrong and face his anger. I knew he'd tell me not to use the swipe key. But I had to use it. The news of Ellen's death disturbed me, and I couldn't get past the idea it might be connected to what was happening here at night.

I needed to know where they took our sleep shells. Just that much. If I could figure out that one thing and see for certain that no one was harming us, I promised myself I would let the rest of my suspicions go.

I left my walkie-ham off and tried not to think of Linus waiting futilely for my call. After midnight, when I knew that the techies would leave for the night, I quietly got up and peered out the window. All the floors of the dean's tower, including the fifth and the penthouse, were dark. The only illumination was a slight glow from the corner of the sixth floor, where I had seen Dean Berg once before.

I could only hope he'd been lulled into inattention by all my nights of obedient sleeping.

Quietly and swiftly, I pulled on my jeans and tucked in my nightie. I threw on a sweatshirt and shoved my feet into my sneakers. Grabbing Linus's swipe key and my video camera, I hurried out the door and down the stairs to the basement. I passed the elevator, and this time, when I came to the service tunnel door, I slicked Linus's pass through the crevice. The light stayed red, for locked. I turned the key over and swiped it again. The light blinked once, and then turned green.

I was in.

I gripped the handle, caught my breath, and pushed the door open.

A concrete corridor flickered to life before me as motion-detector lights came on above. They buzzed faintly. Gray paint was chipping from the walls, but the floor was smoothly swept, and the cool, musty air held a familiar hint of ammonia.

The door closed behind me with a click. I checked quickly for cameras, but the walls and ceiling had none. I was offstage, invisible, and that alone was worth a smile. I hurried until I came to an intersection of more corridors. The three new hallways all led toward darkness, and no signs gave any directions. Behind me, my corridor was going dim as the lights turned off, one by one.

The last light above me went off, plunging me into darkness, and as my other senses sharpened, the combination of mustiness and ammonia brought me an odd awareness: I'd been here before. This scent had penetrated my sleep, which meant I'd been wheeled this way before, in my sleep shell.

I waved a hand to make the lights go on again, and trusting instinct, I turned right. Lights kept coming on above me, and soon the next corridor ended at another steel door. I put my ear to the cool metal, hearing silence. Then I turned the handle and pushed.

I'd arrived in a wood-paneled hallway, with an elevator, a staircase leading up, a set of bathrooms, and a couple of empty vending machines. I checked quickly for camera buttons and found none, which meant I was still offstage. But where?

The elevator dinged.

I bolted back. As the doors whooshed open, I squeezed behind the nearest vending machine.

"Don't mention it," a woman said. She had a crackly, high voice. "I don't mind waiting. It's better than walking back with you-know-who. Good gracious. Would you believe it? Still?"

A bang came against the vending machine and I jumped out of my skin.

"I don't know why we even try," said a second voice. "They never fill these machines. Why do they even have them if they never fill them up?"

"I have to use the can before we go. Coming?" the first voice said.

"This has been the longest day."

A door was opened, and their voices receded into the echoey space of the bathroom. I squeezed sideways a little farther behind the vending machine and tried to peer down past my shoulder so I wouldn't bump into a plug and electrocute myself. The two vending machines were side by side, presenting a united front, but the second machine was farther away from the wall, concealing a narrow, upright space in the corner of the room. Not counting a furry layer of dust, it was the perfect place to hide.

As I slid in farther, my hip bumped against a ridge in the wall. I squirmed to see it was a hinge, and upon close examination, I found the outline of a door cut in the wooden paneling. An unused, secret door was hidden behind the snack machines. It had no handle or keyhole. Intrigued, I pushed the door, and then I palpitated it to see if it would open on a bounce, but it didn't move.

I turned on my video camera to capture what I could of the door.

Then voices came out of the bathroom again, and I held still, listening. The women were moving toward the elevator.

"Did you hear what Bones said to me today?" asked the high, crackly voice. "My boy Burnham was finally talking to Rosie again and I was like, yes! He always gets a spike when he's talking to her, though honestly, I couldn't say why. Her rank's always lower than Burnham's. Bones says that's not his fault."

I listened, curious. The woman with the high voice was evidently Burnham's techie. Bones, I knew, was mine. It seemed like the techies competed.

"I don't want to talk about Bones. He exhausts me," said the other woman.

"I know, right? Anyway. Bones was totally hogging the best angles for his feed on Rosie, and when I told him, quite nicely I might add, that it's okay to share, you know what he said?"

A ding came from the elevator, and I could hear them moving inside. The crackly voiced woman continued: "He said, and I quote, 'greatness isn't made by sharing.' "

Their voices were sealed off by the elevator doors.

I sucked in my belly and squeezed past the first vending machine once more to get out. Considering what I had overheard, I suspected I had arrived in the dean's tower as the last techies were leaving, but this seemed like an unlikely place for anyone to bring our sleep shells.

I knew one person who would have answers. A flicker of fear made me pause, but not for long. I would be careful. I just wanted to see what the dean was doing on the sixth floor. Just for a minute.

I headed up the stairs as silently as I could. One flight up, the stairwell met a big, shadowed foyer. The marble floor shone slick and cold, while above, a shallow, gold-leafed dome in the ceiling was artfully lit. I held back, wary of cameras, and took again to the stairs. The upper stairwell was dark, lit only by EXIT signs. Each floor had a big number painted on its door—3, 4, 5—and when I reached the sixth floor, I paused, staring at the door handle until my breathing slowed. Then I silently pulled the door back a sliver, just enough to see through with one eye.

A big, dim room spanned the entire floor. Deserted desks descended from a central platform in semicircular rows, and along with their large computer screens, they were cluttered with coffee cups, snacks, spider plants, and blankets, as if people practically lived at their workstations. I slipped through the door and closed it noiselessly behind me. Then I dropped to all fours and crept to the aisle to see better.

Far in the lower right corner, close to the windows, a motionless man sat with his back to me, facing a panel of screens: Dean Berg. He was tilted back in a swivel chair while before him, four different scenes were playing simultaneously. No sound came from the speakers, and the screens were too small for me to see any details.

"No, that's not it. The wings were a deeper purple," Dean Berg said clearly.

It took me a sec to realize he must have someone on his earphone. When he spoke again, I crept behind a row of desks and down a step. I pulled up my video camera, and then hesitated. Clicking open the shutter would make a noise I couldn't afford. Uncertain, I lowered it to watch again.

"It's all right," Dean Berg said. "You'll get it. Let me show you again. Synch for me."

He reached forward, and a device the size of a hockey puck shot a narrow beam of light into the air. The light fanned out into a conical shape to make a 3-D field, and inside it, a human body appeared lying lengthwise on an examination surface, in full size and color, but faintly transparent and luminous, like a ghost. It was a young boy, about ten years old. He was sleeping, laid out in a pair of boxers. He flickered once, and then came into sharper focus.

"Cortex," Dean Berg said.

The boy grew so that his body slid out of the frame and his magnified head filled it. Then the visual probe zoomed inside his skull, revealing the cauliflower-like substance of his brain.

"Thalamus. Find the fourth ventricle, and shift to the pons," Dean Berg said. The imaging moved lower and deeper, to a dense shape. "Mag one hundred," he said, and then repeated: "Mag one hundred. You with me, Glyde? How's the acetylcholine level?"

The image zoomed in farther, until the 3-D screen was filled with gray and blue pulsing shapes. I had looked through a microscope at the cells of a leaf once in eighth grade, but this was completely different, like an organic, deep sea city at night, with traffic flowing through streams of liquid light.

"Mag ten," Dean Berg said. "Now wait. Cross-check with the optic tract." He raised his pencil and touched the tip of it to the image. "You see here?" A tiny swarm of white beads flowed into the area he was touching and remained there as he sat back again. "No, don't mine it now. Just observe. Let them settle. It's always better to take your time."

He touched the projector puck again, and a new screen shot up. It expanded virtually to create a second 3-D screen, and after several flickers, streams of reds, yellows, and blues ordered themselves into a brilliant, birdlike creature. I sucked in my breath, fascinated. The bird flew swiftly over a polka dot sea, near to the waves, and then banked to soar upward into the air. It tipped its wings in golden sunlight, and arched them wide in a great, graceful curve of flight.

"Right. Now mine," Dean Berg said quietly. "That's good stuff."

The creature careened back toward a cliff, skimming so close I could see the rippled shadow of its wings on the rock. A feather tore free, and then another, but instead of falling away, the feathers transformed into two more birds. The original one splintered into thousands of exquisite bits and each of those went spinning into a new piece of flight to glide and soar in the sunlight. Like snow on fire. Like something I'd never seen. Never imagined.

Who was this boy? How did he have such incredible things in his head?

"Hold on, Glyde. I have a call coming in," Dean Berg said. "Can you take it from here? Thanks."

He leaned forward and swiped his touch screen.

"Sandy here," he said. He dragged a hand slowly around his jaw. "You do know what time it is here. I haven't shaved." He sat up abruptly, straightened his jacket, and ran a hand back through his hair. Then he touched the little puck projector, and both 3-D screens vanished. "All right. Of course," he said, and touched his screen again.

A woman appeared in a chat screen before Dean Berg, with a mini window of Dean Berg in the corner. She stood on an outdoor balcony, with a snow-capped mountain in the distance behind her, but she was in shirtsleeves and sunglasses, as if she were warm. Black, loose hair framed her paper white face, and deep red lipstick delineated her mouth. Her voice had a lilting accent even when her tone was dry, and I recognized her immediately as the woman I'd overheard him talking with before. What had he called her?

"Working late again?" she asked. Her voice came clearly over a speaker, and then I remembered: her name was Huma.

"I was just heading up to bed. What can I do for you?" Dean Berg said.

"I was expecting more of the Sinclair Fifteen."

"I told you," the dean said. "It's too soon to mine her again. She's fragile."

"Her episode in the observatory was weeks ago, Sandy. I can see for myself she's perfectly fine," she said.

"It's too soon," he repeated.

"I know what you're doing," she said slowly. "You're seeding her, aren't you? That's why you won't mine her for me. I bet you even gave her something about the observatory or Clarence."

"Wrong. It was just stuffy in there. She was dehydrated," Dean Berg said.

The woman shook her head and pointed a finger at him. "You're a good liar, but you forget one thing."

"What's that?"

"I know you. I know how your crafty old mind works."

"Now I'm frightened," Dean Berg said, sounding amused. "Is there another purpose to this call?"

"I want to know if you've banked any astrocytes from Dolan Forty-Seven."

"I can get you those."

"Good. And the Radlewski Twelve?"

"She's almost tapped out, but I can get you a little more," Dean Berg said. "I'll send out a truck tomorrow night. Will that do?"

Huma smiled, and the image of her flickered again. "Of course," she said. "When are you coming to visit Iceland again, Sandy? Bring those lovely twins of yours and we'll take them hiking. How old are they now?"

"Eighteen."

"So old already?"

Their talk shifted to colleges, and I started backing up toward the door.

"Listen, I should really let you go," Dean Berg said. "Give my love to Ivan."

Huma put her palms together. "I will. Always a pleasure talking to you. Bless bless."

Dean Berg leaned forward to touch his computer, and his second screen brought up a view of two dozen sleep shells in a long, dark room. With a pinch of fear, I recognized the dorm room as my own. I shifted backward, clunking softly into a recycling bin. I froze.

"Glyde?" the dean said. He touched a hand to his earphone. "You there? We have a little problem. Rosie's missing."

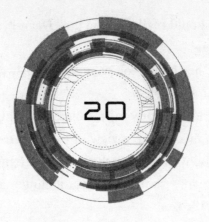

20

THE CAT GUILLOTINE

"LET'S GET YOU back up on the surface. I'd rather not get security involved unless we have to. Most likely she's just in the attic again and I'll see her when she moves. How much longer do you need with the Feinberg Ten?" Dean Berg asked.

I went up the step and crawled behind the row of desks, toward the door.

"No. That's not going to work," the dean said. "She can't be far. Check the last time Linus swiped in. I thought he was too smart to meet her, but you never can tell. Jerry? Can you get on this?"

I was silently opening the door when it hit me what he meant about Linus swiping in. Since I had used Linus's swipe key, they would mistakenly believe that he was on campus. I was bringing trouble to him, too. I should have thought of that earlier.

"I know. She'll be amped up on adrenaline," he said. "Are you up for another prep?"

My veins chilled. He was talking about me. About a prep involving me. I was nothing more than a rat running a maze for him.

I closed the door with the slightest click, and then I flew down the stairs. I rapid-fired my feet down each tread, and spun around the banister at each landing. All I could think was that I had to get away so he would never guess that I'd overheard him. I flew down past the floor numbers: 4, 3, 2. When I reached the basement, I bolted past the empty snack machines, swiped Linus's key in the lock to the service tunnel, and darted inside.

The lights came on as I ran wildly down the corridor. "First left," I whispered to myself. I skidded around the corner. The distances felt shorter, now that I knew where I was going, and soon I was back in the basement of my dorm. The darkness stayed dark and the air had the comforting smell of laundry detergent.

I stopped a second in a dark corner, far from an EXIT light. Uncertain, and half-panicked, I tried to think. I could leave right now. I could run out the door and sprint for Forgetown and beg Linus and Otis to help me get back home. I could go to the attic and move around there so the dean would see me and maybe believe that was the farthest I'd gone from my bed.

What I couldn't do was stay in that dark corner, wasting precious seconds. My gaze landed on the laundry machines. Quickly, I stripped off my jeans, sweatshirt, and sneakers, and crammed them in a dryer. I threw in my video camera, too, and shut the dryer door. Then, in just my nightie, I bolted up the stairs. I tried to stay quiet and close to the darkest shadows. When I reached the fourth floor, I took a deep, calming breath.

Then I pushed into the bathroom and deliberately turned on the light. I blinked slowly, faking sleepiness, and scratched at my back. Then I went into a stall, used the toilet, and came out again as if I had nothing on my mind. No hurry. No concerns. Sure, I was out of bed, but otherwise, this girl had nothing to hide. I flipped off the light and went back to the dorm room.

Moments later, I was back in my sleep shell, tucked beneath my quilt. My heart would not quiet down. Thirst dried my throat, and I couldn't do anything about it except lick my teeth and try to work up some saliva. I didn't dare reach for my walkie-ham.

The dean wanted me for a prep. A prep!

Another minute went by, and the quiet of the dorm stretched out, but I was still tense with fear. The dean wasn't going to believe I'd only gone to the bathroom, not once he checked the swipe lock records for Linus's key. Stupid! I should have left while I could.

And then it hit me. The dean didn't care that I'd left my bed. He had barely been concerned when he saw that I was missing because he was completely confident he could control the situation. In fact, it was perfectly possible that he *wanted* me skipping my pill and *wanted* me getting out of bed.

A soft humming noise started near my head. Startled, I

listened, unsure what it could be. I peeked past the edge of my quilt just as the lid to my sleep shell finished closing, automatically. It had never done that before. My heart ticked in new alarm. Then I heard a soft hissing noise, and a dry, cool smell filled my sleep shell. I panicked. I held my breath and clawed at the lid, trying to push it open. The lid stayed shut. I scrambled under my pillow for my walkie-ham and turned it on.

I had to take a gulp of air, but it was wrongly sweet, like butterscotch. "Linus!" I said.

I yanked at the lid again and banged the glass with my walkie-ham. I tried not to breathe, but my lungs were starved and bursting. My fingers grew weak. I had to breathe in the gas. My panic turned to despair, and then loss, until I collapsed backward, asleep.

>>>>>>>>

I'm slicing off the tail of a tabby cat with a hand-sized guillotine, slowly and mercilessly, while the cat screams and tries to scrape itself away from the blade. I can see the fur of its tail, the angled blade catching and cutting into the blood. I can hear the helpless screaming as the cat scrabbles its feet, trying to run. I feel the pressure of my hand bearing down, and at the same time, I'm straining to get away from the cat's pain, but above all, I am the torturer, and my shame is exquisite.

I woke in a sweat and bolted up in bed, banging into the lid of my sleep shell. I gasped for air and shakily pushed at the lid to slide it back. This time, the lid opened, but my fear

245

was still as real as the dorm room at Forge. It was as real as the early morning light falling in the windows.

Don't hate me, Rosie, said a soft inner voice.

I held perfectly still.

I'd just heard a voice in my head. But that wasn't possible.

I set my fingers lightly on my knees and stared at my quilt. From the other end of the room came the airy drone of a blow dryer.

Close your eyes, said the voice.

No, I said back, speaking in my mind. *Who are you? Get out of my head.*

Whoever it was slid a little closer, a real presence in my mind, just beyond my sight. She stirred softly, like a single leaf turning over.

It's easier if you close your eyes, she said.

"Stop," I said aloud.

She rustled and slipped away, leaving me sweating and shaken. My mind was splintering apart. That realization was even more terrifying than the thought that Dr. Ash and the dean had rifled through my brain last night. Seeding. Mining. Whatever they did to me, was this voice a side effect?

I leaned close to inspect the edges of my sleep shell. Tiny vents rimmed the upper lip, and while I'd always figured that they were used for ventilation, now I saw that they could be used just as easily to fill my sleep shell with gas. The dean didn't even need to bother with sleeping pills when he could drug us with gas whenever he wanted.

How he could he get away with it, I didn't know. I ran my

hands quickly around the edges of my mattress and found my walkie-ham in the crevice. They'd left it for me, inexplicably. Unless they still didn't know about it. Faking nonchalance, I hid it again in my backpack.

I needed to think clearly and figure out a plan, but as I cleaned up and dressed, I couldn't settle. I dropped my toothbrush, twice. The torture of the cat still grated in me like a warning. I had too much I didn't understand. The crazier the things were that I was discovering, the more impossible it was going to be to convince anyone that they were true. My parents would be the most incredulous of all.

"Get a grip," I said to my scraggly self in the mirror.

Half a dozen other girls in the bathroom passed behind and around me like butterflies, completely unaware that a black hole had opened to consume their planet. Paige had a hefty, I ♥ TEXAS cosmetic bag on the ledge over the sinks. She leaned close to the mirror, her mouth slack, as she painstakingly outlined her eyes in black.

My gaze caught hers briefly in the glass.

"Lighten up," she said, and she kept working her liner. "You're on *The Forge Show*."

She was right. Until I decided what to do, I couldn't show how distraught I was inside. I spat in the sink and rinsed my mouth. "Right," I said.

I took a few clothes down to the laundry, and in the process, I managed to bring my things from the dryer back up to my wardrobe. I was relieved to see my video camera was fine. The footage of the hidden door was intact, but since all it proved was that I'd been in the dean's tower when I wasn't supposed to be there, I deleted it.

When I went over to the dining hall for breakfast, Linus was back in the kitchen measuring coffee into a machine. It took a second to remember that the last time the viewers had seen us together, at the lookout tower the day before, we'd been kissing and happy. My heart shrank at the prospect of trying to act like nothing was wrong between us.

I joined the line and moved my tray down the counter. Across the distance, Linus met my gaze coolly. I knew, instantly, that something bad had come from me stealing his swipe key. He snapped the coffeemaker lid closed, and a few minutes later, as I finished filling my tray, he strode over, wiping his hands on a towel.

His mouth smiled, but his eyes were hard. "Hey, Sinclair," he said. "Wise choice on the cinnamon bun."

I hadn't even noticed picking it out. He made no move to close in for a hug or kiss, and I was alarmed that he was going to give something away. Other students flowed around us as if we were two inconvenient rocks in a stream.

"How was your night?" I asked, smiling with an effort.

"Funny you should ask," he said. "I wrote you a poem in my spare time, actually. I had nothing better to do."

Ouch.

"Really?" I said. "I didn't know you were a poet."

"Neither did I," he said.

"Nobody's ever written me a poem before," I said. "Thanks."

"It's not a sonnet or anything," he said. "Then again, it's honest. I know how you appreciate honesty." He dug a small, folded piece of paper out of his pocket. "Don't read it until you're alone."

"Linus," I began. I didn't know how to apologize in front of the cameras.

"Yes?"

I shifted my tray to balance it on one arm so I could take his poem and slide it in my pocket. "Does your poem rhyme?" I asked.

"Should it?" he asked.

I gripped my tray with both hands again. "Not if it's in free verse."

"I guess you'd know more about that than I would," he said. "You've had more schooling."

This was only getting worse. "Listen, do you want to do something later?" I asked.

"Sure. When?"

"I'll come find you after my practicum," I said. "Do you have a break then?"

"I'm helping Otis this afternoon," he said.

I couldn't tell if he was telling the truth, or if he just didn't want to see me. "Maybe later, then?" I said.

"Linus! Are you working here or what?" Chef Ted called.

"Sure," Linus said to me. "See you." He leaned deliberately across my tray and kissed me, hard.

The kiss felt like a favor, a sham to appease the cameras. It was worse than a punch in the gut.

As soon as I could, I ducked into the girls' room and hid in a stall.

Linus's poem was not a poem.

Rosie, I know you took my swipe key. Berg asked me if I gave it to you so we could meet up last night and I told him yes. But then he said you swiped out of the dean's tower and I didn't know what to say. The <u>dean's tower</u>? <u>WHAT</u>?!

You stole from me. I tried to lie for you and it didn't work. Berg told Otis and now Otis is furious. He doesn't want me to have anything to do with you. Berg's letting me keep my job, but he's watching us both.

What do you think you're doing? Why didn't you call me? It's not like you were <u>sleeping</u>. Do you even <u>have</u> your walky-ham anymore?

Don't bother trying to use the swipe key again. It's been deactivated.

I don't know what's going on, but if you're not going to trust me or talk to me, what's the point? Find some excuse to break up with me on camera if you want. I don't care what it is. I'll go along.

I clutched his note to my chest and squeezed my eyes tight. *What's the point?* That killed me. I opened my eyes to read it again, and I could see his anger and disappointment in every sentence. And yet despite everything, he still offered to have a break-up scene with me on camera so our night relationship wouldn't have to come out. He was still protecting me.

I ripped the letter in pieces and flushed them down the toilet.

Somehow, even though I felt both like howling in agony and snarling in my cage, when I walked out of the bathroom stall, I was going to have to pretend I'd just read a love poem. I let out a strangled laugh and blinked hard up at the ceiling.

No. I could do this. I just had to compartmentalize mentally. As long as I didn't have to see him, I would be okay. Forget that he'd be able to watch my feed.

I made myself a promise. It helped me calm down. I would call him that night, no matter what. He had to answer. He had to listen. I would apologize and explain and somehow make him realize that there was, actually, a point.

Until then, I couldn't think of Linus at all.

>>>>>>>>

In Media Convergence, I sat down beside Janice and asked if I could use her phone.

"Sure. What for?" she asked, pulling it out of her bag. "You texting Linus?"

I didn't even have his number.

"I might," I lied.

"I heard he's in trouble," Janice said.

"What do you mean? Who said that?"

"That's just what I heard. Is it true? Like he might get fired?"

251

"No," I said. "Everything's fine."

She nodded at the phone. "Tell me if you find out anything."

I curled up on one of the couches and put my feet on the coffee table. The Forge cameras would see me using her phone, but they couldn't pick up what I was looking for as long as I kept the little screen close. I slumped down, propped my chin in my hand, tuned out the noise of Ping-Pong, and peered down at the screen.

I had little to go on from Dean Berg, but Huma had mentioned Iceland. I tried searching for info on Huma at a hospital or clinic in Iceland. Nothing came up. I tried dream mining and seeding, but there was nothing that looked legit. A couple detours on dreaming brought me to a site about dolphins. They had two brains, apparently, one that stayed awake while the other slept, and this helped protect them from predators.

I wished I had one of those dolphin brains. Half of me would always be awake, vigilantly watching.

I tried to think what else I knew about Huma. She was rich, obviously. She had a husband and kids. She sounded like she and Dean Berg went back a long time, and she had an interest in the school. I checked the donors who gave to the Forge School, and by scanning the annual reports, I discovered a Humaline Fallon who gave in the Guardian's Circle, the highest class of donors.

I had a name.

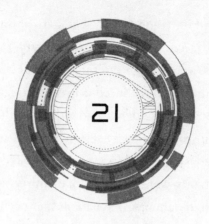

CHIMERA

A PING-PONG BALL came rolling over by my feet, and Henrik followed.

"Want to come play?" he asked.

"No, I'm good." I reached down for the ball and tossed it back to him. I glanced toward the green table and saw his opponent was Janice. Mr. DeCoster, as usual, had his feet up in the corner, and most of the other students were at the computers. Burnham was gnawing at the end of a pencil as he stared at his screen.

I hunched over Janice's phone again.

With a full name to go on, it wasn't hard for me to trace Humaline Fallon to a site for the Chimera Centre, a small hospital and rehabilitation clinic on a private island south of

Reykjavik. Dr. Humaline Fallon was part of a team running clinical trials for a new kind of brain surgery.

I scrolled down through the tiny print. In cautiously optimistic terms, the site introduced a breakthrough, experimental surgery for coma patients and others with severe brain trauma. The hospital was very selective about which patients it took on. They specialized in cases that looked hopeless, but where the patients were younger than thirty and where the accident that had damaged the patient had occurred less than a year previously.

It didn't look like a scam, but it didn't look exactly credible to me, either, especially when it said they sometimes saw results in as soon as forty-eight hours after surgery. That statement alone made me suspect they were feeding on the hopes of coma patients' families. But video footage also showed a towheaded kid with dark-rimmed eyes in a hospital bed. A mini Patriots football was propped next to his elbow. He turned his face slowly to gaze at an older woman, and when he reached a feeble hand toward her, she beamed and cried.

It choked me up.

"What's Linus say?" Janice asked, plopping down beside me on the couch.

"Nothing," I said. I hoped he wasn't watching and thinking I was trying to reach him. "Do you need this back?"

"No, that's okay. You want a turn?" she asked, offering her Ping-Pong paddle.

"Not really."

"Good, because I'm on a winning streak," she said and headed back.

I went back to the Chimera site. In another video, a colorful image of a brain swiveled before a black background. Different sections lit up while an authoritative bass voice chimed in: "Each patient brings a unique case, with its own special challenges. In Kevin's case, his injury occurred deep in the brain stem, impeding motor, memory, and linguistic capabilities. To begin his recovery, Dr. Fallon guides an optical tweezers to certain precise points in Kevin's brain, where the worst damage is located. The laser light at the end of the optical tweezers is tiny, and the doctor can move it so slowly and carefully it doesn't cut anything unless she wants it to. It's delicate in the extreme. Sealing off the so-called dead edges or vulnerable fog can take up to twenty hours. In Kevin's case, it was fourteen."

The shot moved in closer, reminding me of the virtual surgery I'd watched in Dean Berg's office the night before. The voice continued, and colorful computer graphics illustrated his words.

"With nanobots, Dr. Fallon delivers tiny nuggets of regenerative stem cell patch to the most promising places. Then she captures the wave pattern of the surrounding synapses, and sends that same wave pattern into the new nuggets. Before long, the new patches start learning, so to speak, from the circuits around them. They essentially regrow the tiny circuits of the brain."

I watched little wispy tendrils of light spread out in a dark zone, as if someone were drawing dot-to-dots in a galaxy of stars.

In the next video, a young man in a lab coat strolled slowly down a gallery of gilt-framed paintings. "Think of a memory like a pointillist painting, one of those classic Seurat pictures made up of thousands of colored dots," he said. The camera focused on a picture of a garden scene. "Stand back, and you can see the subjects of the painting, the people or the trees or the landscape. You consciously remember such a subject as a dear friend or a favorite holiday at the beach. But step in close, and you don't have enough dots to make the picture clear."

The man moved out on a terrace with a sweeping view of the ocean behind him. "Each dot is a synaptic pattern. Some of our patients have lost the dots," he continued. "They've lost so many dots that whole paintings are missing. But if Dr. Fallon can salvage enough original dots and provide the mind with a new canvas, we can get a pale version of the original painting. And it's alive. Give the painting time, and the dots will fill in the gaps between them. They grow and duplicate, filling in the damaged area."

It was an amazing concept. I wanted more.

"We can't promise anything," the man went on. "At best, it won't be the same painting, the same memory. But the memories will be close. With a successful surgery, the patient will recognize his family and, more important, recognize himself. He can relearn enough of the rest. He has a chance to go forward. Once we essentially reboot the subconscious, the rest can follow."

The video ended, and I went back to watch it again. I

knew the business about rebooting the subconscious was important, but I also knew something was missing. The doctor made no explanation of where the "regenerative stem cell patch" came from. But I knew. I had watched while Dr. Ash had sent those little white circles to cluster around a certain point in that kid's brain last night. She had been taking synaptic patterns, dots that knew how to connect to each other.

They're mining dreams, said a faint voice inside me.

This time, the voice didn't frighten me because I knew it spoke the truth. Slowly, I reached to turn off Janice's phone.

Exactly, I thought back.

Having more information didn't make my decision any easier. If anything, it complicated it. Suppose it turned out that Dean Berg truly was the diabolical evil genius I thought he was, with Dr. Ash as his sidekick. I didn't get why nobody else had discovered them yet. Then again, I still didn't have any real proof that he was harming the students at Forge. I knew for certain that I'd been gassed in my sleep shell, but in a twisted way, that was a logical consequence for skipping my pill.

I still didn't know what to do. Until I did, I had to stick to my normal routine and try to pretend I was fine for the cameras.

>>>>>>>>

Later that Wednesday, after my practicum, I was coming back from a run when I caught up to Burnham outside the pool house.

257

"Hey," I said. "How's it going?" Only after I spoke did I notice he was texting.

He glanced up absently. "One sec. Let me finish this."

With his black sweats riding low on his hips, a blue swimsuit showed below his sweatshirt, and swim goggles were strapped loosely around his neck. I went up a step so he wouldn't be so much taller than me, and pulled my sweatshirt sleeves down over my hands. It was a sunny but brisk afternoon, and the coolness felt nice against my warm cheeks and neck.

"Sorry," he said, putting his phone in his pocket. "What's up?"

"Nothing. Is everything okay?"

"Just family stuff. You know," he said. He rubbed at the back of his head. "Did you need help with your footage?"

"I don't only talk to you when I need your help," I said, smiling.

"But I like to help. Your ghosts are a challenge. I was thinking of taking another look back through your footage, if you don't mind."

"Not at all. Knock yourself out." I liked that he was interested in spying on the campus, too.

He crossed his arms over his chest and did the double jerk with his thumb, indicating the cameras. "Will you do me a favor?"

"Sure. What?"

"Say hi to my mom. She's watching right now. She's a fan of yours."

Really? I thought. I located a little camera button on the nearest lamppost. Then I smiled and did a lame wave. "Hi, Burnham's mom?"

Burnham laughed. "That was perfect." He tugged idly at his goggles, his smile fading.

"You sure you're all right?" I asked. "You seem a little, I don't know, constipated."

He laughed. "Good one."

"But really."

He aimed his gaze toward the horizon. "I don't know," he said. "My family does this group text thing. It's the anniversary of my grandfather's death. We're all thinking about him."

"I'm sorry," I said.

"It's okay." He bounced the toe of his sneaker against the step I was standing on.

"Is your family close?" I asked.

"Yes."

"You have an older brother, right?" I asked.

He nodded. "Yes, Sid. He quit Harvard Medical School to work at Fister," Burnham said. "And I have a sister. Sammi. She's the oldest. She's a civil rights lawyer in Washington."

"That's cool."

"It is," he said. "Except she hates that I came here. This place is the opposite of everything she believes in, like privacy."

A couple of guys jogged down the steps and passed us, while for a moment, the hollow noise and humid air of the pool wafted out the door behind them.

"But you said your brother came here, too," I said.

"Yes, but I'm her *baby* brother. My sister thought she'd taught me better." Burnham absently turned his watch on his wrist, and I suddenly guessed why the old-fashioned piece might matter to him.

"That's your grandfather's watch, isn't it?" I said.

Burnham lifted his wrist briefly. "Yes," he said, and didn't elaborate.

I thought I got it. It had to be kind of weird for him, talking about his grandfather here, with his mom and everyone else watching. He looked like he needed a hug, but I wasn't sure if I was the right person to give it to him.

"It's a cool watch," I said. "It works, doesn't it?"

He laughed. "Yes, surprisingly."

"I'm glad."

He adjusted his glasses and regarded me for a long moment, considering. Then he said, "My grandpa was a great guy. He died eight years ago. When he got lung cancer, he moved in with us so my mom could keep an eye on him. He called me 'Partner,' like we were cowboys."

"Partner," I echoed. Burnham must have been a little kid back then, near to Dubbs's age.

"Yeah, but he drawled it, like a bad western cowboy. Pahtnuh." Burnham tucked his hair behind his ears and settled his foot on the step, leaning into it a little, to stretch. "One night, when my parents were out, Grandpa asked me to bring him a bottle of pills from the medicine cabinet." He shrugged. "I didn't think twice about it. I just did what he asked. I was proud I could read the long words on the labels and find the right bottle on the first try, way up at the top."

Burnham leaned more deeply over his knee. When he didn't go on, I imagined this chubby, helpful kid bringing a bottle of pills to his sick, weak, bedridden, old grandfather.

"Oh, no," I said.

From the other end of the quad, the clock tower bonged the quarter hour.

Burnham straightened up, frowning. "Grandpa was a pharmacist," he said. "He knew exactly what he was doing. My mom found him later that night, after she came home."

"I'm so sorry," I said.

Burnham looked up toward the sky. "The weird thing is, each year, I understand a little better what he asked me to do."

"You were just a kid," I said. "You didn't know."

"Didn't I?" he asked. "Didn't I sort of suspect? That's what I can't quite remember."

"Burnham, you can't blame yourself," I said. "He made the choice, not you."

He shook his head slightly. "You should have seen my mother's face when she put it together that I was the one who got him the pills." He cracked out a laugh. "And now I've said all this in public. Who am I punishing now?"

His phone buzzed in his pocket. He didn't move to answer it.

"I'm so sorry, Burnham," I said.

His gaze, lonely and pained, met mine for an instant before

he turned away. "Anyways," he said, but didn't continue. His phone buzzed insistently, but he still didn't answer it.

I came down a step, and reached awkwardly to give him a hug. "You're still a good person," I said.

"Am I?"

I gave his arms a little shake. "Of course you are."

He smiled tightly, withdrawing from me. "Thanks. I'm going to go dive."

"Good idea."

But he hovered another moment, like he wasn't quite ready to go. A breeze whipped around us, and I dipped my knees as I shivered briefly. We stood there, not speaking, not even looking at each other. I could hear his phone start up again in his pocket.

"Right," he said finally. "I'll see you around. Thanks."

"Of course," I said, and I watched him take the steps two at a time and disappear into the pool building.

>>>>>>>>>

I headed slowly back to the dorm. I hoped, when Burnham talked to his parents, that they would be understanding. I felt sort of honored that he'd confided in me, and uneasy for him, too. I wouldn't have had the guts to tell such a personal story on camera. And that thing he'd said about punishing somebody. I couldn't tell if that was supposed to be his family or himself.

As the hours brought me closer to bedtime, my anxiety

kicked in again. My stomach churned too much for me to try to eat. Or maybe I didn't want to risk running into Linus in the dining hall. Instead, I curled up on my chair in the dorm and pulled out my video camera from home. I had locked some old footage of Dubbs in the memory, and I flipped to it now. Watching her bright face brought me some comfort, and I was able to smile a little.

Later that night, when we were all tucked in our sleep shells and the dorm was quiet, I dialed my walkie-ham to channel four and listened for the static noise to change. Every half hour, I pushed the call button. It was after midnight, finally, when I heard the static go brighter.

"Linus?" I whispered.

"I'm here," he said quietly.

"I read your letter," I said.

"So I gather. I noticed you didn't come break up with me, so that's something."

I rolled to face the direction of the door in case anyone came in, and tucked the little box of the walkie-ham under my ear, where it couldn't be seen.

"Where are you?" I asked. As usual, I kept my voice just barely audible.

"The lookout tower again. I borrowed Otis's keys. He's still not happy with me, but he says I have to make my own stupid mistakes."

I supposed that was a good thing. Sort of.

"I'm sorry about stealing your swipe key," I said.

"You could have asked me for it," he said.

"Would you have given it to me?"

"I don't know, honestly," he said. "Now neither of us has it. I've been restricted to the public doors like a new employee again. What were you doing in the dean's tower last night, anyway?"

"I snuck up to the sixth floor," I said. "You'll never believe what I saw."

"Try me."

As I tried to explain, I wasn't even certain how to put it all into words. I talked through the whole thing, from when I left my sleep shell until I returned. "I *saw* the virtual operation," I added. "Somewhere nearby, Dr. Ash was operating on the kid."

"Are you sure it wasn't a recording of a surgery?" Linus asked.

"It wasn't. It was happening live," I said. "She was doing what Dean Berg told her to do, like he was teaching her."

"And why do you think she was mining the boy?" Linus asked. "Because of the white circles? Did they actually use the word 'mining'?"

I had to think. Huma had talked about mining and seeding, but that might have been during the earlier conversation I overheard. All day, I had thought talking to Linus would make this problem easier, but his questions were making it worse.

"What's it matter what they called it? What else could it be?" I asked.

"To be honest, I don't know what to think," he said. "I'm

sorry to say it, but it sounds a lot like you had a nightmare. The whole thing, the tunnel and everything. Isn't that at least possible?"

I was insulted. And hurt.

"It was no nightmare," I said. "I looked up Huma Fallon online, and she's part of a clinic in Iceland that does brain surgeries on coma patients. She and Dean Berg talked like he's been supplying her with something medical that she needs, and I think it has to be dreams. The medical version of dreams. And you know what really freaks me out?" I swallowed, licking my lips. I made sure to keep my voice down. "Dean Berg knew I was out of my sleep shell, and he hardly cared at all. When I came back to bed, they released a gas into my shell that knocked me out. I think they mined me, too."

"Last night?"

"Yes."

"How can you tell?" Linus asked.

I wanted to tell him about the voice, but I was afraid he would just think I was going mad. "I feel different to myself," I said. "Like the core of me doesn't line up straight anymore. Like it might be a relief to do something crazy."

In the silence on his end, I could hear Linus doubting me.

"You're not believing one word I'm saying," I said.

"I'm just trying to think," Linus said. "I'm trying to put it together."

"I'm telling you the truth," I said. "Every word."

"I hear you," he said. "I'm just wondering if it might be related to something else I found out."

"What?"

"This is why I wanted you to call me Tuesday," he said. His voice turned ironic. "Before you stole my swipe key."

"I'm sorry. You know I never wanted to get you in trouble," I said. "Tell me."

"There was a guy who came through town Monday night," Linus said. "He's this truck driver named Amby from St. Louis. He has a refrigerated truck and he delivers ice cream for the Forge dairy here sometimes. It turns out he also makes deliveries for a pre-morgue."

"What's that?" I asked.

"You know, if you're an organ donor at the hospital and you're dead, they harvest out your eyes or your heart or whatever," he said. "This one pre-morgue in St. Louis realized it's better to ship the organs *in situ*, and let the doctors harvest them at the other end right before they implant them in the new patient."

"Does *in situ* mean what I think?" I asked.

"They ship the donors' bodies intact," he explained. "Instead of sending a heart on ice, they super-oxygenate the whole body, send it on ice, and take the heart out once it arrives."

I tried to grasp the concept of a whole body on ice. Transporting it would be costly and cumbersome.

"Okay, this is grossing me out," I said. I hardly knew where to begin with my questions. "Are you saying Amby delivers bodies in his ice cream truck?"

"I know. It's weird," Linus said. "I just found out about this two days ago. Parker said something about Amby's night job, and it seemed too strange, so I looked into it."

"Wait. Are you saying this guy Amby delivers bodies to Forgetown?"

"I think he might deliver them to the school," Linus said.

22

ROXANNE

"THE FORGE SCHOOL?" I asked.

"Yes," Linus said. "I saw his truck behind the dining hall at two in the morning, but there's no new ice cream in the freezer, and Chef Ted didn't know anything about a delivery."

"Do you think Amby delivered the boy that Dr. Ash was operating on?" I asked.

"That's what I'm wondering," Linus said.

He didn't seem dead. The vivid images coming out of that boy's mind were too alive for him to be dead.

A grumbly bark came from Linus's end of the walkie-ham, and then a soft jangling, like from a collar.

"Do you have Molly there with you?" I asked, surprised.

"Yes."

"Do you always bring her with you?"

"No. She just followed me tonight, so I had to bring her up," he said. "Did you know Berg went to medical school in St. Louis before he came to the Forge School? He has connections there. He studied arts law, too. That's what Parker said today. He had a long stretch of lucidity while Otis was out, and he got to talking about the old days."

"It sort of makes sense," I said. I considered how Dean Berg's background as a doctor and a lawyer suited him to running Forge.

"You know what I can't get my head around?" Linus asked. "The idea of a body in an ice cream truck."

I instantly pictured a blue, frosted body packed in among five-gallon tubs of mint chip ice cream.

"That's incredibly revolting," I said.

"I know."

I kept picturing it.

"So why do I want to laugh?" I added.

Linus laughed. "I know."

I rubbed the back of my thumbnail idly against my lips. "I feel like I'm supposed to do something about all this, like call the police."

"And say what, exactly?"

"Wouldn't you call them?" I asked.

"Me? No. This will sound incredibly annoying, but you don't have any proof."

I didn't. It was true. I was worried about that boy. And myself, for that matter. And Janice, and everyone else. I exhaled slowly, trying to think what to do.

"I have to look for more evidence," I said.

"Maybe videotape something," Linus said.

"I tried that once. Somebody erased it."

"Come again?"

I told him about the night I'd seen Janice taken out. I'd run down to the basement with my video camera, and then back to the attic where I'd seen Dean Berg watching me from the dean's tower, and the next morning, my footage had been erased.

"But how would someone get to your video camera and delete the footage?" Linus asked.

"I don't know, unless someone took my camera out of my sleep shell."

"While you were sleeping?" he asked.

I couldn't tell if his raised voice meant he was angry or incredulous.

"It frightened me," I said.

He didn't answer.

"What are you thinking?" I asked.

He still didn't answer.

"Linus, are you still there?"

"I don't understand any of this," he said. "But I don't think it's safe for you to get out of bed. I think you should say you're sick and you want to go home."

"Leave the school?" I asked.

"I think you should leave tomorrow."

"Now you're scaring me," I said.

"Think about it, Rosie. If half of what you say is true, this school is being run by a madman. A genius, but a pathological one. Nobody's safe here."

Now that somebody else was saying it, and it wasn't only me thinking it, I realized why I couldn't just leave. This wasn't only about me.

"I just have to get some proof," I said. "Then we can go to the police and leave it up to them to get to the bottom of it."

"Don't do anything tonight," he said.

"When else is any better? I have to go tonight," I said.

"No. Dean Berg called in a night crew to run an upgrade of the computer system. The fifth floor of the dean's tower is lit up with techies, and they're going building to building checking some of the cameras. You have to stay in bed."

I craned my neck, trying to see the dean's tower out the nearest window, but the angle of my sleep shell was wrong. I eased my head back onto my pillow and slid the walkie-ham beside my ear again.

"Could they be coming in here?" I asked.

"Possibly, but they're just regular techies. They can't do anything to you," Linus said. "There are too many people around. They wouldn't dare."

"So you think they don't know? What about the teachers and the rest of the staff?"

"No, I don't think so. You can't have a lot of people keeping a secret. It has to be just Dean Berg and Dr. Ash, like you say."

"And one other guy," I said. "There's one other guy with a beard. I've seen him, too."

"Let me talk to Otis about this. We're just making guesses," Linus said. "He knows a lot about the school."

"He'll tell. He works for Berg."

"Maybe Parker, then. His memory's spotty, but when he's on, he's incredibly sharp."

I didn't have high hopes for the man with Alzheimer's.

"Maybe I should write Burnham a note and get him on it," I said. "He's smart. He's been interested in my surveillance of the school."

"The Fisters supply the sleeping pills for the school," Linus said. "His loyalty would be to his family."

"Do you think the Fisters are involved?"

"No, I'm only saying Burnham might not be the best person to confide in at this point. His family business is tied up with the school."

I chewed at the inside of my lip, considering. Burnham was a complicated person, but I trusted him. I needed to think things through before I made a decision. I wasn't sure about Parker, either.

"When's the last time you donated blood to Parker?" I asked.

"Last month. I'm due to donate again tomorrow."

"Really? Do you go to a clinic or something?"

"We do it at home, in the afternoon, when Parker's at his

best," he said. "Otis cooks meatballs and we put on Parker's favorite old movie and watch it all together."

"What's the movie?"

"*Shakespeare in Love*."

"That sounds like a nice tradition."

"It is, actually," he said, laughing.

It made me envious. "Will I see you tomorrow?" I asked.

"I'll be around until lunchtime. Come surprise me."

I smiled slowly. "I can never surprise you. You can always see me on my way."

"Do you think I spend every moment of my day watching your feed?"

"Well, not every moment. I thought you said Franny kept my profile up in the kitchen, though."

He laughed again. "She does. To torture me."

"It's not torture."

"It's something," he said.

I couldn't tell quite what he meant. "Something bad?"

"I've been trying to remember the story of Cyrano de Bergerac," he said.

"Non sequitur," I said. "Tell me what you meant before."

Linus kept going. "That girl Roxanne thought she had just one boyfriend, but he was essentially two men and she didn't know it."

"Cyrano had a big nose."

"Right. Anyway, Roxanne had one boyfriend during the day, and the other one at night," Linus said. "The body and the voice."

"I never thought of it that way, but it's true," I said. "And your point?"

"We're like that, you and I," he said. "By day, our bodies are together, but we can't say what we're thinking. By night, we can talk but we can't touch."

I gazed out the window again, considering the idea. "I think I like the night better," I said.

"Me, too," he said. "I've been trying to remember if the story had a happy ending. I suppose I could look it up."

It was coming back to me. She lost him twice. "I think Cyrano died. In a convent."

"That seems wrong," he said, laughing again. "You know what I'd do if I was there with you?" he asked.

"What?"

"I would talk to you, just like we're doing, but together."

I smiled, closing my eyes. "That would be perfect."

"Who am I kidding? I'd make a move."

I laughed. "That would be perfect, too."

"Sweet dreams, Rosie. Molly says good night."

I whispered good night back.

Then I turned off my walkie-ham and hid it under my pillow. With Linus no longer in my ear, I felt more alone than before. I was afraid to sleep, afraid to let go, afraid to hear a hiss of gas, afraid I'd drop into a nightmare. I tried to tell myself I was safe because the place was crawling with techies, and finally exhaustion released me.

〉〉〉〉〉〉〉〉

I slept through the rest of the night, and woke with the other girls at six the next morning. I listened cautiously for any inner voice to offer a dire warning, but none came. No shadows of nightmares skittered at the edge of my consciousness. For once, I felt fine. Normal. With the sunshine bright outside the windows, I felt like wearing a skirt and leggings, with my brown sweater for warmth.

At breakfast, when I saw Linus, he gave me a wary smile. "Did you like my poem, then?" he asked.

I had to skim back past our conversation in the night and remember where we'd left off the day before. Yesterday morning, when he'd been so cold and angry about the swipe key, felt like forever ago. "Yes, very much," I said.

He pulled me in for a hug and a kiss, a real one, not the fake kind like yesterday's. "You could have written me one back," he said.

"I guess I'm not as romantic as you are."

"Maybe that's why I like you," he said, and kissed me again.

Soon after, when I arrived in Media Convergence, four of the students were playing Ping-Pong already. I had to give Mr. DeCoster credit. When people took breaks to play, it did seem to make them even more creative and productive afterward. He was listening attentively while the painter Harry talked to him about building a sand castle city against the rising ocean. Janice was lying on the couch in her Hamletta scarf with her eyes closed, mumbling. For her impossible project, she was writing a five-act play in iambic pentameter.

Burnham, wearing earphones, was working intently at his computer.

I took the chair beside his. "How was your diving yesterday?" I asked, and reached to turn on my machine.

He took out his right earphone and let it hang. "It was good. And thanks, by the way. My mom says hi back."

"Hello again, Burnham's mom," I said, offering a wave at the nearest camera. "You have a very nice boy here. Very smart and handsome. You should be proud of him."

"Okay, enough of that," Burnham said, shaking his head.

On his screen, an army of cartoon dragons was attacking the clock tower with little bursts of flame.

"You're not failing at that," I said.

"Yes, I am. It doesn't match what I imagine yet," he said.

He had to have some imagination.

"Where's the lady knight?" I asked.

He pointed. "Here. She's running things."

I leaned closer. She still had my hair and a nasty scowl. Her cleavage had been augmented.

"Well done," I said.

I pulled up some of my footage from the graveyard and started working on a ghost I could superimpose into a sequence of scenes. Burnham worked companionably beside me for a while, and then he paused to stretch his hands over his head.

"Hey, I want to show you something," he said.

Beside me, he left his game up on his big screen and skimmed a hand over his smaller touch screen to pull up some of my own footage. He had it arranged in nine miniwindows and he zipped through them all with fluid ease.

"You weren't kidding about taking a look at my footage," I said.

"I ran them through an analyzer," he said. "There were two things that caught my eye. You'll like this."

He set his touch screen between us and shifted his chair closer. Then he pulled up some footage from the clock tower. Purely for the artistic effect of it, I had aimed a video camera down the pit where the weights from the clock dropped on their chains, but even when Burnham ran the footage in high speed so a bit of window light streaked around inside of the cylindrical pit, the chains barely seemed to move. Then the pit went dark as the clock tower was lost to night.

"That's it," I said.

"Just wait," he said.

A flicker of light smudged the screen. Burnham stopped the footage and reversed back to a certain frame.

A circle of light, deep down in the pit, silhouetted the chains and weights dropping down. I leaned closer to the screen, peering.

"Guess what it is," Burnham said.

I slid the time marker through the footage to see that the light lasted about twenty seconds. Then it went off. I stared some more. It wasn't a bright, direct light that would be used on purpose to illuminate the bottom of the pit. And it wasn't a reflection, because if the floor was wet and reflecting light back up, then there would be light in the foreground from the original source, too, but there wasn't. The light at the bottom of the pit was more like refracted light that had bounced down a hallway for a while and lost its luster.

It suddenly occurred to me that Burnham had made a point of showing this to me on the small touch screen, where it wouldn't be readily visible to the cameras.

I glanced over at him. "You're a crafty one. Did you rig this up?"

"I didn't. I swear." He tilted his chair back, smiling. "I knew you'd like it."

"I do."

It made me think. A light down there could mean there was another way to the bottom of the pit, like from the side. Or from another perspective, the pit could lead to a tunnel. I put a marker on the footage, and looked at Burnham again.

"Did you find anything else?" I asked.

"Just a sec."

He leaned in again. This time he pulled up a shot of the girls' dorm at night, with all our sleep shells lined up. The lids glowed faintly, including mine in the foreground. The scene was from the video camera I had set up in my wardrobe, and though I'd checked all of it before myself, I couldn't help fearing he had flagged a time when I wasn't sleeping.

I reached to turn it off. "I've seen this," I said. "We just sleep."

"Hold on," he said. "I know you all sleep. Okay, now watch here."

He pointed to the girl in front: me. I lay in the closest sleep

278

shell, with half of my face visible above the edge and my white quilt snuggled softly over my shoulder. My lips were parted just a hint, and my hair was a fluffy mess. On my bedside table, beside my notebook, I had propped up a photo of Dubbs. I pointed to the photo.

"You gave me that," I said.

"Just wait. There."

On the screen, I still lay sleeping, but my shoulder was bare and my lips were closed. I had moved, but the film didn't show me moving. Instead, it showed a jump cut from one frame to the next. Everything else was the same—the photo of Dubbs, the dimness, the other sleep shells—except for my shoulder and my mouth. Burnham backed it up and I watched it again. I checked the video track, and saw the black line of a splice.

I touched the line with my finger. "Did you put that in?" I asked.

He shook his head, watching me. "I found it like this."

I sat back slowly, my mind racing. For a glitch like that, someone had deliberately taken out a segment of my footage and spliced the loose ends together. It could mean a second had passed, or an hour. With the integrity of the footage gone, anything could have happened in the dorm room that night.

I felt excited and half-sick at the same time. "You know what I've been searching for?"

Burnham nodded. "Ghosts."

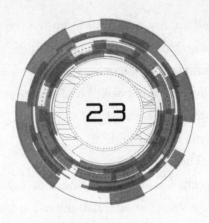

23

GHOSTS

WE COULDN'T TALK about it on camera.

We'd just discovered something huge, and I had to act like it didn't matter. I knew viewers at home couldn't very well have seen what we were looking at on Burnham's small touch screen, and it was doubtful that many of them would have understood the significance of the jump cut, even if they had. I had to keep them uninterested.

I laughed. "I wouldn't say it's definitive proof of the paranormal."

"No, but it makes a person wonder," he said.

"Was there anything else you wanted to show me?"

"That's all I got."

Burnham slid his touch screen back in front of himself and switched it back in synch with his computer game of cartoon dragons. I put some of my other footage up on my main screen, too, so it looked like I was moving on, but I could barely pay even cursory attention while my mind was still racing.

What I liked most was that the splice cut proved someone had something to hide. It was my first actual proof, tiny as it was, and Burnham had seen it, too. I had to laugh. My energy had switched from ho-hum to boundless, and I couldn't possibly stay in my chair anymore. I stood and turned off my computer.

Mr. DeCoster was just finishing his conversation with Harry. He glanced my way. "Everything all right?"

"I'm just getting another one of my video cameras," I said. I grabbed my brown sweater. "Burnham's coming, too."

"I am?"

"You are."

Burnham gave his chair a spin and stood up. "Off we go."

Moments later, we burst outside. The morning was still new, splashing with sunlight, and I filled my lungs with the fresh air.

"You're excited," Burnham said.

"Of course! What a gorgeous day."

"Where are we headed?"

"To the observatory," I said. "Have you been there?"

"Not inside. Isn't it locked?"

"It doesn't matter. My camera's on top."

In the pasture, a shimmer of moisture lingered in the air above the grass. A couple of birds flapped overhead, and a clink came from the back of the dining hall. I looked back over my shoulder toward the kitchen, but Linus wasn't visible through the windows. I gave a wave in his direction, in case he was watching me on the TV screen. Above, from the lookout tower, Otis aimed a camera at us and I gave him a wave, too.

It was just so good to finally have some proof, no matter how small it was. As I led the way down the narrow path, the wet grasses made dark streaks on my leggings and boots. I looked back to see that Burnham was in loafers.

"I hope you're at least wearing socks," I said.

He pulled up his jeans leg to show a bare ankle. "It's no problem," he said. "When did you put a camera on the observatory?"

"A few weeks ago, back when we first started our projects."

"This whole time that you've been looking for ghosts, did you have a plan in case you actually found one?" he asked.

"No. Like what?"

"Tell the police?" he said. "Start an investigation?"

He wasn't talking about ghosts, but I had to answer as if he were.

"They'd laugh their heads off," I said. "Nobody believes in ghosts. Not really. They'd think I'm crazy."

"I don't think you're crazy," Burnham said. "I think you're brilliant."

I laughed, surprised at the simple sincerity in his voice. "Well, thanks. That's probably an overstatement." I tucked my hands in the sleeves of my sweater, trying to figure out what to say without saying anything.

"I wish you had a phone," he said.

Then we could text. "Me, too."

"I wrote you a letter," he said. He took his hand out of his back pocket and passed me a small, bulky envelope.

"When did you write this?" I asked.

"Last night. After swimming. Wait until you're alone to read it," he said.

I could feel something hard inside the paper, but I put it in my skirt pocket without examining it closely. "Thanks. I'm dying of curiosity."

"It's not a love poem or anything," he added.

"Of course not," I said, and wondered if he was aware that Linus had given me a poem.

Through his glasses, Burnham was watching me in a quiet, casual way. I noticed that he was a little taller than Linus. My gaze went to the shape of his mouth, and it took me too long to look away.

"Sorry," I said.

"What for?"

I shook my head.

"Rosie," he said gently. "I get that you're seeing Linus."

A blush of heat burned up my cheeks. "Yes. I am."

Linus could be watching this very conversation, actually.

I spun and continued down the path through the pasture, across the dip and up the knoll toward the observatory. Burnham's letter burned in my pocket, making me feel oddly guilty for accepting it, but I couldn't very well give it back.

My boots crunched loudly as they met the gravel path that

circled the observatory. The dome glinted brightly in the sun-light, but the ladder, recessed back from the main door, was in the shade. I took a quick look up its height. Then I gripped a cool metal rung and bypassed the DO NOT ENTER chain.

"We're not supposed to go up there," Burnham said.

"I went before. It's safe," I said, climbing higher.

The rungs made a hollow, metallic pinging as I ascended. The noise plucked at the edge of my brain. I stepped up a couple more rungs and felt a déjà vu begin. I paused between two rungs. It was an odd déjà vu, different from the last time, because I had truly been here before, so part of my memory was real. It made for layers of being-here-ness.

I kept climbing. "Are you coming?" I asked.

When he didn't answer, I twisted back and leaned into the ladder to look below me. Burnham was standing solidly on the gravel, with his hands on his hips, gazing up.

"I'll just watch. I'll catch you if you fall," he said.

"You look an awful lot like a chicken from this angle," I said. The words tasted familiar in my mouth.

"I'm not a coward."

"Then you should come," I said. "It's beautiful at the top. I mean it."

He reached past the chain, and I felt the ladder vibrate as a rung bore his weight. My déjà vu intensified. I reached higher and paused to brush a little brown spider off the lad-der. It spun out on a new filament of thread and fell grace-fully from my sight, precisely the way I expected it to do.

As I looked upward to see how much farther I had to go,

a whirl of dizziness caught me by the back of my head. I sucked in my breath and gripped the rungs. The ladder tilted dangerously, trying to buck me off. I yanked it back into position. My eyes went tight and black, and with a sense of horror, I realized I was fading out.

I couldn't faint. Not here.

My déjà vu showed me I was about to fall.

I held hard to the ladder, trying to breathe deeply and maintain consciousness, but my upper foot grew limp and heavy. I could feel it slipping from the rung. I wanted to call out to Burnham and warn him, but my head nodded forward on its own, shutting down my jaw and my voice. I concentrated with all my might on my fingers, willing them to clench the ladder. I could still dimly hear Burnham climbing behind me, and then I was falling.

Weightless.

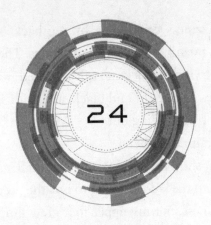

24

THE AFTERMATH

I SURFACED INTO fear.

Before I focused on the grass an inch in front of my eyes or felt my arm twisted in pain, I knew the real crisis was the stillness of the body beneath me.

"Burnham?" I said.

I rolled off of him and turned to look.

He was still. His eyes were closed. My fear escalated toward panic. *Wake up!* I told myself.

But I was already awake. This horror was real.

I leaned close, studying his face for any flicker of motion. His cheeks and eyelids remained smooth. I checked beneath his head and saw that he'd landed with his skull squarely on a stone paver that edged the path. I hadn't even noticed the pavers before, but now they made a hard, deadly line between the grass and the gravel.

"Burnham," I whispered, and set my hand on his chest. "No, no, no."

He wasn't breathing.

I stopped thinking and moved to kneel beside Burnham's head. I opened his mouth, pinched his nose, and bent close to seal my mouth around his. I breathed into him once and let go of his nose. His lips and jaw were slack. I readjusted and tried again, pushing air into him. Then I released his nose again and watched his chest.

Nothing.

Come on, Burnham, I thought.

I gripped his nose and chin more firmly and breathed into him again, a cycle of breaths and pauses, as evenly as I could. With each breath, his unresponsiveness made me panic a little more. I didn't know what else to do.

"We've got him, Rosie," a voice said.

Firm hands gripped my shoulders as a mask was slid into place over Burnham's face. Dr. Ash and half a dozen others were swarming around us with a stretcher and medical supplies.

"Let's give them a little room."

I was guided back and up to my feet.

He has to breathe, I thought. My mind wouldn't go any further than that.

Dr. Ash doubled her gloved hands on Burnham's chest and administered CPR in forced, rhythmic compressions. Someone else was peering into Burnham's eyes with a penlight, and a third stuck an IV in his arm. The doctor gave clipped directions to her team, and then another medic passed her the paddles of a defibrillator. I couldn't see. Too many shoulders blocked my vision.

I tried to shift nearer, but someone was holding me back.

"Rosie," said a calm, low voice.

I jumped as I realized that Dean Berg had me by the arm. "Let me go," I said, pulling free.

Mr. DeCoster and a dozen others were coming down the pasture. A couple girls were pressing their cheeks and covering their mouths in caricatures of shock. Four guys came running over in swimsuits and towels, as if, bizarrely, they'd jumped out of the pool and raced to try to save Burnham.

I glanced across at the observatory ladder. We'd fallen maybe fifteen feet. Not even. It could not happen, it could not be true that Burnham was seriously injured. Things didn't work that way.

He still didn't move. Dr. Ash and the medics were working over him. This had to be a good thing, I thought. They wouldn't bother if it was hopeless. They wouldn't keep pushing on his chest or fit a collar around his neck if he was already dead. A man counted aloud, and on cue, the team lifted Burnham onto a stretcher. I hadn't seen the ambulance come, but it was parked on the grass beside us.

"What have I done?" I whispered, starting to shake.

The medics carefully bundled Burnham into the ambulance,

and the last I saw of my friend, one of his loafers was slipping off his foot.

"Rosie!" Janice cried, charging through the bystanders.

She flung her arms around me. Burnham's ambulance was pulling away. I didn't know where they would they take him. I didn't even know where the closest hospital was.

"You're hurt," Janice said, studying me. "Your arm. Is it broken? Dean Berg, Rosie hurt her arm."

That was when I first felt the pain in my right elbow. Dean Berg turned his soft, grave face in my direction, and when I saw his façade of concern, cold fury hit me. My accident with Burnham was Berg's fault. My déjà vus and my dizziness were because of him and what he was doing to me at night.

"Enough," I said to him. "This has to stop."

Dean Berg looked like he hadn't heard me. His forehead was creased in concentration. He had his normal earphone in one ear, and held another phone to the other. The buzz of a voice in the receiver was loud enough for me to hear.

I pushed up near to him. "I said, this is *enough*."

He smiled kindly and took my hand. "We'll take care of you, Rosie," he said. "Don't worry."

I jerked away from him. He called out to one of the medics and pointed toward me. Then he turned back to his phone call.

"Rosie, hold on," Janice said, stepping between me and the dean. "Let him talk to Burnham's parents."

Burnham's parents were on the phone? I'd hurt their son.

The blame I'd shot at Dean Berg instantly reversed, and I was hit by an onslaught of guilt. I gripped Janice's arm. A medic started asking me questions, but I couldn't answer him. I kept waiting for Dean Berg to look back at me. I had to see the moment in his face when Burnham's parents accused me.

"Rosie, they found a heartbeat," the medic said. "Your friend's heart started again just as they got him in the ambulance. That's a very good sign."

I turned to face him and tried to process his words. The medic was a small man in a tidy uniform, and he gave me a reassuring nod.

"Are you sure?" I asked.

"I'm sure. He has a heartbeat."

Burnham was alive. I gasped for air and covered my face. Janice hugged me again and I hid against her shoulder.

I didn't kill him.

My friend wasn't dead.

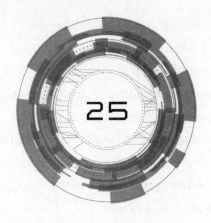

25

THE YELLOW PILLS

NOBODY YELLED AT me. I wished they would. Or rather, my stepfather yelled at me, but nobody who mattered did. According to Larry, I could be charged with manslaughter if Burnham died.

"Don't listen to him," my mother said, taking the phone back.

I was sitting in one of the examining rooms of the infirmary an hour later, waiting for the medic to tell me it was okay to go. Apparently, the police wanted to keep me separate from the other students until they could talk to me.

My arm, in a sling, was numb with a shot they'd given me, but it wasn't broken.

"I feel awful," I said into the phone.

"Do you want to come home?" Ma asked. "Are they

taking good care of you? I could borrow a car from the McLellens and come for you."

"I don't mean physically."

The last thing I wanted to do was leave school. My guilt about Burnham now riveted me to the place.

"It wasn't your fault," Ma said. "It was just an accident, and really, if he'd landed anywhere else he would have been totally fine. It was just that paver in the wrong place."

I slumped lower in my chair.

"You're slouching," Ma said.

"Don't try to tell me it wasn't my fault," I said. "That doesn't help."

"Getting snippy won't help, either," she said gently.

She was right. My problems weren't because of her. I straightened slightly, for her sake. "I just want more news on Burnham."

"Forge has changed his profile picture to a still photo," Ma said.

No surprise there. I fiddled with a penlight the medic had left on the table, flicking it on and off.

"Rosie's blip rank is fourteen. Is that good?" my stepfather called in the background.

Fourteen. My rank had never been so high. Brilliant.

"Dubbs wants to know what Burnham said in his letter," Ma said.

I reached back to touch the bulge in my pocket. I'd forgotten about it.

"I have to go read it," I said. "Talk to you later?"

"Anytime, sweetheart. I took the day off from work so I'm right here whenever."

I hung up, stole the penlight, and slipped into the bathroom. It was a small room with a little sink, a mirror, and a can of air freshener on the tank of the toilet. I examined the walls and fixtures to be sure there were no cameras, and then turned my back on the mirror, just to be sure. With my right arm in the sling, it was awkward getting the envelope out of my skirt pocket, but I managed. Then, as I ripped it carefully open, I was surprised to find three pills inside. They were small, chalky, yellow disks, each one imprinted with a Z.

Since when did Burnham supply drugs? I unfolded his letter.

Rosie,

I've thought about your footage and I've come to the following conclusions:
1. You're spying on Forge for a real reason. Which means,
2. You witnessed something suspicious, and because of the cameras, that could have happened only at night. Which means,
3. You're staying awake at night somehow, at least sometimes.

I thought I was the only one. We have to be careful.

These pills are antidotes to the sleeping meds. You can take one right after your

293

*regular pill and it will keep you up. Never
take more than one. Never take one by itself
or it will fry your brain. I repeat, fry your
brain.*

*Please write me back. I can help. My
parents are going to be unbelievably pissed
if something unethical is going on here,
but they'll want to know. They won't kill
the messenger. I promise. Flush this when
you're done.*

*Burnham
P.S. You're right. The lady knight is you.*

I leaned back against the edge of the sink and read the letter
again. Wow. I wasn't sure what stunned me more: that he was
staying awake, too, or that he'd given me the antidote pills.
Crafty, crafty Burnham, I thought.

A tap came on the door. "Are you okay in there? The police are here to talk to you."

"Coming," I said.

I wrapped the antidote pills in a tissue and stuffed them
down my bra. Then I ripped his letter in shreds, flushed it,
and prepared to go out onstage.

Leave me out of it, said a small voice.

I held still, my hand on the knob. I waited for her to explain, and when she didn't, I tried thinking back at her. *You
know I don't talk about you.*

Then, though I was standing motionless, I felt my balance shift, like she was deliberately doing it to me. I gripped the knob harder.

You mean the déjà vu? The dizziness? I asked. *But that's Dean Berg's fault.*

My mind suddenly filled with an exaggerated image of the dean's face, and his features distorted into ruddy ugliness with bulging, evil eyes.

For your own sake, don't tell them about any of it, she said.

All right, I said. *I won't tell about anything strange.*

She slid back into her murk, appeased, and left me alone.

I took a deep breath and stepped back out onstage.

>>>>>>>>

The police grilled me politely but repetitively about what, exactly, had happened on the ladder. I didn't see the point, considering how many cameras had recorded the event, but I hid my impatience and repeated my story: I slipped and fell. Yes, I had seen the DO NOT ENTER sign, but I had ignored it. It was all my fault, not Burnham's. He hadn't even wanted to climb. Yes, the ladder had seemed safe. I'd been up there twice before with no problems. I wasn't scared by the spider, I wasn't distracted by any noise, I wasn't shaken by Burnham's weight on the ladder below me. I simply slipped and fell, and Burnham had cushioned my impact or I would have been the one in the ICU. Couldn't somebody please get ahold of his family and tell them how sorry I was?

I left out my déjà vu and my dizziness and my inner voice. When they asked to see Burnham's letter, I said it was just a thanks for understanding about his grandpa, and I'd destroyed it out of respect.

News came that Burnham was in a hospital in Chicago. He was on a respirator and suffering from brain trauma. Beyond that, nobody would say. They wouldn't even commit to whether or not he was in a coma. Twice I tried to reach his family to tell them how sorry I was, but I didn't hear back.

The rest of the day was hellishly uneventful. The dean encouraged everyone to keep attending classes, and a counseling station was set up in the library for anyone who was too distracted or upset to stick to routine. I didn't go there.

Instead, I made my way to the kitchen, where the impersonal, well-run activity was distinctly soothing to me. I took a stool near Linus and hitched my heels on the uppermost rung so I could lean over my knees. In time, Franny put me to work peeling and slicing Granny Smiths for pies, which was a perfect, mindless task. I could feel the pain in my elbow as the meds wore off, and I was glad. I wanted something to hurt. It helped me settle back into myself.

Around one o'clock, Otis came in the back door and took off his cap. Linus was deboning a dozen chickens, and though he looked over, he didn't stop working.

"Parker's asking after you," Otis said to Linus. "Ted will let you go."

"It's not a good time."

I looked back and forth between them.

"We had an agreement," Otis said.

"I can do it tonight," Linus said.

Otis turned his hat in his hand. I expected his gaze to shift to me, but I was wrong. Otis didn't say anything more, and a moment later, he went back out the door. Only then did I remember that Linus was due to donate his blood that afternoon.

"You don't have to stay for me," I said.

"It'll be okay," Linus said.

In that one exchange between him and Otis, I'd glimpsed a whole relationship of patience and power, a dynamic completely unlike anything I knew at home.

Chef Ted passed behind Linus with a sack of potatoes, and Franny turned on the mixer at high volume for a minute. Linus kept working with the raw chicken, and I glanced up at the TV screen where a live version of me was sitting on a stool in the kitchen, watching herself on the TV screen. It went on in an endless loop. *Surreal*, I thought.

And then, unexpectedly, I thought of Parker wanting his meatballs and his movie, and it mixed up with Burnham being maybe in a coma, and without warning, I felt prickles rise at the back of my eyes. I had to look up toward the ceiling and blink rapidly to stop from crying. I didn't want to cry today on camera. I couldn't stand the idea of gaining anything from this situation, not even sympathy from my viewers.

"Your friend's going to be all right," Linus said.

He rested the point of his knife on the wooden board, and in his white tee shirt and apron, he looked aggressively healthy and strong and alive.

"We don't really know that," I said tightly.

"His parents will get him the best care anybody could."

That much was true. I couldn't bear to talk about Burnham. His loafer had been slipping off, there at the end. I didn't want to talk at all. I didn't want to think.

"Do you know that story of Cyrano de Bergerac?" I asked.

"Turns out, I do," he said. "Why?"

"No reason in particular."

He took the hint. For now, we could just be bodies in the same room. Later, we would talk.

>>>>>>>>

That night, when Orly came to distribute our sleeping pills, Dr. Ash entered with her. Her red sweater was vivid under the lights as she walked down the length of the dorm directly to me, bringing my own private tray of a pill cup and a glass of water.

"How's the elbow?" she asked me.

"Fine," I said, and rubbed it gently. I had taken off my sling when I changed into my nightie.

Dr. Ash set down the tray, rolled up my sleeve, and examined the bruise. I smelled her faint, familiar perfume as she leaned near. Over her shoulder, I saw Janice and Paige watching curiously. When the doctor turned my wrist, I gasped at the pain in my elbow. She lowered my arm.

"I could give you something for the pain, but once you're asleep, you won't feel it," she said.

"I'm really okay," I said. "Have you had any more news about Burnham?"

"Only that he's still not responding," Dr. Ash said. "They've cooled him down and they're inducing a coma to help him stabilize. It's standard practice. The next twenty-four hours are critical."

Any kind of coma did not sound good to me. "His parents are with him, right?" I asked.

She nodded. "Of course. And his brother and his sister. We might have more news in the morning. From what I understand, he's not in any pain."

"Do you think he's going to be all right? Honestly?" I asked.

"I wish I could say, but it's really too soon to know," Dr. Ash answered. "Each case is so individual, and I'm hardly an expert on the brain. I wouldn't want to give an uninformed opinion."

I was amazed that she could be so convincing when she lied. She knew plenty about brains. She operated on them.

When she lifted the little tray and held it toward me, I noticed a tongue depressor beside the cup. "I'll be checking to see that you swallow your pill," she said.

I felt a prick of adrenaline. She had as good as admitted to viewers that I was at risk for skipping my pill. Did they notice? I glanced back at Orly, who was watching us with her typical dour expression. The other girls had climbed in their sleep shells and were closing their lids.

"Shall we?" Dr. Ash was still holding the tray toward me.

I took my pill, tossed it back, and swallowed it down with

my water. When I opened my mouth, Dr. Ash pressed the little wooden stick inside my cheeks, first one side and then the other. Then she nodded and gestured toward my sleep shell.

I climbed in.

Dr. Ash slid my lid closed for me and gave it a light pat. "Sleep well." Her voice came slightly muffled through the glass.

At the other end of the room, Orly turned off the overhead light, and I could hear Dr. Ash walking away. Night came earlier since we'd passed the equinox, and the room was already dark. My brink lesson came on: a soothing scene of a stream trickling down a mountainside, with delicate spring wildflowers on either side. As I watched, the sleep drugs eased through my veins with twice the speed as normal, and an undertow of exhaustion began to drag me under.

Don't give in, said the voice in my head.

I jolted back awake, but only for a moment. I couldn't withstand the punishing lethargy.

Take Burnham's pill, she said.

Why? There's no point.

As if a lion suddenly jumped on my chest, a jolt of adrenaline charged through my body. Before I could reason, I shot a hand into my pillowcase and scrambled to locate the tissue I had hidden there. I pulled it out and focused desperately on unwrapping the pills.

Just one, Burnham had warned me. I slid one of the yellow pills onto my palm and tossed it back, swallowing it dry. I could do nothing more. My eyelids closed heavily, my arms went limp, and my mind snagged into an uneasy tangle before I descended over the edge.

Except I didn't.

Gravity seemed to stagnate inside my body, causing my organs to neither fall nor float. My bones turned gray, like fog in the early morning, and then a tingling swarmed in my fingertips. It spread into my hands and up my arms. It burned in my sore right elbow and kept going. I could feel each pulse as my heart pumped blood through my veins, and in the space of two breaths, I went from soporific to hyper-awake. Energy and strength lit me up from within, and I couldn't keep my eyes closed.

Nice drugs, Burnham, I thought. *Seriously.*

My first instinct was to jump out of my sleep shell and tear around the room. I fought to resist it. My foot vibrated at a rapid pitch, and my mind clamped onto a single warning: wait until after midnight. I had to wait until the techies went home.

I hid my two extra pills in my pillowcase and pulled out my walkie-ham.

"Linus?" I whispered. "Are you there?"

I listened impatiently to the static. I tried the other channels, then dialed back to four.

Be patient, I told myself.

But it was impossible. My mind clicked like an unleashed train that could go in ten directions at once. It headed toward Burnham lost in his coma, and then it veered to the ladder on the observatory to relive the agony of my fall. It zipped next to the kitchen to revisit Linus cutting chickens, and then to the sixth floor of the dean's tower, where Dean Berg plotted with his projections and screens.

"Linus," I tried again.

No reply.

Burnham's pill had me totally wired. I tried breathing slowly, deliberately, but at the same time, I couldn't stop vibrating my leg.

I gulped back a laugh. I pressed my hands to my temples.

For heaven's sake, said my voice. **Take it easy. They'll see you thrashing around**.

I'm going crazy here, I said.

Unbidden, a redolent memory of Thanksgiving dinner surfaced from the back of my mind: turkey with gravy, mashed potatoes, stuffing, and cranberry sauce. I could taste the meat and the tangy sauce together, and then the cloying, buttery heaviness of the mashed potatoes. A calm worked its way around the buzz in my gut, coating and soothing it until I could breathe more evenly. I managed to stretch out my toes and quit shaking my leg.

How do you do that? I asked.

Have a little more turkey.

I let out a soft laugh, grateful. Soon, I was calm enough to lie still under my quilt and pull together the bits of a plan.

I needed to find out what was going on once and for all, and get evidence about it. Burnham's injury was not, I believed, directly caused by whatever Dean Berg was doing at night, but *my* fall was most definitely connected. It was possible that

Ellen had been damaged by Dean Berg, too. I wasn't going to sit around while casualties piled up, especially now that I had evidence that someone had tampered with my night footage of the dorm. Add what I'd overhead between Dean Berg and Huma Fallon, and it was enough.

If I could just find the operating room, I was certain I'd find evidence I could film, and this time, I would take it public myself, immediately. Once, while Dr. Ash was operating, I had heard Dean Berg talk to her about returning to the surface, which implied that the operating room was somewhere underground.

I had two possible leads: the secret door behind the vending machines in the dean's tower, and the pit in the clock tower. Somehow I had to find a way down, even without a swipe key.

"Linus?" I whispered again into my walkie-ham.

Then, at last, I remembered how Otis had come to the kitchen looking for Linus. He was probably busy with Otis and Parker, donating his blood. I narrowed my eyes at my walkie-ham and touched a finger over the little pockmarks of the speaker. It was all right. If Linus never answered, it didn't matter. It would be better to go without him, anyway, and not risk getting him into trouble.

After the clock tower struck midnight, I gave it another half hour to be sure the techies had all left. A look out the window convinced me that the dean's tower was dark, as much as I could see. I couldn't spot the dean in his dark penthouse, but I took it as a good sign that he wasn't at his sixth-floor station.

I dressed swiftly. Omitting my sling for my sore arm, I put my walkie-ham in my jeans pocket and grabbed my camera and the penlight I'd stolen from the infirmary. I crept cautiously down the stairs, hugging the shadows, until I reached the ground floor. There I peered out a window beside the front door, watching for movement. I tried my walkie-ham one last time.

"Linus? Are you there?"

No reply. I was going out alone.

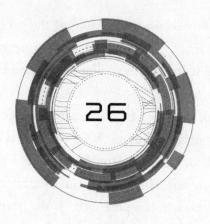

26

THE CLOCK TOWER AGAIN

BY NIGHT, THE fragrant air pulsed with the drone of crickets, and the void of the prairie seemed to encroach onto the campus. Trees and bushes merged into the same lacy black, and the lawns dulled to gray. I stole along the edge of the girls' dorm where the shadows were deep, and at the corner, I darted across to the film building to hide between the foundation and a dumpster. Broken bits of glass crackled beneath my sneakers.

I watched and listened, but nothing moved. Then I hurried behind the hedge of the film building, keeping low, and crouched at the next corner with my back to the foundation. Across the narrow road to my right, the dean's tower stood massive and still, and now that I was nearer, I saw lights in a first-floor corner office. That ruled out any chance of trying to sneak in there. To my left, the expanse of the quad was clear all the way to the auditorium at the other end. Before me, the clock tower ascended out of the rose garden toward a moonless sky. Its face was illuminated, and a green light blinked at the top.

The door of the clock tower was my next goal.

The only hiding points between me and the rose garden were a couple of oaks, an iron bench, and a garbage can. I didn't delude myself. The cameras could easily track me across such an open area, even in the dark. If the dean or a security guard was watching, I would be spotted.

I couldn't go farther, not without a break of some kind. Ten long minutes I waited, and then half an hour while I debated how risky it was to stay put or run for the tower. Nothing moved in the quad, and no one was visible in the lighted office of the dean's tower. I checked my walkie-ham, but Linus never came on. My elbow ached again, and mosquitoes found me.

And then I caught movement beyond the rose garden. A man with stooped shoulders was walking slowly past the library steps. As he moved under one of the streetlamps, the light dropped on his gray hair and the shoulders of his yellow shirt, but I didn't recognize his features. He continued along the sidewalk with a steady, unhurried stride, and when he came to the dean's tower, he set a hand on the stair railing and leaned back to look upward.

"Sandy!" he called. "Sandy, you old devil! Come out and play."

He bent forward, leaning over his shoes, and a moment

later he straightened again. With his back to me, he urinated on the steps. I gasped, holding back a laugh.

A moment later, the door opened and Dean Berg hurried down the stairs.

The old man called out the dean's name cheerfully, and the dean spoke to him in a voice too quiet for me to understand. He set a hand gently on the old man's arm and backed him up a step or two, out of the mess. He passed him a handkerchief. The old man shook his head as he rearranged his trousers.

"Nope. Not going back," he said clearly.

Running footsteps sounded, and Linus came sprinting across the quad.

"Linus!" the man called in a buoyant voice.

"Hey, Parker," Linus said. He leaned over with his hands on his knees, winded. "What are you doing here?"

"I came to see Sandy," Parker said. "We're going out for a drink."

Linus straightened and plucked at the neckline of his dark shirt. "You're not supposed to be up here. I've been look-ing all over for you," he said. "Otis is worried sick."

The man looked uncertain for the first time. "I told you. It's on the calendar."

A security cart passed me then and rolled to a stop by the steps. It was followed by a truck that parked between me and the others, blocking my view. Otis came out of the driver's side and headed around the vehicles, and in that instant, I realized I had my chance.

While all of their attention was focused on Parker, I

crawled out from my hiding place and bolted for the rose garden. I tore through the garden toward the side door of the clock tower. I pulled hard at the door and slipped inside, closing it softly just as someone convinced Parker to climb in the front of Otis's truck.

I'd made it. I listened for a shout or any commotion outside, but the only sound I heard was the pounding of my heart in my ears. The darkness of the tall, narrow room was impenetrable. I looked up, toward the gears, but aside from a faint, crescent gleam on one of the bells high above, I couldn't see a thing.

I pulled out my penlight to cast a cone of thin, white light before me and slid my sneakers forward. The railing around the pit appeared, and then the ghostly chains of the clock. Everything seemed bigger and colder than it had during the day when I'd been here with Linus. I aimed my light down into the pit, where the chains descended into darkness. The ladder rungs projected from the wall of the pit as a series of elongated U-shapes. I kept hoping my eyes would adjust and show me more, but the black of the pit was bottomless.

This is a mistake, I thought. If I fell, I'd be dead.

On the other hand, this was my best lead. I had to go down and see if the pit led to a tunnel the way I thought it could.

I slung the strap of my video camera over my shoulder and gripped my penlight in my teeth, sideways, so I could use both hands. Then I carefully stepped over the railing into the pit and lowered myself down, feeling with my feet for each rung.

My right elbow flared with pain each time I bore my

weight with that arm. Linus had said that the pit was thirty feet deep, and I judged that each rung was about a foot apart, so I silently began my count, one rung at a time. I tasted metal, and my breath came fast around the penlight in my teeth. The farther down I went, the cooler and mustier the air grew, and once, at the count of seventeen, I had to skip a rung that shifted dangerously under my weight.

My progress was painful and slow, but I didn't dare go faster. At the twenty-fourth rung, I heard a winding noise in the clock mechanism far above. I froze. I wrapped my left arm through the rung and seized it in the crook of my elbow, preparing for a dong from a bell. It didn't come.

Shaking, I took the penlight in my free hand and shone it up. The darkness above me was complete. I was very deep, deeper than I'd guessed, but when I shone the light downward, past my feet, only the faintest glint of a reflection came back up to me, like a seam of water between stones. I was still far from the bottom.

I fit the penlight back in my teeth, and kept descending, rung by rung. A rustling noise made me flinch. *Mice*, I thought, listening hard. Or maybe bats. Just as long as it wasn't big black spiders, I would be okay. Those I couldn't stand. I took another step and abruptly touched down against something solid and flat.

At last. With shaking fingers, I took my penlight from my teeth and cast its beam around the bottom of the pit. Through a layer of thick dust, the walls had the perfect flatness of glass. I stroked a finger down one, and found it was a window.

At the bottom of a pit, where even by daylight only a hint of sunlight could reach, I'd found windows. One of them had a small, round, metal knob.

It was a door.

>>>>>>>>

I looked above me one last time, up into the darkness where I knew I had an exit, and then I turned the knob. The door pulled toward me on squeaky hinges, and as I stepped through, I found myself in an old, deep tunnel that surrounded the windows of the pit and extended off in two directions. A few dry leaves were scattered along the corners. I scanned my light up the brick wall to where a broken light fixture dangled by its wires.

A low, mechanical hum came from one end of the tunnel, so I chose that direction, and not long after, a line of light shone from under a door. I pocketed my penlight, listened carefully for a long moment, and turned the knob.

I blinked at the sudden light of a tidy, bright lobby, with an elevator on my left and a fragrant bouquet of flowers on a stand to my right. A door was marked STAIRS. The air smelled vaguely of burned popcorn, and I saw a small kitchenette counter with a microwave, a coffee machine, and a minifridge. Easing farther in, I scanned quickly for cameras. There were none.

Then I looked past the flowers through a large, plateglass window, and my heart went still.

Rows of sleep shells lined an underground vault, making the spacious room glow with the soft light of their lids.

"What is this?" I whispered.

It couldn't be storage because the sleep shells were on. With a prickling sense of apprehension, I pushed through the door and looked into the closest one. Beneath the curved, glass lid, a young woman lay in a gray gown with a blanket covering her from waist to toes. Soft blond hair spread out around her face onto a white pillow, and her expression was a mask of calm. Her eyes were covered with a thick, transparent gel, and two small tabs were attached at her temples.

Her chest rose and fell in soft breaths, proving she was alive, but she was completely, perfectly asleep. I turned to the next sleep shell. A teenage boy lay in a similar state. The wispy fuzz of a first beard showed on his jaw, and his cheekbones were prominent, as if he'd been subsisting on an insufficient diet.

"Can you hear me?" I whispered.

He didn't stir. With expanding horror, I looked into the next sleep shell at a child. A kid no more than five or six. He was asleep like all the others, and so small he was dwarfed by his roomy sleep shell. Stunned, I stared at the bleak rows of sleep shells. Over two dozen people were sleeping in the vault. What were they doing here?

A network of tubes and cords crisscrossed an overhead framework and dropped lines down to each sleep shell. Along the far right-hand wall was another plateglass window and another door. I moved nearer, careful not to bump any of the

311

sleep shells, and peered in at a dark room with a white table. The door opened soundlessly at my touch, and as I reached along the wall for a light switch, I inhaled a familiar scent of vinegar.

I flipped the light. Three empty surgical tables occupied the center of a complete operating room. Trays of instruments were arranged within easy reach, while lights, monitors, and touch screens bulged on retractable arms from the walls and ceiling. This, I realized, was where Dr. Ash had been operating that night I'd watched Dean Berg advise her from the sixth floor of the dean's tower.

As I switched off the light and backed out, the impact of the two rooms hit me. The doctor could operate on everyone here. So could the dean. These people were being stored here on purpose, like living carrion, for the doctor and Dean Berg to mine and seed. What was to stop them from doing the same surgeries to Forge students? To me?

Jerking my video camera around on its strap, I lifted it quickly and turned it on.

"I'm under the Forge School," I narrated in a frantic whisper. I panned the vault, including the entrance to the operating room. "There's an operating room through there," I said. I started quickly back the way I'd come, toward the lobby, and I zoomed in on the faces as I passed. One was a young girl with a scar across her forehead. In fact, at least half of them were children.

I wanted to scream. Stumbling, I knocked into one of the sleep shells, and let out a gasp. The tube connecting to the ceiling swayed, but the boy inside didn't move.

You need to go, said my inner voice.

She was right. I couldn't get caught down here.

Even if the dean hadn't figured out yet where I was, he must have noticed by now that I wasn't in my dorm. He would be looking for me. I did one last, wide sweep with my video camera, and then I rushed out to the lobby. The elevator and the stairs were no good. I didn't know where they would lead. Instead, I pushed through the door to the dark tunnel again and used my penlight to guide me back to the pit.

I slung my camera strap across my shoulder and pushed open the glass door.

Above me, the cylinder of the pit rose as black as ever. I gripped the light with my teeth again, and started climbing. In my hurry, I forgot to count the rungs. Pulling myself up was ten times harder than coming down. My bad right arm was only strong enough to hold on for a moment while I used my left to draw myself up, and I had to keep testing each rung, fearful of depending on the one that was loose.

Finally, my hand met the open space at the top of the pit. My heart nearly burst with relief. Grabbing the railing, I heaved myself over onto firm ground. Every one of my muscles was trembling. I took the penlight from my clenched teeth and flicked it off. I licked my dry lips and tried to calm my breathing, but my fear wouldn't fade.

Dean Berg had a vault full of living bodies hidden under the Forge School.

I had just crawled, hand over hand, out of a nightmare.

27

TRYST

I STEPPED TO the door of the clock tower and listened for any noise outside. Parker, Otis, and Linus must be long gone, but I didn't know where Dean Berg or the security guard was. That guard was an unknown factor. Once before, when I was out of my dorm, the dean hadn't wanted to get security involved. That could be an advantage for me.

I knew what would be smartest: taking my footage public. The best way would be to reveal it during the day, on *The Forge Show*, when hundreds of thousands of viewers were watching. There'd be no way for the dean to undo the exposure, and authorities would have to investigate. All I had to do was make it safely to six o'clock the next morning. Then I could hook up my video camera to one of the big monitors in Media Convergence, and the rest would be cake.

The only question now was where to hide my video camera so the dean couldn't find it before morning and erase my footage. I didn't dare leave it here in the clock tower. Maybe the laundry room would work again. I'd been lucky there before.

I pushed the door open a crack, and when I saw no one, I crouched low and ran for the rosebushes. I crawled between them on the sandy gravel to where the garden met the quad, and stopped to watch again. The crickets were softer now. The first floor office of the dean's tower had gone dark, but the penthouse was lit. When the quad stayed clear and quiet, I bolted for the side of the film building.

Keeping low, I hurried behind the hedge, along the length of the building, and around the corner. I crept into the shadow behind the dumpster. From there, I peeked out. The girls' dorm was next, across one last open space. I hesitated, watching the shadowed area around the back door, and just as I decided to go for it, a dense shape in the bushes moved slightly. I held still. Someone was hiding across from me.

I backed up and pulled my walkie-ham out of my pocket. I could barely see the numbers as I dialed to channel four. "Linus?" I whispered, and lifted the speaker to my ear.

"Hey," he said. "You're awake."

"Where are you?" I asked.

"Right outside your dorm, but don't come down. It's been a crazy night."

"I know," I said. "I'm already out. I'm right around the corner from you."

315

"Where?"

"To your left as you face the door. Behind the dumpster." I peeked around the corner again, and the dark shape shifted in the bushes.

"Don't move," he said, and disconnected.

I shifted back on my heels and braced a hand on the wall, watching the shadows. A minute later, Linus slid in beside me, behind the dumpster, and I cradled my sore arm close so he wouldn't bump it.

"What are you doing out here?" he whispered.

"You're not going to believe what I found," I said. "There's a vault full of bodies under the school. They're alive. I don't know if they're in comas or what, but there are a couple dozen of them at least, and some of them are kids."

"Are you serious?"

"I found them down the pit in the clock tower. I have it all here, on tape."

"Let me see," Linus said.

"We don't have time," I said. "I don't want to get caught here. We need to get this out to the authorities."

"Do you want me to take it?" he asked.

I weighed the idea, uncertain. My video camera might be safer with him. He might be able to give it to the police better than I could.

"Don't you trust me?" he asked.

The question made me doubt. Linus worked for Dean Berg. I'd even seen him in the dean's penthouse.

"What would you do with it?" I asked.

"Whatever you want," he said. "Better yet, you should come with me."

"To Forgetown?" I asked.

His features were barely discernible in the darkness. "Rosie, if what you say is true, what do you think is going to happen once you show people?" he asked.

I didn't have any fear for myself. "Berg is the problem," I said. But even as I spoke, I knew my evidence was going to bring chaos. The entire school was going to be ripped apart.

A flashlight beam scanned across the pavement by the dumpster, and I instinctively crouched down farther.

"Hold still," Linus whispered.

But it was already too late.

"Who's there?" a man called. His beam slowly scanned the steps to the girls' dorm, then the bushes, and then returned to outline the dumpster. I didn't dare breathe. "This is security. Come on out now, before you get hurt." Footsteps came slowly nearer. "Sandy? You with me? We've got a disturbance down here. I think one of your students is out."

I felt Linus's fingers grip mine.

"I know you're behind the dumpster," the guard said. "Come on out of there. There's no use hiding."

My gut instinct was to bolt, but even if I could outrun the guard, the cameras would identify who I was and where I went. I would be caught soon enough. It was smarter to try to talk my way out of this. I started to rise. Linus gripped my hand, keeping me down.

"Give me the camera," he whispered.

Torn, I vacillated. I could leave my footage with Linus and hope he didn't get caught, or I could keep it with me and take my chances with the guard. A flashlight beam shone in my eyes, and I lifted a hand against the glare.

"Rosie?" the guard said. "Who else is there?"

"Nobody," I said, moving more fully into the open.

"Linus? What is this?" asked the guard.

I looked back to see he had stepped out, too.

"What's it look like?" Linus said. "Give me a break."

The guard was a big, strapping guy in a beige uniform with handcuffs and a billy club at his belt. He was shaking his head. "Why am I not surprised?"

A second man came around the corner, a tall, thin guy with a hatchet face and a gray beard. My heart stopped. I knew him. He was the one who had helped Dr. Ash that first night, with Janice. He touched a hand to his earphone, and nodded. "Got that. Sandy wants us to hold them here. He'll be out in a minute."

"Who would you be?" the security guard asked him.

"Jerry Snellings," said the bearded man. "I'm covering for Dr. Ash. We met a couple months ago, remember?"

"Right. The nurse practitioner," the guard said. "Can you believe these two? We'll have drama on the show tomorrow, and that's a fact."

The men didn't normally work together. I made a flash decision.

"Listen," I said to the guard. "We need your help. Something's wrong here at the school. Dean Berg is doing experiments on people."

Jerry laughed. "Not another one of these," he said. "If you want my advice, just stick to the romantic tryst."

The security guard rested a hand on his hip and began to smile.

I spoke directly to him. "You don't believe me. But I can prove it," I said. "I took footage that proves it."

"Let's see that," the guard said.

I hesitated, looking again toward Jerry. "I just want to keep it until morning," I said. "I'll show it then."

The guard reached out his hand. "Nice try. Hand it over."

I backed up, but the guard moved in. When he grabbed my sore arm, I shrieked in pain and dropped my camera.

"Leave her alone!" Linus said, and he dove at the guard.

The guard spun to block him and I was thrown off balance. Linus and the guard wrestled in a tangle of blows. They banged up against the dumpster, but then the big guard pinned Linus facedown to the ground.

"Let me up!" Linus said. "This is ridiculous!"

"I'd watch myself if I were you, love bird," the guard said. "Somebody's about to lose his job, is my bet." And he snapped handcuffs on Linus's wrists.

"Are you kidding me?" Linus exclaimed. "Get these off me."

But the guard left the cuffs on. He gave Linus a pull and he scrambled to his feet, breathing hard.

"Are you all right, Rosie?" Linus asked.

"I'm okay."

I was clutching my sore elbow, but I was more worried about the condition of Linus's face. He rubbed his mouth awkwardly against his shoulder. I looked rapidly for my camera and I spotted it in Jerry's hand.

Hurried footsteps sounded around the corner as Dean Berg burst into view. "Rosie!" he said. "Unbelievable. And Linus. I expected better of you. I really did."

"Make him uncuff me," Linus said.

"Roosevelt? What's going on here?" the dean asked. He pushed up the sleeves of his Forge sweatshirt.

The guard was searching Linus's pockets, and he pulled out the walkie-ham. "I caught them behind the dumpster," he said. "The girl says you're doing experiments on the students."

The dean turned to me. "I beg your pardon?"

"What are you doing to us in our sleep?" I demanded. "Mining us? Seeding us?"

Dean Berg's expression turned from surprise to concern. "Was she like this when you met up with her tonight?" he asked Linus.

"Don't try that. You know exactly what I mean," I said. "I saw you. You had Dr. Ash operating on a little boy. And you've got a whole supply of people sleeping in coffins down under the school. I've seen them."

The dean shook his head sadly. "They get addled when they skip their pills," he said. "They have nightmares. I don't know how this happened after I specifically asked Dr. Ash to be sure Rosie took her meds. Jerry, do you have a sedative?"

"Stay away from me," I said. "I didn't have any nightmare. It was real. I filmed it. It's there." I pointed to my camera in Jerry's hand.

"Let's see," the dean said, beckoning.

"I don't want you to mess with it," I said. "Don't let him," I said to Roosevelt.

The guard was watching closely, but he didn't intervene.

"I think I can turn on a camera without messing it up," the dean said mildly. "Jerry?"

Jerry passed the video camera over. The dean opened the viewfinder and tapped the screen once. He gazed intently for a long moment, watching the footage. Then, with an unreadable look, he passed the camera to me. "Is this what you mean?"

In the viewfinder, I saw footage of my dorm, with the girls all lined up and asleep in their sleep shells. I fast-forwarded through the clip, then clicked to the menu to locate the scene from the underground vault. It wasn't there.

"It was here," I said. "I just shot it. What did you do to it?"

"Did you see Dr. Ash operating on a little boy, too?" the dean asked Linus.

"No."

"The operation wasn't tonight," I said, still checking the menu of my video camera again. "What I found tonight was the vault with all the sleeping bodies. What did you do to my camera?"

"Nothing," the dean said, raising his hands. "How did you get in the tunnels? Neither of you has a pass."

"We didn't go in the tunnels," I said, and I was about to

321

tell him I had gone down the pit of the clock tower when I realized he was fishing for information.

"We met right here," Linus said quietly.

I turned to him. With his wrists cuffed behind him, his shirt was twisted and bunched across his chest. A pocket of his jeans was turned out. His hair was messed and his lip was swollen, but worst of all, his gaze was hard.

"We met to fool around," Linus added. "But she was a little confused. I was trying to get her to go back to bed. Her own bed, that is."

I felt like I'd been punched. "You asswipe," I said.

He gave a crooked smile. "See what I mean about the confusion?" he said.

I spun toward the guard. "You have to start an investigation. What I'm telling you is true. I don't care what the dean or Linus says."

"It's no use, Rosie," Linus said. "They caught us."

"This is not about us!" I said.

Jerry took a step nearer to me. "You want me to take her to the infirmary?" he asked the dean.

"I think that's best," Dean Berg said.

I backed away from Jerry, looking desperately from the dean to the guard to Linus who was now watching me through narrowed eyes. With a shock, I saw that he wasn't only mad. Underneath his bogus claims about a tryst Linus was furious. Like he'd been duped or betrayed.

But *I* was the one who had just been forsaken.

"Thanks a lot, Linus," I said. "That was a great night."

"Rosie, you have to admit—"

I turned sharply away and took two paces before I realized I had nowhere to go. I had no one to help me and no one to believe me. I stared blindly toward the girls' dorm, trying to think what to do.

"Give him a ride home, Roosevelt," Dean Berg said. "And get the cuffs off before Otis sees him. More trouble is the last thing I'd wish on Otis tonight, but there it is. Tell him I'll give him a call in the morning."

"You're not firing me," Linus said.

"Obviously, I am," Dean Berg said. "I warned you once already, remember?"

I turned back to them. "You can't fire him. It's my fault. All of it."

"It's not looking good for you, either, I'm afraid," the dean said. "I can try to appeal to the board, but the trustees have little sympathy for students who skip their pills and meet up with their boyfriends."

"Good. Expel her and send her home," Linus said, staring toward me. "She obviously doesn't belong here."

"Linus!" I said.

"Go on. Take him," Dean Berg said.

"No, wait, please!" I said. "Mr. Roosevelt, you *have* to believe me. You have to start an investigation."

"I hope you feel better soon, Miss. I surely do." The guard prodded Linus in the other direction, and Linus turned away with him.

I glared at Jerry and Dean Berg, just waiting for one of

323

them to crack a satisfied, victorious smirk. Neither one did. Dean Berg merely made a gesture to guide me toward the infirmary.

"Why'd you do this, Rosie?" Dean Berg asked. "Why couldn't you just stay in bed like the other kids?"

"You know why," I said. "You don't have to pretend anymore. Nobody's watching."

He shook his head slowly. "I don't think you understand," he said. "Somebody's always watching."

>>>>>>>>

It didn't take long for a female medic to meet us at the infirmary, and Dean Berg left me in her care. She confiscated my walkie-ham, outfitted me with a nightie and a robe, and showed me to a small, tidy room where I found a sleep shell and a cupboard for clothes. Out the window, the dark shape of Otis's tower loomed high against the night sky, while farther downhill, on its own knoll, the observatory hunkered with its smaller silhouette. It was hard to believe that not even twenty-four hours had passed since my accident there with Burnham.

So much had happened. I pressed my forehead against the glass and tried to put things together. I knew I'd seen the bodies sleeping in the vault, but they didn't show on my video camera. The dean, or more likely Jerry, now that I thought about it, had deleted my footage. After all I had seen, the proof of it was gone.

How can you prove something is true when you're the only one who knows it? Not even Linus believed me. That hurt. He had lied to the dean and the others without flinching, as if he sincerely believed it would make a difference if he could persuade them that we'd only met to fool around. Like that was the noble thing to do.

An agonizing possibility occurred to me. If I had trusted Linus and left my video camera with him, he might have made it safely to Forgetown with my footage. I would have been caught out of bed, but the dean wouldn't have known that I'd seen the vault.

Instead, I was here, and Linus had lost his job.

All those pitiful people down in the vault. Did they even know where they were?

My elbow hurt, and so did my brain.

We need to save them, came the voice from the back of my mind.

I went quiet and alert.

I think I blew it, I said. My discouragement was more than I could put into words, even to myself.

I felt a faint plucking, deep in my mind, delicate as a trembling spiderweb.

"Don't leave me," I said aloud.

Then, unbidden, a barrage of images cascaded rapidly through my mind:

> the fat girl Jill from my old school trying to cover
> her naked body

my mother weeping at the end of the kitchen table
Ellen on the bathroom floor with her kitty purse
Burnham on the pavers, all but lifeless

Stop! I told her. *What's your point?*
It's easier if you close your eyes.

I did, pressing a hand to my forehead, and then, more vividly than in real life, I was back among the rows of sleep shells in the vault, with face after dreaming face, motionless and inanimate. These were the most helpless of all. I peered at one child, at the clear gel that covered her eyelids and clung to her lashes, and from deep inside her, I could feel her mute, desperate begging.

Now do you see?

I wanted to save them. All of them. It was what I had always wanted to do.

28

A DETERRENT

I MUST HAVE slept, because when the clock tower chimed six that Friday morning, I woke in the infirmary. Even before I consciously remembered why I was not in the dorm, my gut pitched with anxiety. Burnham. Linus. The vault.

Dr. Ash knocked on my door and gently opened it. "Rosie? You up?"

"Yes."

"Dean Berg wants you over at the dean's tower as soon as you've showered and changed."

I sat up, swung my legs over the side of the sleep shell, and rubbed my hands over my face. I felt god-awful.

"How's the elbow?" she asked.

I tested my right arm, which was stiff and tender. "Okay."

"Let me see that."

I held up my nightie sleeve while she manipulated my elbow, and I winced at a new stab of pain.

"Just as I thought," she said. "You're wearing a sling and I'm prescribing an anti-inflammatory with a pain killer."

"I don't want anything."

"You're taking it, anyway," the doctor said.

"No, I'm not. It's my body, and I don't want anything else in it," I said. "Just tell me. Have you heard anything about Burnham?"

For a moment the doctor considered me. "He made it through the night. The hospital in Chicago specializes in brain trauma, so he's getting the best possible care."

I nodded.

The doctor crossed her arms and briefly tapped her foot. "You puzzle me, Rosie. I saw you swallow your sleeping pill myself, so I can only assume you regurgitated it afterward on purpose. And then, sneaking out to meet your boyfriend was obviously wrong, but I can almost understand it. You had a near brush with death yourself. You're naturally confused and upset. Is that what this is all about?"

I watched her cautiously. It was like she was feeding me my own story, minus the trip to the vault, and she was doing it on camera. I ran with the hint.

"I wanted to see Linus," I said. "I just wanted to be with him."

The doctor nodded. "The dean is going to interrogate you," she said. "He's called a special session of the board, and four of the trustees have flown in."

328

I clued on the fact that the board could be watching my feed right now, overhearing this conversation. I needed to use that. I had to act as innocent as possible, like someone who knew nothing except the surface level activity of Forge.

"Are they going to send me home?" I asked. "I don't want to go."

"I suggest you tell them the truth, then," she said. "You were still upset about Burnham, and you wanted to see your boyfriend."

I laughed. "Ex-boyfriend now." It hurt to admit it.

Dr. Ash tilted her face and smiled kindly. "I know it seems hard. You've been under a lot of stress. Let's hope the trustees factor that into account."

She had her nice stage persona down perfectly.

"Thanks," I said. I shifted away from her and stood to reach for my clothes.

"Now, about that anti-inflammatory," she said.

"No." I stepped into the washroom to clean up and change.

Soon after, I was headed out the door with Dr. Ash beside me. It was another bright, cool morning, and it was odd to stroll along the busy quad and see the rose garden, the clock tower, and the other students all unchanged. As far as they knew, last night could have never happened. The only difference was a janitor hosing off the stairs of the dean's tower, spraying water where Parker had urinated.

Inside the foyer of the dean's tower, my gaze was drawn to the dome ceiling with its rippled squares of gold leaf. I'd been here not long before.

"This way," Dr. Ash said, and led me to the right, into an office.

I followed uneasily. "Is this meeting on camera?" I asked.

"Of course," she said. "You're still a student here until the board decides otherwise."

The dean's office was a plush, old-fashioned room, with a high ceiling and sweeping drapes. Shelves of books lined the walls, and a fireplace was capped by a portrait of a stern, old woman.

Behind the desk, dressed in tweed and a silvery blue tie, Dean Berg removed a pair of glasses and rose to his feet. "And here she is. Good morning, Rosie," he said. "I'd like you to meet a few of our trustees. All of them have come expressly to consider your case, and I'm indebted to them for their time."

Half a dozen people turned to appraise me while the dean made introductions. Mr. Thomas Joiner was a beady-eyed, balding man in a leather chair beside the fireplace. Across from him, Mrs. Peabody-Lily, a pale, elderly woman in frills, turned down the corner of her lips. Mr. Elliot O'Toole was a distinguished-looking man in his thirties, and his pretty wife, Barbara, a dark woman with a choker of dainty pearls, said hello from beside a tea cart.

Last, a short, elderly man turned from a corner bookshelf, and I was surprised to recognize Otis. Without his hat or his camera, he looked oddly shorn.

"Otis Fairwell, our staff representative, I believe you've met," the dean continued.

"How's Linus?" I asked Otis.

"About as you'd imagine," he answered, unsmiling.

Not a good sign.

Dean Berg leaned back against his desk and crossed his ankles. His ruddy cheeks looked freshly scrubbed, and not a hair was out of place. "So, Rosie," he said. "We'd like an account of what you did last night, from your perspective. Start from the beginning."

I glanced at Otis again before I spoke.

"I was upset about Burnham," I said. "I just wanted to be with a friend, so I called Linus on my walkie-ham and asked him to meet me."

"That's what Linus says, too," Otis said.

Dean Berg gave a slight nod in Otis's direction. "And how did you stay awake, Rosie?"

"I regurgitated my sleeping pill after I swallowed it," I said.

"Have you done that before?" asked Mr. Joiner, the beady-eyed guy.

"No," I said. "It was my first time. I was just going to meet Linus to talk for a little and go back to bed. That's all. But then we got caught."

"According to Mr. Roosevelt's report, he found the two of you behind a dumpster by the girls' dorm," Mr. Joiner said. "That's not a particularly romantic place to meet."

"But it's dark," I pointed out.

Mrs. Peabody-Lily set her teacup in her saucer with a click. "The sleeping policy is for your protection and your health, young lady, not to mention your education," she said.

"If you'd slept, like you were supposed to, you would have had a break from your stress."

"But I didn't want one," I said. "I didn't deserve one." I twisted my fingers together behind my back. "My friend Burnham is hurt because of me. He might die. I couldn't go peacefully to sleep while that was happening."

"So you went to make out with your boyfriend," Mr. Joiner said.

I turned to the beady-eyed man. "Wouldn't you?"

Mr. Joiner's voice was deceptively courteous. "You might mind that tongue of yours, my girl. You're not doing yourself any favors."

"She's obviously lying and using the accident as an excuse," Mrs. Peabody-Lily said. "A girl who will break the rules to sneak out of her bed and meet a boy is not the sort of student we want here at Forge."

"If I may," interjected Mrs. O'Toole. "The point we should be discussing is Rosie's mental health. The girl is falling apart as we speak. Forge has an obligation to see to her welfare. A student shouldn't have to sneak out of her bed to plead for our attention."

"You cannot mean to imply that the school is to blame for her condition," Mrs. Peabody-Lily said.

"I'm saying she might be part of a bigger picture. What about these reports of suicidal alums?" Mrs. O'Toole said. "Were you aware of these, Sandy?"

"What are you talking about?" I asked.

Dean Berg ran a hand around his jaw. "When you asked

the other day about the numbers of Forge alums who have died young, you hit a nerve in our alumni community."

"I haven't heard from anybody," I said.

"No. They wisely directed their comments to me," Dean Berg said. "Apparently, a few others have wondered the same thing, and now they're calling in."

"This is very serious. What have you found?" asked Mrs. Peabody-Lily.

"We have a unique population here," Dean Berg said. "High achieving, but also, if I may say so, highly strung generally. There's no evidence the school itself has a negative impact on its students' mental health. If anything, the opposite is true."

"So you're saying any correlation between attending Forge and early death is strictly coincidence?" Mrs. Peabody-Lily said.

"Absolutely. Strictly coincidence," Dean Berg said.

"But what are the numbers?" Otis asked.

Dean Berg and Dr. Ash exchanged glances.

"What Sandy says is true: any correlation can't be proved," Dr. Ash said. "That being said, I have records of eight young Forge alums who have died in the past two years, three by accident and five by suicide."

"Five suicides," Mr. Joiner said, sitting up. "For a school this size, that's significant. How about it, Sandy?"

"Naturally, we're looking into it," Dean Berg said.

"Did you talk to Ellen's family?" I asked.

"This is a sensitive time for the Thorpe family," Dean Berg

333

said. "We've reached out with our condolences, but anything more would be inappropriate."

"What about suicide *attempts*?" I said. "How many of those have you tracked?"

Dr. Ash answered, directing her attention toward Dean Berg. "We don't have a number for that yet."

Mrs. O'Toole turned to me. "Tell us, Rosie. Honestly. Have you been feeling well? Yesterday on the ladder with young Fister wasn't the first time you felt faint, was it?"

I looked across at Dean Berg, who gazed back mildly at me.

"There was one other time, in the observatory," I said. "Dean Berg was there."

"Any other times?" Mrs. O'Toole asked. "Were you feeling poorly when you snuck out last night, for instance?"

I wavered. I had her sympathy now. Even without proof, I might get the trustees to investigate the vault of sleeping bodies if I told about them. But from the dean's patient, nonchalant features, I suddenly guessed that if I said something about the vault, I'd be playing into his hands. He was ready for me. He had some surefire way to protect himself, while if I spoke the truth, I would prove that I was crazy.

Mrs. O'Toole was still waiting for my answer. "Rosie?"

"I've been fine," I said in a low voice.

"Despite your fall yesterday?" Mrs. O'Toole pressed.

"I'm worried about Burnham, of course, but myself, I'm fine," I said.

Mrs. O'Toole touched a hand absently to her pearls. "I'm not sure what to think," she said. "It does seem, with her friend's fall and how upset she was, that we might have extenuating circumstances. It was Rosie's first offense of any kind."

The dean drummed his fingers on the edge of his desk. Then he turned to swipe his touch screen and nodded toward a low cabinet. With a soft whirling, a large screen rose out of the cabinet. "I believe it's only fair to show you this," he said.

From the speakers came the noise of rushing water. The camera slowly zoomed in on a tile roof, slick with rain, where a solitary figure stood on a catwalk, just below a skylight. I stared, spellbound. A girl in a drenched nightgown hobbled barefoot along the grating. Then she paused and straightened, pushing back her tangle of wet hair. She arched her back, turning to look in all directions, and then, with surprising grace, she spread her arms out to the sky. She flung her head back and opened her mouth wide, drinking in the rain and the night.

She was me, more powerful and beautiful than I'd ever dreamed.

Pride, and sorrow, and a hint of rage triggered inside me.

"You shouldn't have filmed that," I said, turning to the dean. "I thought I was alone."

He froze the picture. "You're at Forge," he replied.

He might as well have said he owned me.

Mrs. O'Toole set her teacup on the trolley. "Well," she said. "That changes things."

"Beautiful," said Mr. Joiner quietly. "Such a shame."

Otis spoke up from his corner. "Explain, Sandy. When did this happen?"

"Very early the morning of the fifty cuts," Dean Berg said. "Rosie's precisely the sort of person we need here. And if I do say so, the viewers agree with me. I couldn't have been more pleased when she passed the cuts."

"That doesn't negate the fact that you should have expelled her right then, the first time she broke the rules," said Mrs. Peabody-Lily. "You were quite remiss, Sandy."

"I could have sent her home then, certainly. But she got me thinking," Dean Berg said. "It's never comfortable for an institution to have its basic principles flaunted. Here was a student who broke the rules to stand in the rain at night. She had nothing to gain from taking such a risk, and everything to lose, but she did it."

Mrs. Peabody-Lily closed her eyes and shook her head. "We already have a school full of artists. They're inherently rule breakers." She opened her eyes again to glare at Dean Berg, but she was half laughing, too. "You're no better than one of the kids yourself."

"I beg to disagree. I take my duties very seriously," Dean Berg said.

"Then what is your recommendation?" Mr. Joiner asked.

The dean shifted his weight against the desk. "I'm torn, frankly. Send her home, and we lose a promising student. I'd be concerned for her health, as well. Rosie comes from a family with few resources and limited access to health care, whereas we could obviously continue to monitor her closely here. Then again, if we keep her, we're setting a dangerous precedent. Other students might feel they can skip their pills, too, which would be disastrous for the entire program."

"Hello," I said. "I'm right here in the room."

"We're not keeping this girl. She's a liar and a cheat," Mrs. Peabody-Lily said.

"We could put it up to the viewers," proposed Mr. Joiner. "Let them vote. It would be good spectacle."

"We are not letting viewers weigh in on a disciplinary issue," Mr. O'Toole said.

"No, Mr. Joiner is on to something," Mrs. O'Toole said. "What's her current blip rank, Sandy?"

The dean leaned over to see the screen on his desk. "She's number four," he said.

I let out a laugh. "Me? Now? I'm in fourth place?" It was my highest rank yet. My heart started thudding. "But why? Do they just want to see me get expelled?"

"It's drama, my girl," Mr. Joiner said. "Our viewers like drama."

"It's not that simple," Dean Berg said. "Rosie's drawing in an important new demographic of viewers to the show. Two new demographics, in fact. She has a vast number of followers among the very poor, like herself—no offense, Rosie— and a small but significant following of elite viewers."

"I see," said Mrs. Peabody-Lily in arctic tones.

I didn't. "What do you mean?" I asked.

"Elite viewers are the hyper-wealthy," Mr. O'Toole explained. "They've been known to donate huge sums to the school, sometimes on a whim."

Mrs. Peabody-Lily rose from her chair. "Be that as it may, we do not make disciplinary decisions based on blip rank. I'm with Mr. O'Toole on this. It would be common."

Otis made a snorting noise. "Common?" he said. "Let me remind you that the entire school is a *reality show*. You've just been calculating Rosie's value like she's a prize attraction at a freak show." He pushed away from the bookshelf. "If you're finished with this nonsense, I've got a job to do."

"Don't leave," I said. He was the closest thing I had to an ally.

Otis crossed his arms and frowned in exasperation. "Then tell me. What do you think we should do, Rosie?"

I looked across at the dean, who watched me curiously.

"Please, Rosie. We'd welcome your opinion," Mrs. O'Toole said. "How do you think we should handle your case?"

"Easy," I said. "The board should send me home and demand the dean's resignation."

The dean's face went stiff. "I beg your pardon?"

Otis laughed. "She's right, Sandy. You broke the rules when you kept that roof scene of Rosie a secret. That's a far more serious offense than hers. What gives you the right? What else have you kept hidden that we don't know about?"

"I believe, as dean, I'm trusted to use my own judgment in certain situations," Dean Berg said.

"Yes," Otis said wryly. "And because Rosie has a few elite viewer fans, you've already made your decision to let her stay. This meeting is a farce and a waste of my time."

"Gracious!" Mrs. O'Toole said, laughing.

"Sandy, with all due respect to Mr. Fairwell and his colorful analogies, I can see the point of keeping Rosie," Mr. Joiner said. "But if we do, what reassurance do we have that she won't break the rules again?"

"There are cameras," Mr. O'Toole said.

"We do leave the cameras on at night," Dean Berg agreed. "It's a health and safety precaution."

"I thought the staff left at midnight," Mr. Joiner said.

"The techies do, but another small team headed by Dr. Ash takes over then," Dean Berg said. "And we have campus security around the clock, obviously. That's how Roosevelt apprehended Rosie and Linus last night."

"Has anyone talked to my parents?" I asked.

"I did an hour ago," Dean Berg said. "They're very disappointed in you, understandably. They'll support any decision we make."

Disappointed. My stepfather was going to be a lot more than disappointed. A clamp tightened in my gut.

"I do have one other idea that might have a bearing on this situation," Dean Berg said.

"Let's have it," Mr. Joiner said.

Dean Berg clasped both his hands deliberately together. "It seems to me the threat of expulsion has not been a sufficient deterrent to keep Rosie in her sleep shell," he said. "I propose that she signs a contract agreeing to follow the rules. If she doesn't, her parents can cede guardianship over to the school, and we can manage her care from then on."

"You cannot be serious," I said.

Mrs. O'Toole laughed. "We are not in the business of becoming legal guardians to our students, Sandy."

"We did it once before. Remember?" Mrs. Peabody-Lily said.

"That's right," Mr. Joiner said. "You may recall I once served as legal guardian for another one of our scholarship students who lost his parents. It worked quite well. In Rosie's case, the point of guardianship will be moot as long as she follows the rules."

I turned to Mr. Joiner. "You can't possibly want to be my guardian."

"Not me. Sandy can incur the risk," Mr. Joiner said. "He's the one who wants to keep you. I say he can assume the responsibility for you if you disobey again."

"It's rather fitting, considering he overlooked your first transgression," Mr. O'Toole said. "He clearly has a soft spot for you."

"And if it turns out she's mentally unstable, the school can foot the bill for her care. That should satisfy my dear Mrs. O'Toole's soft-hearted concerns," Mrs. Peabody-Lily said. "Solves everything."

"I'm not giving up my parents," I said. "Certainly not to have Dean Berg named as my guardian."

"We're not asking you to give up your parents," Mrs. O'Toole said gently. "We're simply asking you to obey the rules, like every other student. Do you want to stay at Forge or not? This is your education we're talking about. Your future."

I glanced at Otis.

The old man shrugged. "They're mad. All of them. But you play their way or you go home."

I thought then of the sleeping bodies in the vault. I was the only one who knew about them, the only one who had a shot at saving them. I looked around at the watching adults and ended facing Dean Berg. He was smiling with grave concern, as if he had nothing but my well-being at heart.

"I'll stay," I said.

Dean Berg's smile expanded warmly. "Wise decision."

29

THE OBSERVATORY

THE DEAN WANTED to confer with the school's legal team about the guardianship contract. He emphasized that my parents would only surrender guardianship *if* I disobeyed the rules. He added that I should talk to my parents and take the day to think it over, and in the meantime, I should attend my classes like normal.

As if normal was possible anymore.

As soon as I made it down to Media Convergence, Janice leapt up from the couch and pounced on me.

"What happened? Are you crazy? What were doing up at night?" she demanded.

"Did you watch the meeting in the dean's office or not?" I asked.

"I did. We all did," she said.

The other students in the room had gone silent, watching us. Henrik and Paige were hovering nearby. Burnham's usual desk was horribly empty.

Mr. DeCoster rose from his desk in the corner. "What can we do for you, Rosie?" he asked.

I shook my head. "I just want to call my mother."

"Here. Borrow my phone," Janice said, and she thrust it into my hand.

I dialed my mom's work number, and got a busy signal. I wondered if she was on the line with Dean Berg. I tried several more times, but the line was always busy. When I tried our home line, thinking to leave a message with Larry, that line was busy, too.

"I can't reach her," I said finally, when I handed back Janice's phone.

"Don't worry," Janice said. "She has to know what's going on here. She'll call you as soon as she can."

I tried to picture my mom juggling calls and trying to keep everything going at the cafeteria, too. I knew she'd call me when she could.

My gaze kept going to Burnham's empty seat until I couldn't stand it anymore. I went over to the Ping-Pong table, snatched up a ball, and strode back to Burnham's desk. I set a paperclip in front of the touch screen he always used, and just like he had done once, I rested the white ball inside the clip so it couldn't roll away. It looked small and fragile there, but playful, too.

The room had grown quiet around me.

"He'll be back," Henrik said.

That was what we all wanted. I wondered how many of the others didn't believe it was true.

For the rest of the day, I was distracted and preoccupied. All of Burnham's friends were. I kept thinking about him, but I also kept thinking about the vault from last night and Linus angry at me. Each trouble gave me a different kind of guilt that hung heavily inside me, like the clock weights in the pit of the tower. As the hours passed and I didn't say anything about the sleepers in the vault, I felt worse, like I was becoming an accomplice to their captivity.

Again and again, I circled back to the way Dean Berg had practically dared me to talk about the vault in front of the trustees today. He had to have some way to protect his secrets. He could possibly, theoretically, close off the tunnel that connected the bottom of the pit to the vault. Somehow.

I felt like a mad girl, inventing bizarre scenarios.

What would happen if I simply told the viewers what I knew? I could even go back to the pit myself, now, during the day.

A fitful wind blew up the quad, and I brushed my hair back, squinting toward the rose garden at the base of the clock tower. Pale, soft petals lingered on isolated blooms, and in the slanting afternoon light, their beauty touched me strangely. Above, on the clock tower, the motto around the face seemed to mock me: *Dream Hard. Work Harder. Shine.* I couldn't do any of those things while a vault of helpless dreamers slept beneath my feet.

They were my real ghosts. My real project wasn't a class assignment at all. I teetered in indecision, weighing if I should go into the clock tower. The cameras of the show would record my movements.

Cameras. They were my best tools now. I simply had to use them right, and I still had one video camera I had never checked. Several posts around the rose garden had button cameras on them, and I found the nearest one and spoke directly to it.

"Linus, if you want to talk, I'm heading to the observatory."

Burying my hands in my pockets, I lowered my head into the wind and headed east out of the quad. I could never pass behind the art building without remembering my first kiss, but today the sight of the wooden spools left me wistful.

I didn't want loneliness. I didn't want longing.

I strode down the pasture path without waving to Otis in his tower, and I headed up the little knoll to stare at the place where Burnham and I had climbed the observatory. The ladder was gone. Even the holes where it had been bracketed to the stone had been filled, since yesterday, with tidy patch.

Slowly, I closed in on the place where we'd fallen, searching for the exact paver where Burnham had hit his head. No grizzly hint of blood remained. I paused with the toes of my shoes aimed at two pavers, undecided. Resentful. I wanted to at least be able to blame a specific stone.

So pick one, she said.

I wiped the end of my nose with my sleeve and sniffed.

Picking one wasn't the same as knowing. I wanted certainty, and I wasn't getting it.

A flapping noise drew my gaze upward, and a dove flew feet-first toward a nook in the eaves. I strode closer and nearly tripped on a ladder that lay in the grass. It wasn't the heavy, old one that had been removed from the wall, but a lighter, portable kind that a worker would use.

Go on, said my voice.

I pictured how bad it would be if I grew dizzy halfway up the ladder, and I rubbed my tender right elbow. *How do I know you won't mess with my balance?* I asked.

She shifted faintly. **If I wanted to hurt you, I would have done it in the pit.**

That was reassuring, in a twisted sort of way.

The road to Forgetown was still empty, so I turned toward another small camera, this one on the wall of the observatory.

"Parker," I said clearly. "If you're watching, tell Linus to come talk to me. I want to see him. He'll listen to you."

Wrangling the ladder up against the observatory, I bounced it a couple times to settle it on steady footing. I looked up the length of the ladder, eyeing the shiny rungs, and started up. My right elbow still hindered me. I'd gone up half a dozen rungs when the ladder did an infinitesimal shift and I froze, waiting to see if it would slip farther. Beneath me, the ground tilted. A muffled cooing noise came from somewhere above me.

Then the tingling began, and the first hint of dizziness.

"No," I said, wrapping my arms around the ladder. *You said you wouldn't make me dizzy.*

That's not me.

Then help me, I said. I focused hard on the rung directly before my face, waiting while a fringe of blackness crowded the edge of my sight. *Make it stop*, I said.

Then let me, she said.

I quit fighting and closed my eyes. A sharp, driving pain scraped through my brain. For a vivid instant, I saw the stiff body of a dead man hanging from a noose, and then he imploded into a cloud of black particles. They shimmered, swirled once, and were gone.

I should have felt wildly unstable on the ladder, but instead, I felt solid again. Purged. Healed.

"What just happened?" I asked aloud.

Pesky garbage. It's gone now, the voice said.

I rested my cheek on the cool rung of the ladder. She wasn't the chattiest inner voice, but she made sense to me. *Am I hallucinating you, or are you my subconscious?*

Ours, she answered. **Our subconscious.**

That fit. I smiled, satisfied.

I moved steadily up the ladder to the dome level, and then up the second, shorter ladder to the satellite dish. As I leaned into the dish, another gust of wind messed my hair, and light reflected brightly in the concave shape. The duct tape and plastic protecting I had secured around the camera were awkward to unwrap, but I worked the camera free and returned with it to the dome level.

Sitting with my back to the sloping dome, I checked curiously through the footage. The video camera had captured one long, uninterrupted, two-week sequence of sky, from the day I'd turned it on until the camera had run out of memory and shut itself off. The summary bar of the video showed alternating light and dark stripes, for the days and nights, with cloud cover and rain. I turned up the little speaker on the camera and skimmed my finger back and forth along the footage, listening for audio spikes, where I slowed the audio to regular speed.

I heard bird noises, bongs from the clock tower, and occasional trucks. Nothing special. It shouldn't have been a letdown, but it was. Another audio spike fell in a nighttime segment, and I switched it to normal speed and lifted the camera to my ear.

A guy's voice came in, thin with a poor connection, but just audible.

"I'm in the lookout tower. You should see these stars," he said.

A girl answered him even more quietly. *"Are you still upset about Paige and the face app?"*

It was Linus and me, I realized, surprised. It took me another second to recognize our first conversation on the walkie-hams.

"Guys don't get upset. *Besides, you were right. It wasn't really your fault. Gorge on Forge took down the footage of me, for what that's worth. Are you awake every night?"*

"Yes. Since the fifty cuts. I skip my pill."

"You know that defeats the whole purpose, right? I mean, it's great to be able to talk to you, but you have to sleep for your creativity to go into full effect."

"I know that's what they say, but I'm not so sure that's the reason. Why did you say that thing about how I'm safe as long as I stay in bed?"

"Because students who leave their beds get sent home. I don't want that happening to you."

The conversation kept going, and I listened, spellbound. How nice Linus sounded. I had been so eager and excited to talk to him back then. It was strange that I'd ended up getting caught out of my bed, just like he'd warned me against. If I had listened to him, things would have turned out so differently. I never would have known about the vault.

When the conversation finally ended, I stared, stupefied, at the video camera in my hands. Another truth sank in. Just as the walkie-hams could pick up a rogue transmission, like mine had during the time I had overheard the dean and Huma, they could also transmit a conversation out to the airwaves. This video camera had picked up the transmissions via the satellite dish, which meant it would have been child's play for the dean to tap the same airwaves and listen in. In fact, all he would have needed was a third walkie-ham on the same channel. I should have thought of this before.

My nighttime conversations with Linus had never been private. All those times I'd poured out my heart and worried and questioned, we hadn't been alone. I felt so stupid. What else had I said into my walkie-ham over the past few weeks? Everything. Assuming Dean Berg had listened in, I had never had any secrets from him. Not one.

It must have been so easy for the dean to play me, all this

time. Did Linus know? He could have been part of the game this whole time. He worked for Dean Berg. Or he used to. Or maybe he still did, and they were only pretending Linus was fired.

"Rosie? Are you still up there?"

I glanced over the edge.

Linus was down below, gazing up.

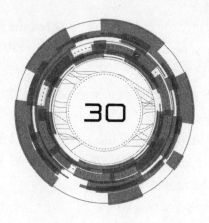

30

REAL USE

WITH THE FORESHORTENED angle and his hands on his hips, he looked annoyed, but not any more annoyed than I felt myself.

"What are you doing?" he demanded. "Do you have a death wish or something?"

"I had to get a video camera," I said, sliding the band over my wrist.

He braced both hands on the ladder. "I can't believe they let you go up there. Are you getting this, Otis? Are you asleep, Bones? You should have sent someone to bring her down."

"I don't need any rescuing," I said, and I turned again to descend backward. I moved carefully but quickly down the ladder, without the least bit of vertigo. My inner voice had fixed the problem entirely.

As my foot met the earth, Linus pivoted me into his arms. He had a new scratch on his cheek and a scab on his lower lip from last night.

"What did you think you were doing?" he said. "You could have fallen again."

"I'm not going to live my life afraid of ladders," I said.

"You have a dizziness problem. When are you going to realize that?" he said.

"You don't have to shake me," I said. "Why are you even holding me if you're mad?"

His lips pressed together in a line, but his grip on me turned gentle. "I'm not mad. I'm here to say goodbye. I'm leaving."

I went very still. Then I touched my fingers softly to his jacket. "Is this because of me? Because of last night?" I asked.

Linus shook his head.

"Yes, it is," I said. "Tell me what's going on."

"It's nothing complicated," he said. "Otis wants me to stay, but there aren't any decent jobs in Forgetown. I can't work here anymore, and I don't count getting bled for Parker as a real job, so I'm moving on."

"Where will you go?"

"I'm heading back to St. Louis," he said. "I can get a ride there later today with a trucker who's coming through."

"You mean Amby?"

I felt his hands slide lightly down my arms, but he didn't let me go completely.

"I might have been wrong about Amby," Linus said. "I haven't found any proof about his deliveries. I shouldn't have told you about that. It just gave you ideas."

I let out a brief laugh. "It didn't give me ideas."

"Something sure did," he said. He stepped back then and released me. "You know what I keep thinking about? I can't help wondering what would have happened if you'd given me your video camera last night when I asked."

"I should have," I said. "That was a mistake."

"But you didn't trust me." He slid a hand in his back pocket. "Isn't that funny? When it came right down to it, you trusted the security guard more than you trusted me. I keep telling myself it's just as well. If I'd taken your camera, I would have watched your footage, and this way, I never have to know for certain how much you made up."

"I didn't make it up," I said slowly. "Everything I've ever told you is true."

"No. It was a good story," he said. "It definitely got me to care about you, but let's be real now."

I searched his eyes. "You've never believed me? All this time?"

"Actually, I did something worse," he said. "I believed *in* you. That was *my* mistake."

I tried to think about it from his perspective, but a tight, aching ball in my chest was making it hard for me to breathe. "Then you think I'm crazy. That I imagine things."

"Don't we all?" he asked quietly.

I took a step back. My fingers felt suddenly cold, and the video camera slid heavily down my wrist. "I know the difference between imagination and reality, Linus."

"Come on," he said. "If you could just admit it once, maybe we could still at least be friends," he said.

I choked on a laugh of astonishment. "Friends? Crazy things are happening at this school. *Crazy* things. But that doesn't mean *I'm* the crazy one."

"Rosie, wait. No one said you're crazy."

"Don't patronize me. That's exactly what you meant."

"I just want you to admit that you make things up," he said.

He reached for me again but I winced away, hugging my sore elbow.

"I don't make things up," I said. "All this time, I thought you wanted to help me, but now that I think of it, you've been no help at all."

He dropped his voice. "You can't really think that. I just lost my job because of last night."

"But you came because I amused you. You came looking to *kiss me*," I said accusingly. "You didn't come to be of any *real use*."

His eyes hardened and his jaw clamped shut. For one last second, he seemed to consider, and then he threw out his hand. "You want me to be of real use? Then be honest. Quit being so cautious. Tell people what you really think is going on here. I've listened to your stories. I've kept your secrets. Go on. You've got a whole world of viewers out there." He gestured even wider. "What's so evil about the Forge School? What's going on here, Rosie?"

There it was. I'd resisted my chance when I was before the trustees, but Linus's goading hit at a deeper level.

"I believe Dean Berg is doing experiments on us," I said. "I think he mines us for dreams while we sleep, against our will."

I could feel the cameras aimed at me and the microphones picking up every word. It was terrifying and exhilarating.

Linus urged me on. "Students like you?"

"Maybe not all of the students, but some of us for sure, and certainly me," I said. "And he seeds us, too. He plants ideas in us. It doesn't show right away. It doesn't seem to hurt or do any damage at first, but it made me dizzy enough to fall off that ladder yesterday."

"When you fell with Burnham," Linus said.

I nodded. "People are killing themselves when they leave here. They're never the same."

"What you're talking about would involve brain surgery, wouldn't it?" Linus asked.

"It's a kind of microsurgery with lasers, I think. Dean Berg studied medicine when he was younger," I said. "Dr. Ash helps him. They have an operating room under the school. They can wheel our sleep shells there at night and bring us back to the dorm before morning without us ever knowing."

"So it's completely secret," Linus said.

"Yes, but the worst thing, the thing I discovered last night, is that he has a whole extra supply of sleeping bodies he can

355

use for experiments," I said. "Dozens. He has dozens of children stashed in a vault under the school, all asleep."

"You mean, in comas?" Linus said.

I felt him guiding me forward with his questions, as if he were beckoning me toward him across a tightrope.

"I don't know what they're in, exactly," I said. "Possibly comas. They're definitely alive."

"And how did you find them?"

"I skipped my pill. I stayed awake. I know I wasn't supposed to, but I did." I pointed in the direction of the quad, beyond the nearest buildings. "I found the sleeping children down the pit in the clock tower."

"Everything you've discovered, you discovered at night?" he asked. His voice had turned unexpectedly gentle. "When you were supposed to be sleeping?"

"That's right. I tried to take video footage for proof, but it all got erased."

"So you're the only one who's ever seen this?"

My heart ticked oddly. "What are you saying?"

Linus turned toward the quad, and then back to me. He spoke carefully. "I just want to understand. I think you're saying, if we go down the pit of the clock tower right now, we'll find a room full of sleeping children. Is that right?"

I paused, searching his eyes. Did he know something that would prove me wrong? Suddenly confused, I flashed to a memory of Dean Berg's smug face. He'd had no fear of me, none, during the meeting with the trustees.

Then the worst happened.

A crumbling of doubt edged through me. I staggered back a step. What if it was all some elaborate nightmare I'd invented? What if I had concocted the whole thing, and none of it was true?

Why hadn't I told the board about the dream mining when I'd had the chance? Maybe I had been afraid to tell my secret because, deep down, I knew it was all false. The more twisted and elaborate the nightmare was, the more special I had felt all this time, figuring it out. Now that Linus had pushed me to say it all out loud, I felt like I was betraying myself.

This wasn't only for the viewers.

He wanted me to see it for myself.

I stared at Linus and backed up another step.

"You think I dreamed it all," I said, awed. "You've been humoring me, all this time."

"If you want, I'll go with you to the clock tower right now," he said. "We can look down the pit. We can climb down, if you want. All the cameras can follow us down."

I could hardly breathe. If we went and looked right now, we should find the glass walls at the bottom of the pit, and the doorway that led to the leaf-strewn tunnel, which in turn should lead us to the vault full of sleepers with their eyes covered in gel. But what if we didn't find that? What if the glass walls weren't there? What if I'd imagined them? They hadn't shown up on my footage last night.

"Rosie, should we go see?"

I backed up yet again. He was totally freaking me out. I was freaking myself out.

My gaze shot to his, and his eyes were warm with pity. "Come with me to St. Louis," he said gently. "Or I can take you back to Doli, if that's what you want."

"I can't," I said.

He had just made me tell.

I was going mad.

"What do you know?" I asked accusingly. "How can you be so sure?"

"I don't know anything. I'm just trying to understand you," he said.

Dean Berg had always been one step ahead of me, even when I was spying on him. He could have fed me anything he wanted me to believe. Anything. Everything. He could have staged whatever he wanted, to lure me in. To punish me. Even a vault of dreamers.

"Can they block off the bottom of the pit? Is that it?" I asked.

"Would you listen to yourself?" he asked, gently. Another gust of wind blew up the pasture and lifted his jacket collar against his throat. "Maybe you need some help."

"Not from you."

"I'm not the enemy, Rosie."

I let out a laugh. "You just work for him. Or you did."

His expression went flat, and then he nodded toward the video camera I was holding. I'd practically forgotten it.

"Good luck with your art, Rosie," he said.

A lonely, aching part of me wanted to reach for him, like I still belonged in his arms. The rest of me wished I'd never met

358

him. I curled my hair back around my ear and blinked against the wind.

"Good luck in St. Louis," I said.

I met his gaze one last time, and then he turned and headed down the pasture, toward the road that led to Forgetown. My cool eye framed up the shot, seeing how photogenic he was against the backdrop of the water tower and the horizon of the prairie, but even though I had a camera in my hand, I turned in the other direction, back toward the center of campus.

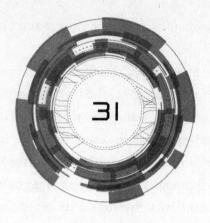

31

CATCHER

THEY SENT A security cart around for me. They said Dr. Ash wanted to check on me. I flared up inside, ready to run, and then I saw their wary eyes. I heard the undertone in their calming voices. The crazy label was clear in the way they handled me, as if they were both sorry and secretly pleased that I'd cracked.

I went with them. I let Dr. Ash check me out. I let her give me some pain medicine for my elbow and wrap it in a sling. She asked me if I truly believed everything I'd said to Linus.

"What's better to say? That I do or I don't?" I asked.

"Just be honest."

I thought rapidly. Honesty depended on whether or not I trusted the person I was talking to, and Dr. Ash was a liar. "I don't want to say anything Linus might hear," I said. "Take me off camera and I'll talk."

"If you go off camera, you're off the show for good. Is that what you want?" she asked.

I shook my head.

"Was this some kind of game you were playing on Linus?" Dr. Ash asked. "Like a performance art piece that went wrong, maybe? That's happened here before."

I glanced down at my hands. "I've been having nightmares a lot," I said. "Maybe I got confused."

"I wish you had told me," she said. "And were you really dizzy on the ladder yesterday?"

I nodded.

"Any voices? Déjà vus? Blackouts? Hallucinations?"

It was hard to tell if they were hallucinations when I believed them. "No," I said.

She set a hand lightly on my shoulder. "Let's let you rest a little, shall we?"

I turned to gaze out the infirmary window, and the doctor left me in peace. Outside, the wind had blown in a change of weather. A mist enshrouded the campus, bringing twilight early, and it thickened to rain as I watched.

I had not known until then that a heart could feel bruised. Mine was bitterly sore, and each time I thought of Linus, it pumped the pain a little harder. I had thought, somehow, that we were starting something small together. Maybe not a family, but something that mattered. Now I couldn't tell if I was angry at him for all he'd done, or if I was angry because he was gone.

I didn't want to need him.

So why did I?

>>>>>>>>

A tap came on the door, and the nurse, Mr. Ferenze, looked in. "A couple of your friends are here to see you. Dr. Ash says it's okay for them to visit for a few minutes. Should I send them in?"

"Sure." I pushed aside my dinner tray and brushed a couple crumbs off my jeans. All I'd eaten was the apple crisp, anyway.

A minute later, Paige and Janice came in hesitantly. Paige wore sweats, while Janice, all in black, looked paler and more chic than ever. Careful of my sling, Janice gave me an awkward hug, and then Paige did, too.

"Thanks for coming, guys," I said.

"You don't look too bad, all considering," Paige said.

"Thanks."

Janice had brought along my brown sweater and my umbrella. She offered me a quaint red flower made of bent plastic, with a string for hanging.

"What's this?" I asked.

"I made it for you. It's a dream catcher," she said. "It's for a window, normally, but you could hang it anywhere."

I laughed, realizing that the flower was made out of swizzle sticks. "That's very nice. Thank you."

Janice glanced at Paige and then back to me. "We wanted

362

to tell you," Janice said. "Paige and Henrik and I went to the clock tower. I climbed down the pit to see what was at the bottom."

"You did?" I asked, surprised.

"Henrik came down, too, and Rosie, we didn't find anything down there but a few leaves and some mouse droppings. It's just a pit." Janice curled her wispy hair behind her ear. "I'm sorry. It's just, I thought you would want to know we tried."

"Thanks," I said. She had just proven that everything I'd said on camera was a lie, but whatever.

"I wish I could believe you," Janice said. "It's an amazing idea."

"That's okay," I said, but my voice came out flat.

She came to sit next to me on the bed while Paige lingered near the door.

The dean had to have some way to seal off the bottom of the pit. A false floor of some kind. But then, that didn't explain why had he bothered having the false floor open at all. He had no reason to ever expose the opening.

"Rosie, are you all right?" Janice asked.

"Of course."

"About Linus and everything? You were pretty tight with him."

"I thought I was, anyway," I said.

"He's a moron," Paige said.

I glanced over at her. "I guess."

"I mean it," Paige said. She arched her back against the

wall. "You have an incredible imagination, and when you figure out how to do everything you want, it's going to be unbelievable."

"So you think I should stay here?" I asked.

"Obviously," Paige said. "You'd be an idiot not to."

Janice nodded. "I think so, too. We've all been feeling horrible since Burnham fell, and you were right there, part of it. It's a crazy time, but it's going to get better."

Another tap came on the door, and Dr. Ash leaned in. "We have a call on the line from Rosie's mother. Can you ladies excuse us?"

I got another hug from Janice before she rose from the bed.

"Thanks, guys," I said.

"We've got your back," Janice said. "Anything you need."

"Thanks."

Dr. Ash let them pass before her out the door. Then she handed me a phone and slipped out again herself, taking my dinner tray.

"Ma?" I said.

"Good gracious, Rosie," Ma said. "What a day it's been. What was that outburst with Linus all about?"

Cafeteria noises sounded in the background as she spoke, and I remembered Friday was her night to work a shift at the prison.

"Ma, you know they can hear me."

"So what? I'm asking for the truth. I need you to be honest, with me and the cameras."

I glanced absently at a camera button on the picture frame opposite me. The picture itself showed the letters of the alphabet formed by different animals: A for Alligator, D for Dolphin.

"I'm not crazy," I said.

"You're something, anyway," she said. "Hold on a second." A mechanical, blending noise came on, and then grew dimmer, as if Ma were moving around a corner. Then the noise abruptly stopped, and Ma's voice was softer. "Larry thinks we should bring you home. He thinks you really have a screw loose up there and you'd be better off back home with the family."

"Seriously? Larry wants me back?"

"He's worried about you," Ma said. "He says that artsy place is ruining you. He thinks you'd be better off here, working at McLellens' and making your own little films on the side. He says McLellen would pay you more because you're famous now. You'd bring in customers."

That was about the last thing I expected from Larry, and yet it made total sense, too. I pulled my legs up on the bed and crossed them, pretzel-style.

"What do you think?" I asked. "Do you agree with him?"

When she answered, her voice was more thoughtful. "What I don't understand is why you were out of bed last night in the first place," Ma said. "I can't believe you risked your entire education to see a boy."

"I didn't."

"No. I can see that," she said. "And that's where I'm stumped.

Because either you really have seen all these things you say about people underground, or you're seriously disturbed."

"Then you believe me?" I said and my heart twisted with hope.

The phone gave a bumping noise, as if she were switching ears. "I don't know which is more likely, honestly," Ma said. "I don't know which would be worse."

I turned to gaze out the window at the rain.

"You've been talking to Dean Berg, haven't you?" I asked.

"Yes. Several times today. He cares about you, clearly. I have no doubt about that."

"There's no way I'm going to have him as my guardian," I said.

"We need to think about this carefully," Ma said. "He's not going to let you stay unless you sign a contract."

I had agreed to stay earlier, in the trustees' meeting, but that was before I told everyone what I knew. I couldn't stay at the school now that the dean knew how much I had discovered.

"Then I'm coming home," I said. "I guess that's decided. Simple."

A soft tapping came from her end. "I've been put in a terrible position," Ma said. "I'm going to look like a monster if I agree to this contract."

I was instantly wary again. "You just said we're not."

"Here's the problem, Rosie," she said. "I've always believed you. I know you're a truthful person. But supposing you're wrong, just in case you've only imagined all of this business and convinced yourself it's true, then you need far more psychiatric care than we can ever provide for you here. I don't want you coming home and going crazy and committing suicide like those other kids."

"So you're saying you want me to stay?" I asked. "For my own health? That doesn't even make sense."

"You're a genius, sweetheart," Ma said. "Forge can provide you with more structure and stimulation than anywhere else. That's just what you need most."

"I'm not a genius. Did Dean Berg tell you this?"

She laughed strangely. "He's seen all kinds of kids like you, kids with incredible imaginations. And he can get you the care you need. He can arrange for a therapist to come right to the school for you. A private therapist, just for you."

"Ma. I'm not staying."

"And this contract, it's actually a good thing," Ma said. "The high stakes will help your motivation. It will give you a chance to show you can follow the rules."

I clenched the phone hard. "I'm not signing it."

"And if, heaven forbid, you can't follow the rules, Dean Berg will get you into the best psychiatric facility in the country," Ma said. "He knows people. He has connections, and he'll spare no expense. He promised me."

She had already decided. I could hear it. She was turning me over to him.

"I don't want to," I said finally, my voice low. "Dean Berg frightens me."

"Please don't make this harder than it has to be," she begged.

"Can I talk to Larry? Let me talk to Larry before you decide."

"I've already told your stepfather."

"Ma, what are you saying? How can you do this?" I demanded. "You're always so weak! Why are you standing up now, for the wrong thing?"

A gulping noise came from the other end of the line. "I'm scared for you, Rosie," she said. "I'm thinking of the years ahead. Don't you see? My heart's breaking here."

I gripped the phone, while inside me, everything stilled.

Ma thinks we're crazy, my voice said.

My own mother. Ma wanted only what was best for us. For a long moment, I couldn't think at all. I couldn't argue. I couldn't breathe.

"Okay, Ma," I said. "Don't cry. I'll be all right."

"Promise me?" she said, her voice tight. "Please, Rosie, will you please be okay?"

"Yes."

32

THE CONTRACT

THE DEAN'S OFFICE felt smaller without the trustees, more hushed and private. Dean Berg took my umbrella for me when I arrived, but I kept my sweater. Fake logs had been lit in the fireplace to counter the chill of the drizzle, but when I reached for warmth, I felt none.

"How are you feeling?" Dean Berg asked me. His pale eyebrows lifted. "Dr. Ash tells me you're doing well."

"I am, thank you," I said. "And you?"

"It's been a busy day," he said. "Something warm to drink? Tea? Cocoa?"

"No, thank you."

A light aimed at the mantel portrait now cast a glare that obscured the stern woman. I saw from her label she was Lavinia K. Jacobs, the show's founder.

The dean leaned back on the front of his desk, where he'd been earlier that day, and his tweed blazer fell open. "That was quite a conversation you had with Linus this afternoon," he said.

"Do you know where he is now?"

"I understand he left for St. Louis."

I nodded. That was what Linus had planned to do.

The dean sighed heavily. "I wish you had told us about your nightmares," he said. "It's unusual for a student to have nightmares at all, and exceedingly rare for one to remember them on waking, but clearly that's what's been happening to you. If I'd known, I would have had Dr. Ash adjust your sleep medication."

"She said the same thing."

"Why didn't you tell us, then?" he said.

I began a circuit of the room. "I didn't know they were nightmares, did I? They seemed real to me."

The dean considered me, pursing his lips. "What do you think now? Did you really climb down the clock tower and find a whole world down there? If you believe that, I seriously question why you would want to stay here."

We were negotiating. We were deciding how crazy I was, but no matter what I said, he had methods to conceal his vault of dreamers. Of that, I was certain.

"You don't need to worry," I said.

"No, I am worried," he said. "I want you to be perfectly honest with me, because if you're truly hallucinating, we need to get you professional help. We'll fully cover the cost. It's no fault of your own. You have no reason to be ashamed."

Shame, is it? said my inner voice.

"I'm not hallucinating," I said.

Not at all, she said.

Don't distract me.

"I'm relieved to hear it," he said. "And you're not having any headaches or dizziness or déjà vus? Nothing unusual at all?"

"No."

Little knickknacks and sculptures were posed among the books on the shelves, but no family photos. On one narrow shelf, beneath a white camera button, lay a miniature set of watercolor paints and a spiral-bound pad of art paper. I reached to open the pad.

"You can leave that," the dean said.

I glanced over at him. "Are these yours?"

"Painting helps me unwind," he said. "Here I am, surrounded by all you artists. I'd prefer you didn't look at them."

I left the pad untouched. "Do you have a family?" I asked, wondering if he'd tell the truth.

The dean reached for a few papers behind him as he answered. "I have twins. They're eighteen. They live in New York with their mother, so I don't see them nearly as much as I'd like."

"Did they ever want to come to the Forge School?" I asked.

"No. It's not their thing."

"What are their names?" I asked.

Dean Berg stroked a hand down his blue tie. "Why the interest?"

"I'm just thinking, if I'm signing a contract where you could be named my legal guardian, I should know something about you. After all, you know practically everything about me."

"Brian and Emma," he said. "But I don't expect to become your legal guardian. That's not how this is supposed to work."

On the next shelf was a small sculpture of a man crawling out from under a shroud, and I traced the silky marble. His label read "Morpheus." The dean liked nice things, I decided.

"Why'd you get divorced?" I asked.

"My wife didn't like me." The dean straightened from his desk and stood to face me as I moved nearer to the windows. "Anything else?" he asked mildly.

"No."

When I came to the edge of his desk, I reached for a spherical paperweight made of glass. It was heavy and etched with the continents of the globe. Little spiky Iceland floated in a smooth sea of blue glass, and someone had placed a tiny gilt star upon it. I wondered if it was a gift from Huma.

"Suppose we get down to business." He passed me a sheet of paper. "Your parents have approved these conditions and they have a copy. Please read them carefully."

I set down the paperweight, skimmed my hand over the

paper, and sank into his desk chair. I expected him to tell me to get out of his seat, but when he didn't, I began to read.

1. Rosie Sinclair will conform to all Forge School rules, including proper ingestion of her nightly sleep pill and remaining in her sleep shell from 6:00 p.m. to 6:00 a.m.
2. Rosie Sinclair will undergo complete physical and psychological screenings at Mr. Sandy Berg's discretion, and he will personally oversee any necessary medical care.
3. Rosie Sinclair will not leave campus for any reason without Mr. Sandy Berg's express permission.
4. Any breach of this contract will result in Rosie Sinclair's legal guardianship passing from her mother, Ms. Joan Sinclair, to Mr. Sandy Berg. Rosie will be promptly expelled and removed from the Forge School. She will be placed elsewhere at Mr. Sandy Berg's discretion and fully cared for until her eighteenth birthday, at which time she will be released.

At the bottom, a line was already filled with my mother's signature, via Legalpen. Two other lines were open for my signature and Dean Berg's. I looked up to find him regarding me.

"I thought it was best to keep things simple. Questions?" he asked.

"Number four is a bit open-ended."

"Not at all," Dean Berg said. "It's a very straightforward agreement. Either you consent to abide by our rules, or you don't. The severe consequences are to ensure your compliance." He gave his ready smile. "We're not going to be made to look like fools."

I tapped the paper softly with my fingers. "Why am I so valuable to you? Why don't you just send me home?"

"All our students are valuable to me," Dean Berg said. "We're deeply invested in each student's success. You've had a rough couple of days here between the accident and last night's episode. Your outburst with Linus today was a sign, I feel, that what you need most is compassion. I firmly believe, as does the board, that with the right support, you'll come through this difficult time very well."

"Despite my nightmares."

He crossed his arms. "Your nightmares, if you can think of it this way, are just the flip side of your creativity," he said. "Handling them is a matter of adjusting your meds and giving you the right outlets."

"For my art."

"Yes. Precisely."

I glanced down at the contract again. "What is this about 'elsewhere at your discretion'?" I asked.

"I could admit you to a hospital if that's what's called for, or I have property in Colorado where I could send you," he said. "It would depend on what I thought was best for you. Naturally, I would confer with your parents, but I won't send you back to them in Doli. That's off the table. Frankly, if you think there's any chance you're going to break this contract, don't sign it."

"And go home now?"

"Right."

My mother didn't want me home. She thought I could get better care here.

"You don't trust me," I said.

"It's just the opposite," Dean Berg said. "I'll trust you if you sign that paper. It's a way for you to take ownership of your situation." He paced nearer and placed his hands on the desk across from me. "Think of it from my side. We're taking a risk with you, Rosie. We're opening ourselves up with a precedent that could impact many future disciplinary decisions. You've already proven you can get out of your sleep shell, twice, and we need to make sure that won't happen again."

I'd been out of my sleep shell far more than two times, and he knew it. But this contract would neatly box me in. Getting down to the vault again would be nearly impossible, and if I was caught, that would be the end of me unless I could prove to the world, once and for all, what a monster Dean Berg was.

I smoothed my hand across the paper. Dean Berg waited on the other side of the desk as I picked up a pen. It grew heavy in my hand as I paused, listening. The sound of the rain touched against the windowpanes. I thought again of those people down in the vault, completely helpless.

Any last thoughts? I asked.

We're taking him down, she said.

I firmed up my grip, put the pen to paper, and signed my name. Then I set the pen back in its holder and stared a long moment at my signature.

Dean Berg straightened. "Thank you," he said. "I think you'll be very happy with your decision."

THE B BUTTON

THAT NIGHT, WHEN we lined up for our pills, the rain had intensified its patter on the vaulted ceiling, and a cool draft ran over my bare feet. Orly came down the row, and I watched as one by one, the girls took their little white cups, tossed back their pills, followed them with swallows of water, and climbed in their sleep shells. Paige took her pill, and then Janice took hers, and I was the last.

"And finally, our star," Orly said. "Dr. Ash has upped your dose."

I took the little cup, tilting it to see the pill inside. It was a round, red pill this time, as shiny as a poisonous berry.

"Have you ever tried one of these?" I asked.

"I'm not the creative type," she said.

"No, I suppose not."

Orly gave the tray a little jab toward me. "No need to be smart," she said.

I gave the pill a quick swirl around the bottom of the cup, and then swallowed it down, for real. I opened my mouth for inspection. Orly used a stick to have a good long look around my mouth, and then she nodded.

"All right. Climb in and close your lid," she said.

"Can't I leave it open? I like to hear the rain," I said. I swore we had discussed this before.

The clock tower began to toll six.

"You know the rule. After your brink lesson you can. But I doubt you'll be awake that long," she said.

She was right about the power of my sleep medication. Even as I climbed in my sleep shell, I could feel a leaden heaviness settle in my limbs. I closed the lid and ignored my brink lesson, watching for the moment Orly turned off the overhead lights. Then I felt along the inner seam of my pillowcase to where I'd hidden the tissue with Burnham's antidote pills. I opened the tissue and spilled out the two remaining yellow pills. They were heavy and awkward under my fingers. With an effort, I tongued one up from the fabric, and it began to dissolve into bitterness on my tongue.

Swallow, she ordered me. **Quick!**

I worked the pill down my throat and quit struggling. I closed my eyes, leaning my cheek deeply into my pillow. The antidote wasn't working. What Dr. Ash had prescribed was too strong.

Open the lid. Rosie, open the lid, said a voice from far away.

My arm was impossibly heavy, but I fumbled for the edge and slid the lid back. Cooler air touched my face and neck. I took a deep breath, trying to remember some elusive, important concept, and failed.

A sniffling, trembling noise came from the sleep shell beside mine. It penetrated to my heart. I forced my thick eyelids open to look across at Janice, who had her lid open. Her pale blond hair glowed in the faint blue light, and her skin shone with phosphorescence. She lay on her side, with her fists bunched under her chin, and her face was crunched in misery. Her sobs became more distinct, a counterpoint to the drone of the rain on the roof. I lifted my face an inch off my elbow.

"Janice," I whispered.

She didn't hear. I called again, but she didn't respond. She couldn't. Janice, who obsessed over Hamlet, who wore polka dots and made me a dream catcher out of swizzle sticks, was crying in her sleep.

I looked helplessly down the row at the other girls. Their faces were washed in the same faint blue, as if they were so many Snow Whites, all but dead. I was failing all of them, my classmates and the children in the vault, and if I didn't get down to the vault soon, the dean would move all his sleeping bodies somewhere else before they could be discovered. However he'd gotten them in, he must be able to get them out.

Burnham had told me only ever to take one pill, but I had one more. I nibbled it between my lips. Instantly, it began to fizz and dissolve between my teeth. I circled my tongue to raise saliva and forced the pill down with a thick swallow.

As I struggled to keep my eyelids open, a faint buzz began in my muscles. It beat back the seaward pull of exhaustion and gradually wired up my nerves. Every restless sob from Janice resonated in me with painful clarity. It took forever for her crying to stop. Then the silence expanded like a violet fog in the air.

I was awake now as I had never been awake before, and I was not insane. I had not imagined anything. I knew what the truth was.

I lay as still as possible, pretending to sleep, plotting. My plan was risky, but possible. I would return to the vault again to film the sleeping children, but this time I would not linger. This time, once I surfaced, I would run as fast as I could for Forgetown. Linus had shown me where he lived, and I knew I could persuade Otis to help me get out of town. Only then, when I was far away and safe from Dean Berg, would I show people what was on my video camera. I would bring my proof to the world. I would demand justice for the people in the vault and anyone who had ever come under Dean Berg's scalpel.

The catch was that I'd have only one chance. If I was caught out of bed, I'd be sent somewhere at the dean's discretion, and since he'd need to keep me quiet, it wasn't going to be anywhere nice.

The clock tower bonged midnight, and I mentally reviewed the contents of my backpack: my video camera, my jacket, a bit of money, a paper roadmap, a penlight, and my two photos of Dubbs. Everything was ready. The dean or Dr. Ash would probably see me the minute I left my sleep shell, but I would be fast and it would take them some time to locate me in the dark.

When finally the clock struck one, I slid back my lid, pulled on some clothes, and grabbed my backpack. I paused only to look out and see that the lights in the dean's penthouse were on, and then I sprinted for the door and tore down the stairs to the first floor.

The pill from Burnham made me feel stronger than ever, with acute hearing and sight. I had an impulse to laugh with giddiness, but instead, I channeled my energy into assessing each shadow and ran lightly to the door. Outside, the rain showed as a halo around a distant streetlamp. The dumpster, which had hidden Linus and me the night before, drummed with a loud pitch.

So far, so good. Now if I could just get to the clock tower.

I ducked my head and tore down the steps into the rain. I leaped over a puddle, hunched my shoulders, and dashed along the film building where I had gone the night before. Because of the rain, it was almost too dark to see, but a grim, reckless thrill was rising in me now. I spun around the corner of the building and dropped into a crouch behind the bushes.

Lightning flashed.

Thin pools of light dropped at the base of each streetlamp around the quad, but otherwise it was dark, with only the lit face of the clock tower floating in the rain high above. Thirty more paces at a dead run would take me through the rose garden to the clock tower, but I waited, watching to be sure it was safe.

We're forgetting something, said my inner voice.

What? I said.

This is too easy.

I peered toward the clock tower and scanned my memory. It *was* too easy. It felt like a trap. Besides, Janice had told me the pit was sealed at the bottom, and I believed her.

I needed another way to get to the vault. I thought over what I'd seen last night, and recalled how the tunnel from the bottom of the pit had gone in two directions. Near the vault, I'd seen an elevator and stairs. The elevator made sense as a way to bring sleep shells down there, which brought me back to the night I'd used Linus's pass to take the service tunnel to the dean's tower.

Then it hit me. The vault could be directly under the dean's tower. It made sense. The underground distance from the pit was about right. The vault would be convenient for Dean Berg who lived in the penthouse. In fact, I had seen the elevator. I had even seen, behind the vending machines, the secret door that could well be the upper opening to the staircase that led down to the vault.

Water dripped down the back of my neck, and I shivered. I craned my head, trying to see along the dean's tower for a way in, but the darkness made it difficult. I sprinted across the road to hide in the bushes beside the dean's tower. Then, quickly, I circled around the building until I found a window with a gap open at the bottom.

I stood on tiptoe and peered inside, into darkness. I scrambled up the wall, shoved the window sash open, and half fell into the room just as another burst of thunder pounded through the air. A light came on overhead, and I dropped instinctively to the floor.

I was alone and dripping in a small, white bathroom. The light, apparently, worked by motion sensor. My heart was beating hard, and I glanced down to see my jeans and sweatshirt were streaked with mud. Cautiously, I stepped to the door and peeked out. No one was in the hall, but I knew I'd be near cameras once I reached the foyer. I wiped at my wet nose and waited for the next flash of lightning.

The instant it came, I sprinted for the foyer. Beneath the gold dome, I bolted right, and skidded toward the elevator. The thunder came just as I was about to hit the down button, and then I realized I couldn't wait there in view of the cameras. Instead, I grabbed the banister and sprinted down the stairs. At the basement level, I spun past the snack machines and slammed my palm against the elevator button.

I cowered against the wall, tense with fear, waiting until the elevator dinged. The door opened with painful slowness and as soon as I jumped inside, I jabbed the lowest button on the control panel, the B button.

The elevators slid closed, but the elevator did nothing. Instead of falling, it remained still. My pulse jolted. I jabbed the B button again, but the button light wouldn't stay on. I looked up, over the door, to the numbers. They indicated I was already on level B.

There was nowhere lower to go.

I'd guessed wrong.

This elevator didn't go down to the vault. I'd walked into a dead end.

"No!" I said.

Hold it in! Push in the B and hold it! my inner voice commanded.

I jammed my thumb into the B and held the button hard. The little disk of a button sank in a click farther, and the floor trembled.

Then the elevator began to fall.

34

THE VAULT OF DREAMERS

THE ELEVATOR ACCELERATED downward, lifting my gut as it dropped. A whisper of memory slid through my brain. We had been here in this elevator before, in our sleep shell, when we were taken down to be mined. We had heard, before, in our sleep, the telltale double click of the elevator button, just as we had felt this same elevator fall and smelled this same stale popcorn tang as we descended.

We're getting smarter, she said.

It was going to be a race. I slid my backpack off and took out my video camera, switching it on and checking the lens for fogginess from the rain. It was fine. I sniffed, wiping at my nose again with my wet sleeve. I had to be prepared. Someone could be waiting to catch me when the door opened. I started my video camera recording, and aimed it at the doors.

When they opened, I was facing the same hushed, dimly lit vault I'd visited once before, and I was alone. I took a deep breath and stepped into the lobby. I had no time to waste. I shucked off one of my sneakers and set it in the opening of the elevator doors so that when the doors tried to close, their rubber edges touched the sneaker and reversed again. It made a fruitless loop. No one else could take the elevator down to where I was, though I couldn't do anything about the stairs.

To my right was the tunnel that led to the clock tower pit. Ahead of me, on the other side of the glass, the rows of sleep shells glowed in the dark vault. As I opened the door and stepped through, the filtered, humidified air filled my lungs.

I lifted my video camera to eye level and scanned it around the room.

"I'm in the basement of the dean's tower," I said. "These people are alive."

In the hush, I thought I heard the faintest stirring, as if one of the dreamers shifted to listen. I aimed my video camera into the first sleep shell at an eerie, deathly young woman. Her voiceless lips were gray, and a pair of black pads was glued to her temples. When her chest moved lightly, I instinctively inhaled along with her, willing her to take a deeper breath.

Go fast, said my inner voice.

I broke away to the next dreamer and the next, filming as I walked swiftly down the row. The first time I'd visited the vault, I'd been shocked to discover the sleeping bodies. Now I was even more dismayed by how passive they all were. So hopeless. I could practically hear a resonating hum from them all, a collective pleading as they mutely begged to be freed.

I aimed my camera up at the tubes and cords that dropped from the ceiling to each sleep shell, and a horrible idea occurred to me. Freedom didn't have to come from waking up. It could come by death.

Don't do this. Get out of here.

She was right. I could not think that way, but a strange immobility was taking hold of me.

In the closest sleep shell, a child lay sleeping. She was a slight girl of five or six—younger than Dubbs. Her stringy hair was smoothed back from her face and her eyelids were thick with gel, like the others, but she was different. She was fresh. A nasty, recent wound that ran across her forehead was held together with butterfly bandages. A tinge of color livened her cheeks and lips. She even had a hint of a tan.

Tucked in the corner of her elbow, like a cruel joke, was a small teddy bear.

My throat tightened up, and my hold on the video camera faltered. I carefully slid open the lid. The girl didn't move. I shifted her gown to look beneath. One fine tube led into her abdomen, and another led to her groin.

"Stop," Dean Berg said. He braced a hand against the doorjamb, gasping for breath. "Don't touch her."

I shot my gaze to the elevator beyond the glass. The elevator doors were closed, so he must have moved my shoe. Other people could be coming soon. He touched a dial switch, and the overhead lights came on.

"Don't touch her," he repeated. "For heaven's sake, don't touch any of them."

"What kind of animal are you?" I asked. "Look at these people!"

Dean Berg was still heaving for air. He licked his lips and raked his hair back from his forehead. His complexion was patchy with color and he gleamed with sweat. "You have to come out of here. You're disturbing them. We can talk, I promise. Just come on out."

Instead, I looped the strap of my camera around my neck, reached into the sleep shell, and scooped up the girl. She was far too light to be healthy.

"You don't know what you're doing!" Dean Berg said, staggering forward. "Be careful!"

I steadied the girl's head against my shoulder and slid my other arm under her knees to lift her body against mine. I caught the lines of IV in one hand, preparing to yank them out of the sleep shell. With my pinky, I snagged the bear, too. "Stay out of my way," I said. "I'm taking her up."

He came to a stop. "You can't! She'll die! What are you doing?"

"Where are her parents?" I demanded.

"Her parents? *I'm* her parents," Dean Berg said. "I'm all their parents. You'll kill her! Stop, please!"

I gripped the girl tight, but I didn't pull her free. "Explain. How did you get this girl?" I asked.

The dean wiped his hands on his Forge sweatshirt and set them lightly on the sleep shell nearest to him. "Her name's

Gracie," he said. "She was legally dead. She was killed in a car accident a week ago. She had no brain function, period."

"Then what's she doing here?" I asked. "Why wasn't she buried?"

"Her hospital moved her to the pre-morgue unit to wait out her demise and finalize her paperwork, but I have contacts there, and when I got the call that she was dead, I was able to bring her here and reignite her basic bodily functions. I saved her."

"I don't believe you," I said. "Why didn't you give her back to her parents?"

Dean Berg spoke with deliberate calm. "She doesn't have any parents. She was an indigent ward of the state. She was slotted for organ donations and research."

"But she never died," I said.

"She *did* die," he said. "She's *still* legally dead, but the minute she wakes up, of course I'll return her to the state. She'll be a miracle. She'll change everything. *I'll* change everything."

The girl in my arms was still breathing serenely, as if in a deep sleep. She was warm. She smelled like she had been playing recently and wanted her nightly bath. I braced her against the edge of the sleep shell, half in and half out, and glanced around at the room.

"Have any of the others ever woken up?" I asked.

"No," he said. "But I'm close."

"Dead people can't come back to life," I said. "You're a sick, sick man."

389

"You don't understand," he said. "They're content now. They're even dreaming. Isn't that worth something?"

"How do you know they're dreaming?" I asked.

He smiled. "Dreams are what I do. They're my specialty."

He was creeping me out, but he was also fascinating me.

"What about this one? What kind of dreams does Gracie have?" I asked.

His expression softened. "She dreams of swinging on her favorite swing. She pumps her legs to go higher. She's wearing red party shoes and white anklets."

"But *how* do you know?" I asked.

"Because I've read her brain waves. I reignited her brainstem. That's what we do here. We give these people a dream life that's only inches away from reality."

"How do you know it's what they want?"

"I don't know that it *isn't*," he said.

"You know it's wrong or you wouldn't keep them hidden," I said.

"I'm keeping them hidden to protect them now. I have to. There's no going back," he said. "They're my responsibility. I've made a commitment to these people."

I shook my head. "We're in the basement of a *school*. This is the last place these people should be. How can you possibly take care of them?"

Dean Berg stepped slowly to the side. I took another glance toward the elevator lobby to see that we were still alone.

"The school and the dreamers go together," he said.

"Students like you are so young and so creative. Your dreams are incredibly vivid and powerful. They can grow in anything."

"You put our dreams in these people?" I asked.

He nodded. "My dreamers are like a farm. We can put a seed dream from you in them, and it takes root. It grows. Slowly and repetitively, but it grows."

"From me, personally?"

"Yes," he said, and smiled again. "I believe I'm safe in saying you have, by far, the most fecund dreams I've ever mined."

I was not flattered. "How many other students have you mined?"

"Over the past few years? A few dozen. Some only once. Some more often. We're getting better at it, definitely." He stroked his hand along the lid of one sleep shell and walked slowly to the next.

"Do you do the opposite? Do you put their dreams in me and the other students?" I asked.

He nodded again. "Your young minds are unbelievably receptive," he said. "Anything we seed into students upstairs takes off like wildfire, and unlike with our dreamers down here, we get to see results once you wake up. We see the effects from the subconscious to the conscious within a day or two, sometimes hours. It's incredible."

"That's worse than brainwashing," I said.

His shoulders straightened. "It's nothing like brainwashing," he said. "We ignite your creativity with a spark, just an image or a movement we find especially evocative, but you make the ideas completely your own. You develop them. That's the beauty of it."

"How?" I asked. "How do you see the results?"

"Henrik took his classical percussion and combined it with dance to set it free. Janice is gender-bending *Hamlet*. It's brilliant."

"What about me? What did you seed in me?"

Dean Berg smiled with genuine pleasure. "You don't even know, do you? It feels completely natural."

"Was it something in the observatory?" I said again.

He lifted a finger to shake wisely. "See, I noticed your interest in the observatory. One of my dreamers down here was perseverating on a hanging. Her father's hanging. I wanted to see if I could make that resonate in you if I triggered it with Clarence's death."

"How could that possibly be a good thing?"

"For one thing, it showed me how receptive your mind is, how thin the barrier is between your conscious and your subconscious. The seed also helped you come up with your ghost hunting idea," Dean Berg said.

I held still, trying to remember. I had been inspired about the ghost angle when I was down in the shop, with Muzh. But I already knew I wanted to spy on the school before that, and the ghosts were just my cover. "No. The ghost hunting was my idea. I had that earlier, before we went in the observatory."

"You sure? How about your idea to spy on the school,

which was a very clever reversal, incidentally," he said. "Where'd you get that idea?"

I thought back. "I can't remember when I was inspired for every idea."

"I can tell you," he said. "It was the morning after we gave you a booster sedation intravenously. You noticed that, surely. Jerry is convinced you were fully awake before he sedated you. We seeded you that night. In the morning, your camera was hanging in your wardrobe, facing toward the dorm. I watched your little 'aha!' "

I remembered then. My idea to spy on the school had seemed like a fabulous breakthrough. "Wait. Are you saying you *wanted* me spying on you?" I asked.

"I wanted you to feel like you were doing something," Dean Berg explained. "I knew you were suspicious about why we were taking out your friends at night, and I wanted you to feel you were taking action. Then, once you started filming the dorm at night, we just had to be careful to patch your footage. It wasn't a problem."

"You came to my sleep shell. You stole my camera and erased my footage."

"I left that to Dr. Ash."

"But she messed up," I said. "Burnham and I saw the splice cut. We saw the light at the bottom of the pit in the clock tower, too."

"Those were mistakes," he admitted. "Burnham was far more astute than I'd expected, but even those mistakes didn't prove anything. You kept doubting yourself with no concrete evidence of the mining. That's where I wanted you. That was the sweet spot."

"Sweet spot?" I said. "You've wanted me to know what you're doing? What could that possibly do for you?"

A soft thump came from the far side of the room.

"Please, keep your voice down!" Dean Berg whispered urgently. "Put the girl back down. You don't want to hurt her. Come out with me."

"Not until you answer my question. Why did you want me to know?" I asked.

"I wanted you aware of the *concept* of the dream mining," Dean Berg said. "I wanted your mind to play around with it, and you did. Your awareness has made your dreams keen like I've never seen before. You're like a magician who knows how the magic is done, or a doctor operating on herself. You're the dreamer who knows her dreams are mined. Can't you feel it? Don't you realize how different you are?"

I recoiled.

Does he mean you? I asked.

She didn't answer. I needed her and she didn't answer.

"You changed me just so you could rip out my dreams," I said.

"It's beautiful, what I've done," he said. "It's medicine and art, together."

I shifted Gracie in my arms and looked down at her rounded cheeks and gently parted lips. A soft breath escaped her. I hugged her harder, glaring back at Dean Berg. One thing I knew: he wasn't an artist.

394

"Those students you mine and seed, they're the ones who commit suicide later, aren't they?" I asked.

"The students who killed themselves were perfectly fine while they were here," he said, shaking his head. "I'm certain."

"How can you say that?" I asked. "They must have been damaged."

He hesitated. "We haven't gotten any of the old students back to do autopsies on them, so I can't say conclusively what happened to them."

"But you know something, don't you?"

The dean crossed his arms over his chest. "Very little. Dr. Ash has asked a few discreet questions. Apparently, some of the suicides had problems with dizziness, déjà vus, hallucinations, and hearing voices before they died. That's not exactly hard evidence of decay."

"Decay?" I said. Those were my symptoms. I took a deep breath. "Is that what's going to happen to me? Am I going to kill myself?"

"You make it sound like that's up to me." He took another slow step nearer. "I watch you all the time, Rosie. You can't possibly guess how much I've grown to care for you. I know you by heart, every minute, but that doesn't mean I control you. You still make your own choices."

"I don't want you to care for me," I said, disgusted. "You're never touching me again."

"I'm afraid you're wrong about that. Your mind, at least, is far too appealing for me to resist."

"You'll have to. I'm going to end this now," I said. "I don't care where you put me, what hospital or whatever. I'm going to tell people what you've done."

"You told people today, remember?" he said. "You told all of your viewers, and you know how many questions we received?"

"I don't know. Hundreds?"

"Four," he said. "Our viewers think your hallucinations are part of the show. They're fascinated. You've established yourself as a delusional, paranoid girl. In fact, I've been fielding calls all day from psychiatric facilities that want to book you in."

I darted my gaze toward the elevator, calculating my best way out of here. He'd kept me talking too long, but I was sure I could still outrun him. I just wasn't sure I could do it with Gracie.

"I'll still convince them somehow," I said. "I won't stop until the police investigate. I'll tell them you get bodies from St. Louis. They'll talk to Huma Fallon."

"Huma is going to be very interested to hear about this night," he said. "Very interested. I clearly have to move my dreamers to be on the safe side. It's very inconvenient, but it was time to relocate them anyway. We're ready for a new phase." An alert, listening expression came to his features. He adjusted his earphone. "You're sure?" he said. His gaze focused back on me. "No, I didn't. I suppose bring him here. Can you manage?"

"What's going on?" I asked.

The dean frowned. "Your boyfriend's arrived."

35

DOLPHIN

"LINUS?" I SAID, stunned. "But he left for St. Louis."

"He must have changed his mind," Dean Berg said. "Jerry just found him in the pit of the clock tower, with a crowbar, no less. I always pegged him for chivalrous. I half expected this."

Linus had stayed to help me! My heart hitched with joy. He must have believed me, at least a little.

"How did you block the pit?" I asked. "Does it have a false floor?"

"It's normally closed," Dean Berg said. "Jerry left it open after he burned some popcorn a few nights ago. A bad mistake, there. He forgot to close it up again, or you never would have found the vault."

At that moment, Jerry appeared in the lobby, on the other

side of the glass, carrying Linus's body awkwardly over his shoulder. Linus's limbs were limp and his head sagged.

"Is he okay?" I asked. "Did you hurt him?" I lowered the girl back into her sleep shell and dropped in her bear. "Did you drug him?"

"He's fine," Dean Berg said. "We just can't have him seeing anything in here."

Jerry carried Linus through the vault and into the operating room. I edged forward, trying to keep my distance from Dean Berg and see Linus at the same time.

When Jerry laid Linus on the table, his head lolled to the side before he held still.

"Where's Glyde?" Dean Berg called.

"She's coming," Jerry said, emerging from the operating room. He gave me a polite nod.

I backed up a step, uneven with one shoe off. The dean circled behind me. I checked anxiously toward the door, but I didn't want to leave without Linus, either.

"You can't hurt Linus," I said. "He hasn't done anything."

"He should have left for St. Louis like he said," Dean Berg said. "It's going to be a nuisance figuring out what to do with him."

I wasn't sure I could evade them both, but if I could get in the operating room and lock the door, maybe I could find an earphone or something I could use to call up to the surface.

The elevator doors opened in the lobby, and Dr. Ash charged into the vault. "What is all this?" she demanded in a savage hush. "You can't all be in here."

Dr. Ash's face came down into view and I stared at her, panting and full of rage.

"I don't understand," Dr. Ash said. "That should have put her out cold." She touched cool fingers to my neck. "You can hear me, can't you?" she asked softly. "Sandy? This is strange."

I squinted. I wanted to shout at her, but my voice came out no louder than a whisper. "You're despicable."

The doctor's eyes lit up. "Very strange, indeed," she said.

Unable to resist, I was turned and lifted by strong hands. I couldn't keep my head from lolling to the side. While my mind was fully awake, my body was fully asleep, trapping me.

"Let's take her back," Dean Berg said. "I have an idea."

He and Jerry carried me carefully to the operating room, and I had a brief glimpse of Linus before they lowered me to the next table. The room smelled faintly of vinegar. From the ceiling, an array of probes, pipettes, and surgical instruments hung, dazzling in the light. Beside me, to my left, Dean Berg began working the touch screen of a computer. A bright light came on above me.

"What is this? You're not seriously thinking of mining her in this condition," Dr. Ash said.

"I just want to read her," the dean said.

"She's not even asleep," she said.

"I know. But as you said yourself, she ought to be," Dean Berg said.

They had a quick exchange about doses of medication while I lay there, watching with my eyes but unable to move my head.

401

"It's like the other night when she should have been out," Dr. Ash said. "She must have taken something else to counteract the sleep meds, some antidote, but I can't see how she could have had access to anything."

"Could she have stolen something from the infirmary?" Jerry asked. He was taking off my second shoe.

"No chance," Dr. Ash said.

"Suppose we ask her," Dean Berg said. "Look here."

The dean, on my left, swiveled up a screen at an angle I couldn't see, and on my right, Dr. Ash leaned over me to take a look. Her concentrated expression didn't change, and she didn't speak. I felt the soft weight of a blanket over my jeans.

"Blot her eyes for me, Glyde," Dean Berg said.

"Why is she weeping?" Jerry asked. "Is she in pain?"

"No. It's the drugs. She can't help it," Dr. Ash said. She shifted back and dabbed at the corner of my eye with something soft. "You want the visa-gel?"

"No," Dean Berg said. "Jerry, we need you back on the surface. Let me know if you see anything unusual."

"What about Linus?" Jerry asked.

"I'll get to him," Dean Berg said. "Can you put in a call to Amby? Ask him to report that he dropped Linus in St. Louis, in case anyone inquires. That will buy me a little time."

"Will do."

I felt Jerry give my foot a friendly squeeze on his way out. I still couldn't move. My tongue felt thick and stupid in my mouth.

Are you here with me? I asked, and listened for a reply from my inner voice.

Instead of words, she sent a current of fear, followed by an image of wild animal eyes hiding deep in the dark of an earthen hole.

A moment later, the dean spoke again. "You see this? Her serotonin levels? What's going on?"

"This isn't a good idea," Dr. Ash said.

"Would you just look? I'm not going to mine her unless it's perfectly safe."

"You said you were only going to read her," Dr. Ash said.

"Yes, but look at this," Dean Berg said.

At the edge of my vision, I saw him skim the surface of his touch screen. Dr. Ash leaned into my field of view again. Her smooth dark hair was back in a neat black headband. I blinked up at her. Despite what she said to caution him, her wide eyes were oddly bright, and color tinged her cheeks. As she saw me watching her, she smiled.

"You're all right," Dr. Ash said to me and patted my hand.

"I'm going to ask her a couple questions," Dean Berg said.

"Don't hurt her."

"I'm not going to hurt her if she answers," he said. His voice came nearer. "Rosie, I need you to answer a few simple questions. You can talk if you try. What's your name?"

I looked fearfully from him to Dr. Ash.

The dean touched his finger to my lips, and at the same time, a jolt of electricity exploded in the depths of my brain.

403

"Your name?" he asked again.

I was tense with pain, sweating with fear that he would blast me again. I swallowed thickly. "Rosie Sinclair," I whispered.

"That's right. Good. See, Glyde? She's cooperating." The dean leaned close and peered into my eyes with a penlight. "And who's your sister, Rosie? What's her name?"

"Dubbs," I said. I had to answer him. It frightened me how much I had to answer him, like the words were being siphoned directly out of my core.

"That's rather an unusual name," Dean Berg said. "Is it a nickname?"

"Yes."

He returned to his touch screen again, at the edge of my vision.

"For what?" he asked.

"For 'W.' "

Dean Berg laughed. "Of course. And what does the W stand for?"

"Wanda," I said.

"A lovely name," he said. "Do the bracket for me, Glyde."

"You know I wouldn't object if I didn't have serious reservations about this," Dr. Ash said. "At least wait until she's fully out. Whatever she's on has to wear off eventually. Have some patience."

"You're such a coward. We may never get another opportunity like this. The bracket, please," Dean Berg said. He shifted nearer to me again, so I could see his pale eyebrows and bright expression. "What did you take to stay awake tonight?" he asked. "You must have taken something. I can tell if you lie, so don't do that."

"Burnham gave me some pills," I said softly.

"Burnham?" Dean Berg said, clearly surprised. He and Dr. Ash exchanged a glance. "Have the Fisters said anything to you?"

"No," Dr. Ash said. "I would have told you immediately."

He turned to me again. "Do you know what the pills were that Burnham gave you? What drug?"

"No," I said.

"You sure?"

"I don't," I said.

"Did you tell Burnham what you suspected about the dream mining? This is serious, now," Dean Berg said.

"No."

"Are you certain?"

Another exploding burst of pain lit up the pit of my mind again, and I squeezed my eyes shut against the hurt.

"She's not lying, Sandy," said Dr. Ash. "See for yourself. You're tapped so deep, I doubt she'll even remember this conversation when she comes around."

"She'll remember it," he said. "She's conscious. She's just sleeping, too."

"That isn't possible," Dr. Ash said.

"Just look."

405

I'm like a dolphin with a double-duty brain, I thought, blinking my eyes open again. I wanted to laugh in despair and pain.

Where are you? I asked.

But she wouldn't answer. I could feel her burrowed deep, trying to hide.

The head of my examining table angled up slightly, and Dr. Ash passed a cagelike helmet above me. Then she fit it carefully around my skull, and I heard the sound of a clamp being screwed.

"You're going to feel something in your ears, to set an axis, and then a prick behind your ear," the dean said. He lowered another light directly over my head. I had to close my eyes against the bright dazzle, and I could feel the texture of the illumination on my eyelids, as if microscopic tentacles were stroking my skin.

Two cool probes poked into my ears, but instead of muffling the sound, they seemed to amplify it. A sharp sting shot under my left ear, just above the hinge of my jaw.

"Felt that? Sorry. It should be okay again now," Dean Berg said. "Are you dizzy at all, Rosie?"

"No," I whispered. Fear was making me cold. I was shivering through the limpness of my muscles.

Dr. Ash dabbed at my eyes again.

I tried to swallow, but my tongue felt thick.

"She's going," Dr. Ash said. "See?"

"I know," Dean Berg said. "It's a natural defense. I thought this might happen. I need one more thing, though. If we can tap fear, we can go directly in. Rosie, are you listening?"

"Yes," I said.

"This is very important. Look at me," he said.

I opened my eyes to find his face filling my line of vision. Fine, blond eyelashes rimmed his eyes, and I could see the individual pores of his nose.

"You've been perfect," he said, smiling. "I want you to know that. Now tell me about something you're afraid of. Something small."

"I'm afraid you're killing me."

"We're not. We're absolutely not," he said. "I'd never do that to you. Think of something else instead. Some small, everyday thing that shouldn't scare you but does, like maybe dogs. Do dogs scare you?"

"No."

"Then what else does? Be truthful now."

"My stepfather's belt."

Dean Berg glanced toward Dr. Ash, then back to me. "Still too big," he said.

"Big spiders scare me," I said. "Little ones are okay, but not the big black ones."

"Spiders," he said softly. "Spiders will do very well."

He nodded to Dr. Ash again, and she aimed a screen in front of me, close up. In growing panic, I tried to look past the screen's rim to Dean Berg, but it was too late. Together, they drew the screen so near it cut off any view of the rest of the room.

"You'll be all right, Rosie. I promise," the dean said reassuringly. Then a moment later, "All set, Glyde? On go, give me a big, black spider, up close and hungry. Ready? Set? Go."

The spider appeared inches from my face, as big as a dog, snapping and biting. Pure horror shot into me. It ravaged through me, igniting and escalating my other fears. Burnham was bleeding to death under my mouth as I tried to breathe into him. My stepfather raised his belt to lash it down on me. Linus's perfect head was crushed by a bludgeoning ax. My sister Dubbs came next, bicycling heedlessly into a rushing train. Wordless terror took over, nothing but teeth and fury, deep in my darkest core.

THE LEAP

I WAKE IN my coffin.

Why call it anything else? My eyelids are covered with gel. I'm too weak to do more than twitch my thumb, but even sightless and immobile, I can hear and think. I am still alive in this world, no matter how tiny my box has become, and my rage has only intensified through simmering.

The lid of my sleep shell makes a distinctive swish as it is opened.

"I wish they'd clean themselves." A lisping, tenor voice comes from directly above me, and I smell a trace of tobacco.

"Careful there." From the direction of my feet, a second man's voice comes deep and smooth. "She's more fragile than she looks. Ready?"

My sleep shell rolls into motion, and my hope goes haywire. I could plead with the men to set me free.

Don't be stupid, she says.

They could be my way out.

They work here, obviously, she says. **See what you can learn before you open your mouth.**

She's right. I concentrate on listening for a clue that I could trust one of these men, but they aren't speaking. My sleep shell vibrates with fine tremors. Then it slows and bumps over a doorsill. Increased light passes through my eyelids, and when I smell a familiar trace of vinegar, my hope shifts to dread.

"How's she look?" Dr. Ash asks.

It's better to have the doctor here than Dean Berg. That's what I tell myself. But not by much. I work my tongue around inside my teeth, testing if I'll be able to form words.

"Good," says the first man, the smoky tenor. "All her vitals are regular. Her heartbeat is up a little. I swear she knows when we're coming for her."

"That's normal," Dr. Ash says. "Half of them do the same thing. Okay, now. Gently."

I'm lifted and placed on a new, cooler surface. By the way my stomach sinks inward, I can feel that I've lost weight. My right elbow is no longer sore. I have no clear way of knowing how long I've been living like this, but it's been more than days. Weeks maybe.

"Can I stay and watch?" says the smoky tenor.

"You've seen this before," says Dr. Ash.

"But not with her," he says. "She's famous."

The other man's voice comes from a distance. "If you don't need anything else, Dr. Ash, I want to double check the rest of the order. You know the pickup is scheduled for four."

"Of course," she says.

His footsteps recede as someone lifts my hand and turns it over. I keep my fingers limp.

"When was she last cleaned?" Dr. Ash asks.

"Two weeks ago," the man says.

"For heaven's sake," Dr. Ash says. "Warm me up some cleanser. Be quick about it." She takes a firmer grip on my hand, and a moment later, I feel her trimming my fingernails.

"Why does it matter?" he asks. "She doesn't know if she's clean or not."

"The body knows," Dr. Ash says. "They rest easier when they're clean."

It frustrates me how little I know. Dean Berg mentioned that he was going to move the dreamers, so I assume we're no longer at Forge. I don't know where Dean Berg is, or what he told my parents, who have to be looking for me despite the contract we all signed. The dean can't just keep me drugged and hidden.

Dr. Ash lifts my right hand across my body, and while she's trimming those fingernails, I surreptitiously rub my left thumb along my fingertips to feel the new shortness. The pleasure in touching my own fingertips is immeasurable.

Play dead. How hard can it be? she says.

You don't get it. They're going to mine me again, I answer.

411

As soon as they finish cleaning me, they're going to mine me, and then they'll put me under again. I don't know when I'll have another chance to try to get out.

It's safer if they don't know you're awake.

I don't want to be safe. I want to be free.

She abandons words and takes control of us by sending me a swell of brown color. Giant turtles pile in a black baby carriage that rolls slowly up a hill, and the bizarre image fills my vision. She's learned how to cross over the barrier to enter my consciousness. I can go her direction, too, into subconsciousness, but I prefer my side, where logic still matters. Where I had free will once.

You could at least send me a dream that will make me happy, I say.

She obliges by sending me Linus as I first saw him, in his white bib apron, leaning back against a giant wooden spool, but without his injury or his ice pack. As he aims his gaze toward the pasture, he is simple, calm, and so familiar it hurts. *Leave him there,* I beg her, but as if she can't resist, she shifts to my last memory of him lying in the operating room of the vault.

Stop, I tell her. My panic rises again.

His table morphs into a black sleep shell and encases Linus like a coffin. When I rush into the dream to push back the lid, his body swells into a putrid mess, and maggots crawl out of his ear. They mutate into tiny flies that swarm at my face.

I jerk back.

Stop that! I say. *We don't know that!*

She tidies up by dissolving Linus entirely. She offers no apology.

My heart's still racing, but I refuse to accept that my nightmare could be true. As far as I know, Dean Berg has never actually killed anyone, and untethered fear is not what I need.

I reassert control and surface into my surroundings again. My body tingles from being scrubbed, and someone is rubbing a soft towel over and between my toes. It tickles, and I almost laugh.

"I love that. See her smile?" the man says.

"Like I said. The body knows," says Dr. Ash.

I feel a hand stroke up my leg, slowly and lightly. That I don't like. He reaches my knee and strokes higher.

"Goose bumps," he says. "See?"

Dr. Ash sets down something with a metallic click. "You'll treat them with respect, Ian, or you're out of a job."

Her concern strikes me as ironic, considering she's part of the team that has confined me here, helpless to defend myself.

"Yes, Doctor," Ian says. "I was just trying to show you. She's responsive sometimes, more than the others."

"She was never damaged like the rest. That matters," Dr. Ash says. "The gown, please. Watch the IV."

A drape of light cotton settles over my body, and I feel like a giant doll as a big hand moves my arms, one at a time. I hear snaps near my shoulders. The cloth is given a final tweak and I'm decent once more.

"What are you going for this time?" Ian asks.

"Same. I want to see how the old gap filled in. It should be regenerated by now, and our partners are eager for more."

"Can't you just multiply it once you mine it?" he asks.

"We can. It's harder to stop once it starts duplicating, though, and that can be just as dangerous as having too little," Dr. Ash says. "Apparently, the surgeons get fewer tumors if they're working with the raw material."

"It doesn't hurt her, does it?"

"Not any more than when I just cut her fingernails," the doctor says. "A little closer, please."

She turns my face to the side, and when I feel a couple of familiar nubs in my ears, I know exactly what's happening. I'm not so much horrified this time as agonized. A stinging prick pinches the skin just beneath my left ear.

This is going to hurt, I say.

Stay calm, she says. **If you want to sleep, I can take you there**.

No, I want to listen, I say.

"See that?" he says. "Is all that activity normal for her? Her auditory is lit up like the Fourth of July."

"That is odd," Dr. Ash says.

I'm startled by the gentle pressure of a hand on my arm.

"Rosie?" Dr. Ash asks quietly. "Can you hear me?"

My heart leaps.

Don't answer her! she says.

But my brain scan has betrayed me already. I'm sure.

What do I do? I ask.

Stupid! she says, and she washes a calm through me. It's pure, serene molasses, and I'm compelled to breathe deeply and evenly. She sends an image of my backyard at home in Doli, when the sunset glows orange over the ridge across the valley. I smell sage in the warm dusk. Dubbs comes to sit beside me, leaning her arm against mine. Even though we're sitting and not walking, she takes my hand and tugs it down.

"It's just a dream," Dr. Ash says. "She might be hearing music. I once mined a bird watcher who dreamed in birdsong."

"What happened to him?"

"He's back there. Stevens Eighteen," Dr. Ash said. "And, we're in."

I feel nothing. Every now and then, I hear a little click, and once I feel the doctor's breath on my face when she leans close. I can picture her narrow features and her straight dark hair. She likes to wear a red sweater.

Then a twinge, like a plucked chord of a guitar, shows me a cupcake with red and white sprinkles. Another twinge makes me plunge into the wet blue coolness of a swimming pool, and then it's gone.

"I bet this dose is going to an old guy, rich as sin," Ian says.

"It's for a young woman," Dr. Ash says. "She had a tragic accident. Her parents have been keeping her alive, praying for a miracle."

"Really?" he says. "That's kind of nice."

More soft ticking comes from my left while on my right, I hear a soft suction sound, like a container being opened.

"Sometimes my heart kind of goes out to them, you know," Ian says. "Especially her. I used to watch her on *The Forge Show*."

"We all have a fondness for Rosie."

I can almost believe her, she sounds so sincere.

"Isn't Mr. Berg supposed to revive her when she's eighteen?"

A couple more soft clicks follow.

Are you there? I ask. *Do you feel this?*

My inner voice answers with a feral, skittering noise from the back of a cave.

"When's her birthday?" Ian asks.

I listen for the doctor's answer, for a hint to know how much time has passed and how much longer I'm expected to stay here.

"He is going to wake her up and let her go, right?" he asks. "That was the bargain."

"I couldn't say."

Don't react, she warns me.

They're never going to let me go!

She sends another burst of calming serum through my veins, but I fight against it.

We have to do something! I say to her.

Another twinge from the doctor brings me an image of my sister Dubbs walking barefoot along the train tracks with me. We're seeking blue cornflowers between the railroad ties, and the green stems stain her palms as she pulls them free. At the same time, impossible, honeyed strands of light spin between and around us, and when we open our mouths to taste them, we laugh. The image is so vivid it shimmers, and I'm not so much remembering or dreaming it as living it right now. "You promised to come home," Dubbs says to me. As she reaches out her arms, I lift her up, flowers and all, into a spinning embrace. Love corkscrews through me like pure radiant power.

Ian's voice comes to me dimly. "That's incredible. See those colors?"

"I know," Dr. Ash answers calmly. "Rosie's a fighter. She's more valuable than all the rest combined."

"Why's that?" he asks.

"Because of this," she says.

I feel a wrenching. A swarm of savage white spheres grabs my sister and tries to rip her out of my arms.

No! I scream. *You can't take her!*

I clutch my sister against me and I try to protect her body as she screams in fear and pain. The universe laughs at us, cold and hard. The swarm pulls harder at Dubbs. Dr. Ash is wresting my sister away from me, and if I let this gem of her go, it will decimate me.

I grasp a sudden, startling idea.

I'm going with my sister, I say.

You can't! she says. **You can't leave me!**

If I stay here, I'll rot in this body. This is my chance.

I summon every particle of strength in my marrow and hold my sister tight. Her arms are wrapped around my neck, practically choking me. They can't take her without me. Going with my sister is my only chance.

My inner voice is a snake of smoke, shriveling and twisting with anger and fear.

You don't know where you're going! What if you never come back? she cries.

I'll be out of this hell, I say. *I have to live.*

She snarls and swells in raging fury, but I summon my fiercest determination. I have no time to reconsider and no time to waste. The white spheres have my sister in their insatiable grip and they give one last, rending pull. I am torn off the railroad tracks, through the swirling web of golden strands, and into a wild, exploding sky. The spheres have stolen my sister, but they're taking me, too.

I break into a disembodied smile of victory.

The dean and the doctor have won. They'll always win. But this time, I've won, too, and I'm more alive than ever.

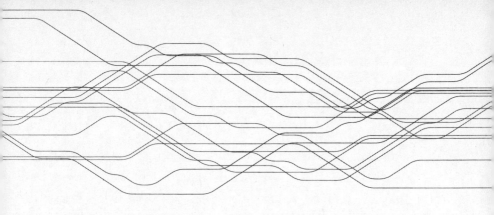

ACKNOWLEDGMENTS

Mine was the rare good fortune to work with two crack editors on *The Vault of Dreamers*, Nancy Mercado and Katherine Jacobs, and I'm deeply grateful to both. Thanks to the team at Roaring Brook Press once again, especially Simon Boughton and Beth Clark. I wish to thank my agent, Kirby Kim, who urged me to chase a daunting idea. I'm grateful to my sister, Nancy O'Brien Wagner, for her insights on key drafts. I'd like to thank William, Emily, and Michael LoTurco, with Lauren Dittmeier and James Moen, whose support and honest feedback were pivotal. As ever, I thank my husband, Joseph LoTurco, for everything.

Caragh M. O'Brien
September 16, 2014

GOFISH

CARAGH M. O'BRIEN

What sparked your imagination for *The Vault of Dreamers*?

I've been interested in dreams and how they might be connected to our creativity for a long time. Dreams seemed to have so much untapped value, and I liked the concept of predatory miners who could steal dreams from innocents. Once I combined the dream mining idea with a reality TV show school, where art students would strive for fame, something clicked for me. I started writing Rosie's story to see what would happen. I was writing blind that first draft because I was experiencing the story in first person with Rosie, and I had no idea how the bad guy was pulling the strings behind the scenes. The story evolved through many layers, and I'm pleased with the result.

Would you have attended a school like The Forge School when you were a teenager?

I would have liked to go to Forge, but I'm not sure I would have had the confidence to apply, and I don't know what my art would have been. I sang, played the violin, wrote, and drew when I was a teenager. Art and music were always my favorite periods of the school day. In fact, I didn't even really think of them as classes. They were what I loved to do.

How much do you think your experience as a high school English teacher influenced your writing of *The Vault of Dreamers*?

Quite a bit. I've definitely been inspired by my students. When I had creative students in my classes, I often felt like my main job was to turn them loose and get out of their way. To me, the teacher Mr. DeCoster personifies that. Also, I saw, over and over, that requiring students to produce work that would be displayed, performed, or read aloud to an audience heightened their investment in the assignment, and I pushed that principle to the extreme with the cameras at Forge. I also hoped the contrast of Forge to Rosie's public school, which was merged with the prison in her hometown of Doli, would resonate with readers. I loved teaching in a public school, but I have serious concerns about what testing and budget cuts are doing to education.

Do you have any recurring dreams?

No. I have great, vivid dreams, though, and horrifying nightmares. Axes, death, that sort of thing. Maybe that's why I can't go to scary movies.

How do you think Rosie's world reflects or contrasts our current society?

On one level, I think Rosie's world reflects our growing fascination with fame and celebrity power. We have these great reality TV shows like *The Voice* and *America's Got Talent*, and everyone can be instantly visible on YouTube. *The Forge Show* taps into our collective Cinderella wish that some big force will magically discover us and launch us to fame and riches. This desire to feel special in a public way is reinforced by our media, but it can lead to a crushing sense of failure and disillusionment when the magic doesn't happen. In the novel,

Ellen Thorpe's breakdown is an example of that. I am much more in favor of internal sources of satisfaction, like what comes with the discipline of the arts. Rosie's world also raises issues of class, the right to privacy, and creativity as a commodity. It feels very real to me.

Do you think some people are innately more creative or artistic than others, and do you, like Paige in the novel, believe they're inherently more valuable than others?
Of course they're not more valuable. Paige is a total snob and quite wrong about that. We all have our own unique contributions to make to the world, and each person is precious. I think there's something dangerous about the concept of inherent talent or artistic genius because it implies that without a natural gift, people can't excel. It's far more important, I think, for each of us to recognize our passions and pursue them with whatever resources we have available, whether that means lessons, practice time, experimentation, or pure determination. Our artistic sides keep us whole. When I see a dancer or a musician in concert, I'm often struck by how effortless the performance seems, but that's evidence of ages of effort and training, and I think that's incredibly cool.

What do you consider to be your greatest accomplishment?
Raising my family.

Why did you end *The Vault of Dreamers* the way you did? Did you know it would make people want to throw the book across the room?
It just so happens that I have heard from a few readers who threw this book across the room. One of them was my daughter

Emily, who read an earlier draft of the novel and warned me that it had a horrible ending. My daughter's distress made me consider what I expected from novels, young adult novels especially, and more particularly, what I expected of Rosie's story. To be honest, I initially wanted to end the novel back a chapter, when Rosie is trapped in helpless pain by Dean Berg, but that seemed so utterly bleak that I couldn't do it. Further consideration helped me realize I wanted to end on a point of hope, even if it was a very strange, out-of-body kind of hope, so I rewrote the last chapter with an eye to that. This version is the result. It might not be satisfying in a normal kind of way, but the entire situation is already too far from normal for anything tidy to work. Rosie sees the chaos and grasps what power she can. I see hope in that.

What challenges do you face in the writing process, and how do you overcome them?

My biggest challenge is that I like to be surprised by what I write. I plunge into novels without knowing where they'll end up. I have a character or two that I like, and a situation that intrigues or troubles me, and I write to see what will happen. This means that I get stuck in many dead ends. I have to throw out huge chunks of my novels and write new sections to fill the gaping maws. Then I have to revise eleven times. The whole process is ridiculous, frankly, and if I could figure out a better way to do it, I would. Fortunately, I have a bizarrely patient editor, Katherine Jacobs, who encourages me to keep exploring. I'm sure I drive her wild, but she's far too nice to say so.

Does this mean you haven't planned out the rest of the Vault of Dreamers series?

It's not that I have no plan whatsoever. I have ideas. I'm just not sure how they'll all fit together yet. I'm wrapping up Book

2 at the moment (*The Rule of Mirrors*), and it has gelled into something I like quite a bit, so I'm sure I'll figure out Book 3 in the same way. I have good characters to work with and a troubling situation. That's plenty for now.

Caragh M. O'Brien welcomes questions and comments from readers. She can be reached online on Facebook, Twitter, and caraghobrien.com.

The entire country watched Rosie Sinclair get expelled
from Forge. But no one knows that Rosie's consciousness has
transferred into the body of another girl—who is pregnant.
Can Rosie make sense of her identity and return to her own body?

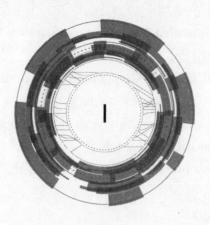

— ROSIE —

THE VOICE THAT STAYED BEHIND

WHEN I FEEL SOFT, breathy pressure on my lips, I open my eyes and grab the guy's throat.

"Stop," I say. It's my first word out loud ever, and the power of it thrills me.

The guy jerks free from my grasp and rubs his throat. He's ugly and young. Mousy hair. Wispy, loathsome mustache. He's in scrubs, like he's a hospital attendant, but I'm not deceived. This is no hospital. It's a vault of dreamers.

"You can't be awake," he whispers. He looks rapidly over his shoulder and then back to me. "Whoever screwed up your meds, it wasn't me." He reaches for the drip that will infuse a new dose of narcotics into my veins.

"No, wait," I say. "Just wait, please. I need to talk to you."

"This is impossible," he whispers furiously. "You must be talking in your sleep."

"Do I look like I'm sleep talking?" I stretch my eyelids super wide and reach up for his face.

"Don't do that," he says, with hushed urgency, and he pushes my arm back to my side.

"I know you like me," I say. "You were this close to kissing me."

"No, I wasn't!"

"No one else has to know," I say. "Is your name Ian? Is that what I heard? Please, Ian. Please talk to me for a second. I'm so lonely."

From my inert position in my sleep shell, lying on my back and dressed in a thin gown, I doubt I could look more helpless if I tried, but I put my every bit of pleading into my eyes, and before I can stop myself, real tears brim over. I hate appealing to him like this. I hate that my loneliness is so true.

He frowns above me, this ugly boy-man with droopy, soft lips. Big ears. Bulbous eyes. Soft everywhere. He might be man height, but I swear his voice never changed.

"Don't cry," he says. "I don't believe this is happening." He touches his sleeve to the corner of my eye, and then he smiles shyly. "All right. I'll talk, but just for a second. I'm a big fan of yours."

"Really?"

He nods. "I used to watch you on *The Forge Show*. I couldn't believe my luck when you came here."

"Where's here?"

His brows lift in surprise. "This is the Onar Clinic, out of Denver. We do sleep therapy and research. You're here to recover. Now hold still. This shouldn't hurt. I just have to check your port." He leans over the place in my chest where an IV goes into my skin and peels off some tape.

I try to make sense of this information.

The last thing I knew for certain was that Dean Berg had me trapped in the vault of dreamers under the Forge School. Linus was there, too, and a pang accompanies my memory of his limp body lying on the operating table. Dean Berg mined me that night, and the pain was excruciating.

Or wait. I recall a span of time after that, too. I was trapped in another vault, maybe this one. I glance up at the supply lines that run along the ceiling. Yes. I'm as certain as I can be that this is the same place. Ian was in that memory, too. I was here a couple weeks or more, and I still had my other voice with me then. We tried to comfort each other. We tried for hope, but then—it comes to me fully now, the last thing I remember, when Dr. Ash was mining me. Us.

The gilded, honeyed lights surrounded our memory-dream of our sister Dubbs on the train tracks, ripping it away, mining it savagely out of us, and when my other voice couldn't bear to lose our sister, she wrapped her arms around Dubbs and held on so tightly that they both were torn away from me. A shattering of star bits swirled around me in the aftermath and broke the night into slivers of gold while I, in disbelief, in agony, screamed and tried to follow.

It was useless. The schism was complete, and my other

voice was gone. I was left behind in our body. Me. The other, lesser voice who spoke only in our head, never aloud. Until now.

Ian slides a new IV into my chest, and the prick hurts. "Sorry," he mumbles. He peels off a new piece of tape to secure it.

This is what I've struggled to wake up to. This hideousness. I've come close to surfacing before, enough to be certain that Ian has lingered over me previously, but this is the first time I've actually broken through.

It's so hard to know what's real.

I always depended on my other voice for reason and logic. She made our decisions while I mocked and doubted, loitered and craved. Of course, I have my own quicksilver, instinctive way of drawing conclusions, and I fall back on that now. Keep him talking.

"How old are you?" I ask.

"What would you guess?" he says.

I have no idea. "Twenty-five?"

He laughs and then modestly adjusts my gown once more. "I'm nineteen," he says. "Three years older than you."

"Four years," I say. "I'm fifteen."

"No. You had your birthday in December. You're sixteen now."

Alarm slams me. "How long have I been here?" I ask.

"Let me think," he says. "You came right before Halloween, I remember. It was wild. Four truckloads of dreamers showed up at the same time, and Berg told us we had to keep a special eye on you. I was like, that's her, Rosie from *The Forge Show*.

I was so psyched. I loved watching your blip rank go up. The show wasn't the same at all after you left."

"But how long ago did I come here?" I insist. "What's the date today?"

A mumbling of voices carries from the distance, and Ian looks over his shoulder until the noise passes. I can't see much from my angle, but from the way Ian keeps turning, I assume a doorway opens in the direction of my feet. He faces me again.

"Today's February eleventh," he says.

My mind balks. I've been here in this vault for more than three months! *Three months!* This is worse than a prison. It's stealing my life! I thrash my hand up in desperation.

"Please, Ian!" I say. "You have to help me. I can't stay here like this!"

"Careful." Ian catches my hand and holds it down.

"Are they mining me? Do *you* mine me?" I ask.

He smiles. "No. Not me."

"Dr. Ash, then? Does she mine me?"

"Look, it's all for your own good," he says. "You have to calm down. It's not right for your heart rate to go up like that. It'll change your metabolism and everything else." He reaches for the narcotics dial again.

"No, please!" I say. "I'm calm. See? I'm fine." I try to smile.

"I mean it," he says. "If you destabilize, they might decide to move you."

"To where?"

"The main research lab," he says. "To be honest, Onar is more of a sorting station than anything else. It's strange for a dreamer to be here this long, but that's what Mr. Berg ordered for you. I think it has to do with confidentiality. He trusts us here."

"I don't want to go anywhere," I say, willing myself to be calm. I know, at some level, he's my only chance. He's the one who lingers over me. I must manipulate him right. "I want to stay here with you."

"You're lucky it wasn't one of the others who noticed you were awake," he says. "I really ought to report this. The doc will want to adjust your meds."

"Don't tell them," I say. "It wasn't luck. I waited to wake up just with you."

"Is that right?" he asks, looking pleased.

"I have an idea," I say. "Why don't you lighten up on my meds so you and I can talk sometimes? I'll keep it a secret if you will."

He rubs his nose and smiles again. "That's funny," he says. "You're asleep all the time. You have nobody to tell."

Duh. Exactly, I think. "I like to see you smile," I say.

He glances over his shoulder again and leans near so I can smell the potato chips on his breath. "I like your smile, too. This is the most exciting thing that's ever happened to me."

"Don't tell anybody," I say.

He whispers confidentially. "Okay."

"Can I ask you something? Do you have a girlfriend?"

Straightening again, he shakes his head, but a touch of color rises in his cheeks. "I never know how to talk to girls."

"You're talking to me," I say.

"I guess. This is different, though."

"No, we are definitely having a conversation, and I am definitely a girl."

He breaks into a quick, private smile and then frowns again. "I really need to put you back to sleep."

"Will you do me a favor?" I ask.

He looks a bit wary. "What?"

"You smell like the outdoors," I say. "Like the forest." This is patently untrue. He reeks of tobacco. "Could you bring me something green to smell?"

"You want something alive, from outside?" He sounds surprised.

I nod. "It would mean so much to me."

He is grotesque to me, this evil troll, but when he pauses to consider, his eyes take on a liquid, dreamy quality, and he looks younger. He pushes back his mousy hair and rubs behind one ear.

"It might help your dreams," he says pensively.

"Is something wrong with my dreams?" I ask.

He hesitates, then shakes his head. "No. They're fine."

He's lying, obviously. Panic tingles at my throat. Dean Berg hasn't killed me in a brief, merciful way. He's been mining me for over three months. He's kept me wasting. Tethered. This is exactly the hell my other voice foresaw when she escaped.

"Ian, please. You have to help me! You can't let them keep me here!"

He reaches for the dial on my IV again. "Don't get excited," he says. "It's your job to sleep."

"Just bring me something green," I say. "That's all I want. Promise me!"

He shakes his head. His lips go straight and firm.

I want to scream at him.

"When can we talk again?" I ask. "Ian?"

His eyes go sad. "That's enough, now. Just close your eyes."

I hate obeying him. He infuriates me. But I do what he says.

It's an exquisite kind of horrible, lying there blind, hearing him breathing and knowing he's turning the dial on my IV. We have a fragile new pact that's built on us both knowing that I'm awake. He could do anything to me, and I'm helpless to stop him, but I have to hope he enjoys the power he has. The control. The mercy. I want him to sense how grateful I am for his decency and gentleness.

Not that he's decent at all. He's a pawn. A Berg tool.

The brown, warm heaviness seeps into my blood. I hold out as long as I can, resisting the meds with will power. If only I knew how to be smart like my other voice was.

Where are you? I call to her.

I listen to the hollow of my mind, waiting while the delicate emptiness plays in my ears, but only my own echo answers back, mocking me. She's gone. I miss her. I hate her, too, and bleating for her won't bring her back. A swirl of bitterness fills me. If she's dead, it's no less than she deserves for abandoning me.

I never asked to be in charge, but I'm all I have left now.

"I'm sorry," Ian says softly. "That was a mistake, talking to you. I didn't mean to get you upset."

He smears a touch of gel on my eyelids. In a moment, he'll close the lid of my sleep shell and walk away. He'll never let me wake again.

"Kiss me goodnight, Ian," I whisper.

"What?" he asks.

It's my last trick to play, and I can't bear to say it again.

Gentle pressure lands not on my lips, but on my forehead—a kind kiss from a monster. It tears at me. I can't tell which of us has won this round, him or me.

Then my lungs fill with pure loneliness, and I'm back to the airless agony at the bottom of my pond.